Maybe I'm Dead

Joe Klaas

AN AUTHORS GUILD BACKINPRINT.COM EDITION

Maybe I'm Dead
All Rights Reserved © 1955, 2000 by Joe Klaas

AN AUTHORS GUILD BACKINPRINT.COM EDITION

Published by iUniverse.com, Inc.

For information address:
iUniverse.com, Inc.
620 North 48th Street, Suite 201
Lincoln, NE 68504-3467
www.iuniverse.com

Originally published by The Macmillan Company

ISBN: 0-595-09037-0

Printed in the United States of America

To my Mother
and the thousands of women she represents,
who have had to wait bravely for their
sons who were behind barbed wire.

Maybe I'm Dead

Chapter One

In the towers the sentries manned searchlights and guns. In the prison the men manned their bunks—all except one. He stood by a cracked open shutter in darkness, watching a man and a dog by the barbed-wire fences. Behind him in darkness another man snored, and the whole prison block sighed with the breath of many sleepers. The man at the window of the tiny room watched the Hundeführer with a firm leash on his steaming Alsatian, halt inside the fence just fifty feet away.

There was a guttural query and "Jawohl" as another guard appeared outside the fences. He carried a ten-foot pole which he poked through the fence at the dog. With a snarl born of savage rage the beast leaped toward the fence, held in check by the Hundeführer's leash. Frightened in spite of the steel maze of barbed wire, the man with the pole cowered for an instant, and then bent forward again.

The dog set up a howling and slavering, attacking the stick in fury and attempting to get at its bearer. The snoring in the little room stopped.

"What in hell's going on?" came a voice from the bunk.

"The Hundeführer is training his dog," the man at the shutter crack said. The snarling increased to a furious howl as the huge dog strained at his leash, steam generating from the foam at his fangs.

Both men now glued their eyes to the crack. The howling of the tormented dog continued until the outer guard withdrew the pole. A guttural exchange, and the Hundeführer continued his way along the inner fence, with the frustrated dog still tugging hard on the leash.

The first watcher closed and bolted the shutter. The second, who was taller and had a black shaggy beard, lit a match and applied it to a tiny lamp made from the lid of a tin can. Both men wore brown sweaters over woolen pajamas, and fur-lined flying boots.

"Want to try cutting out through the wire tonight?" The bearded man's teeth gleamed in the lamp's soft flicker.

"Not tonight, Major," the younger man said, looking at a watch on his wrist. "It's time to set up." With that he carefully opened the room door, stepped through, closed it, and walked with a soft shuffle down a black corridor. A short way down he stopped, looked back, opened a door on the opposite side of the corridor, and stepped into the shadows of a larger room. Its window shutters were open, and ghostly light from the weaving searchlights outside filtered through the frosted glass. From several of the bunks which lined the walls came snores. He bent over to reach down and shake the shoulder of a sleeper in a lower bunk to the right of the door. A figure instantly sat up in the darkness.

"O.K., Junior," the sleeper whispered. "I'll be right in."

Junior Jones left the larger room and retraced his steps down the dark corridor to the small room. He opened the door a crack and whispered, "All set, Major." Then he shut the door and remained standing in the darkness of the corridor, listening to the dull but distinct rumble of shellfire not far distant in the night.

Inside the little room the tall bearded man dragged a small black Hohner accordion from under the lower bunk and placed it on the bunk. Depressing the keys at both ends, he slid the entire keyboard out of the instrument like a drawer. The keyboard contained the innards of a radio receiver. He picked up an earphone and placed it to his ear, at the same time winding a wheel handle in the mechanism on the bunk.

The door opened and closed, and the third man, tall, gray-eyed, wearing an olive-drab greatcoat over pajamas, and a stocking cap of the same color, stood in the soft flickering light of the lamp.

"How's it coming, Major?"

Bearded Major Peter Smith handed the earphone to the newcomer. "Hasn't warmed up yet, Jim."

Jim Weis tucked the earphone under his stocking cap, sat down on the bunk edge with Major Smith, and brought a pad and pencil from a pocket of his greatcoat.

"It's coming in now," he said. "Sounds like Benny Goodman."

The major said nothing, but continued to wind the wheel of the tiny generator. The only sound he could hear was the low grumble of shellfire somewhere in the night.

Jim Weis wrote the date, January 27, 1945, on a clean page of his pad.

"Here it is," he murmured, speaking with the sounds in his ear. " 'This is the BBC, the British Broadcasting Corporation, Robert Donat speaking, bringing you the latest news.' "

Then he began jotting furiously on the pad, scribbling a curious type of shorthand. "Rs" stood for Russian, "adv" for advance, "ks" for kilometers. As he scribbled he grew tense, and his gray eyes widened. He whistled in surprise without ceasing to write. Major Smith continued to wind the generator. For fifteen minutes the only sounds were the scribbling of the pencil and the distant shellfire against the background of muffled snores heard through the walls. Finally he stopped writing, removed the earphone from his cap, and handed it to Major Smith.

"That's it," he said, standing up and stepping to a large hand-crayoned map tacked on the wall. Major Smith slid the radio equipment back into the accordion and returned it beneath the bunk.

Jim studied his notes and the map. The major called out. "O.K., Junior."

Junior Jones entered the room and stood with the major, behind Jim, eyeing the map.

"Where are they now?" Major Smith asked in an eager whisper.

Jim used his pencil as a pointer on the map.

"They've passed us to the north. They're here." He indicated a spot northwest of a prominent X labeled Sagan. "And they've passed us to the south." He indicated another point southwest of Sagan. "To the east they've reached Steinau. They knocked out seven Tiger Panzers when they got the bridge at Steinau yesterday."

"Steinau!" Junior exclaimed, his boyish face flushed. "Why, that's practically here!"

"Twenty kilometers," Jim Weis agreed.

"Less than fourteen miles," Major Smith interpreted. "And they've got pincers around us both north and south. Maybe I ought to wake up the Old Man."

Jim's pencil shook as he traced the horseshoe figure around Sagan on the map.

"Let the Russkies wake him, Pete." He gritted his teeth and shivered nervously. "By God! By God! They're going to get us out of here."

Junior slapped the blond six-footer on the back.

"Old Uncle Joe is on the way!"

Jim Weis shut his eyes and pressed his left hand violently against his forehead.

"By God!" he repeated. "They ought to get here today. Today!"

Major Smith's white teeth gleamed as he moistened the short hairs of his bearded lower lip with his tongue.

"Let's take it easy, huh? We've waited two years. We can wait a few hours without flapping. Now let's log some sack time. And remember: this gen is top secret until the Old Man says to pass it out in the morning."

The major cupped his hand about the little lamp and blew it out.

"Jesus!" Junior Jones swore softly, climbing into the small room's upper bunk. "Only fourteen miles. They've been averaging more than forty a day."

Jim Weis left the room, walked down the dark corridor to his own room, and crawled into his bunk. The iced windows glowed softly from the sweeping searchlights. He lay there listening to the pulsing of the shellfire in the distance. He grated his teeth. Restless, he got up, slipped into unlaced GI shoes, and crossed to the window. Across the snow past the shower house squatted the next icicled prison block. As his teeth continued to grind together he felt a shock of pain in a lower right molar. He turned from the window and reached for the shoulder of a sleeper in the second of three tiers of bunks to his left.

"Huh? Oh, Jim. What's up?"

"Sh-h-h. . . . Tom, I've just got to tell someone. Listen." Jim leaned close to the reclining figure. "Hear those shells?" Together they listened to the rumble and felt tiny vibrations in the wooden prison building.

"What's the gen?" Tom Howard whispered.

"For God's sake, don't spread this around, Tom." Jim's whisper was rapid. "They've got pincers around us to the north and to the south. And they're only fourteen miles to the east."

"Damn. No fooling?"

"I just got it over the canary. This may be the day, Tom."

"Yeah. Yeah. If the goons just don't move us."

"They can't, Tom. They couldn't. They've waited too long."

In the opposite inside corner a man snored evenly and loudly. Tom grinned in the dark.

"Wolkowski's raising more hell than the Russians. He'll scare 'em away."

"Damn it."

"Whatsa matter?"

"I got a toothache. I'm so nervous I think I broke one of my back teeth."

"Take it easy, Jim. Don't go round the bend now."

"Twenty-one months. Twenty-one months in this cage. And now the Russians are only fourteen miles away. Home, home . . . I can taste it. God damn this tooth."

"Yeah . . . yeah. Six months seems like six years to me. I wish you hadn't of told me. Now it'll be hard to sleep."

"Play it close, Tom. Remember, I didn't tell you a thing."

Jim crossed to his own lower bunk, sat down, and removed his shoes. Then he reached up and pushed his fist into the bottom of the tick in the bunk above his. The snoring stopped with a grunt. Jim crawled into his own blankets and lay listening to the murmuring shellfire, eyes opened wide in the darkness, pain burning from the molar into his jaw.

Outside, within the barbed-wire compound, the Hundeführer released the huge, shaggy Alsatian, and the dog howled, blowing steam into the beam of a searchlight cruising the camp from a sentry tower squatting like a great frozen spider over the south fence.

Chapter Two

The dawn came up like the dirty water in a plugged washbowl. Light seeped through the low gray ceiling of murk over Sagan in Silesia, halfway between Breslau in Russian hands and Berlin where the Führer paced. In the five barbed-wire compounds of Stammlager Luft III, shaggy buglers pealed out assembly in the notes of France, Norway, Poland, Great Britain, and the United States, and the echoes bounced back from the wall of pine trees just beyond the barbed-wire fences.

"Roust 'em out," ordered Major Smith, and Junior Jones ran into the hall.

"All out for appel! Everybody out!" The cry tumbled along the corridor.

"Aw, go soak your head!"

"Tell it to the padre!"

Men tumbled after the cry. Prisoners in greatcoats and mittens, some wearing stocking caps, some overseas caps, and some balaklavas, poured out of the rooms on both sides of the long corridor and stamped toward the front of the block.

Jim looked nervously at the thin poker face of Tom Howard, who walked silently beside him. They stepped through the opened block doors onto the trampled snow outside.

"They're still there," Jim said, nodding toward the sentries in the nearest tower.

"Yeah," answered Tom as they took their places in formation. To the left and right and straight ahead across the way, in front of each block building, the great coated prisoners lined up in rows five deep, about two hundred men in each block formation.

Major Smith came from Block 162 and tapped Jim Weis on the shoulder. "The Old Man's room right after appel."

"Right."

Major Smith stepped out in front of the formation.

"Good morning, gentlemen." White teeth glittered in the middle of his black beard. "I trust you all had pleasant dreams."

"I did," cracked a pleasant-looking short stocky man right behind Jim. "I had Betty Grable."

"Don't write that to your wife, Koczeck." The major grinned. He looked to his left and saw that the next block formation was marching in a column of fives toward the parade ground. "Block, tenshun!" he snapped in a deep voice. "Fahrrrd harsh!"

The formation stepped forward briskly.

"By the right flank, harsh!"

Jim scowled with the pain of his tooth as the column slipped rapidly between the rows of prison blocks and past a huge, foul-smelling outside Abort. It was a forty-holer.

"I don't get it. I just don't get it. They must be pretty damned close, but here we are. Appel as usual."

Tom Howard muttered sideways: "Don't let it get you, Jim. Take it easy. What happens will happen."

"Column right, harsh!"

The column turned onto a large snow-packed field bordered by a wooden guard rail and eleven-foot double barbed-wire fences crowned by machine-gun sentry towers. Hundreds of feet thudded in rhythm on the hard-trampled dirty snow. To the right of the column, smoke curled from the hundred chimneys of the snow-shrouded prison blocks.

Al Koczeck, who had dreamed of Betty Grable, was now on Jim's right, blowing frozen breath.

"Hubba," he muttered. "I hope they get us counted fast before we freeze."

"Can the chatter back there! Column left, harsh!"

The column wheeled left parallel with the south guard rail and barbed wire.

"Block, halt. Left face. At heeez."

The men, without breaking ranks, stuffed their mittened hands into the pockets of their greatcoats and began stamping their feet for warmth against the iced surface of the packed snow.

7

"How's the gen this morning, Jim?"

For a moment Jim didn't answer the tall dark man behind Koczeck. Instead he stared across the frozen parade ground around which columns of prisoners were still marching and halting, the clumping of their feet nearly drowning out the distant crump of steady shellfire.

"You know better than that, Bob," Jim finally answered the tall dark prisoner. "But listen," he said softly. "Judge for yourself."

The men immediately around Jim ceased talking. The silence spread throughout the entire block formation. Ears strained behind the wrapped wool mufflers. The shellfire was a low throbbing above the murmur of the two thousand prisoners lined up around the square parade ground.

"Home by Christmas," the major cracked, facing the men.

"Christmas, hell!" snorted a voice somewhere to the right in the formation. "Home by Easter!"

At the northwest corner of the parade ground a group of men marched onto the field and halted in front of one of the block formations. Koczeck began swinging his arms, clapping his mittens against his wide shoulders.

"Let's get this show on the road, Major. Tell the goons I'm ready."

"You tell 'em, Al." Major Smith grinned back.

Jim sighed, blowing out a cloud of white vapor. "How many times I've waited at these God-damned appels, waiting for the goons to get to counting."

"Yeah?" Al Koczeck was making conversation to keep his mind off the cold. "How many times? Exactly how many?"

"Well, two a day for twenty-one months. What's that make, Tom?"

"I didn't bring my comptometer. Let's see. About thirteen hundred times, I guess."

Bob Montgomery, dark brown eyes flashing interest, joined the conversation. "And what about those days after the tunnel broke in Compound 2?" he drawled with a Texas twang. "We did four appels a day for months after that."

"Yeah, and all the pop appels and the bunk appels at night," Jim remembered. "I figure the goons must have counted me more than fifteen hundred times so far. Well, by God, they're not going to be counting me much longer."

A new voice joined in. "They might."

"Oh, yeah? Not this Kriegie. Not any of us."

"They might," the homely red-faced speaker insisted. "They'll probably march us out of here before the Reds get here."

"Fritz the laughing boy. Take it easy, Fritz. You'll be teaching school in Wyoming again before you know it."

"I'll know it when I get there," said Fritz Heine.

"Hubba, hubba." Al Koczeck rubbed his mittened paws together. "Here come the goons."

One of the little group which had halted at the northwest corner of the hollow rectangle of prisoners stepped forward onto the parade ground. He was short and looked fat bundled up in his greatcoat. He threw back his head and bawled out in a powerful voice:

"Cawmmpowwnd . . . !"

In front of the immediate formation, Major Smith faced his men and took up the cue.

"Block . . ."

As the men snapped to parade rest, feet spaced apart and hands gripped behind their backs, they could hear the voices of other block commanders, near and far about the parade ground, repeating and overlapping the word.

"Block . . . Bl . . . Block . . . Block . . ."

And the voice from the northwest corner bawled again:

"Tenn-nn-shun!"

Two thousand pairs of hands slapped simultaneously to their owners' sides as their feet popped together. The sound echoed from the surrounding wall of pines like a single clap of thunder. Suddenly all was dead silence. In the distance the pulse of shellfire became more distinct.

"Listen," Jim whispered.

Two stiff-backed blue-gray figures marched briskly onto the parade ground. They approached the small group of olive-drab figures and saluted. The salute was returned, and the Germans wheeled to pass along before and behind the first formation of prisoners on the north perimeter of the field. Once more the short fat figure stepped forth and bawled:

"Hat heeze!"

The men relaxed as suddenly as they had come to attention, and resumed stamping their feet. The monotonous murmur of their voices reduced the sound of shellfire to the background.

Al Koczeck flexed his short thick arms, his fists doubled up. "Boy, standing at attention ain't for me in this kind of weather."

Jim grinned, showing even white teeth. "You remember the day we didn't?"

"Yeah. That's not for me, either. No, sir. Not for me."

A small man standing in front of Koczeck overheard. "When was that, Al?" he asked in a slow Southern drawl.

"Tell Burt about it, Al," Jim suggested, his gray eyes twinkling. "That's something every new Kriegie should know about."

"New Kriegie!" Burt Salem exclaimed. "I've been here five months."

"Just a new Kriegie. Tell him about it, Al."

"Aw, you've heard about it, haven't you? The day we decided not to pop to for the goons? It was last spring."

"No, I haven't," replied Burt.

"Well, it was just after Compound 2 pulled a big escape. That put the goons in a big flap, so they decided to take it out on all of us, even us here in Compound 3. Four, five, six, even seven appels a day . . . and no set time for them. They just came in and called appels any time, day or night. So one time we decided to show them."

"That was a day," Jim snorted.

"What happened? What did you do?"

"Well, Colonel Akron and Colonel Baker got together and figured out a plan. They called it passive resistance, didn't they, Jim?"

"Yeah. Passive resistance."

"I don't get it."

"Colonel Baker passed the word all over the camp that the next pop appel we would take our time getting out here. We wouldn't march. We wouldn't pop to attention. We'd just slouch around and show 'em, by God, that we didn't go for this stuff of being called out every time the goons took a notion to count us."

"Did it work?"

"Wait. I'm telling you. It turned out the next appel was called just a little after one in the afternoon. A lot of the guys were still eating. Well, they just picked up their cups and bowls and brought 'em out here. We must have messed around about twenty minutes turning out. Then we just slouched around. Old Skullhead walked up to the Old Man and saluted, and the Old Man just stood there with his hands in his pockets."

"Just a minute. Who was Old Skullhead?"

"That was the goon who used to count us in those days. His face looked like a skull. What was his name, Jim?"

"Lemme see. Skiel, I think. One tough son of a bitch."

"Yeah, that's right. Skullhead Skiel. Well, he made like he didn't notice the colonel didn't salute him back, and started counting the blocks. Everywhere the same thing. Nobody popped to or returned his salute. Everybody just slouched in their places eating, smoking, grinning at Old Skullface, and making small talk with each other."

"Jesus, I'd like to have seen that!"

"Yeah. . . . It was a panic."

"What did Old Skullface do?"

"He just went on counting each block, stiff as a board, making as if he didn't know what was going on. He got near two-thirds of the way around the parade ground before the shit hit the fan."

"How was that?"

"Old Skullface was marching along the front row making his count when some dumb Kriegie took a big long drag on his cigarette and then blew it right in Skiel's face."

"No!"

"Yeah. And right there, Skullface quits counting. He doesn't say a thing. Just turns and walks off the parade ground and right on out the gate."

"Jesus, I guess we showed him, huh?"

"Oh, sure. Only, in about fifteen minutes there's another appel called. This time machine guns are set up at the four corners of the parade ground in addition to the goon-box guns. And there are forty goons with burp guns lined up all around. This time Skullface and five other goon officers do the counting with cocked Lugers in their hands."

"Jesus!"

"And that time we popped to," Al concluded.

"Block . . ." Major Smith's voice interrupted, "tenn-shun!"

"Good morning, zhentlemen." A Luftwaffe lieutenant wearing a blue leather greatcoat and polished black boots was saluting Major Smith, and the major was returning the salute. The lieutenant pivoted smartly and began walking along the front row of stiffened men, counting off by fives. He peered over frosted rimless glasses as his leather-gloved right hand penciled figures on a tally card.

"Ein hundert vier und neunzig!" his voice clipped out as he reached the last row of five prisoners.

"Jawohl!" came the voice of the Obergefreiter who had been counting along the rear of the formation. "Ein hundert vier und neunzig!"

The lieutenant turned to exchange salutes once again with the major. "Good day, zhentlemen." The lieutenant moved on to the next block formation.

"At ease," Major Smith ordered.

Once more the stamping and talking commenced.

"Say," little Burt Salem drawled up at Al Koczeck, "they wouldn't really have started shooting, would they?"

Jim Weis snorted. "Who wanted to find out? With cocked guns all around we stood at attention. Besides, don't you know what all those appels were about in the first place?"

"Something about a break in Compound 2, wasn't it?"

"Yeah . . . the big break. Seventy-six men got out by tunnel. We didn't know it when we pulled the sloppy appel, but fifty of those guys were shot by the Gestapo after recapture. They sent the ashes back in little urns. And the Sunday after that appel a Gestapo man stood right over there and rested his rifle on a strand of that fence." Jim pointed toward the place in the fence where the dog had been howling the night before. "He shot one of the cookhouse gang who was standing in the cookhouse doorway."

"What for?"

"Who knows?" Jim shrugged. "It was Easter Sunday. Shot him right through the mouth . . . deader than a doornail. When old Pieber here, who just said, 'Good day, zhentlemen,' came in and saw the body, he stood there laughing. I watched him."

"Jesus! I don't like this place."

"That's what I mean. You're just a new Kriegie."

"All this happened last Easter?"

"Well, the tunnel broke March 24th, last year. It seems longer ago than that, don't you think, Al?"

"Ten months. It seems like ten years. God, I got a kid a year and a half old and I haven't seen him yet!"

"Listen to that Red Army, Al." They listened to the rumble for a minute before Jim spoke again. "That's a lullaby for you."

Once again the voice of the camp adjutant came bawling out of the northwest corner of the parade ground.

"Block commanders . . . dismiss yourrr blawwwks!"

"Block, attention!" The men moved to attention. "At ease. Let's try that over again. Snap it up. Block . . . tennn-shun!" The men popped to. The major grinned. "Dismissed!"

The white expanse of the parade ground turned into a crisscrossing maze of men making their different ways toward the compact city of prison blocks. Tom Howard fell in beside Jim, and Burt Salem joined them as they headed toward their block by way of the track along the south guard rail.

"When you going to put out the gen?" Burt asked.

Jim looked around warily. "Got to check it through the Old Man first. You guys stooging for security today?"

"Yeah," Burt answered, grinning. "By the by, I may still be a new Kriegie, but I got some news for you."

"What's that?"

"The Russians are only fourteen miles away. That's where they were at two this morning. They're probably closer now."

"Oh, Christ! A leak. Who told you that?" Jim looked sideways suspiciously at the placid thin face of Tom.

"Don't worry, Jim. There's no leak. I was awake when you told Tom last night. You had quite a whisper. You ought to write notes when you're excited."

At the corner of their block the three halted. Jim Weis surveyed the prisoners returning to the checkerboard of long low unpainted wooden buildings. He looked along the double barbed-wire fences just forty feet beyond the guard rail, at the coil after coil of jagged wire piled in a maze between the fences to discourage wire cutters. He looked up at the goon box standing like a giant four-legged insect astride the fences with a searchlight for an eye and a machine gun for antenna. His gray eyes glazed as he looked out at the pine trees beyond, now sprinkled with loose blobs of snow.

"I guess I was excited," he said, not looking at his companions. "I guess I still am. Look at this place. Haven't you ever said to yourself, This can't be me? I can't be in a place like this. Sometimes I wonder if I didn't get killed when my plane burned in Tunisia. Maybe I'm dead and don't know it. Did you ever stop to think that if there is such a thing as hell, this is hell? Maybe this idea that we'll someday get out of here is just a way to torment us . . . letting us hear from our families just enough to keep us wanting to see them, keeping us just starved enough to constantly want more food. Look at this God-damned place. Snow all winter, but not clean snow; mud in the spring and fall, and dust all summer. Get into the hole now. Get in while the goon is over at the other side of the goon box."

Without a word Tom Howard stepped into a trench at the side of the block, got down onto his hands and knees, and crawled into a dark square hole cut into the side of the building. Inside, in darkness, he felt his way, crawling in cold dirt along a well worn path. Occasionally his back scraped the beams supporting the floor above him. Crawling and poking, he made his way the length of the block and back to the entrance. Once more there, he called out, "All clear?"

"Just a minute. Now . . . all clear!"

Tom appeared like a mole, brushing himself off with his hands. Then once again he knelt, felt in the snow at the bottom of the hole, and brought forth a frozen strand of string. Smoothing out the snow in the trench, he laid the string on top and got to his feet.

"No goons in there," he announced. "They're brewing some chocolate. I heard them talking through the floor."

"O.K., Tom. Keep an eye on that hole. Let's have a look upstairs."

Jim Weis and Burt Salem stepped through the doorway of the block and walked halfway down the corridor. They halted beneath a trap opening in the ceiling. Jim looked up.

"Need a boost? You're kind of short."

"Yeah, either that or a chair."

Jim made a cup of his hands, and Burt stepped up into it, jumping and grasping the edge of the ceiling trap. As Jim pushed from below, Burt pulled himself up into the darkness between the ceiling and the roof. Crawling on hands and knees along a board catwalk, he toured the length of the roof and back. Back at the trap door he called down.

"All clear, Jim."

Then he crawled to the south end of the passageway in time to hear Jim knocking on Colonel Akron's room below. He heard the colonel's voice distinctly through the thin ceiling.

"Come in, Jim. Come in. How's the gen today?"

"Colonel, they've got pincers around us to the north and south of Sagan, and to the east they're at Steinau."

"Steinau?" The Old Man's deep voice didn't sound very excited. "Let's see. That's not very far from here, is it?"

"Less than fourteen miles. And that was yesterday's communiqué. They knocked out seven Tigers taking a bridge there. Colonel, I think this is it."

"Think so, Jim?"

"Sir, they sound even closer this morning than they did when we were listening to the canary."

"I hope so. We'll see. It's been a long time, hasn't it?"

"It sure has—longer for you than for me. Any more gen from the goons, Colonel?"

"Not since they alerted us three weeks ago to be ready to march. Have a seat, Jim, and give me your news in detail so you can start putting it out. The boys will be champing to hear it."

"Colonel, may I ask your opinion?"

"Surely."

"What do you think, Colonel? Is there a chance the goons may still try to march us out of here?"

In the darkness of the rafters Burt shivered as he heard the Old Man's tired sigh.

"I don't know, Jim. I don't know. Now, let's have that gen in detail."

Chapter Three

Jim Weis walked across the packed snow to the block next his own, entered it, and turned into a small room to the right of the doorway.

"What do you know, Jim?" asked a broad-shouldered, muscular prisoner seated at a small table with a tin cup of brew and a large medical book before him.

"Danny, can you get me on a dental purge? I got a toothache."

"Do you think it's ulcerated?"

"Search me. I don't think so."

"Well, let's have a look." Captain Daniels stood up, took a metal pick from a small box on the table, and then turned to adjust Jim's blond features beneath the room's single light bulb. "C'm' on. Open up." Danny peered into Jim's open mouth. "I don't see anything that looks bad, Jim. Which tooth is it?"

"A lower one. Second from the back on the right."

"O.K. Tell me if it hurts when I tap it." Danny tapped the tooth several times forcefully with the metal pick. "Did that hurt?"

"Nope."

"Then it isn't ulcerated. Sorry, Jim. No dental parade for you."

"Oh." Jim's gray eyes widened. "What's the deal? You got to wait until they're ulcerated?"

"That's right. You ever been out there, Jim?"

"Not yet. This is the first toothache I ever had in my life."

"Well, we don't have any real dentists, you know," the stocky camp medical officer explained. "Just a few guys that maybe went to dental school or worked in a dentist's office for a while before they started flying. Of course, they can put in a temporary filling, but they don't work very fast. About all they can do is to keep up with pulling the ulcerated teeth in this place."

"I didn't know it was that bad. Well, what can be done about a toothache?"

"Your teeth have to be in far worse shape than yours before I can send you on a dental purge. Here, take a couple of these when it starts to ache." Danny dumped some aspirin tablets into Jim's hand from a large jar. "But don't take too many of them. Pretty soon you build up a resistance to aspirin, and they don't work any longer."

"O.K., Danny. Thanks. Say, is that what happened to you?"

"How's that?"

"Were you studying to be a doctor when you joined the air force?"

"No." Danny blushed. "I was a pro boxer. Had a couple of years of pre-med before that, though. I'm going to take medicine up again when we get out of here." Danny motioned toward the book lying open on the table. "I've managed to get in a lot of studying right here."

"It may be sooner than you think. I'll see you, Danny, and thanks."

Jim crossed the frozen space between the two prison blocks and returned to his room. He swallowed two aspirins, washed them down with lukewarm cocoa, and gingerly picked up one of the thin slices of bread and jam. The other men of the room stood around waiting listlessly for the potbellied stove near the door to show some real results. On it stood a metal pitcher of water.

Bob Montgomery, the tall dark Texan, stood looking out of the partially iced window, whistling weirdly in a minor key through a space in his upper front teeth. He whistled the familiar melody, his voice twanging out with the final phrase, " 'Ohhh . . . that Wahhh-bash caaanonnn bawl . . .' "

"Jesus Christ, Bob!" Jim complained. "Don't you know another tune? I been listening to that one for a year and a half now."

Bob Montgomery turned. "Well, I guess I can sing what I want. It's a free country, ain't it?"

"Is it?"

"I was just figuring. Full flying pay. Eleven dollars a day for 546 days. That's $6,006 I got coming today. That's a lot of eggs."

"Yeah . . . that's a lot of eggs."

"Only fourteen miles away." Bob sighed. His brown eyes gazed dreamily over the rooftops to the east. "Man, oh, man, I'm going to turn that hatchery me and my daddy have in Greenfield into a big-time full-sized Texas operation." Bob fell silent and gazed out the window. Suddenly he yelled: "Holy smoke! Look!" He pointed. Fred Wolkowski stayed in his bunk, but all the rest of the roommates fell in beside and behind Bob and looked. Jim was the first to speak.

"Refugees."

A column was approaching outside the south barbed-wire fences. Leading the column was an old unpainted two-wheel cart, loaded high with furniture and bedding, drawn by the stooped, shawl-shrouded figures of an old man and an old woman. Other figures, equally stooped and ragged, followed carrying bundles wrapped in sheets on their backs.

"Where are they coming from?" Tom asked of no one in particular.

"Just out of them woods," Burt answered.

Another cart, this one with four wheels, appeared, drawn by a skinny horse and an ox, and behind that more figures bent over under loads almost bigger than themselves. The leading cart was almost even with the block now, but the old couple drawing it looked neither to the right nor to the left. Now came a long line of ragged old men and women and skinny children trudging silently, steadily past.

"There must be hundreds of them," muttered Fritz Heine, his voice reduced to a croak, and then, as the column seemed to be without end, added, "Maybe thousands."

"God, look at that cow!" exclaimed Burt.

Led by two children, with an old man beating its flank, the cow was almost buried under a huge bundle tied to its back and sides. More animals appeared, all loaded down, with more ragged peasants trudging along.

"By golly," cried Fritz Heine, "they're on the run! The Russians have got 'em on the run!"

Jim snorted. "Hell, they've had 'em on the run for weeks. We've just never seen 'em before. And there's a good reason. Do you know why?"

"Why?"

"That's not even a road out there. What's happened is, they've taken to the woods."

"What's that mean?"

"Maybe the Krauts are using the roads to move up equipment. Or maybe the Russians are using the roads. Maybe they aren't so safe any more. How do I know?"

They watched the strange parade of defeat straggle past for another minute before Fritz spoke again.

"Well, I'm glad of one thing. I'm glad I made me a pack."

Several of the men groaned, and from his bunk Fred spoke for them. "Why bring that up again?"

"Because if the whole German population can march out of here through the woods, I don't see any reason why they won't march us out, too. And, by golly, I'm ready."

"Aw, tell it to the padre. We ain't been ordered to walk yet. Are they still coming?"

Still watching the never ending line of refugees, Bob answered. "Sure they are. Why don't you come down and have a look?"

Fred Wolkowski stretched himself out on his upper bunk. "I'll look at 'em after a while. Wake me up when the Russkies get here."

Al Koczeck moved away from the window and pulled a cardboard box from beneath a lower bunk. He lifted it onto the bunk beneath the pinned-up photographs of a dark-haired girl and a baby and stretched his short thick body out on the blankets. Pulling a handful of old letters from the box, he began to read them.

Jim looked over at Fred's back. He was asleep facing the wall. Tom Howard had spread out a solitaire game on his bunk. A round-faced youth across the room sat with his feet propped up, writing a letter.

"Hey, Noble," Burt called from the bunk beneath Tom's. "Writing to your fiancée?"

"Yeah," answered the round-faced youth, still writing.

"Come on over for a game of gin. There's no use writing that letter."

Jack Noble looked up innocently. "Why not?"

" 'Cause if the Russians get here before the goons march us out, you'll be with your gal in Pittsburgh long before that letter. And if the goons do march us out, it'll be pretty damned quick. They won't be packing the mail along. So why write the letter?"

Noble's round face scowled in thought for a minute. Then he stood up. "Yeah, I guess you're right." He crumpled the unfinished letter into a ball, crossed to the potbellied stove, and threw the wad of paper into the fire.

As the room quieted, the prison camp seemed to do the same. Bob still stood at the window watching the long line of refugees with their bundles and their carts and their animals slogging along just beyond the barbed-wire fences.

"Six thousand and six bucks today," he murmured to the ice-framed window. "Cripes, that's a lot of eggs. . . ."

The window rattled as a Soviet shell exploded in the frozen earth somewhere beyond the wall of pines.

Chapter Four

Colonel Akron, the Old Man, powerfully built, portly, and wearing a perfectly creased olive-drab gabardine shirt, sat alone in his small room unconsciously rubbing the blue stone of his West Point class ring along the right spear of his trim brown mustache. He studied an open book on the table before him. He sighed sleepily as the words on the pages began to blur in the light from the room's single dangling electric globe. He started to yawn but stopped, instantly composing his florid middle-aged face at the sound of a knock on his door.

"Come in," his rich voice invited.

The door opened, and Colonel Baker bent over to duck under the top of the doorframe, his freckled face glowing from the cold. Colonel Baker was Big X in charge of all escape activity.

"Oh. Hello, Red," the Old Man said, and nodded toward a chair across the small table.

The tall officer closed the door and removed his cap, revealing cropped blazing red hair, and sat down.

"I've found another one," he grinned, pulling a large wooden cribbage board from the pocket of his greatcoat and laying it on the table. "Brother, is it cold outside!" He loosened the heavy wool scarf at his throat. "I just passed the cookhouse thermometer. It's forty below. The German radio says it's the coldest winter in twenty some years."

The older officer pointed at the cribbage board. "What's in that one, Red?"

"I haven't opened it yet." The redhead carried on the conversation while he studied the cribbage board carefully, moving it so that its white varnished surface reflected the light. "Down at the theater they're watching the new show with overcoats on. The stove isn't doing any good at all. Say, George, how is it you aren't down there? You've always been a first nighter, haven't you?"

"I wasn't in the mood for a play tonight. I saw that one on Broadway. Saw the picture, too, with Jimmy Stewart, Lionel Barrymore, and Claudette Colbert. I don't think any of our boys can do it like Claudette. Anyhow, the real show is going on out there." He nodded his head toward the shuttered windows and the faint sounds of shellfire beyond.

"Yeah," Colonel Baker agreed as he pressed long fingers experimentally against different parts of the cribbage board. "I wouldn't want to be out there long on a night like this. There. Now I've got it." His long fingers drew the cribbage board apart, revealing a secret drawer. "More money," he said, extracting a neat bundle of new German currency.

"Genuine or counterfeit?"

"Who knows? Our people can make just as good German money as the Germans can." He slipped one crisp note from the bundle and tossed the rest across the table toward the Old Man. "If they keep sending this stuff we can start an inflation."

The Old Man chuckled. "The British already tried it. One night the RAF dropped nothing but tons of counterfeit Reichsmarks. But what really raised Ned with the Nazi economy was the night the Limeys dropped thousands of Third Reich food-ration books. This stuff looks good enough. Who received the parcel this time?"

"Fellow over in Block 158. They were playing a game on the board when I walked in to get it."

"Same source?"

Colonel Baker nodded. "War Prisoners Aid Association, New York. Usual thing. Towels, soap, food, cards, and the rest. Nice parcel. The goons haven't tumbled yet that about one parcel in ten contains a trick cribbage board."

An explosion louder than the steady distant rumble rattled the window and the wooden shutters.

"It's that German 88 again," the Old Man analyzed. "They've got it set up pretty close by."

"You know," Colonel Baker said, "any minute now the boys with red stars on their hats are going to come walking through those woods out there, and you and I will be out of a job. Especially me. We won't need a Big X any more."

The Old Man laughed softly. "They'll probably send us both back to the Point, Red, to teach courses in How to Be a Good Kriegie and How to Find Money, Maps, and Radio Parts in Cribbage Boards. Meanwhile you're still Big X and I'm the senior American officer. Better get this stuff stashed away." As he tossed the neat pack of currency across the table a cry penetrated through the walls of the room.

"Goon in the block!"

Colonel Baker clutched the pack of currency and rose halfway out of his chair.

"Goon in the block!" A nearer voice relayed the call.

Colonel Baker reached for the two parts of the cribbage board, quickly slipped the currency into the secret compartment, slid the two parts together, and shoved the innocent-looking board over against the window sill. A sharp knock sounded on the door behind him. It opened immediately, and a thin youthfully blond German in a Luftwaffe blue greatcoat walked in and saluted Colonel Akron, who was rising.

"Colonel Akron," the German clipped with a slight accent, "you will order all of the men to prepare immediately to march. At once. It is the Kommandant's order."

The senior American officer's florid face changed to gray. "To march?" His usually rich voice quavered. "Now? You mean tonight?"

"Yes," the German said, looking at a watch on his wrist. "It is now nine o'clock. We march in half an hour."

"But, Hohendahl," the Old Man pleaded, "not tonight. A forced march in half an hour? It's forty below zero out there!"

The thin German shrugged. "I am merely relaying the Kommandant's order. He has received orders. From Berlin. We march in half an hour. Now I must go and prepare too. It is the war, nicht?" Hohendahl saluted, turned, and walked out of the room. The echoes of his bootheels fell back through the open doorway.

The Old Man and Big X leaned against the table top and stared across at each other.

"It's finally come," breathed the Old Man. "Almost one whole year on half-rations, and now I've got to order them to march. In half an hour. In forty below zero. And I don't even know where to."

Big X straightened up. "Shall I spread the word, George?"

"Yes. Please." Muscles twitched beneath the splotched floridness of Colonel Akron's face. "Somebody will pay for this," he grated. "This goes in the little black book."

Colonel Baker picked up the cribbage board and turned to leave the room.

"Better start with the theater," the Old Man called after him. "There are 344 Kriegies watching a play, not to mention the actors and stagehands."

"Oh, my God. That's right." Colonel Baker ducked through the doorway, crossed the hall and knocked on a door. "Major Smith! Junior! Colonel Akron's room on the double!" Without waiting for an answer he turned, pushed open the block's south door, and stepped out into the shocking cold of the night. Straight white beams of searchlights rayed motionless into the compound. The guttural shouting of scurrying guards came from beyond the tangled fences. Colonel Baker moved with long-legged strides along the inner guard rail toward the black bulk of the Kriegie Theater at the west end of the night-shrouded compound.

In the darkened auditorium of the hand-built Kriegie Theater packed rows of overcoated, smiling prisoners sat in unpainted seats made from Red Cross packing cases. Al Koczeck and Bob Montgomery from Block 162, Room 8, watched the glaring rectangle of the stage before them.

"Not bad, huh?" Bob nudged Al as a prisoner costumed and made up like a pretty ballerina cavorted on the stage.

Onstage, Mervin Cahn, a skinny New Yorker playing a mad Russian ballet teacher, boomed out a line:

"Confeedenshally . . . shee steenks!"

The Kriegie audience covering the floor that sloped down toward the stage waited a split second and then let go with a roar that shook the building. The laughter suddenly stopped as the tall olive-drab figure of Colonel Baker strode incongruously onto the painted stage set and up to the footlights.

"The show is over, gentlemen." The colonel's voice rang clearly over the startled audience. "The Germans have decided the Russians are close enough."

Al poked his elbow into Bob's ribs. "The goons are going to surrender the camp!" His whisper was a falsetto.

"File in an orderly fashion out of the theater. Go to your rooms and pack," the tall speaker calmly instructed. "The Kommandant has ordered that we be ready to march in less than thirty minutes— so take your time."

With the hint of a smile the tall West Pointer turned and walked off the stage. Somebody started to pull the curtains, but left them hanging partially closed. The fluff-skirted ballerina yanked a blond bobbed wig from short black hair and quickly left the stage.

"Son of a bitch!" Al shook his head at Bob's shoulder level as they moved with the jabbering file out into the crowded aisle. "I never thought they'd do it. How in hell are they going to march ten thousand men out of here on a night like this?"

Bob, whistling softly, made no answer. They stepped out into the bitter cold. The breeze was as thin and sharp as a razor blade.

In Room 8 Jim Weis laid a notebook down beside him on his bunk, stretched, and ran his fingers through his unruly blond curls. He swung out of the bunk and walked across the room past the center table at which Ed Greenway and Fritz Heine mechanically pegged a game of cribbage. Jim stared vacantly at the heavy closed shutters blacking out the windows. Above the constant murmur and shuffle of the crowded prison camp, the rumble of shellfire to the east pulsated steadily. From the north came the intermittent louder bark of a Nazi big gun returning the Red fire.

"I don't see what's keeping them." Jim talked to anyone who cared to listen. "If they had kept moving the way they were going last night they'd have been here by noon today."

"It's the Oder River," twanged Bill Johnston, his angular length draped over an upper bunk by the window as he gazed at the knotty boards of the ceiling. "The goons stopped 'em at the Oder."

"But not for long." Jack Noble's chubby face registered wisdom as he lay on a lower bunk speaking up to the seven bed boards supporting Bill Johnston's burlap pallet. "That river must be frozen over solid. It's forty below zero outside."

"God . . . if they just don't move us first." Jim still gazed at the black shuttered window. "I don't think they can do it now. They've waited too long. I just don't think they can."

Suddenly confused shouting and pounding of feet exploded in the hallway. The door crashed open. Major Smith burst into the room.

"Pack up, men! We march in half an hour!"

Jim banged his back against the upper bunk jumping to his feet.

"Tonight, Major? Tonight?"

"That's it, Jim!" The Major's white teeth flashed in the middle of his shaggy black beard, but he wasn't grinning. "So get packed as quick as you can. Don't try to take too much, but eat as much as you can. We may not see much food for a while wherever we're going. I'll see you in front of the block in half an hour. Oh, yes. And wear all the clothes you've got. It's forty below out there."

The major left, and they could hear him shout in the next room.

"Well, let's get at it." Fritz Heine's voice trumpeted above the confused shouting of men throughout the block. His homely red face was almost gloating. "Who said it was too late to move us?"

Five of the six men present in Room 8 began violently to pull blankets from their bunks. Suddenly Jim remembered Fred Wolkowski.

"Fred!" Jim shouted, bent over his own lower bunk. "Fred! Wake up!" Jim knocked his head against the upper bunk and grabbed the spot through his thick blond hair as he straightened up. With his other hand he grabbed the shoulder of the sleeping man. "Fred!"

"Hunh . . ." Fred moaned and rolled onto his back. "Wassa matter?"

"Get up, Fred. We've got to march. The goons are marching us out of here tonight!"

Fred yawned. "The dirty bastards." He eased his slender body with increasing speed down the five-foot drop to the floor. "The dirty mother-loving bastards." He stepped over the olive-drab blankets that Jim was hastily spreading on the floor and crossed to the wooden food cabinet nailed to the wall.

"I'll bet they don't make it." Jim smoothed out two blankets one on top of the other on the floor between his bunk and the center table. "I bet you anything the Russkies overtake us."

"You know, they might at that." Wolkowski studied the cans on the shelves of the food locker, selected one filled with Red Cross jam, and calmly dumped half its bright red contents onto a slice of dark German bread.

"Hey, take it easy with that stuff!" complained Fritz Heine. His prairie-bred face was even redder than usual as he dragged a gleaming back pack from under his tier of bunks. It was made of tin cans carefully beaten flat and fastened together in sheets. Attached to its shiny metal bulk were shoulder straps made from the sleeves of an old khaki shirt.

"We can't pack all this." Fred nodded toward the shelves loaded with canned food, sacks of sugar, coffee, and tea, cartons of biscuits and cheese and other hoarded reserves. "I'm eating as much as I can hold." Fred stuffed his mouth with the bread and jam.

"Oh, no?" boomed Fritz. "Well, I'm going to take as much as I can carry." He crossed to the cabinet, gathered up an armful of canned meat, and took it back to his huge pack in the opposite corner.

"Hubba hubba, hubba. Let's take a walk, men." Al Koczeck strutted into the room rubbing his hands together like a baseball player.

"Yeah, let's take a leetle walk." Bob Montgomery, towering behind Koczeck, grinned. Both men crossed to their corner bunks and began pulling blankets to the floor.

"Well, how'd you like the show?" Bill Johnston's voice went up a notch in irony.

Bob looked around at the other seven busily milling men. "Where's Tom and Burt?"

The two entered. "What's all the flap about?" Tom inquired, his thin face calm. "A little evening stroll?"

Fred spoke through a mouth full of bread and jam. "Yeah. In forty below zero."

"Boy, that's for me. Let me at it." Al Koczeck reached up into the food cabinet with both thick arms and dragged down a shower of dried peaches and prunes, a can of Spam, and some C-ration biscuits.

"Hey, you guys take it easy on that stuff, for gosh sakes!" Fritz yelled as he made another trip to the food locker. "We been saving that for weeks. Out of half-rations, too."

"Oh, dummy up, Fritz," Bob Montgomery jeered. "We can't pack all that stuff out of here."

Jim Weis stood up and pushed his blond hair back. "Hold everything. If we go off half cocked we've had it. Let's get organized."

Fritz, his features set with determination, kept on stuffing cans and cartons into his pack. The rest paused.

"All right, Jim," Bob said. "You're the room Führer. Start organizing."

"O.K. Well, in the first place, when the major briefed us for this kind of emergency he recommended that no man try to carry more than seven pounds."

Fritz snorted. "You can carry seven pounds if you want to, but don't come to me when you're hungry. Just because you were all too lazy to make packs."

"All right, Fritz." Jim's slightly edged voice contained authority. "You can carry all you want. Only let's organize, say, four pounds of food per man. Meat, dried fruit, oatmeal, and chocolate. Those are the important foods. Spread it out, Bob."

Bob handed the items out of the cabinet and Koczeck lined them up in ten rows, one row for each man. Quantities of food still remained on the shelves.

"Too bad you weren't cooking last week, Jim," commented Al Koczeck.

"Yeah," Fritz answered. "If he had been we wouldn't have had anything to take with us at all."

"Well, now we've got more than we can handle," Jim retorted, "and we've been depriving ourselves of all this out of half-rations. Now, each man take a pound can of meat, a pound of fruit, four chocolate bars—Jesus! What are we going to do with all these chocolate bars?"

Tom Howard's thin face broke into a smile. "I just left Room 4. They could use some. They've been losing at poker in there."

Jim nodded. "And one pound of oatmeal per man. If you eat it dry it swells up in your stomach and you don't feel hungry any more. Those are the staples. You can take anything extra you want. Who'll take a pound of sugar and some salt? We may get to cook the oatmeal someplace."

"I'll take it," Bill Johnston volunteered.

"All right. Let's get cracking."

"Hubba!" Al Koczeck helped himself first, and the rest followed. The stock of cigarettes was large. Each man grabbed from ten to twenty packs from a cardboard box. There were still many packs left over.

"By golly, I'm going to take some of those, too." Fritz grabbed an armful.

"What for?" asked Burt Salem. "You don't smoke."

"They might come in handy for trading." Fritz dumped the loose packs into the rapidly filling maw of his tin pack.

The rest of the men of Room 8 made bedrolls in prescribed fashion. Two blankets were placed on the floor. A towel, some soap, toothbrush and tooth powder, razor and spare blades, the food and cigarettes, extra pairs of socks and long underwear, small mirrors, pencils, and other sundry personal effects such as photographs and letters were placed in a row along the center of the blankets.

Jim Weis hauled a box from under his bunk and extracted a heavy YMCA POW gift diary, several paper-bound notebooks, and some pencils. Ruthlessly he tore the heavy binding from the diary, ripped loose the empty pages, and tossed them back under the bunk. The pages covered with fine handwriting he placed with his other belongings on the blankets.

"Hey, Jim," Tom Howard called across the room, "you going to pack that stuff? It must weigh four pounds alone."

"Four pounds of my sweat. I'm going to damned well try." Jim then folded the blankets once lengthwise over the articles along the middle and rolled the bulging fold toward the edges to form a long lumpy tube. This he folded endwise, making a large horseshoe of the whole thing. With pieces of clothesline he bound the ends and tightly tied them together. Slipping the loop over his shoulder he tested it. It felt secure. He took it off, leaned it against his bunk, and looked around the crowded room.

"What time is it?"

Bob looked at his wrist watch. "Nearly a quarter after nine."

Munching on a biscuit piled more than an inch high with canned Canadian butter and marmalade, Jim Weis ambled through the dull light of the corridor. His bulky pants legs rubbed together until he came to Room 11 at the south end of the block.

"How are your boys in Room 8, Jim?" Major Smith looked up from his task of securing the ends of one of two blanket rolls resting on the lower bunk. "All set?"

"As set as they'll ever be. You know, Major, I don't get this."

The major grinned through his beard. "Who does?"

"No. What I mean is, why are we knocking ourselves out to get ready in such an all-fired hurry? Why aren't we stalling? We got nothing to gain by marching out of here in a big rush, have we?"

Major Smith straightened up. "I don't originate the orders around here, Jim. I just pass them on. Stooge for me a minute, will you?"

Jim stepped into the tiny room, swung the door to until it was open just a crack, and pressed an ear to the crack. Behind him the major stepped up to the opposite wall and with a razor blade pried loose an innocent-looking board. From a hidden trap behind it he brought out a large bundle of currency and thrust it into his combat jacket pocket. From the opposite end of the block came a shout.

"Goon in the block!"

Another voice picked it up. "Goon in the block!"

Jim turned and whispered quickly. "Step on it!"

"Goon in the block!"

"Goon in the block!"

The cry was rapidly relayed from room to room, voice to voice, until it completely faded. Hobnailed boots could be heard approaching. Major Smith quickly replaced the board over the wall cache.

"O.K. Open the door, Jim."

Jim opened the door and once again munched at the food in his hand. The major bent over the lower bunk and tested the ropes of the two bedrolls.

"Good evening, Major."

Big and bundled in drab Luftwaffe blue, Obergefreiter Glimlitz paused to show gold teeth in a smile and then turned to knock gently on Colonel Akron's door across the hall.

"Glimlitz," Major Smith called. "Where are we headed for?"

Glimlitz shrugged. "Who knows?"

The resounding deep voice of Colonel Akron carried through the door of Room 12. "Come in."

Glimlitz showed his gold teeth once again, opened the door and went in.

Jim grunted. "That old fart probably doesn't know at that."

The major grinned and sat down. "Well, Jim, I've said it before and I'll say it again—"

"Yeah, I know: 'Things'll get a lot worse before they get better.'"

Jim opened the food locker of the small room. "What you got to bash, Major?"

"Help yourself."

Jim chewed some raisins and offered the box to the major. Both men munched the fruit quietly, listening to the rumble of the battle somewhere beyond the blackout shutters, hearing the never ending background of blending voices from up and down the prison block, trying to catch even a glimmer of meaning from the muffled sound of conversation between Glimlitz and the Old Man across the hall.

Jim absently watched the major's shaggy black beard work rhythmically up and down with the chewing.

Major Peter Smith, Jim thought. Regular army. One of the first big heroes to taste glory. Wonder how he felt during that thirty seconds over Tokyo, and those thirty days of bond selling afterward back home. It's funny that he should have had all that and two Distinguished Flying Crosses for only flying two missions—one with Doolittle over Tokyo and the last more than two years ago over Bizerte. Or could that be called two missions? Wasn't it only one and a half? How must he feel sweating out a march in forty below zero and most likely thinking of his wife and two kids? An old Kriegie. One of the oldest. An old soldier at thirty-three. He'll make it out of here. He'll make it . . . and those who stick with him will make it if he doesn't die.

And while Jim regarded the major, the major studied Jim, thinking: If the rest were all like him. Not very old, but not just a kid. Second Lieutenant Jim Weis, maybe ten years younger than me. The major looked at the full, unruly blond hair, at the clear face unlined except at the corners of the eyes from staring too long and too often into the ball of the sun, at the full lower lip that could have been sensuous except that it was too constantly set. It beats me, these Eagle Squadron guys . . . especially this one. When he had flown his fifty missions why didn't he go home? When he had a hundred why didn't he pin on his medals and quit? What was he trying to prove? Well, he's no bookkeeper or he'd have known he couldn't keep gambling his chances forever. There were only two prizes for his method. One was death, and the other—well, here he is, and he still has a chance at them both. But he's a soldier. He obeys orders. He'll make it . . . if I make it.

A shot of camphor in the air made Jim turn to watch gold-toothed Glimlitz step out of the Old Man's room and on through the block's south door into the frigid white beam of a searchlight. The Old Man's door opened again. Redheaded Colonel Baker's long frame filled the way.

"Major," he called. "Colonel Akron wants to see you."

Major Smith crossed into Room 12. "Yes, sir." He addressed the stocky, mustached American senior officer.

"Are the men ready to march, Major Smith?" The Old Man's voice was both strong and tired.

"Yes, sir, if you mean are they packed."

"Good. Now that they are ready, pass the word around to stall for time."

Major Smith smiled through his beard. "Right ho, sir." He looked at Colonel Baker, whose freckled face grinned.

"Get Junior Jones to pass the word along from block to block. We may as well give Uncle Joe a few more minutes to get here."

The three men listened briefly to the crumping of the nearby shell-fire and felt the thin wooden floor shake. The major threw a friendly salute to the Old Man and crossed over to his own room. Jim and Junior Jones waited with eyes glittering. Jim asked the question.

"What's cooking, Major?"

The major shut the door carefully and turned. "Junior, see if you can get word from block to block. Tell everyone to be ready to form outside, but to stall for time. When the order comes to fall in, tell them to keep messing around in their rooms. Stall. We want to stall as long as we can."

"Yes, sir!"

"Now that's more like it."

"O.K. Get going, son. Jim, you take care of this block."

"Yup."

Junior dashed down the corridor toward the north door. Jim stepped next door to Room 10, entered, and faced twelve bundled-up Kriegies inside.

"What's up, Jim?"

"Orders from the Old Man. Stall. Stay ready to march, but when the order comes, stall."

"What do you mean, stall?"

"When you get the order to fall in out front, don't do it. Mess around with something in here. Make like you're still packing. Only, don't fall in until you have to."

"How'll we know when we have to?"

"You'll know. The goons have got guns. Make them use them."

"Oh, that's great!"

Jim looked back briefly. "No. That's an order!"

In Room 8 Tom Howard was drinking a rich mixture of Klim when Jim made the announcement.

"Jesus!" Burt Salem exclaimed. "What time is it now?"

Bob Montgomery looked at his wrist watch. "It's almost nine-thirty."

Tom finished his drink leisurely, put the container down on the table, and wiped his mouth slowly with his sleeve. "There's only one thing wrong," he said casually, his thin face unperturbed. "We're not holding the cards."

Chapter Five

Colonel Baker's six foot four was well padded beneath a greatcoat and a neat blanket roll coiling over his right shoulder to his left hip when he opened the door of Room 11, stepped inside, and shut the door.

"Is your canary taken care of, Major?"

"All set," answered Major Smith, who was second in command below Colonel Baker in all escape and underground activity. He nudged the broken remains of the Hohner accordion on the floor with his feet.

"How are you doing it?"

"I took it apart and gave each piece to a different man to carry."

"Good men?"

"All old Kriegies."

The Big X's freckled face broke into a smile. "Well, that's all of them. We're keeping one of them operating along the way."

Major Smith looked surprised. "That's a good trick. How can we do that?"

"A pocket canary with batteries."

"Shorty's?"

"That's right. I wanted you to know, Major, because you're Little X. That makes five of us who know. Shorty, two stooges for him, and you and me. This block will be next to the last in this compound's column. Shorty will be up ahead. If he should drop out, pick up his canary when you pass him."

"Yeah. Oh, hell. Shorty won't drop out."

"That's why I picked him. But it's forty below outside, Pete. Remember, this is where most of Napoleon's army froze in the retreat from Moscow; and they were the finest foot soldiers in the world. None of us are foot soldiers. We're all fly boys, and we've been on half-rations for nearly a year. This probably isn't going to be very nice. Last winter when Shorty broke out of here he managed to hard-ass it more than a hundred miles over the mountains into Czechoslovakia before the Gestapo caught him, so I figure he'll probably make it now as well as anyone. But if he doesn't, you pick up his canary, Pete, when your block catches up to him."

Major Smith grinned wryly through his beard. "Who's going to pick me up?"

Both men stood looking at the floor, listening to the outside sounds of nearby shellfire and the babbling murmur of voices in the prison block. Suddenly, as always, they started at the familiar alarm of Junior Jones's voice in the corridor.

"Goon in the block!"

Lieutenant Pieber, followed by Glimlitz, entered the north end of Block 162.

"Ah, yes, Mr. Junior Jones," the German officer said through a knowing smile. "By all means. Goon in the block."

Junior, pink face unperturbed, fell in beside the rapidly striding Pieber as other voices echoed the alarm. "Where are we going, Herr Pieber? Do you know?"

Pieber shrugged his thin square shoulders. "Time will tell. We shall see."

"But we're not going far, are we? We can't go far in this kind of weather."

"But why not?" Pieber asked in mock surprise. "Why not? Listen." They could hear the soft rumbling shellfire outside. "Good German soldiers are fighting bravely in that weather."

"Yeah, and so are the Russians."

Pieber stiffened as his gaunt cheeks tightened. He rapped his gloved fist sharply against the door of Room 12. Colonel Akron's deep voice answered calmly, "Come in."

Pieber stepped inside and closed the door, leaving the heavy-set Glimlitz in the corridor with Junior.

"Well, Glimlitz, what was that job you were going to take over after the war? Gauleiter of New York?"

Glimlitz grunted.

"Who do you think is winning the war now, Glimlitz?"

The gold teeth gleamed as Glimlitz forced a grin. "I think maybe now they are winning this war." Glimlitz jerked his heavy head in the direction of the battle rumbles outside. "Yes, I should now think they are winning, nichtwahr?"

Junior's young face quivered with nervous glee. "Well, well. Well, well. I never thought I'd see the day when Lagermeister Glimlitz would admit that we're winning."

The gold-toothed grin of the German relaxed a little. "You don't understand what I think. I think they win the war, not you. Not the United States. Not England. When the Bolsheviki wins, then all Western Kultur is kaput. But there is still hope."

"You're doggone right there is. Hope for us."

"I think maybe your Frahnklin Rosenfeldt, he will figure this out, too, and come on our side. Then we beat the Bolsheviki together."

"You must be chewing opium. Say, where do you get this Rosenfeldt stuff? The name is Roosevelt."

"Ach, but he is a Jew. No matter. I am a soldier, not a politician. I have volunteered for duty on the Ostfront when Breslau fell kaput. But I am too old. They will not take me, so here we are, all of us together, running from the Bolsheviki together."

"Why Breslau?"

"When they entered Breslau, I knew all was kaput for Deutschland." An unfocused look came into the blue eyes of Glimlitz. "My wife, my son, my daughter, my home—all were in Breslau. . . . "

The door of Room 12 opened. Colonel Akron and Lieutenant Pieber stepped briskly into the hall. The colonel's voice rang out sharply. "Colonel Baker!"

The door of Room 11 opened instantly, and Baker ducked through. "Yes, sir."

"Order the entire compound to fall in in front of the blocks ready to march."

"Yes, sir." Both men wore straight faces. Colonel Baker turned around. "Major Smith, order your men to fall in out front ready to march."

"Yes, sir." With a perfectly straight face Pete addressed Junior. "Lieutenant Jones, order each room to fall in out front."

"Yes, sir." Junior threw a snappy salute, about faced, and made a dash for the nearest room to get there before he broke out laughing. Jumping inside the crowded room he called out loudly: "Fall in out front. Fall in out front ready to march!"

In the corridor Colonel Baker saluted the Old Man and turned to

Pieber. "How about it? If I start walking between the blocks is some guard liable to take a shot at me?"

"But of course not. Please hurry."

"I don't know, Herr Pieber." Baker shook his head slowly. "I don't think the men have had time enough to be ready yet."

"Nonsense. They have been ready for weeks. Please hurry, Colonel Baker. The Kommandant is waiting."

"Well, I'll see what I can do." Baker unhurriedly ducked out of the block through the south entrance.

"All out in front ready to march!" Junior darted from room to room reshouting the command, but stepped far enough inside to gesture with downturned palms.

"Hey, Junior. Wait a minute." In Room 8 Jim Weis looked up from the dummy task of packing and unpacking unwanted food in cardboard Red Cross cartons. "Any gen from Pieber or Glimlitz where they are marching us?"

Junior shrugged in imitation of Pieber. "Ve shall zee. Ve shall zee. Say, did you know Glimlitz's wife and kids were in Breslau when the Russians took the place?"

"Yeah?" Bob Montgomery snorted. "Now isn't that just too bad." Bob was rolling surplus blankets into a huge useless bundle. "Here's a first-rate pack for you, Junior. You can take it with you."

"No, thanks."

"Better yet," suggested Jim, once more beginning to unpack the food cartons. "Give it to Pieber and tell him to stuff it."

"Can it," whispered Junior. "Here comes Pieber now." Junior raised his voice. "Come on, you guys. Fall in out front of the block!" He backed out of the room, bumping roughly into Pieber. "Oh, excuse me, Herr Pieber." Then he vanished down the corridor.

Pieber peered through his spectacles at the elaborate confusion in Room 8. All ten of its occupants appeared to be frantically packing and sorting.

"Zhentlemen, zhentlemen," Pieber admonished in hurt tones. "Kom. Kom. You must march now."

Jim looked up soberly. "We'll be ready pretty quick, Herr Pieber. You kind of caught us all flat-footed. Say, where are we marching to, anyway?"

Without replying, Pieber watched for a few more seconds, then turned abruptly back into the corridor. As he strode toward the south end of the block he peered through his spectacles into the rooms to right and left. All were scenes of similar confusion. He walked swiftly to Colonel Akron's room and opened the door without knocking. Colonel Akron was squatting on the floor piling books into a box.

"Colonel, Colonel, what is the meaning of this? Why aren't your men falling in?"

The Old Man's deep voice answered in dead seriousness. "I guess we're not quite ready yet. Just give us a little time. You must have patience."

Pieber stared down at the American senior officer who remained squatting, systematically studying the cover of each book before he placed it in the cardboard box. Abruptly Pieber turned and stepped into the hall where Glimlitz stood.

"Kommen!" Pieber's voice was brittle. Glimlitz followed the lieutenant out through the south door into the night.

The colonel's door remained open, and he looked across the corridor into Major Smith's room. The major grinned. "That did it, Colonel."

"Yes," answered Colonel Akron solemnly, "I suppose it did. Well, tell the men to relax. We might as well wait in comfort."

Major Smith stepped into the corridor, where the confused noises of the stalling tumbled from every room. He threw back his head and his voice roared: "Take it easy, men! All clear! All clear!" He called again. "All clear for a while! Room Führers, front and center!"

The floor clattered as the senior prisoners from each room clumped down the corridor. The major grinned at the huddle of faces which formed around him.

"Well, the fat's in the fire now, men. Pieber is wise to us. So I think when they come back every man had better have his greatcoat on and be ready to march."

"No more stalling, Major?" an unidentified voice asked.

"Just a little," he answered. "Be ready to move fast, but take your time and move slow." A twinkle appeared in his eyes. "But use your own judgment. If they get tough, you have my permission to move as fast as you want to."

"Gee, thanks," another voice responded.

"One more thing," Major Smith said. "Somehow I don't think it would be smart this time to yell 'Goon in the block.' Lieutenant

Jones, you stooge the north end of the block, and, Tom Howard, you take the south end. When you see them coming, give us a 'Hi yo, Silver.' Got that? Hi yo, Silver."

"Awayyyyy . . ." someone called.

"That's all, men. Keep a lick upper stiff, or something like that."

The huddle broke up and scattered. Jim and Tom Howard entered Room 8 and headed directly for their lockers.

"Coats on, men," Jim told the curiously waiting members of the room. "Be ready to march, and be ready for anything when the goons get back. This time we fall in, but we still take our time about it."

"That's—uh—something we got plenty of—uh. Time." Al Koczeck was having difficulty stuffing his wide padded shoulders into his greatcoat.

"Well, I'm going to be all ready." Fritz Heine, already wearing his greatcoat, bent backward and slipped his arms into the slings of his gleaming tin pack. "It takes time to get this pack secure."

Burt Salem buttoned his greatcoat snugly about his short body and frowned. "Say, isn't this apt to be something like that appel deal you were telling me about this morning?"

"You ain't just awoofin', brother."

They waited fully clothed and sweating. Some lay with eyes wide open on their bunks. Others sat silent or talked softly. For what seemed a long time there was almost no sound louder than the pulsing of the explosions outside, beyond and remote from the stifling heat of the room. Suddenly all started.

"Hi yo-oo-ohh, Silverr-rr!"

Tom's voice ripped through the block. Men jumped to their feet. Jim looked up, tensely calm, from the novel. "Take it easy, boys. Take it easy."

The nervous men assumed relaxed positions which their faces belied. Tom ran into the room and quickly began slipping into his blanket roll.

"They're coming. Lots of them—with guns."

"Yeah. Sure." Jim's voice remained calm. "Sit down and take it easy, Tom."

Tom sat down beside Jim on the lower bunk. The ten men in the room waited.

There was a crash as the door at the block's south end slammed open. The floor quaked under booming, hobnailed jackboots.

" 'Raus!" A guttural voice screamed the command. Boots clattered. " 'Raus!" The men in Room 8 looked at one another. " 'Raus!" Another guttural voice rasped out the order. More boots crashed along the corridor. " 'Raus! Aufstehen! Heraus!"

"Yeah . . . yeah. O.K." Voices of fellow prisoners could be heard. Their footfalls joined the tumult. Footfalls exploded toward Room 8. " 'Raus!" The deafening screech came from a glowering guard in a gray-green greatcoat and dark blue steel helmet, with a full square military pack on his back. " 'Raus!" The eyes of the goon glared, and he held a burp gun ominously by its stock and long magazine. "Aufstehen! Schnell!"

The men in Room 8 began slowly to move. Bill Johnston stood up and stretched luxuriously. "O.K., Doc. Hold your horses. We're coming."

"Verdammte Luftgängstern!" screamed the goon. " 'Raus!"

The burp gun exploded in an ear-splitting roar in the guard's hands. Splinters flew from the table and the shutters, and windows crashed in pieces. Bullets ricocheted from the table, which tumbled against the wall. The men dived into bunks or flattened themselves in the corners. Jack Noble cried, "No . . . no . . ." Jim Weis cowered on his bunk behind his locker waving his arms and shouting: "Nicht schiessen! Bitte, nicht schiessen! Don't shoot! Wir kommen schnell! Bitte, nicht schiessen!"

The burp gun stopped spewing. The guard backed into the corridor and motioned along it with the gun. "Nun. 'Raus!"

"Jawohl, jawohl." Jim almost whimpered as the men tumbled into the corridor and joined the swarm of prisoners heading toward the opened front doors of the block.

Major Smith appeared from somewhere and fell in beside Jim. "Anybody hurt in there?"

Jim shook his head, attempting to control the slight chattering of his teeth. His bad tooth began to ache. "Major," he said as they stepped into the frigid shock of the outside night, "you can take this room Führer's job and shove it up your ass."

The major wrapped an arm about Jim's back and gave his right shoulder a squeeze. Then he pushed on through the rapidly gathering block formation to its front. He came face to face with Lieutenant Pieber. The German's steamy breath rose from a cold grin.

Beyond the immediate quiet which settled over the two thousand shivering prisoners German voices shouted orders down by the west gate. Sparks from overheated stoves belched into the blackness from a hundred chimney stacks. The men listened tautly to the shells exploding unseen, as the low swirling ceiling of mist glowed with the lights of the camp. Major Smith's dark beard towered over the men of Room 8 as he approached the end of the formation.

"Men," he said in a lowered voice, "who'll volunteer to carry this guitar? Tex was going to leave it behind, but it might be a good thing if we had a little of Tex's music in a day or so . . . wherever we happen to be."

The men of Rooms 8, 9, and 10 who heard the request looked shivering down at the hard-packed snow and said nothing. Then Bill Johnston's Midwestern twang lifted their eyes.

"Oh, what the heck. We'll take it."

Major Smith grinned and passed the guitar to Bill. "Good lads. We may need a little entertainment before this is over." He walked back to his place in front of the formation.

Al Koczeck danced a little jig and clapped his hands to fight the frozen air. "Did you hear that? 'We'll take it. We'll take it!' I like the way he said that 'We'll' business. What are you trying to do? Get a promotion or something? They don't give out promotions here, mister. Didn't you know that?"

"Aw, what the heck. It don't weigh much. It'll be good for morale."

Bob Montgomery snorted. "You ought to be in the U.S.O., Johnston."

From up the line, Tex's voice boomed out. "What are we waiting for, Major? What's the delay?"

Major Smith looked west between the long formations of cold, restless prisoners toward the gate. "Search me. It's just like our own army, I guess. Hurry up and wait."

From that direction, the short, stocky figure of Captain Daniels strode into view. He stopped and faced the men. "Any disabled men in this block?"

"Yeah," somebody cracked from the pack, "my balls are frozen."

"What's the deal, Danny?" asked Major Smith.

"I don't know. The goons say any disabled men can fall out now."

"And then what?"

"I don't know. Anybody sick? Anybody lame? You can fall out now and take your chances on what the goons will do with you."

"Would they leave us behind?" a voice asked.

"I don't know. But if you think you're too lame or sick to march, you can fall out now."

Tom spoke sideways to Jim. "You know, I think I'm developing a sore toe."

Four men stepped out of the ranks and stood beside Danny. "Last chance," he called. "But if you're not really disabled, better stay with your block. There's no telling what will happen to the disabled men, but there's some safety in numbers."

"What about your toe?" Jim muttered.

"Pain's left it. The goons are liable to shoot those guys."

"Yeah, but they might be left behind and liberated by the Russians."

"What's the difference? I think the Russians will catch up with us tonight, anyhow."

Danny said something to the disabled men, and they walked west toward the gate. Two of them limped badly.

Suddenly the ground trembled and continued to tremble for a few seconds before the rumbling of a prolonged explosion which passed over them from the south. When it stopped, the prison camp erupted into a babble of chatter.

"Man, oh, man!" exclaimed Fred Wolkowski, chuckling between his rounded shoulders. "They must have hit an ammunition dump!"

"Hubba, hubba, hubba!" cried Al Koczeck, playfully punching Jim's shoulder. "They're coming, men. They're coming!"

Tom Howard reached to the back of his neck and pulled up his woolen scarf until it formed a hood over his knitted GI cap.

"Say, that's an idea," observed Bob Montgomery. He adjusted his own scarf. "My ears were about to fall off."

Jim and several others began adjusting their scarves over their heads. Guttural shouting sounded from the direction of the gate. The shuffling of boots joined the sounds as the formations of blocks on the other side of the road began moving in a long shadowy column toward the gate.

"All right, men!" Major Smith's voice gained attention. "It looks as if we're going to get started, so here's a final little pep talk. I'm in command of the block. The room Führers take orders from me. The rest of you take orders from your room Führers. So try and stay with your own room combines. If we stick together, we ought to be all right."

A voice down the line asked a question. "What about escapes, Major?"

The major looked quickly to the left and right and behind him. There were no Germans nearby. "When we leave here you're on your own as far as that is concerned. I can't tell you not to escape; but remember, it's forty below zero. If you do make a break for it, you'd better know what you're doing. And don't forget, there are Russians all around us. There's a good chance they'll overtake us before morning anyway. But it's up to you."

The formations to the west of Block 162 could be heard scuffling off toward the gate.

"I don't know where they are marching us," Major Smith continued, "but ten thousand men are going to make a mighty big column. If any Russian planes buzz over on the deck, dive for the nearest cover and pull it in after you. From the air they won't be able to tell we're Allied Kriegies. And from what I hear about the Russians, they shoot first and check dog tags afterward."

The major grinned and blew steam into the near darkness. "That's all I have to say men, except"—he paused, and everyone knew what he was going to say—"before things get any better they'll get a hell of a lot worse!"

To the left, the commander of Block 161 called his formation to attention. The bulky figure of Obergefreiter Glimlitz came from that direction. "All right, Major. Now is it time to march."

"Block. Ten-nshun!"

The men snapped to rigidity beneath their heavy layers of clothing.

"Left, face. Route step, harsh!"

As they shuffled over the ice-caked ground, some of the men glanced back over their left shoulders at the squatting length of Block 162.

"Take a last look at your old home," suggested the major. "You'll never see Block 162 again."

Beneath the flames and sparks boiling from half a dozen red-hot chimney stacks, the long sloping roof gave off a ghostly blue-white glow from its shroud of snow. Icicles gleamed like a long row of giant sharks' teeth from the eaves. Warm yellow light flowed from every window onto the crusted snow of the compound. Unexpectedly Jim's vision blurred, and two tears froze instantly on his cheeks as he faced forward and marched away from the block with the formation.

42

"Well, we're off," Koczeck muttered from behind.

"Any change is a holiday," Montgomery's voice added.

Almost immediately the formation was halted in a widened space between the end of a prison block and the front of the Kriegie Theater.

"Hey, where you guys going? Why don't you stick around with us to welcome Uncle Joe?"

The shout came from a large group of men standing before the theater.

"We're going out to meet him!" Koczeck called back.

Jim spotted the long grinning-faced figure of Mervin Cahn, the skinny actor from New York. "Hey, Merv! What you doing in that outfit?"

"The show must go on," Merv called back. "Goin' to finish it after you noisy guys leave."

Behind Jim, Bill Johnston twanged: "What's Cahn doing with the disabled guys? He's the biggest rackets guy in camp."

Jim answered softly. "He's got T.B."

"I'll bet he has," snorted Bill. "I'll lay odds it's just another racket to get out of marching. Look at all the old Kriegies in that bunch."

Major Smith listened to the talk and stepped over. "Johnston, did it ever occur to you that spending a couple of years in a place like this might increase your chances of getting sick?"

"Heck, don't jump on me, Major. I was just making conversation."

Up by the gate the voice of Lieutenant Pieber interrupted. "Now, Major, you vill bring your men forward, please."

"O.K., boys. Let's go."

As the column moved, Jim turned and waved. "Take it easy, Merv. See you on Broadway."

"Halt. Halt. In fives, zhentlemen."

Pieber and Glimlitz walked down both sides of the column, counting the men off by fives.

"Ein hundert zwei und neunzig," snapped the lieutenant.

"Ein hundert zwei und neunzig. Jawohl," replied the Obergefreiter.

"And where, please, are the other four officers?"

The major waved an arm. "Over there. Too disabled to march."

"Ah, ja." Pieber shook his head sadly. "There are so many of them. It is a pity. I do not know what we shall do with them. Now you may pass through the gate. Turn to the right and follow after the others onto the road."

43

"All right, men. Let's go."

The two great gates made of thickly strung barbed wire, heavily stapled to stripped young pine logs, were open. The column passed shuffling between the red- white- and black-striped sentry boxes, each occupied by a guard standing with rifle held at ease. A few feet ahead, across a narrow frozen road, rose the rusty lacework of another double barbed-wire fence, and beyond that the squat buildings of another prison compound. In it men stood in yellow-lighted doorways cheering as the men of Block 162 turned right.

"Ain't you guys coming?" a marcher boomed out toward the neighboring compound.

"After you, sir! You got here first!" came a voice from one of the distant doorways.

Fritz Heine, trudging bent forward under his bulky tin pack, lifted his voice so that Major Smith could hear it. "They ought to be leading us. The senior officer in that compound has had 'em all marching around the perimeter four miles a day for the past two weeks to get 'em in shape just in case this happened."

"Well, look at it this way, Fritz," the major called back. "That means they've already marched four miles today. We're starting out fresh."

Fritz grinned sheepishly under his pack. "Say, I never thought of that."

"Well, boys," the major said cheerfully, "you've always wanted to walk out of here. Now we're doing it."

"Man, oh, man!" Koczeck chortled. "Look at the superrace!"

Everyone grinned at the guard who took his place beside the block formation.

"He must be in his sixties!"

The old soldier's face was pinched under the weight of a blue steel helmet. His shoulders were pulled back under the huge pack that seemed almost as big as he was. From the webbing at his bulging waist protruded canteen, mess kit, ammunition pouches, flashlight, and bayonet. He leaned miserably on his rifle as if it were a shovel.

"Do you speak English?" Jim asked.

"Nein." The voice was meek. "Nur Deutsch."

"Wohin gehen wir?" asked Jim.

The German removed one hand from the rifle and held its heavily gloved palm upward. "Weiss ich auch nicht," he moaned.

"What did he say?" asked Burt.

"He says he doesn't know where we're going either." Jim turned to Tom. "Take it easy. Ehay aymay ownay ouray ingolay. He's probably from Brooklyn."

The old guard turned and walked a few steps ahead. In addition to everything else, a trench shovel thrust its handle up the back of the pack. Fred Wolkowski shivered. "That load must weigh sixty or seventy pounds."

Jim watched the lanky figure of Colonel Baker walk toward them along the endless columns stretching into the night. The Big X walked up to Major Smith, and they stepped away from the formation. The major gestured violently with both arms. Colonel Baker shrugged and walked on toward the rear of the column. Major Smith stepped up close to the head of his formation.

"Men, gather around me." As many as possible pressed forward. Jim and Tom squeezed together near the front of the cluster.

"Men," the major said soberly and softly, "about this business of escaping. There's something I have to tell you. I don't like to."

Jim and Tom stared tensely at the major, whose eyes met theirs briefly before sweeping on over the cluster. He licked his lips before going on.

"I have just been told by Colonel Baker that Colonel Akron has been handed an ultimatum by the Germans. It is this. For each man who escapes—two prisoners will be shot!"

The frigid night breeze carved daintily into the stiffened backs of the men.

"It may be a bluff. It's strictly against the Geneva Convention. But we've never caught them bluffing yet. Colonel Akron does not feel it's his duty to order you not to try to escape. But he wants you to know what the Germans say. For each who escapes, two will be shot."

Far up ahead, almost out of hearing, some kind of command was shouted in German, then in English. The men of Block 162 strained to hear it. It floated back again from somewhere nearer, but still they could not make it out.

"Hey there! Pipe down a minute." The major directed his order to some who were still talking.

The distant command came again, a little nearer. Tom called to the major. "Sounds like 'Forward march!' to me."

Again the command came from up ahead. "Forward march!"

"Here we go, men."

"Forvert march!" Still nearer, in a German accent. Again and again it came, closer each time, until it was loud and just ahead. The formation ahead began to move at the command. The short fat old soldier guarding Block 162 turned and screamed it in a high-pitched command.

"Fourfart mersh!"

Perhaps fifty men laughed loudly as the 192 former residents of Block 162 started to walk loosely forward. As the command was repeated over and over until it began to fade behind them in the distance, many looked over their left shoulders for last looks at Stalag Luft III.

"It doesn't seem real," Jim said.

"It's real, all right," Tom said, almost slipping off balance on the iced surface of the road.

"What I mean is that for nineteen months I haven't been more than half a mile in any direction. I've never been outside the barbed wire in all that time."

"Well?"

"Well, here we are marching. Marching where? Jesus, I feel funny. It seems like I could force this out of myself and pull my eyes open, and be grabbing the sheets of my own bed in Seattle."

"Try that for me, too, will you?" Tom Howard wasn't laughing. "Only, drop me off in Oklahoma."

Jim shut his eyes so tightly his eyeballs ached. He bumped into someone on his right. It was Fred Wolkowski.

"Hey, watch where you're going! This blanket roll is beginning to feel kind of heavy."

"Yeah," Al Koczeck agreed behind him. "How's that tin turret of yours, Fritz?"

Fritz Heine shuffled along. His clumsy flying boots slid on the ice. His body bent forward to support the jogging tin pack on his back. "Oh, I'll get along all right. Only I don't know about these boots. It's kind of hard walking."

"Jesus!"

Jack Noble looked at Ed Greenway. "What's the matter?"

"The shellfire! It's stopped! I can't hear it!"

"It's the sound of your feet," Bill Johnston said with a sigh. "It's drowning out the shellfire."

Around them, up ahead, and to the rear, thousands of feet beat out a constant muffled tattoo on the thick ice of the road. Burt Salem spoke between puffs of sudden exertion and the rapid pace. "How long do you reckon this column stretches?"

"It must be miles," someone answered.

Like an army of ants they marched, each man at his own pace and bearing his own load. The prison camp lights dotted the tangled barbed wire to the left. The miles of men moved on into the frozen night. Each man guessed why. No man knew where. The murmuring footfalls fed their hearts with hope that the Russians would catch up before dawn.

Jim Weis: "There I was. . . ."

I once owned a real canary named Ping Pong, black and yellow and full of wing-cocked fight. Couldn't keep him in a cage. Gave him freedom of an apartment. Couldn't keep him in the apartment. He flew away—I hope. There were cat tracks in the soot of the window sill.

I never got another real canary, but I got wings of my own. I shed the earth and soared the blue. And, Christ, it wasn't easy! Not for a boy labeled Nazi in the Land of the Free. For the boy labeled Nazi was me.

"I'm putting you in full charge of the Cadet Club in town," lean Captain Clark said briskly when I was still a dodo flying cadet in the Class of 41G.

"Yes, sir," I replied, surprised.

"You should make a go of it," the young base commander said. "You have the quality of leadership."

Yes, I started out great. Big fat Mr. Murray, my civilian flight instructor at the California Army Flying School, climbed out of the blue and gold biplane unexpectedly at the practice field one afternoon.

"You sure you never said you had any flying lessons before you came here?"

"Only what I've read in books."

"Well, you're doing all right." The sunbrowned face grinned. "Only six hours and fifteen minutes dual, but you're ready to solo. I don't believe in letting this particular time get stale. So hop off and take it around."

A slap on my back and I was alone. Solo!

Point the Stearman down the field. Gently pour the coal. The clacking prop a symphony as the ground slips away and its grass streams downward to the rear. Up, up, easy . . . the altimeter hand points to one thousand feet . . . and level off. Soft right rudder and stick tipped lightly right. Watch the struts and the cylinder heads aiming like Vickers guns at the wheeling brown horizon of mountains. Level . . . 120 miles per hour . . . as fast as a Spad or a Nieuport . . . turn and bank. Look around. The bulbous white bulging of clouds. The slanting gold streaks of the sunshine. Look below. The oil wells like black asparagus. The golf course a green puddle. Mr. Murray's white helmet a pinpoint on the brown square of the field straight below. Turn again, light pressure at the seat of the pants. Cut the throttle and let the nose drop, wind singing just right through the wing wires. Cough the motor and turn pointing down the field. Watch it swell up like the tide, up and around on both sides as the airspeed slides back with the stick. Back, back, ever so lightly . . . all the way back and roll, bumping gently on the soft swishing brown grass. Toes touching brakes . . . slow down, wheel and taxi, heart beating with the whap-whapping prop, over to fat, smiling Mr. Murray.

"O.K., son," he said, lumbering up onto the wing. "Now you've done it. But let's not say anything to anyone about it. You got that? I'm not supposed to solo anyone until eight hours of dual."

The body can land, and the soul stay aloft making friends with the clouds by day and the stars at night.

"I've got to tell someone, Toy," I bubbled to the Cadet Club hostess as we walked to the hotel where I had rented a room before the club closed. "It's a big secret, but I've soloed already."

"Jim, that's terrific. You must be the first one in the class." She hugged my arm a little closer as we walked past the front desk that was always unattended late at night.

"I know something you don't know yet." Toy smiled as we lay in bed sipping rum and Coca-Cola. "You're going to be cadet commander."

"What makes you think so?"

"I heard the upper-class officers talking at the club. They said you've got the quality of leadership. You're it, Jim, honey. Cadet commander as soon as the upper class graduates. You've got quite a life ahead in the army, punkin."

"Well, I'm leading a pretty good life right now." We put down the drinks for a while.

A week later I was washed out. I didn't ask why. A good flying cadet never asks why. I was a good flying cadet right up until I suddenly wasn't any kind of flying cadet at all any more.

"It beats me," fat Mr. Murray complained. "I'm thinking of quitting. You were my best student."

Why? It gnawed. There were too many other washouts for me to be sure why.

A traveling board came to the town just then, giving IQ tests and recruiting workers for an aircraft factory near Los Angeles. I didn't want to go home.

When a fellow wants to fly, is ready to die to fly, he's guilty of self-abuse when he takes a job in an aircraft factory. Planes all around are not the stuff for peace of mind for the pilot whose wings have been clipped.

The tightrope of security twanged when I reported for work at the huge plant, for they made me a personnel investigator. It was my job to check and recheck to make sure no second-generation Germans, Japs, or Russians were employed there. And I was supposed to make triply certain that no one even suspected of being a Fascist or a Communist—or a Nazi—was hired. Investigation reports and so-called credit reports containing intimate facts and gossip about the private lives of twenty-eight thousand job seekers oozed over my desk before I saw a way to get back into the air after six weeks on the nosy job.

"Mr. Poole"—I addressed the supervisor of Department 42—"I have a chance to take flying lessons in the daytime. May I work on the night shift?"

Mr. Poole's face reddened. He wouldn't look at me. "What do you want to do that for?" He made doodle marks with his pencil on a pad before him. "The Air Corps has already told you you can't fly. Besides, I was going to send for you. I have to let you go entirely."

"Oh." Here it was again. "Something wrong with my work?"

"We've decided you're not suited for this type of work."

That was all. Two or three more tries, but still the same answer:
. . . "not suited for this type of work."

I joined the Washout Club at Santa Monica. Six other washouts from my army class and I shared an apartment by the beach, worked at another aircraft factory (I didn't tell them about my last job) and took flying lessons under the Civilian Pilot Training Program at Mines Field.

I was elected president of our Washout Club. My "quality of leadership" took us all down to the Hollywood Roosevelt Hotel, eighth floor, where the Clayton Knight Committee recruited trained pilots for the new Royal Air Force Eagle Squadron. We all needed more flying time to qualify.

At the new aircraft factory I typed tooling orders, and pornography for fellow employees when the orders ran out. At the request of the supervisor, I worked overtime nights when there was no work to be done, and thereby helped keep the costs up so the cost-plus profits would be higher. After seven weeks I was called into the personnel office. On the way through the plant I passed a festive group guiding Paul Mannix, a former employee and now an Eagle Squadron hero home on leave, on a tour of inspection.

"We hear you're only working here so you can build up enough time flying to join the RAF," a personnel man in a checked jacket said.

"That's right."

"Well, we have to let some people off in your department. We only want to keep those who intend to make a career here, so pick up your check on the way out. It's already made out."

As I left, plant publicity photographers were posing Mannix with his sky-blue uniform before the fancy administration building.

I became a grease monkey at Mines Field, taking care of the planes I was learning to fly, living on eighteen dollars a week, and putting all the rest into flying time.

I was the leader of the CPTP class. I got the highest flying and ground-school grades in southern California. But I was alone again. The big defense dough looked too good to most of the Washout Club. Only Whitey Stock was left, and he was washing out again as a civilian pilot. One evening Whitey told me a man had called at the apartment who wanted to see me at the Santa Monica police station. A man named Nichols. The desk cop directed me down the hall to an unlabeled door.

Nichols showed me his identification. Federal Bureau of Investigation.

"Having a rough time, aren't you, Jim?"

"Not too rough."

"Did you know you've been tailed night and day for the past three weeks?"

"I have?"

"You have. When you were at home, your apartment was watched."

"I'll be damned. What did you learn?"

"Every day you went to Mines Field and flew. Your instructors say you're pretty good. Every week night you went to ground school at UCLA. Pretty good there, too. You're working hard, Jim. Why?"

"I want to be a good pilot. What's wrong with that?"

An easy smile softened Nichols's thin face. "Nothing. You play pretty hard, too. After ground school you are picked up each night in a big LaSalle by a very attractive feature dancer from MGM. She's married, but then you know that."

"Whose business is that?" I muttered.

"Yours and hers, and I suppose her husband's. Then there's another girl, one of these starlets, a French refugee. You see her on Saturday nights in Hollywood. That's the night the dancer's husband isn't working at the studio."

"She's drawing me a map," I said. "I'm going to shoot up her family's wine cellars in Burgundy. The Germans have taken them over."

"Last Saturday," Nichols continued, "you called at the offices of the British Aviation Corporation at the Hollywood Roosevelt Hotel —used to be the Clayton Knight Committee. You arranged for a flight test at Montebello next Saturday."

Nichols paused. He wasn't using notes. I said nothing.

"Trying to clear your name, Jim?" he finally asked.

"I've got nothing to clear. I don't get this at all."

Nichols's smile was rather sarcastic. "You don't get it. Flying cadet, doing fine, washed out, just like that. Job in an aircraft factory. Fired. Job in another aircraft factory. Fired. No reasons given, and you don't get it. What happened back there in Seattle, Jim?"

"You seem to know everything," I snapped. "You tell me."

"Yes," Nichols said, drawing a card from his wallet and toying with it, "we think we know everything. Don't you imagine we do, Jim?"

"I suppose so."

"Well, suppose we do know everything. Anything you're ashamed of?"

"No."

"All right, Jim," he tossed the card toward me. "If you've done nothing to be ashamed of, you've no reason to be afraid of me. I'm really not supposed to do this, but I'm playing a hunch. I think I do know what you're doing, and maybe it's all right." Nichols stood up. "Go to it, Jim." As I was leaving, he called after me. "My phone number is on that card. If you end up in any more blind alleys, use it."

My girl's husband drove me to Montebello for the flight test. He didn't have anything to worry about. I passed it.

"It's out of the question," a guy at the Hollywood Roosevelt Hotel said next day. "We can't take you."

"You've got to!"

"Not a chance. Sorry."

"God damn it!" I blew my top. "I know what you think you've got against me! I've got to talk to you!"

We left the room with the big brightly colored Hurricane specifications chart on the wall and went to a private room. I talked for two hours, and then remembered the card. He called Nichols.

"Come back tomorrow at three o'clock."

The next day at three I was in. It was in November of 1941, more than three years ago. As the assorted group of army and navy washouts and other misfits boarded the bus across the street from Grauman's Chinese Theater, we were addressed by Captain Benway of the first war's Lafayette Escadrille.

"You boys are getting in on the ground floor. You're the leaders who are showing the way. All America will follow. Good luck, and good hunting."

So I made it in spite of the libel. In spite of the series of Seattle newspaper articles which hinted at, but did not name, my father as "a disseminator of Nazi propaganda." In spite of the schoolboy amateur who authored the articles and later testified before the Congressional Committee on Un-American Activities that I was the Nazi propaganda agent on the University of Washington campus. Well, I suppose I shouldn't have sued and won the libel suit against the Seattle newspaper. They had an excuse. The author wasn't a staff reporter. The series of articles made a good circulation stunt. How was the newspaper to know the punk would later be called before the Dies Committee to identify us by name? It stands to reason they didn't expect to have to settle all that cash out of court with five of us. I can see it now in a pig's eye, because there really was a sort of evidence against my father and me.

My Missouri-born dad served both in the U.S. Navy and in the U.S. Marine Corps. He couldn't speak a word of German. But there was irrefutable evidence. He was a businessman. Until the war started he represented two German steamship lines. He sold tickets on the German transatlantic luxury liners. Wasn't that enough to justify the articles and the Dies Committee publicity that made anonymous patriots make midnight phone threats to cut our throats and remove our balls? It made my chances of becoming a military pilot pretty slim. But I took all the chances and got to England first.

"You boys are getting in on the ground floor," we were told. Ground floor. How low can you start?

The quality of leadership. The major thinks I've still got it.

Chapter Six

"So that's it."

The miles of barbed-wire fence were replaced by a dull open field of snow. Tom looked sideways at Jim.

"What?"

Jim nodded toward the open field. "The last camp of all." Row upon row of weather-stained unpainted crosses stood black against the dull snow.

"Say, it's kind of nice out here." Marching at Jim's right, Fred Wolkowski grinned beneath the hood of his wool scarf at the beauty of the snow-tufted trees now walling both sides of the road. "It doesn't seem so very cold."

"It reminds me of a hike I made once," Jim said. "A bunch of us kids with the YMCA. We camped overnight by a glacier on the side of the mountain. We got hotter than hell climbing up to it. Then we built a fire and nearly froze to death. During the night it snowed and the snow turned to rain. When we hiked down in the morning we were a mess."

"What mountain?"

"Mount Rainier. You ought to make a trip out west when we get back, Fred. You got nothing around Chicago like Mount Rainier."

"Yeah, but you got nothing out west like Chicago. I hear a man in uniform can't buy a drink in Chicago any more. Somebody else always pays for it. Man, that's for me."

To the right the wall of scrubby trees ended. The backs of large, tightly shuttered houses loomed toward the black mist of the sky.

"Sagan," Jim said. "It's larger than I thought. This must be the outskirts."

The column crossed an intersection, and the men looked down a dark, empty street between silent snow-covered houses. From that direction came the shrill high squeal of a train whistle. The block formation ahead was trudging over the rise of a railroad crossing.

"Jesus!" Al Koczeck's voice came from the rear. "Maybe they're going to load us onto a train."

The short German guard held up his hand, and Major Smith did the same. Block 162's formation halted.

"Here she comes," someone said. Down the track, approaching at high speed was the train, running without lights. As the small German locomotive pumped past the glow from its firebox raced along the snow between the rails. Boxcar after boxcar flipped by, their open doors yawning blackly.

"It's empty!" Tom shouted.

Standing still now, the men began to shiver in the frigid night air stirred to motion by the clattering westbound train. Soon the last of the long line of cars flipped past and slithered off into the woods.

"Ain't that a hot one?" Tom demanded. "The trains are going west empty, so they march us west on foot."

"Let's go!" the major shouted up front. They crossed the tracks.

"Bitte, schnell, bitte," the old German soldier pleaded.

"Pick 'em up and lay 'em down, men," the major called above the tramping. "We've got to catch up." Ahead the road curved emptily into the carefully planted forest of pines.

"How about somebody spelling me with this guitar?" Bill's Midwestern voice drawled from behind Jim.

"I can't," Fritz's voice rasped. "I don't think I should have worn these flying boots." Jim looked briefly over his shoulder at Fritz, bent forward under his oversized pack, feet scraping the ice in their oversized coverings.

"Give it here," Tom said. "We'll take it for a while."

"Thanks." Bill passed the guitar forward. Tom shouldered the instrument, holding it by its handle.

"That damned Bill Johnston," Jim complained in a low voice. "Always trying to be noble. Abe Lincoln in Illinois stuff. Sometimes I think he thinks he is Abe Lincoln. If that character Tex, who plays the damned thing, didn't want to tote it himself it should have been left behind. Take a look back at what that Texas guitar player *is* carrying. He's more loaded down than a B-17. Stuff to stuff his gut."

They marched awhile without talking. They were not required to march in step, yet the pace was such that their feet automatically beat out a rhythm: 1,2,3,4; 1-2-3-4.

Ahead, the figure of a man on a bicycle approached out of the darkness of a bend in the road.

"Ride 'em, Hohendahl!" Tex's voice boomed from the rear. Gefreiter Hohendahl tried to slow his bike to a halt and had to wrestle with it as it slipped out from under him. He retained his composure and turned to Major Smith.

"Major, why have you fallen behind?"

The major trudged on, forcing the thin German noncom to follow wheeling his bike. "We got held up by a choo choo," he answered. "How come we couldn't ride out on it?"

Hohendahl ignored the question. "Please hurry. After five kilometers you will be permitted ten minutes' rest before we go again."

"Hey, Hohendahl," a voice called above the pattering boots. "How's about borrowing your bicycle?"

Sad-faced Hohendahl mounted the bike and pedaled out of sight to the rear.

Fred Wolkowski grinned. "Leave it to Hohendahl to scrounge himself a bike."

"He can't walk," Jim commented. "Got hit in the thigh by a twenty millimeter when he was a gunner on an ME-110."

"Too bad it didn't hit him a little higher."

"Maybe it did," Al Koczeck chortled. "If it didn't, the Russians will probably fix him up in the morning."

"If they catch up by morning," Fritz grunted under his load.

"Perk up, Fritz," Bill twanged. "Look around. This is a winter wonderland."

Throughout the column the men made small talk. The barbed wire was behind them, and the open road ahead. Nobody paid any attention to the squat old man who trudged laboriously beneath the weight of steel helmet, rifle, and full military pack. Bob began to whistle "Wabash Cannon Ball." Cigarettes glowed in quick motion and smoke mingled with the trailing vapor of a multitude of breaths. In the formation several voices began to sing:

" 'A troop ship was leaving Bombay . . . ' "

Other voices joined in.

" 'Bound for far distant shores. . . . ' "

More voices rang out:

" 'Heavily laden . . . ' "

The men marched along and sang with a new buoyancy.

" 'Bless 'em all! Bless 'em all!' "

Some blessed 'em all, and others used the other verb as all the voices joined in time with the marching.

" 'Bless all the sergeants and W.O. ones; Bless all the corporals and their bastard sons. . . . ' "

The men sang and marched with smiles on their faces and life in their boots. The major grinned back over his shoulder, teeth white in his black beard.

" 'You'll get no promotion this side of the ocean, so cheer up my lads. . . . ' "

Ahead and behind, hundreds of voices boomed out the finish. There were cheers, and the cheers echoed from the snow-tufted black trees on either side.

"You know," Fred said, "this ain't bad at all. I'm even beginning to sweat some. It doesn't seem like forty below zero."

"It's no colder than the cockpit of a Spitfire," Jim observed, "and I've sweated there lots of times."

"I'll bet you have," Fred grinned.

"I'll never forget one time," Jim reminisced. "I got separated over Abbeville at about 26,000 feet. We were tangling with the yellow-nosed boys, Goering's flying circus. There must have been four hundred of them and that many of us. Everywhere I looked I could see formations of planes, but they were just far enough away I couldn't tell which were theirs and which were ours."

"I've been in that spot," Tom interrupted. "Over Ploesti. What did you do?"

"I said to myself, 'Brother, this is no place for you!' So I just rolled over on my back and headed straight for the deck. I must have traveled down at about eight hundred per, and when I leveled off I just barely cleared the ground and headed west, and that's the way I kept heading—due west with all that speed. About ten minutes later I was across the channel and over Merry England. When the rest of the boys got back, I was already dressed up in my best uniform waiting for the next bus to London. They thought I'd bought it, back there over Abbeville. What did you do over Ploesti, Tom?"

"I just looked around until I spotted some big birds—bombers.

They were bound to be ours. I flew back tucked safely under the bomb bay of a B-24. I was glad to see them, and they were happy to have me along; but if we'd got bounced I wouldn't have tackled the Luftwaffe by myself. No, sir. I'd have probably just climbed right on up into that bomb bay."

Jim and Fred laughed, and Jim's laugh trailed off to a smile. "You know a funny thing? I just zoomed over that French coast. I still had a lot of speed from the dive left—must have been doing six hundred. But just as I hit the French coast there was a little wharf sticking out into the channel right in front of me. And there were three Germans on the end of it with some kind of machine gun on a tripod. I just barely saw them and had time to pull the trigger. I used twenties and thirties both. You should have seen them go shooting off the end of that wharf. I didn't even look back."

Jim, Fred, and Tom marched on in silent thought for a couple of dozen steps before Jim sighed and said: "Ah, them were the days. Fighting the war in England: beds, women, all you wanted to drink —you know, that old blue uniform with the Eagle Squadron patch on the shoulder was all the money you needed. You lived like a millionaire on eighty-three bucks a month. You could even save part of it."

"It wasn't like that when I was there," Fred grunted. "We had to pay through the nose."

"Ah, but you had plenty of money, Fred, and the Limeys knew. Hell, I remember when the first GI's came over waving fistfuls of pound notes and raising holy hell with the women. They ruined the place. Why, when I transferred, the price of the room I always took when I was in London went up ten shillings. When I asked how come, the clerk said, 'You've changed the color of your uniform, old boy.' "

"Personally," Fred said decisively, "I think the Limeys stink. Give me Chicago."

"That goes for the Eyties, too," added Tom.

"Well," Jim admitted, "I'd rather be back home in Seattle myself. You know, I haven't even walked down an American street in uniform yet. I don't even know what it's like."

Fred grinned. "You'll do all right. With all the fruit salad you'll be wearing, you'll do all right."

"Whew." Tom blew out his breath. "I don't know about you men, but it seems to me we ought to be about at the end of that five kilometers. I'm getting downright hot. I'm sweating."

The long icy road wound gradually ahead between the trees.

"Listen," someone said.

Ahead they could make out voices singing: " 'That was a very fine joke. Sing us another, please do. . . .' "

As they approached the singing, they could make out the obscene humor of the limerick that followed.

"We must be catching up," Jim said. "Jesus! I don't know if I could even fly a plane any more. It's been nineteen months since I've seen a cockpit."

"Well," Tom said, "with the Russians catching up to us you'll soon have another chance. Going to volunteer for the Pacific, Jim?"

"Hell, no! I didn't have sense enough to go home when I could have, the last time. I'm going to take some of that Stateside duty I've been hearing about. Only, I wish those Russians would hurry up and get here."

The road unwound ahead.

"There they are."

Under darkness, against the white of the snow up ahead, the singing column of men had halted, stretched across a gracefully arching stone bridge over a creek.

"Hey, where you been?" A voice from the tail end of the column started a series of jeerings. "Why don't you guys get a horse? What'sa matter? Couldn't you get your wheels up?"

"Stopped off for a little poontang in Sagan!" someone yelled back as the German guard and the major held up their arms for the column to halt.

"Have a weed," Jim said. Fred and Tom took cigarettes, and Jim clumsily cupped a match book in his mittened hands while the three lit up. The men stood around chatting, not bothering to remove the blanket rolls and packs from their shoulders.

"Jeez, listen to old Uncle Joe," Al Koczeck said. To the north and south could be heard the same steady rumbling accented by the bloop of greater explosions.

Fred grinned. "Hot damn. That's getting closer."

Tom and Jim, cigarettes dangling from their lips, held their scarves an inch away from their ears and looked skyward, listening.

"That is closer," confirmed Jim. "Funny we couldn't hear it while we were marching."

"I wish I could sit down," muttered Fritz, straining erect under his pack.

"Why don't you?" asked Jim. "Here, I'll give you a hand."

Jim stepped behind Fritz, took a firm hold of the pack and lifted as Fritz wriggled out of the shirtsleeve straps.

"Wow! This thing's heavy. No damned wonder you want to sit down."

Fritz seated himself on the tin pack. "I'll be all right when I get these boots off." He unzipped the flying boots and fumbled with the pack, trying to hang the boots on it.

"Oh, for Christ's sake!" jeered Bob. "Throw the damned things away."

"These are valuable," complained Fritz. When he found there was no place on the pack for them, he stood up and held the boots aloft. "Anybody want a pair of good flying boots?" There was no answer.

"Throw the damned things away," repeated Bob.

Fritz looked at the boots a moment and then tossed them into the snowbank at the side of the road. Without saying anything, Jim walked over to the snowbank, picked up the boots, and one at a time heaved them into the ice and running water of the narrow river.

"Come on, you Russians," Tom Howard prayed, still listening intently to the shellfire.

Fred removed the cigarette from his lips and chattered his teeth. "You can tell it's forty below zero. And a couple of minutes ago I was sweating."

Throughout the column the men began stamping their feet and swinging their arms. Here and there men sat on big packs. Down its narrow ice-banked channel the water of the river rustled. Thumbs against his chubby cheeks, Jack Noble blew vapor into his cupped, mittened hands. "I'd rather walk," he muttered, "than stand around like this freezing to death."

"Aren't any of you fellows tired?" asked Fritz, looking up from his seat. No one paid any attention.

"Pipe the goon," Jim muttered to Tom. The old guard had eased his pack to the icy road and was furtively removing the trench shovel and the metal gas mask container. Looking to right and left, he hastily flung the heavy articles into the woods.

"He'll be throwing away more than that if we have to go very far," predicted Tom.

Fred grinned with chattering teeth. "If I was him I'd have kept that shovel to dig a hole and pull the hole in after me when those Russians catch up."

"What the hell are we standing around with our blanket rolls on for?" asked Jim, lifting his own over his head and laying it on the ice before him. "We might as well take it easy."

Tom handed the guitar to Jim. "Here, hold this." He lifted his own blanket roll from his torso. From up ahead came a long high-pitched unintelligible command.

"Here we go again, men," called Major Smith. "I think." All listened, and then from closer came an unmistakable order. "Let's go!"

Koczeck and Bob lifted Fritz's pack so that he could arm his way into it. The old German guard struggled into his unassisted. Tom quickly looped his blanket roll into place and then picked up Jim's to help him into it. Jim held out the guitar. "Here."

"You carry it for a while, Jim."

"Oh, shit." Jim resignedly angled the instrument over his left shoulder. The formation ahead began to move across the bridge. Block 162 followed.

"By golly," boomed Fritz's surprised voice. "I'll be doggoned!"

"What's the matter?" asked Bob.

"All of a sudden I can't bend my shoe soles. They're stiff as boards."

"Well, it was your idea marching in new shoes."

"That's not it," Koczeck said. "Mine are stiff, too, and I got on old shoes. I think they're frozen."

"By golly," said Fritz again. "That's it. My feet must have been sweating in those boots. Now the soles are frozen."

"My feet sweat anyway, without boots," said Koczeck. "Christ, I hope they thaw out! This isn't very comfortable."

"Gosh, no," agreed Fritz.

"I think they will," Koczeck reassured him. "I've had something like it happen before, ice skating back in St. Paul."

"How are your shoes, Tom?" Jim asked.

"O.K. A skinny guy like me don't sweat in the feet much."

"You know," Fred observed, "my shoes are kind of stiff, too. But I'm beginning to feel warm again."

Once again the slapping of thousands of feet against the ice allowed only the voices nearest to the listener to be heard. Ed Greenway nudged Bill Johnston with his left forearm. "Look."

"Hey, Fritz," Bill called. "Look over there. You weren't the only Kriegie carrying too much payload on your feet."

Embedded in the snowbank to their left were three pairs of flying boots discarded by the prisoners ahead.

"And on your back, too," Burt Salem added. As they continued, other items could be seen where they had fallen in the snowbank: Y.M.C.A. logbooks and rolled-up German newspapers and magazines. Suddenly the trees on either side grew thinner until they found themselves trudging through a neat, totally darkened village.

"Say," Fred commented, "these are pretty nice houses."

The two-storied clay houses with large slanting roofs rose tightly shuttered and silent on both sides of the road.

"Yeah," agreed Jim, "and they're not as new as they look. I'll bet most of them are a couple of hundred years old."

Tom peered from beneath his cowled scarf at the seemingly lifeless buildings. "Do you suppose there's anyone inside of them?"

"Sure," snorted Jim. "With their fat Kraut asses sweating in fat Kraut feather beds. Can you imagine ten thousand P.O.W.'s marching through an American town like this without anyone even coming to the window to have a look?"

"Not in Oklahoma. Besides, we wouldn't be marching ten thousand P.O.W.'s across country. We'd put 'em in passenger trains and feed 'em ham for Christmas. Nothing's too good for our P.O.W.'s. I saw 'em—before I got eager."

"What got you eager, Tom? You had a good set-up."

"Sure I did. Head of the whole business-machine department—safe in a Long Beach shipyard. I was essential. But every time a P-51 flew over I wanted to be in it. Well, here I am. A year and a half and nine missions later. I made it, and here I am. Now I'm not essential any more."

"What the hell! You just did a short hitch. We'll be heading home tomorrow."

The column snaked its way steadily on through the ghostly blacked-out village. Tom looked back as they left it. "Not a damned sound or movement in the whole town. You'd think something like this happened all the time."

"You don't understand the Germans," Jim said as they tramped along the road into woods again. "They're so used to other people's misery they don't pay attention to it. I remember before the war.

I was standing on a second-floor balcony of Maximilian's palace in Munich, looking down across the front steps toward the street. A guy came down the street toward the palace on a motorcycle. Then he turned the corner too fast and the motorcycle whipped out from under him. He landed smack on his head right in the middle of the pavement and stayed there—out cold. People walking along the sidewalk glanced at him and then walked on. Do you know, by God! I watched for a couple of minutes, then walked back into the building, down to the first floor, clear down that long flight of front steps and out onto the street—and I was the first one to reach the guy. He had the damnedest bump you ever saw on his head. It stuck out the top of his head like a fist. I figured the guy would die sure. And yet nobody else paid any attention to him . . . and there were plenty walking by, too. Finally a policeman came by and we carried him over to the gutter. Still nobody paid any attention. These people just don't react when they see an accident or a fight, or a killing, even. They're hard."

Jim's left shoulder ached slightly from the weight of the guitar. He shifted it to his right shoulder, but the blanket roll was in the way. He handed the guitar to Fred. "Here, you take this damned thing for a while." Fred leaned it over his shoulder.

"What happened to the guy?" Tom wanted to know. "Did the cop get an ambulance?"

"I don't know. I got sick and had to leave."

"You wouldn't get sick now."

"No. Not now. But I still wouldn't leave the guy lying there like that."

They walked along in silence for a while before Tom spoke again. "Back home everybody always flocks to the scene of an accident."

"Yeah," Jim agreed. "And college kids get drunk and want to look through the morgue. They've never seen blood and guts before. That's the difference between the American and the European."

More silence. Blowing steam, Tom sighed loudly, using his voice. "What's the matter?" asked Jim.

"My shoulder's beginning to get numb. This blanket roll feels heavy now."

"Mine, too. Let's shift shoulders."

As they walked they clumsily lifted their blanket rolls from their right shoulders over their heads and then looped them over their left shoulders.

"That's more like it," Tom said, "but it still feels heavy."

Jim looked back over his shoulder. "How you making out, Fritz?"

Fritz looked up from the hunched position in which he was walking under his pack. "I could do with some more rest. How much farther you think we've got to go before the next rest period?"

"On and on. Your shoes thawed out yet?"

"Golly, I'll say they are. They're soaking wet. I'm sweating like a pig."

Beside Fritz, Burt Salem was shifting his bedroll to the other shoulder. "Do pigs sweat?" he grinned.

"They do in Wyoming."

Right left right foot left foot right left . . . each step caused the pack straps to snap against the shoulder bones, and the freckle-faced straight-haired Elvie smiling in a desolate Wyoming doorway appeared in Fritz's thoughts. . . . Right foot left right. Fritz beneath his burden in the darkness suddenly chuckled aloud.

Burt looked at him curiously. "What's funny now?"

"I'm going to get my wife drunk when I get back."

"So what? We're all going to get drunk."

"But Elvie doesn't drink. Neither do I. But I had some champagne in London. I'm going to get a bottle of it and take it home to Elvie. She'll think it's pop."

Burt grinned. "Oh, you dog, you!"

"Yes, sir. That'll be a doggone good joke on Elvie. Wait'll she finds out she's been drinking liquor."

Rifle fire. Plap! Plap! Plap! Up ahead. The column stopped. Machine guns suddenly chattered in the night. An airplane roared overhead and to the left.

"Down!" Jim yelled. "Strafing!" Jim and some others hugged the ice, faces pressed against its slight wetness. Fritz kneeled, and the shifting weight of his pack made him fall to the ice sideways. Up ahead, the burst of machine-gun fire stopped. The unseen aircraft was gone. Faces lifted from the ice, and those who remained standing were glad they hadn't ducked.

"What the hell's going on?" someone shouted. From up ahead somewhere came angry, hysterical shouting in German.

Tom and Jim crouched on hands and knees side by side. "What was it?" Tom asked. "A Russian plane strafing?"

"That's what I thought at first," answered Jim; "but that wasn't any aircraft fire. Sounded more like a burp gun."

In front of the formation, Major Smith, who had stood erect, called ahead to the next formation. "Anybody know what happened?"

The men who had fallen rose, wiping their cold faces with their scarves to remove thin layers of ice. Fritz stretched out on his side and struggled helplessly, weighted down by his pack. "Somebody give me a boost, will you?" Burt Salem and Al Koczeck reached down and lifted the pack, and with it Fritz got to his feet.

"What do you suppose happened?" asked Bob, and his mouth remained puzzledly open.

"Golly," complained Fritz, "I think I wrenched my back."

"Golly, he says," jeered Burt. "Doesn't anything make you cuss?"

Fred twanged two discords on the guitar. "I thought I broke it, but I didn't."

"Too bad you didn't smash hell out of it," spat Jim.

"What happened?"

"Jesus, what's up?"

"Somebody's bought it for sure!"

The length of the formation shivered, and men looked at one another shivering and asked the unknown of the unknowing and kept on shivering without an answer. Up ahead, the unseen hysterical guttural continued and made as much sense as the yapping of dogs. Jim lifted his blanket roll over his head to the road. Others did the same.

"Well, Fritz," Jim said, "here's your rest period, ready or not." Jim and Tom lugged the pack from Fritz's back. Fritz stretched and reached back to his ribs. The men sat down on their packs and blanket rolls. Jim watched Junior Jones confer briefly with Major Smith and then slip forward into the mass of the formation ahead.

"It beats me," Tom Howard muttered. "Something must have happened."

The cold crawled up ankles and backs, and the squatting men began beating their knees together and slapping their thighs.

"Maybe it's the Russians," somebody said; and they listened again to the shellfire.

"I'll bet a Russian patrol caught up with us," said Koczeck. Jim shook his head, and Tom looked blankly past a snowbank into the woods. Fritz buried his face on his forearms, supported by his knees.

"Fritz," Jim commanded, "get rid of some of that crap."

Fritz did not look up.

"God damn it, Fritz, chuck some of that crap away!"

Fritz looked up. "No. I carried it this far, and I can carry it the rest of the way."

"You dumb son of a bitch," Jim whispered hoarsely, "I'm the room Führer and I'm giving you an order. Throw some of that crap away!"

Fritz's upper lip quivered in the darkness. "You've got no right talking to me like that."

"You shithead!" spat Jim. "I'm trying to save your life!"

Tom put a hand on Jim's knee. "Hold it, Jim. Hold it. It's his life. Let him croak if he wants to."

Jim got to his feet and walked between the squatting men to where Major Smith stood at the head of the formation.

"God damn it, Major. What the hell happened?"

The major grinned. "That's a good question. But whatever it was, it wasn't good. What's eating you, Jim?"

"That Fritz! He's carrying so much he can hardly stand, let alone walk."

"That's his business, not yours."

"Well, Jesus, Major! I don't want to lose anybody."

A voice called back from the formation ahead. "Some guys got shot, Major Smith! They tried to make a break for it."

"Who got shot?" the major called back. "Who tried to make a break?"

"Some guys in Block 154."

"Oh, oh," Major Smith muttered softly.

"The damned fools," whispered Jim.

"That's Shorty's block."

"Yeah, and Bud's and Hank's and Sammy's. Ace is in that block, too."

"Shorty's the one I'm worried about."

Jim looked strangely at Major Smith. "He's a good man, but so are the others."

"Jim, I want you to do something."

"Huh? Oh. Shorty's hot, huh?"

"He is. When we get up to where whatever in hell happened, you get on the other side of that fat little goon there and talk to him. Ask him where he lived, how many grandchildren he's got, and a lot of other crap like that. Just keep him turned away from me, and I'll see what I can do."

Jim's whole body began to shake, and he slammed his right foot down against the ice to stop shaking. "Sure, Major." The adrenalin was up, and he could watch the vapor of his own breath curling up between him and the major's black beard. "Only tell me a little. Why do you think Shorty's dead?"

"I don't think so. But I've got to check if I can."

"What's he packing?"

They felt alone in the few feet of icy road between the rear of one squatting formation of men and the ragged front of their own formation.

"A canary. A live canary. He's listening as we go. If Shorty was one of the guys that bought it, we've got to get it."

"Here comes Junior," Jim said. "Maybe he knows."

Junior Jones's face was a blotchy gray under the cowling of his scarf as he crossed the short distance from the squatting formation ahead to Major Smith and Jim.

"O.K., Junior," the Major said. "What's the gen?"

"Wait'll I get my breath. God, this air is cold!" He stood there panting, every breath a frozen torture to his lungs. "Well, I got up there. It's blocks 152, 153, and 154."

"Three of them?" the major said in surprise. "I thought it was a break."

"That's what the goons thought," Junior explained. "As near as I could get it, a plane flew over and some guys flapped. They thought it was a Russian plane."

"I heard it," interrupted Jim. "I kind of had an idea—"

"Somebody yelled, and a whole lot of guys headed for the ditches. The goons flapped too. There were only two of them, but one goon had a burp gun. Three or four of the guys ran into the woods, and the goon with the burp gun mowed 'em down. From what I can gather they're deader than hell."

Major Smith looked off into the woods at the side of the road for a minute, audibly gritted his teeth against the steady rumble of shellfire, and then turned back to the still panting Junior Jones. "Did you see Shorty?"

"No."

"Did you ask who was dead?"

"Jesus, Major, I did what I could. Nobody seemed to know who got shot."

"But you didn't see Shorty?"

"No."

"Who did you see?"

"Aw, Major . . . I saw lots of guys. Christ, what are you getting at?"

The major said: "Skip it, Junior. Jim, the plan goes. When we get up there you divert the goon."

Jim said, "Yeah." He stood slapping the toe of his right boot against the ice. Then he said, "Yeah," again. Then: "Major, your plan stinks. You're the only head man around here. Don't get me wrong, I'm not trying to be a hero; but if you left the road and I talked to the goon he'd wonder why the hell I'm talking to him and then look around and find you gone. Let me do it."

"Do what?"

"Look at the corpses. And you talk to the goon. He's a Kraut, and the fat little son of a bitch will be so tickled to talk to a major he won't see me going."

"And besides," Major Smith said, "they'd much rather shoot a major than a lieutenant."

"Yeah." Jim grinned. "And if I don't have something more to worry about than that Christ-awful guitar and that God-damned hick navigator Fritz, I'm liable to kill a couple of guys who are our allies just like the United States Navy. Where's he packing it?"

"In the breast pockets of his battle jacket, under his greatcoat."

"O. K., Major, you con the goon. I'll reconnoiter the dead men."

Jim walked back to his own group and sat down on his blanket roll. Tom looked at him. "Why would anyone make a break for it when it might get other guys shot?"

"It wasn't a break," explained Jim. "A kite flew over and they thought it was a strafing. They flapped and so did the goons."

"Did Junior find out who got shot?"

"No."

They watched Fritz reach down and tug at the toes of his shoes. "They're frozen again," he said, "and I'm getting blisters back of my heels."

"New shoes," Burt jeered. "God, what will the Russians do with us? We'll probably have to march back to the camp again. I wouldn't mind being there right now in my little fart sack." Burt felt a back snuggling up to his back and looked over his shoulder. "Noble, what are you doing?"

"We can keep each other's backs warm." Jack Noble's voice vibrated between chattering teeth.

"Think about that fiancée of yours back in Pittsburgh," Burt said, not moving away. "That ought to keep you hot."

Noble sat holding his head down between his shoulders. Instead of huddled dark shapes in the night, he saw a warm face in a warm room, and a warm body.

"Hadn't we better wait?" she was saying, her blouse open and lighted by the fireplace glow. The picture faded, and once more he was watching the shivering men. And he was still waiting.

All talk ceased as the cold gnawed deeper and deeper. The men gazed dumbly at the icy road, and were roused suddenly by a shout from Major Smith. "Let's go!" Ice had formed on his beard. The men labored to their feet and lumbered into their blanket rolls and packs. The column started forward.

"Even my shoes are frozen now," Tom muttered, and Jim nodded. Cans and packages of discarded food spotted the snowbank on both sides of the road. Major Smith angled to the left, fell behind the old German soldier, and increased his pace until he was walking on the old soldier's left. Jim watched.

"Here's where it happened," Fred said. Ahead and to the right, about twenty feet into the woods a German stood over two dark lumps. Jim casually slipped from the ranks and waded through the snow. The German was Glimlitz, who gestured with an arm for Jim to get back in the ranks. Jim still approached.

"Go on," ordered Glimlitz. "Keep going."

"Please, Glimlitz," Jim said, kneeling by the two corpses. "Friends of mine." The bodies were lying face up, but the night and the trees made it too dark for recognition. Glimlitz turned the beam of a flashlight first on one of the faces and then on the other.

The open eyes did not blink.

"Now, go on," Glimlitz ordered. "Keep going."

Jim turned and waded quickly to the road where he trotted to catch up to his place in the column. Major Smith left the old German guard abruptly and fell back into the column. "Did you make it?" he asked.

"Yeah, there were two. Neither was Shorty."

Fred held the guitar up and looked over his shoulder. "Somebody else take this thing," he begged.

"Who were they?" the major asked. "Anybody we know?"

"Give it here," Al Koczeck volunteered, and took the instrument.

"I knew one of them," Jim answered. "Jew kid from Chicago. I can't remember his name."

"Well, anyhow, Shorty's still up ahead." The major moved forward to the head of the formation.

"This thing is heavier than it looks," Koczeck complained, weighing the guitar in both hands.

"Throw that damned thing away," Jim barked.

"Should I?" Koczeck asked.

"Throw it away," Jim repeated. "We got enough to carry."

"How about it, Bill?" Koczeck asked over his shoulder. "You were the guy who volunteered. Should I heave it?"

The column moved out of the woods into another small silent village.

"It makes no difference to me," Bill answered. "Chuck it if you want to."

"Throw it away," Jim snapped.

"Here goes," Koczeck said, and raised the guitar to throw it.

"Wait, Al," Fritz interrupted. "That's valuable. I'll take it."

"Oh, for Christ's sake!" Jim gritted through his teeth.

Without saying anything, Koczeck passed the guitar to Fritz, who trudged along under his pack, holding the guitar clumsily dangling before him. After a moment, Jim spoke rapidly. "God damn you, Fritz, I'm through pissing around with you! You're already beat from that pack. Now throw that guitar away, and I mean it!"

"Well, all right; you don't have to get hot about it." Fritz stepped from the column and leaned the guitar carefully against a fencepost at the entrance to a silent house in the village. Before he could turn around, Jim stepped from the formation, snatched up the guitar, and smashed it to splinters on the fence. Then he heaved the tangled remains violently against the door of the house and stepped back into the moving column.

"Gee," Fritz said in a surprised voice, "what did you do that for? I thought somebody might find it there who would enjoy it."

"Yeah," spat Jim, still through clenched teeth, "some dirty mother-lovin' son of a bitchin' Kraut!" They marched on steadily, each man looking at the feet of the man ahead. They came to the end of the village. Jim looked up and let frigid air strike his throat. "God, oh, God," he whispered, "where are those Russians?"

The long column of men trudged steadily onward into the woods.

71

Fritz Heine: "There I was. . . ."

By golly, I don't care if I never see another airplane again. I like to grow things. My wife, Elvie, says I've got a green thumb. Well, I ought to have, by gosh. I grew up on a farm and so did Elvie, the farm next to ours. Only, I went to college. Well, not college exactly. Normal school.

That's sort of like growing things—teaching school. We didn't get a very big school in a very big town, but then there aren't very many big towns in Wyoming. But I had a lot of kids to teach because I was teaching the fifth through the eighth grades. And it was nice.

Elvie and I had a little house a little ways out of town and we had a garden. I didn't make anything at all like what I'm making now with flying pay, but we grew our own vegetables, kept chickens and raised our own bacon, and we could trade pork for beef. Every month we mailed thirty dollars to the bank. Gosh, I guess we're saving three hundred now.

I got drafted, and they let me try out for aviation cadet training. I used to watch the airliners fly over, and thought it would be nice to be a pilot. Gosh, I didn't even know how to drive a car. They put me in front of a panel of different colored lights, and I was supposed to push certain buttons when certain light combinations come up. I guess I wasn't fast enough, but I knew Euclid. So they made me a navigator. They sent me to Florida for three months to school, and they had me flying all hours of the day and night, practice-navigating old Pan American clippers.

"You're doing fine," the instructor used to say, "only can't you get the fix a little faster? You're really moving along at a couple of hundred per, you know."

They sent my class along and kept me for an extra month. Pretty soon I could get the fix as fast as anyone, and you know, some of those other guys got the wrong fixes. Mine were always right. I knew I could get a plane where it was supposed to go.

"Moses Lake for you," the base adjutant said when he handed me my travel orders. "Four fans. B-17's."

I hitched a ride with A.T.C. and saved eight cents a mile all the way from Miami to Spokane. All I had to pay was bus fare from Spokane to Ephrata . . . just a few dollars. Boy, you sure can make money in the Air Force!

And they sure do train you! I trained some more at Moses Lake. For three months I trained navigating Forts all over Washington, Idaho, Oregon, Montana; and once, just for the dickens, I navigated right over our house in Wyoming. I'll bet Elvie didn't know that was me flying over.

"The following officers are to report to the base adjutant's office for orders," the notice on the bulletin board said. They listed my pilot, co-pilot, and the bombardier, but not me. Those fellows were all sent to B-29 school, and I was without a crew.

"Take off for Great Falls," the C.O. said to me next day. "You'll get on a new crew there."

They didn't give me travel pay that time. Just flew me over in a Fort. Gee, we trained three more months. I could have navigated anywhere. I got on a crew with a swell bunch of fellows; only, the pilot didn't think much of navigators.

"I don't need a navigator," Phil said. "I like to know where I'm going myself, not have somebody else figure it out for me."

That darned Phil. He used to get my goat; but I shouldn't say that, 'cause now he's dead. But, anyhow, I figured he'd need me sure when we flew across the ocean to England.

"Vector eight-two degrees," I said over the intercom when we had left sight of the coast.

"Relax and enjoy the ride, Fritz," Phil called back. "I'm following the guy up ahead."

Gosh, I didn't even do any navigating flying clear across the Atlantic. They assigned us to the 350th.

"When do we see action?" Phil wanted to know.

"After you've flown some practice missions right here in England," the C.O. said. He assigned a captain who had finished his missions and was waiting to go home to fly with us. We practiced for two weeks. Then we got to go on a mission.

Schweinfurt!

It was dark when we were being briefed. I took a lot of notes so I could navigate good. Phil and the rest of the crew just sat there in their flying gear, smoking and drinking coffee.

It took us more than an hour to climb, circling through the overcast, and to form on the striped marker planes. Finally we headed east over the channel. By golly, you never saw so many B-17's. Everywhere you looked there were B-17's . . . up, down, both sides, and ahead. The sky was full of B-17's. And we were flying tail end on the right of our squadron. Heck, there wasn't any navigating to do. There must have been a couple of thousand B-17's, and in every one was a navigator—just sitting there. Some fellow way up ahead out of sight was doing the navigating.

And then they came up after us, just as we crossed the coast of France. Planes with yellow noses. The Spitfires went after them. I could see German fighters diving at formations of B-17's to the right and to the left. They'd roll over on their backs and fly upside down right through the formations, and every time one or two Forts would teeter out of the formations and go into long spiral dives. I got scared. The earphones were going:

"Bandits, one o'clock high."

"Bandits four o'clock, level."

"Those aren't bandits. They're friends."

"Bandits twelve o'clock low, coming up."

Gosh, everywhere I could look I could see bandits. But they didn't hit our squadron at first. Sometimes fellows would drop out of the Forts that were hit, and you'd see the chutes open up; but then you'd be past that, and seeing it all over again up ahead. It was awful.

"Here they come, boys." I heard the C.O.'s voice in my earphones. "Close up the formation."

Phil eased our Fort in tight under the wing of the B-17 ahead. I couldn't see the ones the C.O. was talking about. I looked all around and couldn't see them. Then the plane we were tucked under just suddenly exploded. I couldn't hear anything, but there was smoke and pieces flying. I ducked and we flew right through it. Our plane lurched, like something hit our wing, and then settled as Phil eased us up into the next place in the formation.

I forgot all about my maps. I didn't know where we were. Mike, the bombardier, eased up beside me in the plexiglass nose.

"Here they come again," the C.O. said. "Two o'clock high."

This time I could see them. They were heading straight for us. Two-engined planes. I think maybe they were ME-110's.

"Grab a gun!" Mike shouted, and I grabbed the fifty-caliber on my side of the nose. I pointed it right at one of the planes and started shooting, but I don't think I hit him. He disappeared over us, and the plane shook some more. I figured we were hit somewhere behind.

"Target ahead," the C.O.'s voice said over the earphones.

Mike looked straight ahead and called, "Bomb bays open."

Another voice answered, "Bomb bays open."

I could feel the plane shudder. Mike looked straight ahead and fingered the toggle button.

"Aren't you going to use the bombsight?" I shouted.

"Naw," he snorted above the plane's noise. "I just toggle when the planes ahead drop 'em. They don't need bombardiers on these things. All they need is togglediers."

"Three o'clock high," the C.O.'s voice called.

I looked over that way and saw some ME-109's coming down. I tried to swing my gun around but it wouldn't go that far. I could see white tracers from a 109 coming right at me. I ducked my head. The plexiglass and part of the fuselage splintered around me; explosions in the nose stopped all hearing. I cowered with my head in my arms.

"Bombs away," the C.O.'s voice called.

I looked around at Mike. Gosh, he was sagged against the broken plexiglass on the other side, and it was all full of holes and bloody, and the wind was pouring in and blowing streams of blood back from Mike's neck. His head was gone. It was just gone. I reached over and took the toggle switch out of his hand and pressed the button.

"Bombs away," came a voice in the earphone. "Captain, we're hit pretty bad back here."

I took my eyes away from Mike's bleeding neck and looked down. That's where we were going—down.

"Navigator to pilot," I called. No answer. "Phil, Phil, are you all right?" No answer. We were still heading down. "Bail out!" I called. "Bail out!"

I crawled back uphill to the forward hatch, and pulled the emergency release. It fell open and snapped off. I dove through and pulled my ripcord.

Suddenly, everything was quiet—at least I thought so at first. Then I could hear it way up above: the distant sound of planes. They were small, and didn't seem to be doing much, except flying. I looked around. There were no other chutes. I landed in a field where a farmer was stacking wheat. He smiled and took me into his house and tried to feed me, but I wasn't hungry. Some soldiers came and got me.

Golly, all that training. I'm a good navigator, but I never got to navigate at all. And Mike didn't get to use his bombsight. But I'm better off than he is, I guess.

Gosh, if I hadn't been here last summer the fellows in Room 8 wouldn't have had fresh vegetables. None of them know how to grow a garden. My wife, Elvie, says I have a green thumb. By golly, with all the money I'm saving now, Elvie and I'll be able to make a down payment on a farm. I can teach school and have a farm besides.

Wait till Elvie sees the souvenirs I'm carrying.

Chapter Seven

For a long time they had been marching without talking, each man concentrating on putting each foot ahead in turn. At intervals one of them would let out a low, weary moan. The old German guard staggered along under his heavy pack muttering the same word over and over.

"Listen to him," Tom said. "He's gone nuts and is asking for his mother."

Jim listened for a minute. "That's 'Müde, müde.' It's German for 'tired.'"

"How long we been marching?" Fred asked.

"Hours," Jim answered. "It's after four."

Fritz reeled along, zigzagging under his pack. The men gave him a wide berth to keep him from bumping into them. With every step he grunted a little. All in the formation who carried back packs now swayed from side to side as the weight shifted with each monotonous step forward.

"Mort," Jim muttered between clenched teeth. "Mort."

Tom looked sideways at Jim. "You talking Italian?"

"Hmmh?"

"Mortay. That's Eytie for dead."

"Oh." Jim was breathing hard. "No. I just remembered the name of that Jew kid who got shot back there. Mort. Mort was his name." As Jim trudged on he could see the kid's living face distinctly. "I had to blot out his eyebrows with nose putty and paint new ones," he said.

"What are you talking about?" asked Tom Howard, also breathing heavily of the frozen air.

"Mort. He was a chorus girl in one of the shows. I made him up every night. You get to know a face that way."

The face that Jim was seeing now as he plodded over the ice was dull pale against the snow, eyes blankly open, reflecting the gleam of a flashlight; teeth dull and fragile, exposed like a dead rat's. Jim shivered. Snow particles floated down, tingling against the eyelids of the marchers.

"Jeesus!" Bob Montgomery's voice crackled. "It's starting to snow."

Some of the men ignored the new development. Others looked up.

"Naw," disagreed Bill Johnston, studying the tops of the corridor of trees. "It's just falling off the trees." The tops of the trees swayed like moving black shadows.

"Wind," somebody stated.

"Huh, what was that?" Jim wanted to know.

"There's a wind coming up," answered Tom Howard, studying the darkly moving treetops. They marched on, snow wafting coldly down upon them, sprinkling shoulders and scarves with tiny crystals.

"Müde . . . müde . . ." moaned the old German guard.

"I wish that old bastard would shut up," growled Bob. "He's moaning along like a God-damned nigger."

He'd said it again. Nigger it had always been, all his life in Texas; only now, every time he said it, he noticed he was saying it.

"God-damned Kriegie camp," he muttered.

Al Koczeck wiped some of the snow dust from his face. "Just what we need. Wind."

Bob agreed. "I ain't cut out for this kind of weather."

"It's not the cold that's getting me," said Al. "It gets damned near this cold back home in St. Paul. It's this friggin' marching. My arches are aching something awful."

They trudged on wearily, automatically. "I wonder how Thunderbird is making out up ahead," Bob mused. "This ain't the kind of thing for a nig—a Negro, neither."

"About as good as you, I reckon." Al grinned sideways. "There's not much difference between a black boy and a Texan."

"Up you," snorted Bob. "Thunderbird's different. He ain't like the rest. You can talk to Thunderbird. Did you know he's got a master's degree from Duke University?"

"Yeah, that's why I can't figure out how you can talk to him."

"Up you," repeated Bob. The rustle of the trees could be heard now above the relentless patter of boots on the icy road.

"How long did you bunk with Thunderbird?" asked Al.

"About two weeks," answered Bob. He was remembering those two weeks, following the surprise of two Negro fighter pilots arriving at Stalag Luft III as prisoners of war.

"Aw, hell, the goons shoot them," the white Kriegies had always said when speculation arose as to what happened to Negro flyers after they were shot down. But, finally, two had arrived safely at the camp. Bob was one of the men called to the adjutant's office in the emergency.

"Men," the short, fleshy adjutant said to the twelve Kriegies in the little room, "we've just received two nigger officers in this purge today, and that presents a problem. Now, I'm a Southerner, and I've called all you gentlemen here because you are Southerners. I reckon we know how to handle niggers. Don't get me wrong: these are good niggers, educated niggers. They been to college and they're fighter pilots. One of 'em is an ace—has seven Air Medals, two D.F.C.'s and a D.S.C., so we got to treat 'em right. Still, you all know as well as I do, we've got to draw the line somewhere. I figure if we put 'em in with Northern Yankees they may get swell-headed and get out of hand. Sometimes there's nothing worse than an educated nigger. So I've done some shuffling of billets so you men will be divided into two rooms at opposite ends of the camp. I'm putting one nigger in each room with you. Now, you gentlemen are used to handling niggers down home, so I figure you'll have little trouble keeping them in line. Now here are your new billet assignments. . . ."

Crunching along the icy road with snow slivers spanking his cheeks, Bob smiled to himself at the elaborate precautions and some of the complaints of the selected overseers.

"Sonovabitch! On top of everything else, now we gotta room with a dinge."

"Why in hell don't they let the smokes live with the Northern fuggers? Most of 'em are nigger lovers, anyway."

"God damn! A nigger for a messmate. What's this here army coming to?"

"The goons should have shot 'em like the rest. You know, sometimes the goons have got somethin'."

Bob chuckled.

"What's tickling you?" grunted Al, lifting his blanket roll slightly above his shoulder to shake the stale snow from it.

"I was thinking about Thunderbird and his gunsight," Bob

answered, teeth flashing beneath the cowl of his scarf. "One night some of us were playing pinochle in the room, and Thunderbird was lying on his bunk, just looking straight up. All of a sudden he rolled over onto his side and propped his head on his hand. 'Say,' he says, 'did I ever tell you about the new Mark VII automatic gun sight?' 'No,' someone answers, 'tell us about it, Thunderbird.' 'Well,' says Thunderbird, 'you get on the tail of some Messerschmidt 109's and squint through that gun sight. A little sign lights up and says: *No, Not Yet. Closer.* So you pour on the coal, get a little closer, and squint through the sight. The sign lights up again. *Not Yet.* You fly a little closer to those 109's, and the sign lights up and says *Now!* Then all you do is squeeze the trigger five times and four Air Medals and a D.F.C. drop out the side of the gun sight. Man, it's sumpin!' "

Al's chuckle was inside himself, appreciative, but held inside by the cold. "He must be quite a boy."

Bob stumbled slightly as Jack Noble's shoe behind him scraped down the back of his ankle. He said nothing and kept marching until the shoe scraped him again.

"Jeesus Christ!" he cursed over his shoulder. "Look where you're walking, Noble."

Noble's head was bent low. He looked up. "Huh, what?"

"Look where you're going. You're stepping on my heels."

Noble blinked his eyes. "Oh, 'scuse me." His eyes opened wide. "Say, I think I been sleeping."

"Well, you better wait until you can lay down someplace."

"I was. I really was. I was sleeping and walking at the same time."

"Don't teach Wolkowski how you do that," cracked Koczeck. "He'll sleep the rest of the march."

"When you woke me up I was dreaming that the Russians had caught up with us." Noble bundled the scarf tighter under his chin, watching the heels of Montgomery in front of him as he trudged.

Abruptly they popped out of the forest of rustling trees.

"Oh, God . . ."

The road cut across a gentle slope. The wind screamed down a field of snow from the northeast, right through the column and on down the slope of snow to the southwest. Men held their elbows and upper arms twitching against their sides as they walked. Tom's teeth chattered audibly above the tramping boots.

"Close your mouth," ordered Jim through the slit of his own.

"Mmm-m-mother of G-God, that's c-cold," chattered Tom.

"Keep your mouth shut," Jim hissed. "You'll freeze your lungs."

"Let's have some more trees," prayed Fred Wolkowski.

Phosphorescent ripples of snow crept down the slope toward them. A sharp stinging spray cut through the formation and joined the ripples crawling down the slope to the left.

"W-What's this ahead?" muttered Tom.

Ahead and to the left at the side of the road was the dark shape of a hay wagon piled high with chairs and mattresses and other effects, and with pots and pans and farm tools tied to its sides. As they drew nearer they could see at least three people in the wagon, their heads peeking out of a single huge cone of ragged quilts and featherbeds.

"Refugees," Jim said. "Part of that bunch that went by yesterday."

Fred twisted his whole body to have a look, holding his chin tight against his chest in the knifing wind. "They picked a hell of a place to stop."

They marched abreast of the wagon and past it, staring curiously at the gray belly and stiff legs of a dead horse where it had fallen in the traces. Fritz staggered under his pack and looked up briefly as they passed. Then he resumed looking down at his feet.

"Müde . . . müde . . . müde . . ." wailed the German guard with each step forward.

Fritz picked up the cadence and groaned with each step.

"Oh, Christ!" Jim whispered through gritting teeth.

Behind Fritz, Montgomery and Koczeck looked at each other. Montgomery reached out his right mitten and put it under Fritz's pack. Koczeck reached out and lifted with his left.

"Don't let it get you, Fritz," Montgomery said quietly.

The groans stopped. Fritz let out a big breath and lifted his head.

"We're due for another rest pretty soon," encouraged Bob.

"Yeah, yeah," mumbled Fritz. "I'm O.K. now."

Montgomery and Koczeck released their awkward holds on the pack, and Fritz immediately began to stumble again. Soon he was moaning as before.

The noise, mingled with lesser moans and grunts throughout the column, brought a confusion of memories to Jim. As he trudged along in his own weariness, he was once again on a cot in the Luftwaffe Hospital at Tunis. He could even feel his legs and buttocks throbbing against the shell splinters imbedded in them. The cot was one of many crowded into a hall of the hospital, and he was looking through a doorway at a nude, handsome blond officer lying in a bed, moaning with each breath and clutching at the gauze wadding which plugged up a gaping hole in his belly.

"Schwester. Schwester!" the German would scream between groans, and the Italian nun would come running, and always the German would want a bed pan. His intestines were splattered to ribbons, and always he felt that his bowels were moving. Again and again, as darkness fell, the nun placed the bed pan under the blond giant, who would curse her hysterically in German. The moaning was horrible, and gradually it developed a grating quality as if the terrible wailing were being forced through loose and rattling gravel. Finally the nude giant raised his torso on one elbow and forearm, clutching and ripping the wadding from the raw hole in his belly, and screamed all the invective of hell in German. The nun was not there, but all the hospital heard it, and cringed, before the screaming stopped and the giant flopped back on the sheet, purple with rage. Jim remembered the three distinct breaths the man had inhaled and exhaled, rattling like the snore of a Goliath, before open-eyed and gaping-mouthed death brought silence. Then the arrogant purple fury had turned to mottled blue. They had carried the corpse away as the nun smoothed the sheet for another patient.

Fritz's moans grew louder and more like sobs.

"God damn it, Fritz, do you have to do that?" Jim spat over his shoulder.

Fritz seemed not to hear as he staggered on and on. "Müde . . . müde . . . müde . . . ." The German guard kept mournful cadence with Fritz's misery. The relentlessly freezing wind made the moans of others in the formation a faint background to the immediate sounds.

The scene shifted again for Jim, and he was forward on the cargo deck of a huge ME-323 Gigant, its six engines throbbing, carrying himself, an Englishman, and sixty desperately wounded Germans across the Mediterranean from Tunis to Sicily. There were the shattered and bandaged Germans stretched out on the floor of the canvas monster, screaming constantly at the pains aggravated by the vibration of the engines. There was the thin English prisoner with a bullet hole through his lungs vomiting sourly his first time up in an airplane. There was the jittery Luftwaffe gunner peering nervously past his guns through the two open ports in the nose through which the wind sped freezing back over the wounded. There was the German standing beside the gunner stuffing cotton compresses into a stinking mouth where his tongue had just been removed, constantly changing the compress so that the never ending slimy green discharge streamed back in the wind from the gaping hole in his face in ten- and fifteen-foot long streamers, stinking and falling rotten and bitter over the stretcher cases. Jim could feel the green slime catching and clinging to his beard stubble. The screams cut out the sound of the engines.

The horror faded, and Jim let out a disgusted snicker as he marched. He suddenly remembered how he had crept up behind the gunner and the man without a tongue and very carefully reversed the bullets in the belts of the two machine guns so that they would jam if the gunner had to use them.

"Jesus, Fritz," he pleaded, "try to control yourself."

But Fritz moaned on and on as they trudged on and on in the icy wind and darkness.

In the Regia Marina hospital at Trapani there had been a wop kid in the next room who called nothing but "Mama" for a day and a half. "Mama . . . Mama . . ." he had cried, over and over again. He had stooped over to pull a dud frag bomb out of the ground at the Luftwaffe base. It had blown his hands off to the elbows and his face off to the ears, and a hell of a big hole in his chest. "Mama . . . Mama . . ." He had cried it, screamed it, wailed it, whispered it.

"Why don't they knock that son of a bitch out with some dope?" Jim had wanted to know.

"They don't have any," the American sergeant in the next bed had explained, chin wiggling above a plaster cast that encased everything but his head, arms, and legs. "Hell, the Krauts got medicine, but these Eyties got nothing; and the Krauts won't give 'em nothing, neither. They even set my busted back without an anesthetic."

"Jesus, that must have been something!"

"Yeah, they put my ass up on a metal rod, set my tailbone in a little ring. Then they tied ropes to my arms and legs and my head. They were running through pulleys in the ceiling. Then a bunch of Eyties grabbed hold of the ropes and just tugged to beat hell. I bet you could have heard me yellin' clean back in Africa. I thought that was rough, but do you know? There was another GI here then. They cut his eyeball out without an anesthetic. You should have heard him yell before he passed out."

"The dirty bastards."

"Hell," the sergeant had said, "it ain't their fault. They just ain't got any anesthetic, and the God-damned Krauts won't give 'em any. It ain't that, I'm pissed off with the Eyties about. It's this bitch of a cast. The stupid bastards left a hole in it to piss out of, but they didn't leave any place to crap out of. I ain't had a crap in two weeks."

"How do you hold it?"

"I can't hold it much longer. One of these days I'm going to let her go, and then you'll know it. Brother, it's going to stink in here."

"Mama . . . Mama . . . Mama . . ." the gory freak in the next room had kept crying.

"Why don't they shoot that son of a bitch?" Jim had said. "What good is a wop with no hands and no face?"

Why had he called that freshly deformed kid a bastard? Jim wondered as he walked along, his memories a barrier against the numbing wind and the monotony of Fritz's moanings. He suddenly realized that he was semi-conscious, and that Tom Howard was saying something.

"Huh? What's that, Tom?"

"Looks like we're going to go uphill . . . over a bridge or something. And there's some more refugees."

Ahead, through the swirl of drifting snow, the crawling column rose darkly against the white of a long incline. At the foot and to the left was the black box shape of a covered wagon, with several figures moving around it. As they slowly approached they could see it was not a refugee cart. One of the figures turned. It was Lieutenant Pieber, the Lageroffizier.

"Major Smith," he called. "Put your men to pushing this wagon."

Major Smith lifted his arm and the formation halted. One of the other figures beside the wagon was Hohendahl, who left immediately, pushing his bike up the incline.

"Brot," said Montgomery. "It's full of Reichsbrot." The black loaves of bread completely filled the cavernous interior like cordwood stacked for a furnace. Two roan horses were hitched to the wagon.

"Push it?" the major questioned, walking over to Pieber. "What's the matter with your horses?"

"Too much ice," explained Pieber. "The horses can't haul it up the hill. Please have your gentlemen push."

The exhausted men quivering in the cold wind looked with dread at the heavily loaded wagon.

"God, that's worse than a load of bricks," complained Montgomery. "Them loaves weigh at least four pounds each."

Fritz stood bent under his pack, arms dangling like an ape's.

"You expect us to move that?" Major Smith asked incredulously.

"We will try," Pieber said. "These are the rations for the march. The horses will help."

"I dunno." The major shrugged his heavily padded shoulders and turned, beard in the wind, facing the formation. "O.K., men. Let's get our asses into it."

Cursing wearily, the men lumbered over to the wagon. Some grappled the sides, others the spokes of the wheels, and others, three deep, got behind. Jim, Tom, and Fred put their shoulders to the tailgate, other arms pushing them from behind.

"God damn it, Fritz!" Jim roared. "Get the hell out of here, you dumb son of a bitch! You can't do any good." Without a word Fritz squeezed from the crowd. Major Smith stood at the right rear corner. The soldier-driver began grunting commands at the horses and cutting their flanks with his whip.

"Heave!" the major yelled, throwing himself into the pack. The wagon did not move. "Heave!" The wagon moved forward an inch and then back. "Heave!" An inch and a half forward and back an inch, clouds of steam from packed breathing spending itself in the wind. "Heave!" Loud grunting in unison mingled with shouts and the snapping of the whip. "Heave!" Forward, grudgingly, the wagon crawled, horses' hoofs clapping and digging the ice. "Heave! Here we go!" Forward, slowly, in ponderous rhythm, the men moaning. "Heave!" Snap. Snap. "Heave!" Major Smith looked ahead up the icy ramp. It looked endless. "Heave!" The men grunted, groaned, and shoved, their feet slipping and skidding on the ice. "Heave!" Tom quit pushing and allowed his skinny body to be pressed flat against the tailgate by those shoving behind. "Heave! Look out! Watch it!" The front of the wagon began sliding to the left, down the camber of the icy road. "Hold it, men! Hold it!" One of the horses whinnied, blowing huge clouds of steam. "Hold it, for God's sake!" The whinnying changed to screaming. "Jump clear, men! Jump clear! Clear—for God's sake!" The men scrambled, falling, rolling clear, as the wagon began sliding backward. The horses' hoofs clattered, and one of them slipped to its knees, sliding back with the wagon. Finally the wagon came to a standstill, turned sideways, back at the foot of the ramp.

The animals neighed and blew noisily, one horse still on his front knees. Men stood, sat, and lay on the road, emitting mighty pants of steam.

"To hell with it," panted Major Smith to Pieber. "It's impossible. We could never make it."

"We must," countered Pieber. "Ozzerwise you must carry the rations yourselves."

"I didn't even know you were hauling rations for us."

"Ach, but of course, Major." Pieber pretended to be surprised. "Naturally, we must take care of you."

"Well, you can see for yourself." Major Smith waved around at the exhausted men crouching with hunched shoulders against the bitter wind. "We are in no shape to push that wagon uphill."

"Very well," said Pieber bundling the lapels of his soft blue leather greatcoat closer around his chin. "March on, then. You will find the column waiting up ahead."

Major Smith turned and heaved a big sigh. "On your feet, men. Let's go!"

"Aw, Major, what's the hurry?"

"Let's park for a while."

"Come on, men," the major called again. "Just a little ways farther and we stop for a rest."

Burt and Bob helped Fritz, who seemed in a daze, to his feet.

"Let's go!" shouted the major, and the formation began the long uphill struggle, some lumbering like the major and Jim and Fred, some walking fairly easily like Tom, Bob, Al, and Burt, others staggering slightly like Bill and Ed, and a few stumbling from side to side like Fritz and the old German guard. As they climbed higher and higher along the ramp, the frozen blast of the wind became even more piercing, but the drifting clouds of snow crystals were escaped.

"Hey, Jim," Bob called ahead, "what the hell is this? A bridge?"

"Search me," Jim called back.

"Look. Lights," Koczeck called.

Two pinpoints of light approached far to the left and below the ramp.

"Look's like a car with blackout shields on the headlights," Tom said.

The uphill trek strained thigh muscles, and the increasing blast of cold from the northeast bit sharply into the right side of each man's neck and shoulder and back. Going uphill each pack and bedroll seemed heavier. The twin lights approached beneath the column ahead and below and vanished.

"It had to be a car," Tom said between pants.

As they approached the top of the ramp, on what must have been a half-mile climb, two wide parallel ribbons of gray could be seen stretching out of sight below to the southeast and on the other side to the northwest.

"An Autobahn," Jim said. "That's what it is, one of the Autobahns, the highways that lead to Berlin. This is an overpass."

"Yeah, that's what it is," agreed Tom.

The formation reached the top of the windswept overpass and leveled off. The wind whistled and sliced through each man like a frost-glazed knife.

"We g-gotta stop soon, now," Bob chattered. "W-We j-just can't go on like th-this."

"Not up here," Koczeck protested. "It's—that wind. It's colder than a witch's tit."

Right in front of them the staggering Fritz was exhaling long dry, broken sobs, oblivious of their sound. Burt Salem stumbled to his knees and clambered exhaustedly to his feet as those behind him veered to avoid collision. Each man watched the ice and the heels of the men in front of him, and each man stopped automatically at the sound of Major Smith's shout from up ahead.

"Hold it, men. Hold it. Here we stop!"

The men looked up bewildered, as if they might have imagined the command in the terrible steady blast of cold which ripped across the overpass. They saw that they had caught up with the column. The formation ahead was made up of sprawling, squatting, stamping shapes.

"Looks like this is it. Take a rest," the major called.

"Jeesus," Bob swore. "Not here, huh? Not here you said?"

Koczeck was already sitting on the ice, wriggling out of his blanket roll. Fritz stumbled forward onto his face and rolled over on his side on the ice, his huge pack to the wind.

"They're trying to kill us off," Jim said to no one in particular, his shoulder blades pressing through his heavy clothing against the hardness of the road. All of them, exhausted from the night's marching and the effort to push the rations wagon, lay numbly on the ice. They stayed there for perhaps five minutes as the sweat-saturated insides of their shoes froze brittle against numb feet. Finally Major Smith sat up and gazed about at his sprawled command. He looked up at the faint sound of aircraft engines filtering through the loud hiss of the wind. It was a twin-engined plane. Its dark silhouette droned into the east.

"JU-52," Jim mumbled, looking straight up from his bed of ice.

"Say, men," the major called from his sitting position. "I've got an idea. Let's build a fire."

The suggestion was greeted with moans. No one stirred from the ice.

"How about it?" the major called again. "Let's build a fire."

"Sure, Major," Bob jeered from flat upon his back. "We can all toast marshmallows!"

"No. I mean it," Major Smith persisted. "I'll bet we can do it. Most of us are carrying things that'll burn. Things we don't really need." He climbed stiffly to his feet, stooped over, and began untying one end of his blanket roll. He brought forth four bundles of letters and picked his way among the sprawling figures to the center of the formation. He held the letters above his head. "Here, I'll start it with these. Letters from my wife and kids. Three years of letters. When the Russians catch up we'll soon see our wives and kids, so what are we packing the letters for? They're just paper. C'm' on. Who's got some letters for the fire?"

Several men sat up with a start.

"The Russians!" Jim exclaimed. "Where are the Russians?"

They listened, startled that they had forgotten to listen for the shellfire in their cold exhaustion. Softly, muffled by the wind, the rumble of exploding hope came to them from the north.

"There it is! There it is!" exclaimed Bob. "They're still acomin'."

Beside Bob, Al Koczeck, his head propped on one elbow against the ice, fumbled with his blanket roll.

"How about it, men," Major Smith repeated, looking about at the sprawling forms. "Who's got something for the fire?"

"Here, Major," Koczeck called from the ice. "Here's my letters." He handed him a couple of bundles. "I knew I was saving 'em for something."

Other prisoners began working at their blanket rolls and packs. "Here, Major. Goon newspapers."

Men began to lumber to their feet, bringing old newspapers, copies of magazines, and souvenir logbooks to add to the pile the major was building up.

"How you going to light it?" asked Bob, edging toward the pile. "You'll never get it started in this wind."

More and more paper mementos and souvenirs landed on the pile as the men gathered around it, huddling together to keep warm.

"Form a tight ring around it, men," Major Smith instructed, squatting and fumbling with a match. "Come on; close up the circle." The men formed a barrier against the wind. The major scratched a match against one of the brass buttons of his greatcoat. It went out. "Here, Major." Someone handed him a box of German safety matches. He held it close to the base of the pile of paper and struck it to flame. The paper caught, and the flame grew upward. "That does it."

"Hubba!" exclaimed Koczeck, slapping his mittens together.

"We need more fuel," Major Smith called as the fire burst to full life. "This won't last long."

"Who's got more paper?" The shout went up as the scroungers set out to find some.

"How about you, Fritz?" Bob Montgomery called down at the still figure. "I bet you got enough fuel in that pack to start a bonfire of our own."

"No," mumbled Fritz, cheek against the ice.

"Whatta ya mean, no?" Bob sneered. "You packed dozens of magazines and newspapers. I saw you. All your letters, too."

"I'm saving 'em for my wife," Fritz said wearily. "She'll get a kick out of 'em."

"Look," said Bob disgustedly, "your wife's sitting home by a nice warm fire or sackin' in a nice warm bed—if she's not out with some 4-F—and here you are freezing to death and packin' a God-damned load like a God-damned nigger just so she'll get a kick out of it." Bob felt doubly guilty for a second, but he continued. "Come on. Dummy up, Fritz. Let's have the paper."

"Leave me alone," Fritz moaned.

Jim, who had evinced no interest in the fire until now, was lying flat on the ice nearby. "Don't be a damned fool until you're dead, Fritz," he called emotionally. "Give it to the fire. You'll never make another five kilometers with it, and you know it. Put it in the fire."

Fritz did not answer.

"How about it?" demanded Bob. "Do we get the paper?"

There was no answer.

"Take it," Jim said, still looking at the swirling sky.

Bob and Al Koczeck fumbled with the fastenings of the pack, which was still attached to Fritz's back. Fritz buried his face in his arms against the ice as they rummaged through it.

"Jeesus, look at this!" Bob withdrew a fat roll of copies of *Der Adler*. Al brought forth a Y.M.C.A. P.O.W. logbook complete with heavy stiff-backed binding. There were only a few letters. These were shoved back, and then a big bundle of German newspapers and a notebook were pulled forth. "There's about seven pounds right there you won't have to tote any more," Bob said, refastening the pack. Fritz didn't lift his head from his forearms as they carried his mementos to the packed ring of prisoners round the fire. As they squeezed into the flickering circle, Jack Noble squeezed out.

"Might as well try to get warm by a flashlight," he said. He sat down on the ice behind Tom, who was also sitting. Noble wiggled up behind and astride of Tom. "Hey, Jim," he called, "get in behind me. This is the way to keep warm." Jim complied, and soon there was a chain of men stretching across the road, sitting belly to back, each man hugging the man in front of him.

"Here comes Hohendahl," Tom announced from the front of the chain. Hohendahl approached pushing his bike. He was followed by a large group of prisoners without packs heading toward the rear of the column.

"Block commander," Hohendahl called. "Block commander."

Major Smith turned from the huddle at the fire, his black beard silhouetted against the glow. "Yeah?"

"Six men, please, to carry rations. We must lighten the wagon. Six men, please."

The ration details waited with Hohendahl while Major Smith diplomatically asked six shivering men to volunteer.

"How about it, Casey? It's better than standing here freezing to death. Osgood, Junior! Go with Hohendahl here and pick up some Brot, will you? Maybe you can pick up some gen."

The men moved off with Hohendahl, heading back for the stalled wagon at the foot of the ramp.

"Hey, Major," someone at the fire called, "we need more fuel."

Other chains of men had formed, hugging each other on the ice, fighting the wind.

"Let's change places, Noble," Jim said at the head of the first chain. "My back's fairly warm, but as far as the front of me is concerned I'm end man on the daisy chain." They changed places and Jim hugged Noble tightly into his crotch.

"Say, Noble, you're not bad. All you need is tits and a cookbook."

Montgomery left the fire and walked to the chain. "We need more paper, Jim," he said. "How about it?"

Jim looked up seriously. "How about what?"

"How about all that paper you're carrying? You got plenty?"

"Yeah, and I'm keeping it."

Fritz, still lying with his pack on the ice, raised his head to watch and listen.

"Come on, Jim," Bob urged. "It's just paper. It'll burn good."

"Forget it," Jim snapped, face taut in the cold.

"Yeah," Fritz whined, "it's all right to burn up my souvenirs, but not Jim Weis's. No, not Jim Weis's."

"How about that?" Bob sneered.

"There's plenty of paper in my roll," Jim spoke tensely, "but it's not souvenirs, and it's not for burning."

"God damn you, Jim Weis!" The men of Room 8 looked at Fritz in awe. He had never sworn before. "You're no better than anybody else!"

"Aw, shut up," Jim said weakly, nervously.

Bob looked down a minute. "Chicken shit," he murmured, turning and walking back to the fire.

Jim shivered, tensely silent in the chain of men.

"Hey, leggo. Leggo, Jim," Tom complained. "You're holding me too tight."

Jim relaxed his grip and remained silent, furiously gritting his teeth. Finally he spoke. "God damn it, Tom. I'm no chicken shit."

"Easy does it, Jim."

"I'm not a chicken shit. It took me more than a year to write what I'm carrying. There's 130,000 words in my roll and 71 poems."

Tom didn't answer. The cold wind hissed past the immediate silence around Jim. Suddenly Jim extricated himself from the chain of men and stood up. "All right. So I'm chicken shit." He walked over and sat down against the bank of snow at the edge of the overpass.

"Ah, nuts," he sighed at the hurt in his breast, then violently, "Nuts!" He wriggled further into the snowbank to ward off some of the bitter wind and listened half sick to the faint rumble of battle blowing down from the northeast.

Major Smith, blowing into his mittens, walked away from the fire and found Jim sitting alone.

"Kind of anti-social, aren't you, Jim?"

"I'm always anti-social."

"Got no friends, eh?"

Jim ignored the question. "How's the fire?"

Major Smith sat down beside Jim. "Confidentially," he whispered, "it ain't worth a damn." Then, in a louder voice that still wouldn't carry, "But it gives the boys something to do, and it has lightened a lot of loads we shouldn't have been carrying in the first place."

Jim motioned northeast over his shoulder toward the distant explosions. "They don't sound any closer."

The major listened. "No, they don't."

"Remember what they did at Warsaw?" Jim asked.

"Yeah. What's that got to do with us?"

"The Red Army got right up to the city. Then they stopped and let the underground fight until the Germans wiped it out. Then the Reds moved in—after the Poles who had held out for nearly four years were dead."

Major Smith shook off a spasm of shivering. "What's that got to do with us?"

"What time is it?" Jim asked.

"After five."

The major turned his face into the cold wind. "It's a gloomy time of night—or morning. I've got a lot of imagination, and all my friends are dead." The rumbling of the guns swelled and faded like surf in the wind. "I wish they'd close the gap or shut up."

Bob approached them and leaned into the wind. "The fire is just about out, Major," he reported, looking at Jim. "No more paper."

"It was a good fire," the major answered, and stood up into the wind. "Here comes the ration detail."

The prisoners got up from the ice and descended upon Junior and the others who were carrying armloads of the heavy black loaves and square blocks of margarine.

"Two-sevenths of a loaf for each man," Bob informed the members of Room 8 who were staring at the two and six-sevenths loaves resting on Bob's blanket roll. "That's two days' rations." He began cutting the loaves with a sharpened table knife and passing them out.

"This stuff weighs a ton," Tom said, chewing off a piece. "I'm not carrying mine," he sputtered.

"Stick it on the fire," Koczeck suggested. "It ought to burn real good. It's made out of sawdust."

Bob divided up the margarine.

"I just remembered something," said Jim. "Eat the margarine. It's carbohydrate . . . supposed to keep you warm."

"Who told you?" jeered Bob.

"My mother is a dietician," Jim said, eating the margarine like candy.

"Br-r-r-r," chattered Noble. "It's terrible cold. Let's form the chain again."

Jim picked up a bread ration and a margarine ration and carried them over to where Fritz was still lying. "Here," he said, tossing them down by Fritz's head.

Fritz looked up. "Thanks," he said weakly.

"And get up on your feet," Jim ordered. "It's a wonder you aren't frozen to death. Come on. Hey, somebody, give me a hand."

They pulled Fritz to his feet, but he could only stand by holding on to his helpers. Jim began rubbing his legs briskly through the many layers of clothing, and Tom did the same to his back and chest.

"What's the matter?" Major Smith asked, approaching.

"He's damned near frozen to death," Jim said, still rubbing.

The major looked at Fritz's pack, lying on the ice.

"You better lighten that pack," he told Fritz.

"W-We c-could-dn't b-be going much f-farther?" Fritz asked.

"I don't know. We could be." Major Smith looked at Jim, who shrugged. From up ahead came shouting. Guards were standing at the left side of the overpass, waving their rifles. Major Smith turned. "All right, men! On your feet! Let's go. Let's get out of this wind!"

The men left Fritz to gather up their own bedrolls.

"Come on, men!" the major shouted. "Off we go into the wild blue yonder! Let's go."

Fritz looked dumbly down at his pack. Slowly, without any help, he reached down, grabbed it by an arm loop, and torturously lifted it until he could slip an arm and shoulder into it.

"Another day, another ten dollars," the major shouted.

As the formation moved forward, Jim felt the weight of his bedroll.

"My shoes are really like rocks this time," Fred Wolkowski complained. "Frozen solid."

The wind slapped its frozen fingers across the faces of Montgomery, Noble, and Koczeck as they watched Fritz staggering ahead of them, trying to force his left arm into the other sling of his great pack.

"Like a nigger—a Negro," Bob muttered. "Like a God-damned Negro totin' cotton."

The going was easier down the ramp at the other end of the overpass. The wind lessened a little as they reached the slope beyond. But then the drifting snow began to sting their faces again as the long column moved forward through the night.

Bob Montgomery: "There I was. . . ."

People are always mistaking me for something. In this screwy war I've been mistaken for a movie star, a paratrooper, and a Southerner.

When I went to San Antonio to sign up for aviation cadet training the word got around that a movie star was joining the Air Corps. Somebody made a gag of it. While I was taking the six-four physical, dogfaces kept running in to have a look at Robert Montgomery. Well, that's my name, but I ain't no movie star. The same thing happened every place the army sent me for bombardier and B-17 phase training back in the States, but that was nothing to what happened in England. I joined the Key Club in Cambridge, and every time I checked in between missions the word got around and half the twists in Cambridge would show up. I ain't no movie star, but I did my best . . . but then I ain't no stud horse, either.

Lead bombardier, I got to be. Another week and I'd have made captain. But one day we picked up too much flak over Hamburg and had to hit the silk. I already got my membership card in the Caterpillar Club, but I ain't just a bird-turdin' when I say I got it the hard way.

There was a lot of wind that day, but with old Betsy Bomb Sight I steered the pay load right into the sub pens O.K. Hittin' the silk in that wind was something else again. Jeesus! it takes a few minutes to float down from 19,000 feet, and that old umbrella was rockin' like nothin' I ever been through. I never been on a boat, but, brother, I sure got seasick bobbin' around in that chute. It was bombs away for my bomb bay about halfway down, and I watched my own puke stream right down where I was headin'—into the drink—some kind of lagoon. I never learned to swim in Texas, so I figured I'd had it.

I pushed the CO_2 lever and inflated my Mae West; and do you know, when I hit that cold water my chute just billowed out and drug me along with it? I was scootin' over that water at maybe twenty miles an hour until finally the silk snagged in some reeds near the shore. It was shallow and I could hear some kids yellin', so I undid the harness and waded through the mud and reeds toward where the shouts were coming from.

"Hi," I called as I pushed through the reeds and stepped up on the bank. There were two boys, maybe ten years old, wearing short pants and suspenders and brown shirts. "You fellows speak American?"

And . . . wham! Just like that, one of the little bastards points a pistol at me and lets me have it. He hits me right up here in the chest near my left shoulder. I still wear the shirt with the hole in it. Gonna take it home for a souvenir. An inch lower and he'd akilled me.

"Now what'd you want to do that for?" I asked, laying flat on my back. The kid said, "Ferdamnty paratroopin'," or something like that. I felt like heavin' again, but there was nothing left to heave, and my chest was bleeding like a stuck hog. Then the kid points his gun at me again, and I know I'm a goner. I'm too pissed off to even yell; but somebody yells, and the kid doesn't shoot. A German soldier walks up, pats the two little bastards on the head, and tells me in good English that the Hitler Jugend thought I was a paratrooper.

Well, that explains everything. That makes everything just dandy. Even the kids in this God-damned goonland go around shooting people.

Then the movie-star business starts again. The goon soldiers, the goon nurses, the Russian women working in the hospital—the minute they hear my name they think I'm the movie guy and nothin's too good for me. Christ, what a country!

Then this Southerner business starts up when I finally get to Stalag Luft III. They put me in this room where Jim Weis is room Führer. He needs a haircut pretty bad and has a big bushy mustache when I first see him. He looks maybe thirty-five years old and must have been born overseas and packs a lot of weight. But he spends most of his time writing in notebooks or reading or down at the Kriegie Theater rehearsing shows, or—I didn't know it then—working with the X Committee, and we get along fine until one day.

Hell, I was just telling about something that happened back on our chicken ranch in Texas.

"We had one lazy buck nigger workin' on the place," I was saying.

"One day my old man found him buckin' in the saddle on top of an old nigger gal in a ditch on the place. Well, sir, my old man starts kickin' that buck nigger in the ass until he jumps up off that old gal and starts runnin' up the road with his pants in his hand and my old man achasin' him and peltin' rocks at him. 'Don' hit me, boss. Don' hit me,' that buck nigger keeps a yellin'. 'Don' hit me no mo'. Ah wuks. Don' hit me, boss. Ah wuks. Ah wuks! Ah's a good niggah, boss. Ah's a good niggah! Ah wuks!'"

Well, I'll be damned if that little story don't set off a rip-roarin' argument about race prejudice and that kind of stuff. After it's going good and loud for a while, Jim gets into it.

"Just what in hell are you over here fighting the Nazis for?" he asks.

"Well, it ain't for no niggers," I answer.

Jeesus, I never seen anybody blow his top so suddenly before! "That's the trouble with you God-damned Southerners," Jim yells. "You God-damned Southerners think just because you're white you're better than a man whose skin happens to be a different color. The fact is that you God-damned Southerners are mostly just plain stupid!"

"What the hell you callin' me a God-damned Southerner for?" I yells back at him. "I ain't no God-damned Southerner. I'm a Texan!"

Jim just snorts and walks out of the room. Jeesus, I figures, you got to be careful what you say around some of these characters from the North. These Northerners are nigger lovers. Only Jim ain't from the North exactly. More northwest.

That blew over just like most things do. Jim hardly ever blew his top like that about anything. He'd been a Kriegie long enough to know you can't pop your cork every day or so living in a room full of men.

But then there was that time when the adjutant moved me into the room with Thunderbird, thinking I was a Southerner. Then the shit really hit the fan. I've never seen anyone so mad as Jim was.

"That bastard!" Jim cussed while I was gathering my things together. "I could pump a bullet into that fat face without even blinking. You taking a whip along, Montgomery?" he asked, looking at me like I was a wormy rat.

"Jeesus, Jim," I tried to explain, "it ain't my idea. Hell, I'll treat the nigger all right. The colonel just don't want him to get out of hand."

You ever seen anybody so mad he cried? That's the way Jim was. He just rolled over on his bunk facing the wall and didn't say anything. I knew he was crying.

It wasn't bad in that room. Not bad at all. All the white guys were Southerners but me, and I didn't know how to act at first. Hell, a guy with seven Air Medals, two D.F.C.'s and the D.S.C. is no ordinary nigger. But Thunderbird sort of took care of that by himself. He did his share of the work. He could play cards as good as anybody. He had more college than anybody else in the room. There was a guy from Florida named Ace—not a real ace, he only shot down three planes—used to fly with Jim. One day he asks Thunderbird in a friendly way:

"Tell me, Thunderbird, how've those nigger fly boys in your outfit been making out?"

"All right," Thunderbird answers, smiling. "I suppose you've heard the one about Four Four Four?"

"No," says Ace, "don't believe I have."

"Well," says Thunderbird, "we were coming in at Corsica after a rough mission. Some of the boys were a little shot up. 'Hello, Ox Star. Hello, Ox Star,' one of the boys calls the field. 'Cleah the runway. Cleah the runway. This is Foah Foah Foah comin' in foah foahced landin'.' "

After everybody got through laughing, Thunderbird smiles gently at Ace and says:

"Ace, I'm from the South myself, so I can understand why some people feel sorry for us Southerners. But we can beat it if we think about it. It's just as easy to say 'Negro.' Or, better yet, why not just use names? That's why I call you Ace instead of White Boy."

Ace's mouth falls open, and then he grins. "O.K., Thunderbird."

First thing you know, we're all pals. Thunderbird is quite a boy. I've walked many a circuit with Thunderbird, and he's O.K. The same thing happens in the room where they put the other Negro pilot with a bunch of Southerners. Then one day two more Negro pilots arrive in camp. Thunderbird announces they've all arranged to room together, so he's moving out on us.

"Anything we've done?" I ask Thunderbird.

"Hell, no," he grins. "You boys are tops. We're all from the same outfit and want to be together, that's all. You guys will always be my friends."

We were sorry to see him go; but what the hell, he was still in the same camp. We broke up the arrangement the adjutant had set up and returned to our old rooms.

"Welcome back to Nooky Nook," Jim says grinning when I moved back in. The old son of a bitch had got a haircut and shaved off that big bushy mustache. All at once I realized he wasn't a day over twenty-four.

Somehow, that Jim Weis gets my goat every so often.

Chapter Eight

The creeping dawn was dull, dirty gray, yet the snow was white in contrast to the gray slick of the icy road. The moans of the weariest were as natural a sound by now as the constant shuffle of feet.

"Daylight," Burt Salem panted to no one, "and the Russians haven't caught up." He watched dully the staggering, moaning figure of Fritz and wondered how anyone could endure such misery for so long.

"Son," Burt remembered his dad had said before the last farewell back home in Florida, "I don't suppose you'll run into much physical wear and tear in the Air Corps, but if you were going into the infantry like I was last time you'd probably learn something like I did. There may be some things you think you can do and some things you think you can't do. But in a war, that's all changed. In a war you find you can do things you wouldn't imagine trying. You do 'em because you have to. War can make a superman out of you, give you strength you never knew you had. But, of course, you won't have to do anything like that in the Air Corps. It'll be clean white sheets and three squares a day for you, not like it was for me in the trenches."

For miles, now, Burt had been wondering what was holding Fritz up, what kept him staggering forward under that ridiculous hulk of a pack.

I couldn't do it, Burt decided, and the thought made him concentrate on the aching numbness of his own back, the grating of his ankles against the trouser bottoms stuffed into his shoe tops, and the cold which seared the membranes of his lungs. Not with that pack, Burt was sure, feeling the clinging weight of his own lighter blanket roll and the cold burning where it rubbed against his right shoulder.

In the half-light beneath the shroud of swirling mist above the corridor of snow-weighted pines, the gray-brown column of lurching ragged men curved ahead and uphill. A low snow-covered building appeared on the right, tucked in the wall of trees, pale yellow squares of electric light at the unshuttered windows.

German military packs and rifles were piled against the building, and soldiers were milling about, keeping careful distance from several Hundeführers standing beside their Alsatian and Doberman dogs. Glimlitz called something from the group. The staggering old German guard broke away from the column. One of the dogs let out a prolonged minor yelp as his Hundeführer took the old German's place, marching beside the formation.

"How about some of that for us?" a weary voice called as a door opened revealing German soldiers holding steaming cups. Then the building was behind them and only the new guard, his straining dog pulling him along by the leash, was different as the weary legion slogged on and on in the whitening gray.

"I wondered what they did with the dogs," Fred murmured, looking down at the heels of the man in front of him. To each that was the vista—the heels of the man in front, and the heels beyond and to each side—a forest of brown bootheels swinging forward beneath the drooping, tucked-in trousers.

"Somebody's had it."

Tom's voice brought Jim's eyes up from the blur of bootheels and ice. Ahead, two figures stooped over a third, sitting in the left snowbank. As they drew near, the two figures managed to haul the sitting man to his feet. The guard with his dog passed them, and the three stepped in ahead of Jim. The center man limped weakly, his arms about the shoulders of the men who supported him.

"What's the trouble?" Tom asked.

The man on the right, puffing, called over his shoulder, "Mac, here, he just gave out for a bit."

"Come on, Mac, you can make it," they heard the other flanker coax. "Come on, Mac, you just need your second wind. It'll come."

"What block you from?" asked Jim.

"One fifty-four," the first speaker grunted, stumbling under the arm of Mac.

Tom and Jim looked at each other. Mac let out a low groan. "Lemme go," he cried weakly. "Lemme sit down."

"We're with you, Mac," the man on the left pleaded. "We'll make it. We'll get there."

"Lemme go. Gotta rest. Lemme go." Mac half walked and half dragged his feet over the ice. "Please," he whined. "Please."

"No, God damn it. No," the first man grunted fiercely. "We're sticking with you, and you're sticking with us."

But both the men supporting Mac were panting heavily and stumbling to keep up.

"Who's got your blankets?" Jim asked. "Where are your packs?"

The three seemed not to hear him, and struggled on, pleading with Mac, refusing his pleas to let him go.

"That's no good," Jim said softly to Tom Howard. Tom grunted. Watching Mac's booted feet first erratically moving ahead, then dragging, soles backward, on their sides, then attempting to march again, was no good. Jim felt his own shoulders sagging, and his vision bleared.

"God damn it!" the man called Mac sobbed. "Lemme go. I can't, I can't, I can't . . ."

"Shut up," the staggering supporter on Mac's left kept saying. "Shut up, shut up, shut up. . . ."

"Jesus, Jesus, Jesus, Jesus . . ." Someone behind in the formation was keeping the same cadence.

Jim realized that his tooth was aching. He had not noticed it because his shoulders and thighs were aching at least as much, and a great weight was pressing unmercifully on three of the vertebrae of his neck. He concentrated on the toothache now to relieve his awareness of the pains of the march.

"Who are these guys?" Fred asked out of the side of his mouth.

"Some of the newer Kriegies, I guess," answered Jim through teeth clenched tightly against the sore molar.

Fred glanced back at the miserably plodding Fritz. "I'd rather be carrying what Fritz has than that guy," Fred commented, breathing heavily.

"We're over the hump," Major Smith called back from up ahead. "Easy does it now, men!"

The formation had reached the top of the grade, and the road broke out onto the side of a wooded hill and curved undulating down. For an instant ahead and below they could see the endless rising and falling snake of the column. Then, as the formation started downward, the man called Mac gave out entirely.

"Oh-hh-hh-hh," he sighed between his struggling comrades, as if with relief at reaching the top; "oh-hh-hh," as if the top were all they had to reach; and fell to his knees between the two men, who, grunting horribly, dragged him along over the ice.

"Mac . . . Mac . . . Mac . . ." It was all the man on the left could say. The man on the right turned sideways and walked backward, stumbling, but still hauling Mac by his right wrist. No one offered to help them.

"You guys had better decide what you're going to do," Jim advised.

"Christ!" sobbed the man on the right. "Somebody help us. Can't somebody?"

No one offered to help. The man on the right fell, clambered to his feet, fell again, and once again got up, frantically pulling along the sliding figure of Mac.

The formation passed the dark brown form of a prisoner lying motionless beside a large pack on the ice at the left side of the road. Eyes shifted from the struggling trio to the new sight, and then it was left behind.

"C-Come—c'm' on," breathed the man pulling Mac's left arm, and then the three of them pulled out of the column and collapsed at the roadside, Mac sliding head first a few feet down the bank among the trees.

"Damned fools," Jim muttered between his clamped teeth.

Tom Howard grunted and looked back at Fritz. He grunted again and looked ahead and down at the clopping boots which had replaced those of the trio. They blurred under the weight of heavy eyelids and the ache of overexposed eyeballs.

The formation passed a stump upon which huddled a sitting prisoner, his face buried in his arms.

"How long does it take to freeze to death?" asked Fred.

"I don't know," answered Jim. "Not long in forty below zero."

"I hear you just fall asleep and never wake up," mused Fred.

Up ahead Major Smith slackened his pace and allowed himself to fall back in the formation between Tom and Jim.

"They're beginning to drop out," he said.

"Yeah." Jim glanced back at Fritz.

"Did you get a look at that last one?" Major Smith asked.

"No. We were past him almost before I saw him."

The major marched along with them in silence for a moment.

"We've got to get on the ball," he finally said. "Let's not take any more chances."

Tom pressed a fist against Major Smith's arm. "Here's another one," he said.

The major slipped out of the column to the left and took a hurried look at a figure lying face up in the loose snow at the road's edge. He stepped back into the column.

"Dead?" asked Jim.

"I dunno. Maybe sleeping. Jim, you walk on the outside and check. There'll probably be more. Wolkowski? You know Shorty, don't you?"

"Yeah, sure." Fred looked puzzled.

"Well, check anyone that's dropped out on that side. If it's Shorty, yell Tallyho! I'll halt the whole formation. You know what to do, Jim."

"Right."

"I don't get it," Fred said, moving obediently to the right side of the formation.

Tom looked questioningly as Major Smith moved forward and Jim crossed to Tom's left.

"Just a precaution," Jim said. "Shorty's hot."

The formation passed two prisoners who had fallen out on the right. One was propped up against the steep snowbank and the other was slapping his face. Fred could tell at a glance that neither was Shorty.

Behind Tom, Fritz suddenly lurched diagonally through the formation toward the right snowbank.

"Stop him!" cried Bob.

Burt looked up and caught Fritz trying to cross in front of him. "No, you don't." Burt flung the tottering Fritz back toward the center. Bob caught Fritz by his pack, straightened him out, and gave him a shove forward. Fritz nearly fell, but recovered.

"You ain't dropping out, you son of a bitch," said Burt Salem.

Fritz reeled forward, a sobbing hulk under a pack. Bob shook his head and looked down at the ice. He tried to spit, but his mouth was dry and there was no spit.

The road leveled off on the side of the hill. Jim stepped out and looked ahead.

"There's another one," he said. Tom and Jim stepped out of the formation. They could see a prisoner sitting on a roadside rock.

"It's Shad," Jim said. "Hey, Major," he called. "There's Shad."

Major Smith angled to the left to have a look. As they drew up to the seated figure, the formation ahead came to a stop. The major held up an arm. "Hold it," he called. The formation came to a halt. Many of the men dropped to the ice where they were.

Major Smith and Jim walked over to the seated figure.

"What's the matter, Shad?" Major Smith asked the slightly built prisoner. "You're not giving out, are you?"

Shad looked up beneath the folds of a heavy brown wool stocking cap. "What the hell, Pete? Why should I kill myself? I'll catch up when I'm ready."

Major Smith turned to Jim. "Ask the Hundeführer how long we're stopping."

Jim crossed to the German, keeping just out of range of the dog which prowled at its leash, tongue out, panting steam.

"Wie lange bleiben wir hier?"

The German shrugged. "Ich weiss nicht. Vielleicht fünf Minuten, zehn Minuten."

"He doesn't know," reported Jim. "Five or ten minutes, maybe."

"Chow up while you've got a chance!" the major called to the formation. "Eat while you can!"

"You were with Shorty, weren't you?" Jim asked the seated prisoner.

"Yeah. He's all right."

"Any gen?" Major Smith asked.

"He picked some up from BBC this morning," Shad said. "But it wasn't good."

"What was it?"

"The Russians are right where they were yesterday morning."

Jim squatted and grasped a handful of snow.

"What?" cried the major. "They haven't advanced at all?"

"Not an inch. They're mopping up and preparing for a new drive."

Jim stamped to his feet. "Son of a bitch!" he gritted, and turned, walking back toward his friends.

"Jim, come back here!" Major Smith clipped.

Jim turned and stamped back. "It's just like Warsaw," he snapped. "The Red bastards don't want us liberated."

"I don't know about that," the major said. "Listen."

They could still hear the rumbling of shellfire, distant now, and to the south.

"I don't hear anything to the north," said Jim.

"Sometimes we can't hear anything to the south," said Smith. "It's these hills."

"The bastards want the goons to move us out—or bump us off. They don't want to be bothered with us, that's all," Jim complained. "Them and their God-damned second front. They don't give a shit what happens to us."

"Go get something to eat. Keep your mouth shut about this."

"Huh?"

"Jesus Christ, they're dropping out right and left now. If we lose hope we're through. So keep your mouth shut. You've heard nothing. Understand?"

"Yeah." Jim turned and walked back to the formation. The men of Room 8 were unfastening the ends of their blanket rolls, all except Fritz, who was lying with his face against the ice, his pack still strapped to his back.

"What the hell are you doing?" Jim asked the others in an angry voice. "Don't go through your own rations. Take some of the dead weight off him!" He nudged Fritz's pack with his toe.

"You mean eat his food?" asked Bob incredulously, looking up from a squatting position.

"Yeah, sure. The dumb son of a bitch won't last another ten feet with that load. He might not without it."

"I brought my own food," said Bob.

Jim sat down beside the sprawled Fritz and quickly jerked the bows of the pack. "Either you eat it, or I throw it away," he said gritting his teeth. "Here." He pulled out a pound tin of corned beef and tossed it on the ice beside Bob. "Somebody pull him out of this damned thing," he ordered, extracting boxes of raisins, Spam, and boxes of biscuits.

Tom and Fred worked the pack straps loose and over Fritz's shoulders. Jim ripped the top off a box of raisins and thrust them into Fritz's face. "Here, eat some of this," he ordered.

"You're stealing my food," Fritz moaned. "You got no right—"

"Shut your mouth!" Jim bellowed. "We'll see you get enough to eat. Now start eating and shut up."

"Take it easy on the poor guy," Bob said. "He packed it. It's his food."

Jim stood, deliberately wound the top off a can of Spam, and started munching it. He turned away and looked down the wooded white slope, chewing great bites. Bob looked around. The others were busy eating food from Fritz's pack. Bob picked up the can beside him and opened it. Tom walked up beside Jim.

"Want some raisins?" he asked, proffering the box.

"Yeah," answered Jim. "Have some Spam." He looked back over his shoulder. Fritz was sitting up, chewing at the raisins.

"We could have made a break," Tom said with his mouth full. Jim said nothing. "With all these guys dropping out, how're they going to know who's escaped from those who've bought it?" Jim still said nothing. "The Reds have probably taken Sagan by now, and we'd have been liberated," Tom continued. "I think that business of shooting two for each escaped was just a bluff."

"So what?" asked Jim.

"We could still make a break," said Tom. "If we'd done it before, we'd be free 'men now."

"No, we wouldn't."

"Sure we would. The Russians are bound to be in Sagan by now. What say we make the break now, Jim? They'll still catch up."

"No." The raisins had frozen. Jim was tearing away the cardboard and biting hard chunks from the block of fruit. He turned and walked over to Fritz. "How you feeling?"

Fritz wouldn't look up. Jim bent over the pack. "You got any rope in this mess?"

"Hey," Fritz whimpered. "Leave that alone. You've stolen enough."

Jim rummaged in the pack, throwing away some handmade tin dishes and a lamp made from a can. He pulled out a heavy rusted steel bar about fourteen inches long and hefted it in his right mitten. "What in hell is this?"

"That's my pranger," pleaded Fritz. "Put it back."

"This thing must weigh three pounds," said Jim as he tossed it over the bank and down the slope. He pulled out a bundle of rope. Selecting a piece about six feet long, he doubled it and tied the ends to the pack straps. He tied the lid down on the pack and stood up, holding the loop of the rope. He tossed the loop down before Fritz. "Here. Now you don't have to lug it on your back. We can't be going much farther. You can drag it along like your ass."

Major Smith's shout came from up ahead. "Come on, men, here we go again. False alarm. Let's go."

The men lumbered slowly to their feet, breaths white in the daylight, and shouldered their loads. The column moved forward.

"Hey, Shad," Jim called. "Ain't you coming?"

Shad, still seated on the rock, waved an arm and the formation moved forward, leaving him behind. Jim fell in beside Tom and looked back. Fritz was following, dragging his pack by the rope over the ice. "It must be ten pounds lighter," Jim said.

"Yeah," Tom agreed. "What's wrong with making a break now?" he asked.

"Aren't you kind of tired?" Jim asked.

"I'm pooped."

"And a little cold, maybe?"

"God, yes."

"Well, I know something you don't. Escaping is no good now. We've got to stick with the column."

Already they were panting again.

"Who said so?" asked Tom. Jim marched on as if he had not heard the question. Behind him Fritz, dragging the pack, was staggering violently from side to side.

Suddenly the column stopped again. Fritz fell to his knees and elbows. Most of the men sat down on the ice, removing their blanket rolls.

"What's going on up ahead, Major?" Tom called.

Major Smith turned, gestured with his arms that he didn't know, and sat down. The cold morning air pressed down like a lid on the sitting men. To the south the distant shellfire whispered. Jim's eyes closed and he started to fall asleep, but his sagging body woke him with a start. He looked around and saw Fritz crawl with his pack over to the border of piled snow at the road ledge.

"What you doin', Fritz?" Bob called from where he was seated. Fritz nestled against the snow on his belly, resting his face in his arms.

"You're not quitting, are you?" called Bob. Fritz nodded, only the back of his head visible. Bob and Al Koczeck looked at each other, got to their feet, and crossed to stand over him.

"Don't quit," Al said. "If you quit you'll freeze to death."

Fritz rolled his head to one side. The tears froze white on his face. "I can't go on," he whispered hoarsely. "I can't walk any more."

"Sure you can," said Bob. "We'll take turns pulling your pack for you."

"No!" shouted Jim, who had been watching from where he sat in the formation. "We won't pull his pack. He can leave it!"

Bob glared across at Jim.

"I can't walk," Fritz whispered. "My feet are hurt."

"What do you mean?" asked Al. "How are they hurt?"

"I don't know, but they're hurt. I can't walk any more."

The formation ahead began to move forward, and Major Smith rose to his feet. "Here we go!" he called.

Bob and Al looked down at Fritz's back, heaving with sobs. "We can carry him," Bob suggested.

"No, God damn it!" shouted Jim. "If he can't walk, leave him." Jim turned his face forward.

Bob and Al stood undecided. The rest of the formation stood watching.

"Come on!" the major shouted, with a big sweep of his arm. "Leave him. We've got to get going!"

The men in the formation started marching. Al and Bob took a last look at Fritz, sobbing into his pack, and then rejoined the march.

"Poor bastard," whispered Tom beside Jim. They marched on in silence, the mass of men stretching ahead in a blur.

"We couldn't have carried him," Jim said after a few minutes.

"No," agreed Tom.

"If you try to help a straggler you both get it," said Jim. "Noble!" he called over his shoulder.

"Yes, sir," answered Noble, his chubby face grinning sheepishly as he realized he had addressed Jim as a superior.

"When you get a chance, write down the location and the date." Jim looked ahead again. "It's just like those first three guys," he said. "Two tried to help one, so all three pooped out."

"Yeah. Forget it, Jim," Tom said.

They trudged along cold and silent before Jim spoke again. "What did they put a married farmer like that in the Air Force for anyway?" Tom didn't try to answer. Major Smith held up his arm and the column stopped again. Jack Noble made his way between the sitting and standing men to Jim.

"I don't know the location," Noble said, pulling a small paperbound notebook from his greatcoat pocket.

"Just put down Silesia," Jim directed, "thirty-five or forty kilometers west of Sagan. The date is January 28th."

"What about the time?" Noble asked, writing clumsily with a short pencil stuffed into his mittened fingers.

"About nine o'clock Kriegie time, 6:00 A.M. goon time," Jim said. "What the hell difference does the time of day make?"

Noble folded the notebook shut, stuffed it in a pocket, and sat down, twining his legs around Tom's hips. From far up ahead and out of sight came the faint sound of cheering.

"Something's up," muttered Fred.

Another cheer rose, closer. Major Smith stood up and faced the formation. "Sounds like good news," he called.

Jim rubbed his ears through the scarf looped over his head. "Good news," he muttered. The cheering came closer until the formation ahead exploded with the sound.

"What's the gen?" the major called.

A man sitting at the rear of the formation ahead called back: "There's a town up ahead. We're stopping there!"

The men cheered, followed by the cheers of the other formations fading to the rear. Once more the men lumbered to their feet and the column moved forward.

"We could have dragged him this far." Jim heard Bob's voice behind him, stifled sudden anger, and kept walking, concentrating on his toothache. The column halted and started again and again, the men remaining on their feet each time, shivering and stuttering curses at the cold.

"There she is." Major Smith grinned back as the formation crossed a rise and the snow-mantled buildings of the town appeared on both sides of the column.

"Graustein." Fred read aloud the name of the town from a small black and white rectangular sign posted on his side of the road.

Lieutenant Pieber and Colonel Baker, both grinning, faced the oncoming formation.

"Pass by fives, Major," Pieber directed, pad and pencil ready in his gloved hands.

Major Smith turned. "All right men, snap it up. The quicker we form up by fives, the quicker we hit the sack!"

"What's the deal, Colonel?" somebody called as the men passed to be counted.

"Warm barns with straw," Colonel Baker smiled. "Four hours' rest in warm barns with straw."

"Well, that's something," said Fred between pursed lips, "but, Christ! only four hours. I could sleep forty."

"How far we marched, Red?" asked the major, jogging from foot to foot, waiting for the formation to be counted.

"Forty kilometers," answered Colonel Baker. "Not bad for men who have been on half-rations for a year."

"Not good, you mean," said Major Smith under his breath as Pieber turned from the counting.

"You are two men short," clipped Pieber suspiciously.

"Casualties," the major snapped back. "That's two more for the little black book we're keeping."

Pieber shrugged. "A pity," he said. "Fortune of war. You may go on."

The formation passed a house on the left with latticed windows at waist level. In a center window, standing in a vase, a tiny black and white German flag and a small red and black Nazi flag were crossed. A fat Hausfrau, bundled up in shawls, stood at the gate pouring steaming coffee into china cups for a cluster of guards. The Hundeführer tied his dog to the fence and joined them. They passed some young boys standing silently, arrogantly watching them. As the road took on the appearance of a main street, the buildings on either side grew larger.

The column was moving ahead in spurts, buzzing with the promise of warmth and rest. "That God-damned Fritz," Jim said without changing the pace of the conversation, "insisting he could carry all that crap on his back like some kind of superman. Fritz Heine. It must have been the goon in him."

"You're not pure Irish yourself," Tom said.

"No . . . I'm not."

"Personally," Fred shivered during another halt, "I'm pure cold and pure tired. Where in hell is this barn we're getting?"

Ahead, the street angled abruptly to the right so that now they faced a bulky gray stone building of four stories. They could see prisoners filing into its large arched doorway.

"Hey," Tom said, "they're putting us in that hotel up there. That's no barn."

"That's the town hall," said Jim.

"It don't look bad to me," said Fred. "It beats a barn all to hell."

Enthusiasm swept the formation as it approached the town hall. It changed suddenly to shouts of protest.

"Aw, what the hell?"

"God damn!"

"Oh, no!"

Gefreiter Hohendahl and a fat amply overcoated civilian halted the flow of men halfway through the formation ahead. Hohendahl, ignoring protests, disappeared inside.

"Any more hotels, Major?" someone called.

"Ik awk vise nix," Major Smith tried to joke.

Hohendahl reappeared and motioned another group of prisoners to file into the building. The men cheered. The cheering died. Hohendahl motioned Block 162 to march on around the bend in the street and past the big inviting building.

"Barns ain't so bad," Major Smith called over his shoulder.

"This way, gentlemen." Hohendahl indicated the opened gate beside a two-story building with a thatched roof about a hundred yards beyond the town hall.

"Barn it is," said Tom as the column wheeled to the left between the stone gateposts. Ahead, to the rear of the two-story house, rose the gray clay shape of a large barn, as large as the house itself. The exhausted throng fought for dirty hay which they spread over the ground of the barn. Tom pointed up at the bare walls. "Jesus, look!" Daylight glared through hundreds of little square holes. The frigid wind whistled across and out through identical holes in the opposite walls.

Jim shivered. "It's a God-damned wind tunnel."

"They got it that way to ventilate the hay."

Jim untied the ends of his blanket roll and changed socks before crawling, shivering, in. Men stowed personal food and belongings in the hay beneath them with their shoes, and squeezed together, comforting each other like worms in a cold, cold can. Tom sighed in disgust. "Warm beds with straw."

In the windy barn Jim's body twitched only once, when Fritz's face appeared in a dream. But he did not wake up.

Chapter Nine

Jim awakened, eyes closed, aware that someone had just stepped on his arm. His whole body between the blankets and the hay was numb with cold. With instant revulsion he remembered the man-packed barn in which he had gone to sleep. He squirmed onto his left side. When he tried to open his eyes he found that they were granulated shut. He brought a mittened hand from beneath the blankets and rubbed the scabby accumulation loose from his eyelids. His eyes opened.

He saw the face of Fritz Heine! It was no dream. Not two feet away from his own face, stark against the dirty hay, the swollen red face of Fritz slept between blanket edge and wool cap.

Jim sat bolt upright, dizzy, his body aching, and stared. It was Fritz, all right. The tin pack lay between Fritz's blanket mound and the lump of another man beyond.

"What time is it?" Tom Howard's voice sounded casual down at Jim's side.

"Look," Jim said.

Tom rolled stiffly over onto his left elbow and saw Fritz. He sat up. "What do you know?" Tom sighed.

They stared dumbly at the sleeping face, then at each other. About them in the huge cold cavern of the barn, shaggy figures picked their way gingerly back and forth among the sprawling, blanket patchwork of those still sleeping.

"What do you know?" Tom repeated. "He made it."

Al Koczeck approached from the direction of the big square open entrance. When he got to them he leaned close and whispered: "Hey, you guys, bring your cups and some butts and follow me. Hot water and a warm kitchen."

"Look." Jim nodded toward the sleeping Fritz.

"Yeah," said Al. "I saw him. C'm' on and bring your cups."

Al waited while Jim and Tom pulled on their GI shoes and tied them. Then each reached into the hay beneath him for the cups fashioned from British Red Cross biscuit tins.

"We can't leave this stuff here," Jim said softly. "Somebody'll swipe it."

"No, they won't." Al grinned. "Guys are getting rid of stuff now, not swiping it. C'm' on."

In single file the three laboriously made their way through and over sleeping men. Occasionally they stepped on blanket-hidden arms and legs.

"Man, I'm stiff," Tom complained when they stepped out into the dirty trampled snow of the barnyard. With each movement their groins throbbed; their thighs and calves ached. Their ribs and back muscles seemed to be fighting each other. Their shoulders, biceps, and feet were dull and stiff.

"What time is it?" Jim asked, looking up at the low gray ceiling of solid clouds.

"It's after two!" said Al. "The four hours are up already. C'm' on."

He crossed the yard to where Kriegies crowded in and out of the back doorway of the house. Major Smith lowered a steaming tin cup and grinned at them.

"Well, Jim," he said, "I left you a present while you were asleep. Did you find him in your stocking when you woke up?"

They stopped before the major. "Where in hell did he come from, Major?" Jim asked.

"Remember that Brotwagon we pushed last night? Well, when they unloaded most of it they got it over the Autobahn. It trailed the column, picking up stragglers. I guess there weren't too many."

"That's a good deal," said Tom. "On the next lap I'm going to drop out and ride. When must we start again?"

"That's a good question." The major shrugged. "Better get yourself some black market hot water before the thundering herd wakes up." He nodded toward the already crowded inner porch of the house.

They pressed in through the doorway and waited with the chattering crowd there for turns at whatever was beyond another doorway.

"It isn't much warmer outside." Tom shivered.

"Somebody said they saw a thermometer," Al said. "They say it's thirty-three below."

"Pukka gen?" Jim asked.

"Search me," Al answered. "Just gen."

Men ahead of them in the pack stood on tiptoe trying to look inside the house.

"Hey, you guys!" somebody yelled ahead. "How about dragging your asses out of there and giving somebody else a chance?"

"You payin' rent?" another voice shouted.

"You ain't just a bird turdin'," a voice inside called back. But the pack squeezed aside to let some of them wriggle out. Then the crowd surged in, Tom, Jim, and Al with them.

"Hubba, hubba, hubba," enthused Al, rubbing his hands together. "Feel that heat?"

It was a large German kitchen, crowded with men, and an extremely large coal range was loaded with steaming pots and kettles. A fat lady wearing a sail-sized apron tended the pots and pans, chattering loudly to a skinny teen-aged girl who poured the hot water into tin cups, taking cigarettes or soap in exchange. A shelf above the range was already covered with loose cigarettes and small bars of Red Cross soap.

"How much they getting?" Jim asked, pulling the scarf down from his head to let the unfamiliar warmth sting his ears.

"Three butts or a bar of soap for a cupful of hot water," said Al. "I could end the war right here."

"Three cigarettes," Jim said. "That must be worth a fortune to these bastards. Do you know what the German ration is?"

"Hush, boy," Tom admonished, and moved ahead in the line. "There might be such a word as 'bastard' in German. We don't want to get the old heave ho."

"A German civilian gets no cigarettes," Jim answered his own question. "A non-combatant soldier gets two a day. A goon soldier in combat gets only six. Jesus, these people will be millionaires!"

"Not for long," grinned Tom. "The Russians will take care of that. Here." He extended an open pack. Jim and Al each took four cigarettes. Al struck a match and the three lit up. The skinny girl poured the hot water from a small saucepan.

"Danke," she said without smiling when he handed her three cigarettes.

"Bitte," responded Jim, last of the three to receive his out of a big teakettle when the saucepan ran out. He had hoped to get a smile with this courtesy, but got none. He crowded over against a wall.

"I brought some Nescafé," Al said. With a teaspoon which he produced from the pocket of his greatcoat, he scooped a measure into each of the three cups.

"Now I know how Dan McGee felt," Jim said, taking the spoon from Al and stirring his coffee.

"Who?" Tom asked, taking the spoon.

"Dan McGee—the guy in the poem that got cremated in Alaska."

"Oh, yeah."

"Hey," came a shout from the kitchen's crowded doorway, "how about getting out and giving us a chance?"

"I'm only just beginning to feel warm," Tom complained.

"We'd better make room," Jim said. A group of prisoners stood packed against a door which probably led into the house. "Let's see if we can ease through there," he suggested.

They squeezed between the crowding men, holding their cups high. Jim looked back over their heads toward the two females busy at the huge stove. "Now," he said, and pulled the knob. The door opened against the weight of the prisoners packed against it. He slipped through, followed by Tom and Al.

"Now this is something like it," Tom said, as the door closed, muffling the clamor from the kitchen. They were standing in a small pantry alcove, heavily woodworked in ancient brown timber. "Man, I'm stiff!" Tom added, placing his cup on a shelf beneath a glass cabinet full of dishes and glassware.

Jim walked on to look through an archway to the left. "We're sure to get chased out of here," he said, looking beyond into a dining room and living room well furnished with old furniture and rugs. "Better not touch anything. The goons might be touchy about looting."

"I don't want nothing," Al said, "except to get warm." He leaned against a wall and wiggled his right foot slowly. "You guys' feet sore?"

"Chilblains," answered Jim. "We're bound to have them." He gazed into the dining room beyond at a framed portrait of Hitler hung above the empty fireplace. Then his eyes lowered to the mantelpiece. "Hey, there's a radio in there."

"So what?" muttered Tom between loud slurps at his cup.

It was a small table-model radio. Its modern design contrasted sharply with the other furnishings. Al stepped up beside Jim, and both sipped the luxuriously hot coffee as they looked at the radio.

"Boy, what a canary!" Jim sighed. Tom walked over to have a look.

"So what?" he repeated.

Jim entered the room, crossed to the fireplace, reached up and slid a mittened hand along the electric cord until he found the plug near the floor. He pulled it out, grabbed the radio, and tucked it under his greatcoat. "Let's get out of here," he whispered, and shouldered open the door against the noisy pack of men in the kitchen. Holding the radio clumsily against his hip beneath his greatcoat, he squeezed his way through. The fat Frau and the skinny girl were still busy retailing hot water at three cigarettes per cup.

"Find the major," Jim ordered as they squeezed out into the bitter cold yard. The piercing breeze circulated under Jim's unbuttoned greatcoat and around the radio resting on his hip bone as he crunched over the trodden snow to the barn.

Al found the major talking to a spread-footed guard at the gateway to the house. Waiting a few feet away, Al heard the distinct sounds of shellfire in the chill air. The wall of the house deflected the sounds so that he could not be sure from which direction they were coming. Finally he caught the major's eye.

"What's up?" the major asked, falling in beside him as they walked toward the rear of the house.

"Jim liberated a Kraut canary."

"What?"

"We were in the house," Al explained. "One minute Jim says we've had it if we touch anything. You know, somebody might get shot for looting. The next minute he spots this canary, grabs it, and we walk out with it under Jim's coat."

They entered the barn. Most of the sleepers were awake and either sitting or moving about on the scattered hay. A group of curious prisoners stood around Jim, who was squatting beside the sleeping Fritz.

"All right, you men," Major Smith ordered, "break it up. Scatter. What you trying to do, draw a crowd?"

The group dispersed meekly. The major and Al sat down on the hay beside Jim.

"Let's see," Major Smith said.

The contents of Fritz's tin pack lay on the hay. Jim held the pack so that they could see the radio in the bottom of it. The major grinned.

"What's it weigh?" he asked.

"Six or seven pounds," Jim answered.

"Cheeze it!" Al whispered suddenly. "Tallyho!"

They looked up and saw Gefreiter Hohendahl standing with his bicycle in the barn doorway. Jim stuffed his own four and a half pounds of notebooks down on top of the radio in Fritz's pack.

"Major Smith," Hohendahl called, "have your men get ready please. We must march again."

"You heard what the man said!" Major Smith shouted, rising to his feet. "I hope you can get that thing out of here," he said softly to Jim. "If you get caught with it, they're liable to shoot you." He walked off among the milling men. "All right, let's get packed!"

Beside Jim, Fritz awakened and sat up rubbing his eyes. "Hey, what you doing to my pack?"

"It's my pack now," Jim said, and stuffed his own food and effects into it. "Now don't flap, for Christ's sake! I'm packing a canary in it. Here, use my rope to make a blanket roll."

"What's the big idea?" Fritz blinked down at the pieces of rope in his mittened hands.

"If you couldn't make it with all that junk last night, you won't be able to tonight," Jim said. "Now make a blanket roll and put as little as possible into it." Jim shoved his own blankets into the pack and hefted it up. Even with the radio the pack was only about half as heavy as it had been with Fritz's stuff in it. "Now leave most of that junk behind," he ordered Fritz again.

All over the hay-covered floor of the barn men jostled one another, stooped and squatted to remake their packs and bedrolls.

"I'm getting out of here," Fred Wolkowski said, and looped his blanket roll over his shoulder. He headed through the crowd toward the doorway, followed in file by Al Koczeck, Tom, and Jim. "How about that?" Fred grinned as they stepped out into the shock of a freezing breeze. "All last night he bitches about that pack of Fritz's. Now he's carrying it himself."

They crossed the yard toward the gate. A small covered wagon entered it, slowly drawn by a black ox. The driver was a woman. As they approached, the woman turned, her young face smiling out of a tightly wrapped black silk shawl. She shouted something.

"Hey," said Al, "that's Polish."

"Yeah," said Fred, and he shouted something back to the woman in Polish. She pulled on the reins to halt the ox, and clambered back through the wagon to say something more in Polish.

"What's she saying?" Jim asked.

Al joined the conversation, and the three of them chattered in the foreign language.

"She's Polish," Fred explained.

"No fooling," Jim said sarcastically.

"She says she's been traveling for over a week just ahead of the fighting." Fred talked some more Polish. Other prisoners gathered around curiously, listening to the strange language.

"Hey!" Fred turned excitedly. "She's got a baby in there."

The woman reached deeper into the wagon and faced them again with a baby wrapped in a quilt in her arms. Prisoners crowded close around the tailgate of the wagon. They peered at a tiny sleeping face. The mother said something more in Polish.

"She came in here to see if she can get some milk," Al translated, "only it's not very easy to get. The goons don't like her because she's Polish."

"There must be a cow around here somewhere," Tom said. "All that hay is for something. Has she got any money?"

More and more prisoners crowded around for a look at the baby. "She has occupation money," Al reported, "the kind the goons put out in Poland."

Tom drew an unopened pack of cigarettes from his pocket and tossed it into the wagon. "Tell her to buy some with that," he said. "You can probably buy a cow for a couple of packs of butts."

The mother placed the baby back in the wagon's interior and then picked up the cigarettes to examine the pack curiously. Somebody else in the crowd threw a pack, and it spun into the wagon.

"Give her some weeds," somebody yelled. Other packs sailed through the air. Prisoners came running to see what the excitement was about. More and more packs of cigarettes dropped into the wagon.

"Hubba, hubba!" exclaimed Al, clapping his hands together. "She'll be the richest dame in Deutschland."

"Fall in!" The major's roaring command interrupted the party. "Fall in!" he roared again.

The men broke away from the wagon, cigarettes still tumbling into it, the woman on her knees laughing with tears running down her cheeks.

"Cute little guy," Al said as the men of Block 162 took their familiar places in the formation. "What a deal! Mine's a lot bigger than that by now. I wonder what he's like."

"By the time you get home," Jim said, "your kid'll probably be big enough to paste you in the eye for trespassing. Boy, it's going to be another cold night!"

Ahead, beyond the gate and across the street, they could see another column of brown-bundled prisoners file out of a space between two buildings and turn west.

"Here we go again," Tom said. "Where in hell are those Russians?"

"They're still shooting," shivered Fred, listening to the long, familiar rumble. "They must be still coming."

Packs and blanket rolls on the snow at their feet, the men shuffled about in their places to fight the cold. Some puffed cigarettes and others munched Red Cross food. From the rear of the house a short fat old man wearing a black fur coat and a black felt hat stalked forward with Hohendahl. The civilian waved a pitchfork, talking loudly as they passed toward the gate.

"Oh, oh," Fred murmured softly.

"Looks like somebody tried to listen to a radio," Tom muttered sideways, "only it wasn't there."

The tin pack leaned heavily against Jim's left knee. He inhaled and exhaled slow drags from a cigarette held between the mittened forefinger and thumb of his right hand.

"Maybe he wants us to pitch his hay back up!" somebody to the rear yelled, followed by catcalls.

"Verdammte Luftgängstern!" bawled the German, shaking his pitchfork.

"I wish I wasn't standing quite so close to you," Tom cracked softly to Jim.

Major Smith stood ahead and to the side of the column, regarding the old German nonchalantly. Lieutenant Pieber's boots clacked briskly on the ice as he rounded the corner followed by Hohendahl wheeling the bike.

120

"Nun," Pieber authoritatively saluted the old German with the pitchfork, "was ist los, mein Herr?"

The fat smooth-jowled German flapped his fur-clad arms and shouted incoherently. Pieber left the old man and crossed to the major. The men in the column listened silently.

"Major Smith," Pieber clipped, eyes snapping behind his glasses, "you will please return the wireless at once."

"Huh?" The Major acted bewildered. "Return the what?"

"The wireless," snapped Pieber. "We shall tolerate no looting during this march."

"What do you mean, 'wireless'?"

"The receiving set, please. It was stolen from this house. Where is it?"

"Look, Pieber," Major Smith said sincerely, "there must have been three or four hundred men in that house. All of 'em weren't my men. The people who live in that house made a fortune in cigarettes and soap selling plain hot water."

The German officer stared up at the tall American for a few seconds and then said flatly:

"Instruct your men to produce the receiving set. Then we will leave here and nothing more will be said. Otherwise . . ." He shrugged slightly, still staring into Smith's face. A chill, additional to the bitter cold, enveloped Jim's back.

Major Smith turned. "Well, men. You heard Herr Pieber. Has anyone got a radio?" He scanned the entire column slowly, but his eyes avoided Jim's. "If anyone has a radio, speak up." No one spoke up.

"Verbrecher! Criminals!" shouted the fur-coated man, shaking the pitchfork like a spear.

Major Smith gestured with mittened palms upturned and faced Pieber. "Sorry. That's all I can do."

"So," Pieber grunted, and began a slow walk staring into the ranks at the men. "So." He worked his way slowly back toward where the men of Room 8 were standing. "If we must conduct a search," he said, pronouncing each word separately, precisely, "then we must find the thief." He looked separately at Tom, at Fred, at Jim. "Then we must shoot him like a dog. The penalty for looting is death."

Jim could feel the pack pressing against his knee. Pieber passed on. Jim followed him with unblinking eyes. "And who," Pieber's flat voice clipped on and on, "would be so stupid as to die like a dog for a silly, ridiculous little wireless?"

Jim could hear the flat cold voice of Pieber working toward the rear of the formation. He could feel the cold sweat above his hips, and the silence of the men and the whispering of the frigid breeze. Then Jim heard the clop of Pieber's boots approaching rapidly from the rear.

Suddenly the German officer was up to him! And past him!

"March out!" Pieber snapped, passing Major Smith and heading out the gate. The old German shouted at Pieber. Pieber shouted something back, and the old German backed slowly against the gate pillar, his pitchfork drooping.

Major Smith turned. "Let's go!" he shouted, blowing out a cloud of steam. "Load your backs and let's make tracks! Let's go!"

Jim heaved a sigh and bent to grab the tin pack. "No search!" he almost shouted.

Fred and Tom grinned, holding the pack while Jim slipped his arms through the shirtsleeve straps.

"Hell," said Tom, "they could never make a search here. Their men are too busy herding Kriegies all over town."

"Say," said Fred. A light came into his eyes. "Are you the one who's got it, Jim?"

"Sure he is," grinned Al Koczeck. "Didn't you know?"

"Well I'll be damned," breathed Fred. He grinned and adjusted his own blanket roll. "I wondered why you traded packs with Fritz."

"Let's get out of here!" shouted the major up ahead. The column began to move forward, and turned out of the driveway onto the ice-covered cobblestones beyond. Al looked back as they turned. The black-scarfed Polish mother was standing, bent over and waving from her covered wagon, a lighted cigarette dangling from her lips.

Up ahead, Major Smith grinned back and held up a mittened fist, thumb pointed upward. "Up the Jerries," he called in a stage whisper.

"Up the Jerries." Jim returned the thumbs up.

Behind Jim, Fritz trudged under his lighter load, looking wearily down at the ice-packed street, uninterested in the talk of the men or in the buildings lining both sides. Behind Fritz, Jack Noble rubbed a sleeve across his chubby face as he walked. "Boy, it's awful cold," he said. "I hope we don't have to march as far as last night. I'm sore all over."

"Well, at least nobody volunteered to carry any guitars this time," Al said, grinning over his shoulder toward Bill Johnston and Ed Greenway.

122

"You know," Bill countered in his Illinois twang, "I looked all over for a good guitar for tonight, but I couldn't find one."

Ed nodded ahead toward the bobbing tin pack on Jim's back. "Looks like Jim volunteered to tote something this time."

"You think so?" said Bill. "Say, you think maybe Jim swiped that radio back there?"

"Yeah, I think so," said Ed.

Bill scowled. "I can't figure that guy out," he drawled slowly.

"He's a goon hater," Ed said. "He'd do it just to annoy the goons."

The yelping of dogs was louder now. Grayness was settling over the already gray buildings of the town. Obergefreiter Glimlitz stood in the street up ahead. The yelpings came from between two buildings to the left of Glimlitz.

"Sounds like we draw a Hundeführer again," Major Smith commented loudly over his shoulder. "I hope they've fed those critters."

Glimlitz gestured. A guard with an Alsatian, shaggy in the gray light, left a line of men and dogs between the buildings to fall in beside the formation.

"Where we headin', Glimlitz?" Major Smith called.

"First turn to the right," Glimlitz answered. "You will join the main body there."

The column clopped raggedly on past the Lagermeister.

"It's getting pretty dark," Fred observed. "Who said the goons could never move ten thousand men at night?"

"Some damned fool like me," Jim said, trying to wriggle his shoulders under the unaccustomed weight of the tin pack. "It's hard to believe."

The column came to a guard standing at an intersection. The guard pointed, and the major led the formation to the right around a hairpin corner. Ahead the main column waited, stretching out of sight up the side of a barren snow-covered ridge. They came to a halt beside the Brotwagon they had struggled with the night before at the Autobahn. Only one horse now stood in the traces. A Luftwaffe officer wearing a soft blue leather greatcoat motioned to the major and spoke with him briefly.

"Room stooges," Major Smith bellowed, "front and center."

Jim glanced at the drooping Fritz. "Al, you take it," he said to Koczeck.

The room stooges walked over to Major Smith by the wagon.

"There's your Greyhound bus," Fred said to Fritz. Fritz looked

123

up at the wagon and back down at the ice again. Jim shouldered out of his pack and lowered it to the ice.

"Man," he said, "I don't feel like walking up that hill." The balls of his feet and his heel bones ached. It was nearly dark, and an increasing pressure of frigid wind blew down the length of the column. Men complained quietly about the cold, the ache of muscles and bones, and the blisters on their feet and ankles. Inside the wagon, guards were passing out bread and margarine to the room stooges, who broke away one by one to return to the formation.

"Half a loaf per man," Al said as he returned.

"Good God-all-Friday," Jim snorted. "What in hell are we going to do with all that?"

"It's all we get the rest of the march," Al explained. "Hey, take it off of me, will you? It weighs a ton."

The men paired off. Each pair took a loaf and a block of margarine. Tom hefted the loaf he had taken for himself and Jim.

"A man could build a mighty strong house out of this stuff," he said.

"They bake it in kilns," Jim agreed. "If you hit a man over the head with one it'll kill him sure. See if you can break off a couple of chunks to go with this marge."

Tom wrestled with the black loaf. He held it across his knee and tried to claw some of it loose.

"Can't budge it," he said. "It's like iron."

"Here." Fred handed Tom a sharpened table knife. Tom pushed it into the loaf and worked it back and forth until he had sawed off a ragged end of bread, which he handed to Jim. Jim unwrapped the hard frozen block of margarine and bit into it, using a tough mouthful of the bread as a chaser.

"Eat as much of the marge and as little of the bread as you can," he said, handing the block to Tom. "That bread is just so much dead weight, inside or out. So we may as well chuck most of it away."

Throughout the formation men were arguing or discussing what they should do with the heavy loaves.

"What I don't savvy," Bob said, "is why they're giving it all to us at once."

"Maybe they want to get that wagon completely empty so it'll hold more guys when they drop out," Bill said.

"Hmmn," Burt sputtered through a mouthful of bread. "That

wagon ain't going far with that horse pulling it. Look at his front foot."

Frozen blood was smeared around a deep red gash in the horse's left front foreleg. The horse held the injured leg cocked away from the ice, standing on three hoofs.

"On second thought, I think I'll walk," muttered Tom.

Up the column the wind blew back a distorted series of shouts.

"Load up!" the major called, half a loaf of bread in one hand and half a block of margarine in the other.

Jim hefted the tin pack onto his back and slipped his arms through the shoulder straps. "How you feeling?" he said, turning to Fritz. Fritz shook his head mutely and stared down at the ice.

"Let's go!" the major roared, and the men began to trudge forward up the climbing road. It was completely dark now. Below, to the right, the snow-blanketed rooftops of Graustein loomed a dull ghostly white until they were cut sharply from sight by a high white bank.

At the head of the formation the major tossed the larger part that was left of the bread into the bank. It buried itself in the snow.

"Here goes," said Tom. He flung the heavy loaf he was carrying into the bank. Other loaves followed as the column climbed and climbed.

"We're heading east, aren't we?" Tom asked. "I wonder how come."

"It's a switchback," Fred guessed.

The men looked neither to right nor left as they bent into the wind which blew stronger and colder as they climbed. Al Koczeck mechanically watched the dark blur of Fred's bootheels as the road turned abruptly. They continued climbing, heading west again.

"The poor little bastard," Al muttered, but no one heard him above the crunching of boots and the deep hiss of the icy wind. He was thinking of the strange young Polish mother and her tiny infant back at Graustein. And, thinking of them, he was also thinking of his own wife and the year-old son he hadn't seen. "The poor little bastard," he repeated as the wind sliced through the back of his greatcoat like a thousand frozen needles, and the big broken blisters of his feet burned against the rough insides of his heavy shoes.

Once more, to the left now and far below, the rooftops of Graustein appeared, a gray-white checkerboard. Tiny snowflakes began to fall, wide-spaced and given velocity by the wind.

"That's all we need," Jim grunted. "Snow. More snow."

"It might cut down the wind some," Tom said.

But it didn't. The wind continued to increase, knifing steadily, unmercifully into their backs and concentrating torture in their right shoulder blades and necks. Had it not been for the wind, the men might have been able to breathe easier as they reached the top of the barren plateau. Instead they marched gasping along the road which now cut straight across a wide frozen plain. The wind grew, whistling shrilly and drowning out nearly all other sounds.

"Looks like we're in for it," Fred shouted, his voice barely audible.

The snow increased, and the flakes, slanting almost straight forward, clung to their greatcoats and packs until every man's bobbing back was a dirty white mass in the darkness.

The snow fell heavier and heavier, blasted harder and harder by the wind which wailed low and loud without letup. Jim lifted his face in an effort to press the back of his head against the agony of his shoulder blade. To his surprise he discovered the snow was so thick now he could see only the men a few feet ahead of him. Major Smith was out of sight somewhere beyond a writhing screen of white. Pushing his head back against the shoulder blade did not ease the piercing pain, and the whipping snow swirled around and down the front of his neck.

"Jesus!" he said, and the word was whipped soundless from his mouth. "Jesus!" he called again. He looked sideways through the beating snow toward Tom.

Tom Howard screamed to be heard. "It's a blizzard!" His voice matched the hysteria of the wind. "A God-damned mother-loving blizzard!"

The snow lashed against Jim's face as he took a hurried glance over his shoulder. He could barely see the hunched form of Fritz.

"Dumb son of a bitch," Jim whispered fiercely as he bent forward again under the wind and snow. And a chill of guilt was added to his misery, for he knew that in some strange way he hated Fritz, here to haunt him alive instead of already dismissed as dead.

Al Koczeck: "There I was. . . ."

What a spot for a mother and baby to be in! Huh. What a spot for a father to be in! If only I could have finished my missions and got back in time. I almost made it. The twenty-fifth mission is the last one, and the one most apt to get you. It got me.

Jim says flying combat ought to be a bachelor's business, and I guess he's right. Thoughts run through your mind that shouldn't be there when the flak comes and the Messerschmitts are queuing up for passes at you and your wife four thousand miles away is going to have a baby.

"Does it show yet?" Willette asked me that last night, standing sideways, naked and white and beautiful, beside the bed in the motel we had rented near the air base at Boise. No, it didn't even show. I've not seen even that much of my son.

She went back home to St. Paul. And I went to war.

Twenty-five missions. I don't suppose it sounds easy, but it sounds like it wouldn't take long if you're lucky. You know something? It takes months to fly twenty-five missions in a B-17. I know, because I flew twenty-four and a half missions . . . and that takes years.

The officers' club on the base in England was closed. Many of the men were already asleep. I sat at a table in our room, the little framed photo of Willette before me, and my silver St. Christopher's medal lying beside the paper and pen.

"Got the good luck piece out, huh, Al?" said Rocky, my first pilot as he carefully folded a GI blanket into a small square. Rocky had his cap and battle jacket on.

"Where you going, Rocky?" I asked. "You ought to turn in early tonight. Briefing time is going to roll around awfully soon in the middle of the night."

"Gotta get my good-luck piece." Rocky winked and patted the blanket. "Gonna log a little pasture time with that barmaid at the Baron of Beef. She gets off in just a few minutes."

"You can have that kind of stuff," I said.

"I never like to fly with a load of ashes," Rocky grinned. "It makes my wings droop. Sleep tight."

He left, and I was alone to write the letter.

> HELLO BABY:
> Well, honey, it looks as if I'm going to make it back in time to be with you when the baby comes. Gosh, how I miss you and think of you and the baby we're going to have! I still say it's going to be a boy, but you know I don't care as long as it's yours and mine.
> Tomorrow, in just a few hours now, before this letter gets off in the mail, I'll be headed across the channel on the twenty-fifth trip. Darling, you know what that means. By tomorrow night at this time I'll be through and packing to come home to you. It's so wonderful that it's nearly all over I can hardly believe it.
> Give my love to your folks and mine, and tell them the good news. And when my darling wife has her darling baby I'll be right there with you both.
> Got to turn in early now, as briefing is before dawn. Hope it's a milk run this time. Lots and lots of love to you. Bet you're real cute with that big belly.
>
> Love,
> AL

It was no milk run.

The target was a synthetic rubber factory near Stuttgart, and the Germans didn't want it disturbed. We disturbed it. But we flew only one way.

I looked out through the bars of a fourth-story jail at the dirty brown stone buildings of Stuttgart and thought: This can't be me. It can't be. It happens to other guys, but not to me who's lived a clean life and been faithful to my wife, even in England, and confessed to the priest only yesterday, and am soon to be a father.

But there I was.

"Would you like to speak to your family over a shortwave broadcast?" asked the smiling German at Dulag Luft near Frankfurt. Would I like to speak to my family? He was really asking, "Would you like to act as bait for American listeners on one of our Nazi propaganda broadcasts?"

I sat in the cooler—the tiny solitary cell at Dulag Luft—for days because I wouldn't answer questions. And I looked at the walls and the window that was frosted so that it was impossible to see out of it. I thought of my wife and wondered what worry would do to a pregnant woman whose husband has been reported missing in action.

Finally they let me write a post card.

> DEAREST WILLETTE:
> I'm so sorry, darling. I thought I'd be with you. Be brave. I know it must be soon now, maybe before this reaches you. I pray for you all the time. God will look out for us both. I am well. Bailed out. Not wounded. Nothing can happen to me now. For me the war is over. So keep a stiff upper lip and remember I love you very, very much. Write to me every day. The address will be Stammlager Luft III, Sagan, Deutschland. I love you.
> AL

"How long before your next of kin are notified you are a prisoner?" I asked Jim ·Weis, the old Kriegie, the first day I arrived at Stalag Luft III.

"Oh, a month, two months, sometimes three," he answered.

"It's been a month now since I was shot down," I said. "Do you suppose my wife knows yet?"

"Figure a month minimum from the time you got let out of the cooler at Dulag Luft," Jim said.

"But, Jesus! That was only last week."

Jim had a mustache then, and I remember he was tugging at one end of it with his fingers. "Then your wife doesn't know yet," he said.

Later in the day, Jim said, "Come on, Al, let's take a circuit."

"A what?" I asked.

"A walk around the camp."

It was summer then. The sun was hot, and the ground inside the new south compound was still covered with pine needles and dotted with the stumps of the trees that had been cut down.

"Something is eating you," Jim said as we walked along the guard rail that stood twenty feet in from the barbed-wire fences. "What is it, Al?"

"My wife is going to have a baby. Maybe she's even had it already. It ought to be about now. It's driving me nuts. How long before you begin to get mail from home?"

"Not much before four months," Jim said. "You'll just have to grin and bear it."

"But, God, I don't even know if she's alive! And she doesn't know I'm alive."

"I wish we were still in the north compound with the British," Jim said. "I'd like you to meet some guys over there. They've got a club called the Society for the Protection and Preservation of Pregnant Kriegies. All the members became fathers after they were shot down. You'd be surprised how many there are, Al, in the same boat as you. And do you know something? It always turns out all right. Always."

"You mean nothing ever goes wrong?"

"Never has so far," Jim smiled under his curly blond mustache, "so why should it with you?"

"I can't help worrying."

"Course not," said Jim, "but just don't flap. You can't flap for three or four months, you know. And besides, it wouldn't do a damned bit of good. Your wife is back in the good old U.S.A. with friends and relatives all around her, and good doctors and hospitals."

"Yeah, I suppose so."

"Tell you what," Jim said. "I think I know how we can find out how things are going. There's a fellow named Tracy Strong working for the Y.M.C.A. in Geneva. He's from my home town in Seattle and I got a letter from him about a month ago. The mail between here and Switzerland is a hell of a lot quicker than between here and home. You give me one of your letter forms and I'll write and ask him to check up for you. Maybe he can send a cable or something."

To actually be doing something about it. It was the first time I'd felt good since I was shot down. Of course, nothing happened right away after Jim sent the letter to this Tracy Strong in Switzerland, but I had the feeling that everything that could be done was being done. Weeks passed. I'd get to flapping again, and Jim would take me on a walk around the circuit and tell me more about the Society for the Protection and Preservation of Pregnant Kriegies. He even suggested I organize a chapter in the south compound, but I couldn't find anybody else who could qualify.

"A representative of the Protecting Powers is visiting the camp today," the major told us one day when we were formed up on the parade ground for appel. Protecting Powers are what they call the neutral countries who send Red Cross workers to try and enforce the Geneva Convention. "He will see the following men at the adjutant's office right after roll call," the major went on. "Lieutenant Weis, Lieutenant Brown, Lieutenant Jones, and Lieutenant Koczeck. If anyone else wants to see the representative . . ." But I didn't hear the rest.

We had to wait our turn to see the representative in a small room, and I just about dropped a baby myself right in the hallway. Jim went in first.

"Tracy Strong sent me his regards," Jim said when he came out. "You're next, Al." I brushed right past him.

"Lieutenant Koczeck?" the man sitting behind the desk asked. I nodded. "My name is Soderberg," he said, standing to shake hands. "My home is in Stockholm, but I have just come from Geneva. Relax, Mr. Koczeck. Everything is all right. In fact, you are to be congratulated. You are the father of a fine baby boy. Let me see. . . ." He consulted a notebook. "Yes, eight pounds, two ounces, and the mother is doing fine. She sends you her love, and the boy is named Allan, after his father."

I felt kind of dizzy. "When?" was all I was able to say.

"Oh, yes." The representative smiled, looking at his notebook again. "The birthday was July 14th, just three months ago."

July 14th—why, that was the day I was shot down! When it happened, she didn't know I was missing or anything.

When I stepped back into the hall, Jim was there, all out of breath from running. "Here," he said, "I got these in a parcel from home last month and figured you might be needing them." He handed me a box of cigars.

I let out a whoop. They must have heard me all over the camp.

Maybe you've been a father and had to pace for a few hours until the big event was over. But try it for three months some time.

And do you know something? I found out later there isn't, and never was, any such thing as the Society for the Protection and Preservation of Pregnant Kriegies. If there were, I'd make Jim Weis honorary president.

Chapter Ten

Hours back, during a miserable halt in the brutal sting of the blizzard, numb-fingered men had taken blankets from their rolls and packs. Now they trudged on and on with the white-caked blankets cowled over their heads and packs. From beneath the hood of his fiercely clutched blanket Jim peered at a small black and white sign through the swirling snow in the night.

"Poslau," he read aloud, his voice drowned by the hum of the wind.

As they passed along the snow-beaten road between the few almost invisible houses and barns of the tiny village, he twisted his neck to look backward around the edge of the blanket.

Fritz, like an aged nun beneath the shroud of his blanket, was still there.

Fritz, a nun among nuns, slogged on like the rest, head forward and drooping, spine aching and cold, the bones of his feet bruised against the sides of his shoes, his mind in a delirium of fatigue.

" 'I pledge allegiance to the flag of the United States of America,' " he could hear himself saying. The moan of the wind was a dull background to the dream. He was in a tiny schoolroom leading small boys and girls in the Pledge. Their pudgy arms stretched out toward the colors in the corner. There he was on his first day back. His silver navigator's wings gleamed, and Elvie stood just inside the schoolroom doorway with her arms full of flowers and smiling with pride.

" '. . . one Nation indivisible . . .' " Mr. Struthers, the fat baldheaded superintendent, stood beaming and nodding beside Elvie.

And the cold, cold wind pierced steadily into the bones of his back.

" '. . . with liberty' "—the little kids peeked sideways at him as their high twanging voices joined his—" 'and justice for all'!" The little kids dropped their outstretched arms and scrambled forward around Fritz —the good little kids!

"School's dismissed!" he shouted, eyes full of his smiling freckled-faced wife, Elvie.

"Huh?" shouted Al Koczeck, his voice snapped off by the wind and muffled by the torrent of snow. Fritz trudged on without answering, his shins throbbing with each shuffle forward. Beside him Al retreated into the privacy of his cowled blanket.

"Hearing things," Koczeck muttered. The cold sifted steadily through to his back. "I'll never be able to tell Willette about this."

He could see himself seated in his folks' house, Willette beside him before the fireplace, a drink in his hand, trying to tell her, and her folks and his.

"Well, next to worrying about news of the baby, the march was the worst. You see it was cold—forty below zero."

"That's pretty cold, all right," his brother would say. "It gets that cold around here."

"Yeah," he would answer, "but we weren't in Minnesota. Say, did you ever hear of a blizzard—I mean a full-scale blizzard with all the snow in the world coming down—at forty below zero?"

"Must have been rough," someone would say. "Have another drink." And Willette would sit there smiling, maybe holding the baby.

But that wouldn't tell it, he thought. Forty below. Snow. Wind. Sore feet. Sore back. Sore neck. Nuts. It couldn't be told.

"How'd the Germans treat you, son?" his father would say.

"Not so bad, most of the time," he'd probably answer.

A dark something in the snowbank at the right side of the road caught his eye. He reached up and pulled the blanket back on that side. Snow slapped against his cheek as the column passed the prone figure of a prisoner, already partially covered by drifting snow.

They only have to treat you bad once.

Their part of the column came to a fork in the road, and the formation followed to the right. A clump of trees momentarily thinned the snow blast, and for the first time in hours Al could see ahead to where Major Smith led the formation.

Another one fallen, thought the major, who had also observed the corpse in the snowbank. That makes eight, or is it nine? that I've seen. As they passed the shelter of the trees, the full fury of the blizzard slammed against him again and made him stagger. He wondered if any of the men in his own formation had dropped out.

Christ! You can't march backwards to keep watch, he thought. His beard was stiff against his face, brittle with ice. He was thinking he should have stayed in the cavalry. But he'd had his days of glory. He knew how it felt to return home a hero. And he knew how it felt to find yourself alive when you'd had every reason to believe you would be dead.

"Thirty seconds over Tokyo," Ted Lawson had called it, and had written a book about it. Old Ted had lost a leg in the deal. Pete sure wanted to read that book. But he knew how it felt to receive a medal on the Capitol steps, and to ride between the cheering crowds in an open car, and to have to turn over the cash gifts of grateful citizens to charity, and to keep only the little piece of jade from Chiang Kai-shek as a souvenir. He carried it still for good luck. He'd managed to smuggle it past all the Germans.

Good luck? Was it good luck to have been shot down on his second mission—the very first one over Tunisia—not nearly as dangerous as the first which he had survived?

"Well, I'm alive," he assured himself, the wind freezing the marrow of his bones, "and I saw my wife and two boys again, safe and secure in a nice home in Texas, and I'm no worse off than the rest up ahead and back there." He staggered sideways in the blast of the blizzard to look back at his command. He could see only as far back as Tom, whose thin face was blurred behind the curtain of swirling snow and his blanket hood.

I'll go back home to Oklahoma, Tom Howard was thinking. I'll go back to the farm just out of town, and Pal, my airedale, and my old man in his overalls. No business machines for me for at least a year, and no more flying at all.

Tom's thinly fleshed bones grated against each other as he trudged forward, the blanket roll sawing his neck and shoulder.

I'll never walk again, he was thinking. I'll buy me a big Buick convertible with red leather seats and I'll find me plenty of women to keep me warm.

His teeth chattered as he thought of good Bourbon smuggled across the state line and a hammock slung between cottonwoods in the sun. He could smell the pungent cottonwood leaves, like the perfume of a woman.

Maybe I'll get me a wife, he thought, but not before I've tried out a lot.

He could see himself making love in the sunshine and on light warm evenings on the red leather seat of the convertible. And he could see the green felt top of a poker table in town.

Man, won't I show those guys what I've learned in the army?

His shoulder blades were scraping together. Surely he was walking on the bare bones of his feet.

I'll stay where there's sunshine and plenty of room, he thought. No cities for me for a while. He twisted sideways to peer at the humped cowl that was Fred Wolkowski.

Sleep . . . sleep . . . sleep. The thought of sleep was a fester in Fred's chilled mind. From under the cover of his blanket he noted another form curled up in the snowbank to the right as they passed.

Oh, to curl up and drop off to sleep like that! But the needle-sharp snow curling in toward Fred's face didn't feel warm.

I could sleep for a week, Fred was thinking. I could sleep for a year. I could sleep in a pile of manure.

He could almost sleep as he walked if it were not for the burning of the broken blisters so close to the chilblains on his toes and the wind gouging into his back. He could see himself sweating between his old lady's featherbeds.

Even with a woman I would just sleep, he thought.

He remembered the sleepless night in a hotel room where he and his pilot traded beds and the girls in them three times before dawn.

That was a long time ago, he thought. Year and a half now and I've only seen three or four girls.

He recalled, with a fury that roused him almost fully awake, the afternoon last summer when two teen-aged Fräuleins undulated their hips under their thin cotton dresses just outside the barbed wire of Stalag Luft III and made obscene gestures with their fingers toward the Americans within. He could see the sex-starved officers forming a crowd to follow them along the fence, until finally the girls had lain down and spread their legs toward the camp, laughing wickedly at the hunger within. Major Smith had been right to order that audience broken up. It was not right for American officers to let the goons see them drooling over such stuff as that.

I wouldn't piss on the best looking Fräulein in Germany, Fred swore in his thoughts. When I get a girl again she'll be Catholic and Polish and I'll marry her in the Church. With my back pay and commission maybe I can find a good wife when I get back to Chicago.

He saw himself returning to his Polish neighborhood. His shoulders,

135

drooping under the steady torture of the wind and snow and the weight of his blanket roll, straightened up and he walked with the pride of a returning officer.

There's not many guys in that neighborhood officers, he thought. There's not many guys get to be officers with no college at all.

Suddenly the column halted, and with the halt the storm seemed fiercer than ever. The men stood looking down at the ice while the wind and snow howled through them. Fred glanced around to see where they were. All he saw was a cloud of furious snow. A few feet behind, the dazed faces of Bob Montgomery and Jack Noble reminded him that there were others who had risen to be officers without going to college.

Bob Montgomery gazed glumly down at the heels of Fritz and at the turmoil of snow drifting like steam over the ice. He noticed with dull curiosity that Fritz's lower legs seemed to lean at an acute angle over his insteps. The angle increased until Fritz was kneeling and his blanket cowl had dropped down to hide his feet. Bob's eyes lifted slightly to note that Fritz's blanket was shaking in addition to being whipped by the wind. Fritz was shivering violently, and the sight of it was all that was needed to start Bob doing the same, erect in the storm.

It'd be warm at San Antonio, Bob Montgomery was thinking. God, I hope they let me go to Randolph Field!

He remembered the studying he had done in the back room of his family's hatchery at home in Texas, how he had labored over unfamiliar mathematics and history so that he could pass the test and become an aviation cadet.

I sure as hell didn't do it to become a bombardier, he remembered bitterly. I wanted to be a pilot.

They had given him an aptitude test and sent him to bombardier's training without giving him a crack at flight training. But there was still hope. New Kriegies said they were letting returned bombardiers take officers' flight training if they wanted to.

Randolph Field for me, Bob assured himself. Then three years of duty as a pilot and I'll be happy to go back with my old daddy in the chicken hatchery.

Bob was shaken from his dream with the realization that the column was starting to move forward again and that Fritz in front of him was still kneeling humped over.

"Come on!" Bob snarled in angry decision, his voice drowned by the whipping wind. He bent over and grabbed Fritz by the right shoulder. Jack Noble grabbed the other shoulder and they flung Fritz to his feet, let him go, and quickly marched on. Fritz staggered after them.

Noble looked back briefly. He saw Fritz following. Another figure beyond, anonymous in the terrible night, staggered from the formation and sank toward the left snowbank to fade from view in the blizzard. The column wheeled to the right at a white-swept, unmarked intersection.

What am I doing here? Noble asked himself, tiny knots of muscles clenching within his soft flesh. "I've worked so hard all my life, but not for this—not for this—"

He felt himself, all jelly and knots, somehow plugging along. The wind and snow now slapped furiously into his face, no matter how he clutched the blanket around it.

I'm not made for such stuff. He'd said it before, early in high school in the little community that existed for making steel, just outside Pittsburgh.

He wasn't like the other sons of steel workers, who seemed to inherit the muscles and love of blast fires for making steel. So he'd learned in high school how to use a T-square, and afterward had got a job copying blueprints in Pittsburgh.

"We'll pay your tuition so you can go to Tech nights, and work here in the daytime," the great J. S. Bellemer himself had said unexpectedly one day after watching over Noble's shoulder for a while. "Then some day you can fit in with us, if you like, as an engineer."

To be an engineer was better than shoveling coke into a white-hot vat of seething wet steel. But the night classes at Tech were not a far cry from the Air Force navigation classes at Coral Gables, and they in turn had inexorably led to this frozen inferno in Silesia. And away from a waiting fiancée and a waiting opportunity.

"I'll be waiting for you, darling," she said that last night when they decided to wait. "Your job and your future will be here just like you left it," J. S. Bellemer had said, months before when his number had been called. "You can pick up right where you left. You'll be an engineer for us yet."

The muscle knots clenched in the weakness of his thighs. The wind seared his lungs, and its howl seemed to be saying: "Noble, you soft son of a steel town, you're not made for this. . . ."

But on and on he felt himself going nevertheless. There was no choice. He let out a weary wail of loneliness and remembered he was not alone, and looked sideways bewildered at the short blanket-shrouded figure of plodding Burt Salem.

Burt bumped into the shrouded back of Fred as the column came to a halt. To his left, beyond Fritz, who once again sank to his knees, Burt made out the figure of Junior Jones moving forward against the pounding snow. Junior faded from view in the swirl up toward the head of the formation. Burt wondered what the halts were for.

Up ahead, Junior spotted Major Smith, walked over and shouted, "What are all the stops for, Major?"

"Who knows?" the major shouted back, voice faint across the few inches of snow that blasted between their faces. "How are things back there, Junior?"

"Pretty rough. I think we've lost several men. These stops aren't doing us any good. You can't rest in this!"

From up ahead, unseen beyond the barely visible men of the next formation, came a weird grumble of sound. Major Smith and Junior faced that way and pulled down their blanket cowls and stretched out their scarfs to listen.

"Go see what's up, Junior," Major Smith yelled. The iced formation of his beard gave his face the appearance of a marble statue. Junior left to disappear in the boil of the snow, the major staring after him. As he waited, the cold tore through him. He refitted the blanket over his head, suddenly aware that Jim had come up and was standing silently beside him.

"How you making out?" Major Smith shouted.

"Fritz looks bad," Jim shouted. "I don't feel very good myself."

The major reached an arm from his own blanket to feel Jim's and the hard bulge of the tin pack beneath it. "You can throw that canary away if you want to," he said a little more softly, leaning very close to make the suggestion.

"Not yet," answered Jim, and they both turned forward as Junior appeared, excitement obvious in the darkness.

"Jesus Christ!" Junior yelled. "We've had it!"

They waited while Junior took a big breath.

"We're lost!" he yelled. "The goons took a wrong turn someplace and we're lost. The goons don't know where we are. We were supposed to have hit some town a few kilometers past Poslau, and we didn't!"

The major and Jim stared open-mouthed at Junior.

"That does it!" Major Smith finally exclaimed, breaking the ice of his beard with the back of a mittened fist.

"Poslau!" Jim cried. "Why, that was miles back!"

"I'm telling you!" Junior screamed, almost in glee. "We've had it!"

The scream blended into the wail of the lashing wind and carried it off with the lacing drive of the snow.

"Hey, they've gone on!" Jim yelled, pointing ahead. Blackness and swirling white filled the space where the rear of the next formation should have been.

Major Smith turned. "Let's go!" he bawled at the top of his lungs and started forward.

Jim and Junior waited at the side of the road while the formation began to move past. Jim noticed that at some time during the night the Hundeführer and his dog had been replaced by the fat old guard who had started with them from Sagan. He stepped into the formation as the men of Room 8 drew abreast.

Junior's face was half turned from the pelting snow as the old guard, now carrying no more equipment than a rifle slung over his greatcoat, lumbered past. Junior fell in at the rear of the formation behind the broad towering pillar of blanket that was Tex and bent forward, cold muscles throbbing, into the march.

Now where am I going? he thought. What the hell? I didn't know anyway, and now the goons don't know either, so that makes us even. And when did I ever know where I was going?

He remembered going to Hotel Management School in Kansas City for a summer. For a time that had been the answer. Then he could graduate and say:

"Here I am, healthy and eighteen years old and educated. So give me a hotel and I'll manage it."

And he remembered quitting his job as night bellhop and relief desk clerk in Okmulgee, Oklahoma, and going north. First stop, Denver. He had to see if it was true what they said about that hotel in Denver.

"Hello." He had called the desk. "Send me up a quart of whisky and a woman."

It was true . . . real service. Next stop, Canada. All the time it took them to teach him how to fly he wasn't sure where he was going, but it was a pretty good bet. Seeing as how the Battle of Britain was going on, it would be to England. It was.

"Night fighters!" he had exclaimed when at Bournemouth they had assigned him to O.T.U.

"It's something new, old boy," the penguin flight lieutenant had assured him, "and quite the thing, really. You're fortunate to be selected for it because of your night vision."

Night vision. Junior peered about him now through the swirling white snow that even hid the blackness of the night. He could see only as far ahead as the stumbling old guard, marching along beside a tall skinny blanket-draped figure that must be Bill Johnston. Night vision You needed night vision to fly Beaufighters like you needed tail feathers.

He remembered sitting in his throbbing office high up in the blackness one night, watching the ultraviolet glow of the instruments and following the directions coming through the earphones from the sergeant out of sight in the nose with the radar grid.

"Fire!" the voice had crackled. He pushed the teat, and what do you know? A flash of light up ahead and then blackness again. "We got one!" the voice in the earphones crackled.

"Sorry, old chappy," the intelligence officer had grinned at him after landing. "It was one of ours, not a Hun. The bugger must have left his I.F.F. off."

When you fly night fighters, you don't know where you're going. Well, he knew where he was going if he ever got out of goonland. Being a bellhop in Okmulgee isn't so bad. Besides, with his $7,000 back pay, maybe he could make a down payment on the joint and put in service like that hotel in Denver. Yay, man!

Suddenly Bob Montgomery turned sideways and fell back beside Junior.

"Hey, Junior," Bob yelled above the wail of the wind, "you heard the gen? We're lost! The goons have gone and got us lost!"

Junior's blanket hood bobbled as he nodded, eyes straining curiously to peer through the snow. Up ahead the old German guard let the rifle slip from his shoulder and slide down his arm. The fat little figure stumbled frantically, trying to catch the gun. Bill Johnston reached down and grabbed it, and handed it to the panting old man.

"Danke," wailed the guard as he staggered along, dragging the heavy gun by its leather sling.

What kind of a deal is this for an old fart like that? Bill Johnston thought, the bones in his frozen back biting into his flesh. What kind of a deal is this for any man?

Bill remembered how he had wangled and wangled to get out of the infantry so he wouldn't have to march. It was tough wangling because he was a sergeant and a regular. But he'd made it and got sent to aerial gunnery school.

"The way to keep from going overseas," he had confided to a buddy, "is to get such good scores they make you an instructor."

And he'd wangled that, too. It had kept him safe and Stateside for six months. Then the combat gunners who had completed their tours started coming back, and Bill had seen the light again.

"They're going to start replacing us with these war-weary guys and send us over," he had predicted to another new buddy. "I'm going to apply for glider-pilot training. I hear that takes several months."

And the wangling had worked again. He'd spent three months in the sun at 29 Palms. But there was still wangling to do.

"Jesus!" he had confided to another new buddy over some beers one hot night, "I don't like this glider business at all. They drop you and a load of GI's behind enemy lines and where are you? You can't take off again in a glider. You're just back in the foot army again with a gun in your hands. That's not for me. I'm applying for aviation cadet training. It takes a good year Stateside to train a pilot."

As always, the wangle had worked.

"No, sir"—he was lecturing a group of fellow cadets in the barracks at Luke Field just a few days before graduation after thirty weeks of flight training—"I've got it all figured out. No combat for me. I'm going to wangle a job as instructor and fight this war Stateside."

"Your name's Johnston, ain't it?" a cadet who had just entered the barracks jeered. "Well, I got news for you. You're assigned to four fans. Go take a look at the bulletin board. The assignments are up."

And in the crowd that quickly formed at the bulletin board he read the bad news:

> All graduating officers whose names begin with letters A through M are assigned to heavy bombardment O.T.U. Officers whose names begin with N through Z are assigned to single-engine-fighter O.T.U. The following officers . . .

And there was no wangling out of B-17's. As of that date all training-command assignments were filled with returning combat pilots. Bill, who was in the infantry the winter of 1941, was shot down and captured in the winter of 1944.

And I wangled it all to get out of marching, Bill thought to himself, gritting his teeth at the pain of his pumping muscles as he slogged through the blizzard beside the old German guard. Why couldn't it have been a short war?

The fat old German stumbled over his dangling rifle and lifted it to clutch it painfully against his breast.

"Why don't you throw it away?" shouted Bill.

The German looked at him dumbly as he stumbled along. Bill reached out and tapped the rifle. "Throw it away!" he shouted again, gesturing toward the side of the road.

"Ach! nein," cried the German. "Das ist verboten." He clutched the rifle more tightly, and gestured with one hand across his throat.

"He can't throw it away," Ed Greenway shouted beside Bill. "It's a court-martial for a German soldier to lose his gun. He might be shot for it."

Bill shrugged and turned his face away from the stumbling old man.

Beside him, Ed looked ahead between two blanket backs and noticed that Fritz was staggering along like a wino that's out on his feet. And beyond Fritz, Jim, the tin pack bulging grotesquely under his blanket, was also staggering slightly under the load. Ed looked down at his sore pumping feet to see if he was staggering too. The movement of his boots through the surface of drifting snow reassured him.

"Gon-na make-it, gon-na make-it, gon-na make-it," he began repeating over and over in time with his marching. After a while the watching his feet and chanting became exhausting, and his head hung as if by a wire at the top of his spine. With an effort he lifted the weight of his head and stopped chanting.

It's endless, he thought, dazedly following the undulating maze of blanket-draped snow-peppered backs. It's just being pushed around like always from the first day they induct you into the army. It's like everything they do from when they make you wash out your first latrine until they send you out over Romania in a B-24 that you know is too slow and too low and not well enough armed. They just shove you around till you're dead, and then they shove you into the ground.

He remembered the funerals of the gunners after each miraculous return in the B-24 that was shot so full of holes it should never have returned even once.

"What's it all about?" he used to ask the mute boxes being lowered under the Italian rain. "What have the Germans or the Hungarians or the Romanians ever done to me?" And the only answer he got was the tattoo of rain on the dark coffin lids when the flags were pulled away.

Am I lucky to be alive? he wondered, sludging along in the vast crawl of blanketed men who all seemed hooded strangers and hardly men at all. Only the gnaw of the bitter wind and the constant sting of the snow against his face and the soreness of bone and flesh from heavy head to slogging feet made it real. Once again he let his muffled chin fall against the rough front of his greatcoat and watched the dark darting of his boots.

"Gon-na make-it, gon-na make-it," he resumed chanting. He was still chanting when he bumped into the back of the man ahead as once again the column came to a halt.

"Schwer, schwer," moaned the old German guard, letting his rifle drop to the ice where the drifting snow immediately began to pile against it. "Ach, ich bin müde . . . müde. . . . "

"The poor old fart," Bill shouted to Ed. "He's almost as beat as Heine." His hooded head nodded ahead to where Fritz crouched, knees and elbows against the ice.

Several figures broke away from the formation and sat down in the snowbank to the left.

"Jesus!" shivered Ed. "Wherever we're going I wish we'd get there. Let's make a tent like Jim and Tom up there."

Jim and Tom were leaning forehead to forehead under a cone formed by each holding the edges of the other's blankets to his own.

"How about some chocolate?" Jim suggested in the darkness. "It'll give us energy."

"Yeah," answered Tom, voice hollow in the flimsy privacy. "Got some handy?"

The wind poured in when Jim let go of the blankets to reach into his pocket. He pulled out two C-ration bars and handed one of them to Tom. In order to handle the bars they abandoned their shelter plan. Jim tore away the paper wrapper with his teeth and looked down toward the huddled, snow-pelted form of Fritz.

What's keeping him going? Jim wondered. What's keeping me going? occurred as an afterthought as he felt the ridiculous extra weight of the radio he was carrying. He knew he would carry it on and on, if only to justify the investment he had already made in fear and fatigue. He poked the chocolate bar into his mouth and bit down forcefully into its frozen solidity.

"Oh-h-h!" he cried, dancing in pain as shock from his decayed molar screamed up into his brain, nearly blinding him. He swallowed whole the chunk of chocolate that had broken off and inhaled lungfuls of the freezing wind until he got a grip on himself.

"Let's go!" came the major's voice faint in the wind.

Jim noted that someone was dragging Fritz to his feet. He saw Bill Johnston, out of hearing, talking to the guard.

"Müde, müde, müde," the old soldier was sobbing. "Ich kann nicht weitergehen. Hier bleibe ich. Ach! es ist schwer, schwer." He nudged the rifle on the ice with his boot toe.

"What's he saying?" Bill shouted at Ed Greenway.

"Search me," Ed shouted back. "I think he's pooping out. The rifle's too much for him. Come on."

Bill hesitated, looking pityingly at the old German. "Kom," Bill urged.

"Nein, nein," cried the German, new tears freezing over the old. He kicked the rifle again and shook his head.

Suddenly Bill reached down, picked up the rifle and slung it over his own left shoulder.

"Kom," he said, placing a hand on the old soldier's back. "Kom, I'll carry your God-damned piece."

Mutely, the old man obeyed, limping along very close to Bill.

"Well, call me a son of a bitch!" cried Junior Jones, watching as he marched at the rear of the formation. "A Kriegie carrying a gun for a goon!"

Onward the column burrowed unseen and unseeing through the blizzard.

"Müde . . . müde . . . müde . . . " wailed the old guard as every so often they passed snow-spattered forms lying by the side of the road. "Müde . . . müde . . . müde . . . " The wails grew louder until finally he reeled away from the column, tottered, and fell face forward into the snowbank. Bill unslung the rifle from his own shoulder and flung it at an angle backward like a spear.

It landed muzzle first in the snowbank beside the guard so that the stock leaned with the wind. The swirling snow blotted out the sight as they marched on.

"What a chump I was!" Bill muttered to himself as he rolled his sore left shoulder trying to restore circulation. "The old Kriegies will ride hell out of me." He eased to the right in the formation to allow Fritz, who was staggering horribly, to fall back a bit.

"Look," shouted Ed Greenway, pointing into the snow driving toward them across a plain from the right. "A house. Two houses!"

The black shapes of the houses, perhaps a hundred yards across the plain, were barely and intermittently visible between undulations of the hard swirling snow. They stared at them, the first houses they had seen since away back at Poslau.

"Maybe we're getting someplace at last," Bill shouted and looked ahead, hoping for more signs of population. Up ahead he saw Jim, Tom, and Fred, who had been looking back at the houses, turn their hooded heads forward again.

"Those two houses looked familiar," Fred yelled at Jim.

Jim thrust the last of his aspirins into his mouth, swallowed, and threw the envelope away.

"They all look alike," Jim said.

"How's the tooth?" Tom shouted into the wind.

"No worse than the rest of me," answered Jim, and they stopped talking. It was true. The tooth ached violently, but so did his bruised feet. His groin felt as he remembered it when his leg wound was infected and the Luftwaffe surgeon had wanted to amputate. The pack straps, pulled down and back by the extra weight of the paper and radio he was carrying, felt as if they had sawed at least halfway through his shoulder. And he felt colder than a corpse.

The poetry of nature, he thought, remembering the words from some travelogue he had seen years before. They passed a small clump of trees which swayed furiously above them, and stared at the familiar but ever unbelievable fury of the snow and shuddered with the bitter blasting wind. "Nature is hell to men who freeze," he decided, and made a mental note to write a poem on the theme. . . .

The column suddenly halted, and a cry from Fred interrupted Jim's thoughts.

"Jesus God!" Fred cried. "Look!" He pointed at a sign at the side of the road. They had seen it before. It was black and white and it spelled out POSLAU. They stared at the sign and at one another, and back at the sign.

"We've been marching in a circle," spat Tom. "For hours we've been marching in a circle. Those stupid bastard goons got lost and marched us around in a circle. We haven't gotten anywhere at all."

Jim turned bewilderedly and looked at the astonished, angry faces of the men behind him, mocked by the snow slapping their cheeks. Suddenly Jim's stomach tightened up like a fist.

"Where's Fritz?" he cried. The men of Room 8 looked about and behind.

The full blast of the wind pelted streams of snow straight into Fritz's face as he waded wearily through the deep drifting snow toward the growing dark shapes of the two houses.

"They'll take me in. . . . They'll take me in. . . . " He said it to himself aloud, over and over, as he struggled knee-deep through the snow. "They'll take me in. . . . " His thighs were like water, his feet like heavy molten lead, his back, neck, and shoulders numb, aflame and freezing, all at once. He fell, staggered again to his feet, and stumbled ahead covered with the clinging snow. The houses grew larger and larger, but none the less dark as he got nearer. "They'll take me in. . . . They'll take me in. . . . " With a great moan he staggered and fell against the heavy wooden door of the first house and stood there panting. Then he began to pound on the door with his fists.

"Help! Help me. . . . Help me-e-e," he wailed with all the voice left in his lungs. He heard a deep guttural shouting within, and pounded harder with new energy of hope. "Help!" he cried. "Please . . . please help me-e-e. . . . "

A woman's shrill voice within blended with the guttural voice of a man.

"Please help . . . please . . . please . . . " sobbed Fritz as he slid down the door to his knees.

The guttural within came sharp, a strange tongue falling like a club on the sobbing Fritz.

"Please . . . " he cried, and there came an answer to his knocking as someone kicked at the unopened door from within.

"Oh, Elvie . . . Elvie . . . Elvie . . . " he sobbed as he sank to the snow before the unopened door. The deep voice within growled something once more, and then there was only the wailing of the wind. "Elvie . . . Elvie . . . Elvie . . . " he sobbed over and over, his deep voice changing to a faint high whine. "Elvie . . . I tried . . . "

As the wind and snow beat down on the figure, the crying stopped and a faint smile came over the face of Fritz. Lying there, eyes closed, he began to feel warm. A pleasing numbness began to blot out the pains in his body. He dreamed of a schoolroom in Wyoming, and the little kids, arms outstretched, and Elvie, freckled face smiling, standing in the sunny doorway.

" 'I pledge allegiance to the flag,' " the little voices were chorusing, " 'of the United States of America' "—Elvie was holding flowers—" ' . . . one Nation indivisible' "—the picture was growing faint with the voices—" 'with liberty . . . and . . . ' "

"He's gone," Fred shouted flatly when the men of Room 8 had finished looking through the formation. Jim said nothing.

"This time I guess he's really had it!" shouted Tom.

Jim nodded.

"Let's go." Major Smith's wind-muffled command drifted back.

The snowfall began to lessen as they trudged unseeing once again through the small village of Poslau. The column slogged on and on down the left road of a fork where hours before they had taken the road to the right.

"It's a hell of a night," shouted Fred to no one in particular. There wasn't much talk after that.

Jim Weis: "There I was. . . ."

He remembered standing on the lip of the gully in pre-dawn darkness nearly two years ago, the same gully where the night before he had scanned the dusk skies, hopelessly hoping for Barney's Spitfire to speck into sight.

"C'm' on, Jim. Chow express!" someone had called from the man-covered jeep, engine jazzing among the cones of pyramidal tents.

"No, thanks, I'm not hungry," Jim called back, and the jeep pooped off, billowing dust over desert grass in the dull light of dawn.

Now, shuffling along dazedly over ice through forty below, Jim wandered again over the half-mile from the bivouac area to the operations dugout as the African night turned to rosy promise of day.

"You through breakfast already, Lieutenant?" the ops sergeant said as Jim stepped down into the carbide-lit cavern lined with black cast-iron sewer pipe.

"Yeah," lied Jim, watching the sergeants hang tickets beside the letter identifications of planes on a board mounted beside the large pin-marked briefing maps. The sergeant hung a ticket marked U.S. beside the letters MSV. "What's the matter with MSV?" Jim asked.

"Your plane's out for an engine change, Lieutenant."

Three days at least, Jim figured halfheartedly. Fastest Spitfire in Africa. He and his crew had carefully filled every crack and indentation in its fuselage and wings with plastic wood, then emery-papered it smooth, and kept it polished daily with floor wax. Got an extra twenty miles per hour out of her that way. Jim watched dully as the sergeant hung a longer, plain white card over the letters MSU. That was Barney's place, and now it was blotted out. His eyes shifted from the plain white card to another board, upon which were hung cards proclaiming the names of the squadron pilots, and after them the number of missions each had flown in the African campaign.

After Barney's name was a ticket reading, "43." Beneath Barney's name was Jim's and a ticket that said, "42." That's the way it had been for days. First Barney would get ahead one mission, and then Jim would catch up. It was a sort of race. As Jim watched, the sergeant removed the placard bearing Barney's name and the ticket "43" and took them over to the table that was being used as operations desk.

Jim could never remember anything about the time that passed while he sat on a bench in the large cluttered dugout waiting for the business of the day to get started. Now as he slogged along, dazed, through the merciless night, his memory jumped, as in a vivid dream, to the sound of the field phone ringing in the dugout full of ready fighter pilots. . . .

"Major," the sergeant called, and the jabbering of the flyers stopped, as Pat, the C.O., placed the phone to his ear.

"Yes, sir. Right. Middle cover. Right. And you're leading this squadron. Right. Yes, sir."

Pat, a short man for his authority, walked over to the ops map, and Jim joined the other twenty-odd pilots of the squadron in a semicircle for the briefing.

"Same thing as yesterday," Pat smiled, pointing to a pin already stuck in the map. "La Fauconnerie. Every hour on the hour. First mission in"—he consulted his wrist watch—"about seventeen minutes. Escorting B-25's. This squadron is middle cover, bouncing squadron, and Colonel Proffer is leading."

Jim watched his own last name being hung on a board upon which were painted three flights of silhouetted Spitfires. "Number four, blue flight," Jim noted, "tailend Charlie outside." He was long used now to flying in the most dangerous, least authoritative position. This was a peacetime squadron come over from the States. All its older members were first lieutenants. The RAF men who had joined it in England were still second looeys.

"Art," Jim said to the Harvard man with the crew haircut who was to be his element leader for the mission, "what if I see something like I did last time, and can't get you over the RT? We're bouncing squadron this time."

"Go ahead and bounce it, Jim," was the nasal reply. "I'll follow you, in that case."

Jim turned to the major. "Whose kite do I fly, Pat? Mine's unserviceable."

"Let's see," the major pondered, studying the list. "Take O."

MSO. It had belonged to Ace before he had been transferred out of the squadron for leaving top cover to get himself a Hun. Jim solemnly nodded, even though he felt a superstition. Barney, Alligator Mitch, Ace, and Jim—the Unholy Four. They had started out together. "The God-damnedest fighter team that ever hit the skies," Ace had predicted. And now Mitch was gone . . . shot down at Kairouan. Ace was kicked out of the squadron, or at least asked to get out. And Barney . . . shot down yesterday, or at least he didn't come back from La Fauconnerie.

Outside the dugout Jim climbed into a jeep. Hamhocks, another RAF transfer, was acting as chauffeur as punishment for sleeping in, one morning. "I'm flying MSO," Jim told Hamhocks, "but take me by my dispersal spot so I can pick up my gear."

"Not that tin can," Hamhocks grunted, kicking the jeep along.

"What's the matter with it?"

"Well, it's full of holes, for one thing," Hamhocks reported.

At the dispersal point where his ship usually stood, Jim's three crewmen climbed in, piling his chute, helmet and mask, and fleece-lined jacket on the front seat beside him. Jim wriggled into the jacket as the jeep bounced.

"Where's my St. Christopher's medal?" he yelled back at the enlisted men, fingering the jacket breast where the silver-winged medal had been.

"Jeez, is it gone, Lieutenant?" the crew chief yelled back.

Hamhocks, mouth curling beneath his black mustache and Jewish nose, skidded the jeep to a halt in its own dust before the nose of a parked Spitfire. "I'd rather drive a jeep than that thing."

Jim noted the patches that had been riveted over bullet and flack holes in the wings of the yellow and tan desert-camouflaged Spitfire, but he was thinking about the St. Christopher's medal. It had been sent to him by someone he'd never seen, the janitor of a museum in New York who had read about him in a newspaper.

"Oh, well, I've still got my red scarf," he assured himself, fingering the blazing garment where it contrasted with the blond curly hair at his neck. He climbed up on the wing and sidled into the cockpit onto the hard dinghy seat of his chute. The crew chief looped the straps over his shoulder. He clicked the loops and the straps up between his legs into the round British chute buckle.

"You didn't make your inspection, Lieutenant," the crew chief commented, slipping the key through the Sutton harness while Jim fastened the helmet straps beneath his chin.

"To hell with it," Jim mumbled, and the crew chief looked surprised. There came a faint droning in the sky to his rear, followed by the coughing and wheezing of the colonel's motor kicking over to start somewhere up ahead in the mile-wide maze of dispersed Spitfires gleaming in the sunrise. The crew chief slammed the cockpit flap shut, and Jim began pumping the primer on the instrument panel.

"Clear?" he yelled as the motors sputtered to chattering life about the dispersal area.

"All clear!" came a shout from up front. Jim turned on the two magneto switches and placed two left fingers over the starter buttons.

"Contact!" he yelled, and pressed the buttons. The three-bladed prop wheezed and whined around, Jim held the control column between his knees, reached up with his right hand and gave the primer another pump, and the two thousand horses roared to life, the prop blast blowing the crew chief's hat off. Jim throttled back; the crew chief, still clinging to the side of the cockpit, held his thumb up. Jim returned the salute, and the crew chief jumped down from the wing.

Here we go again, Jim thought, looking out at the various clouds of dust being blown up and back by starting and taxiing Spitfires. Looking up and back he saw the formation of B-25's, eighteen of them in three neat rows of six, swinging wide to the south on the beginning of their routine rendezvousing circle of the field at ten thousand feet. Jim released the loop catch of the hand brake, and the Spit began to roll forward. Zigzagging gently, he quickly taxied along a maze of pathways and out onto the flattened-out yellow grass stubble of the field, where thirty-five other Spitfires were wheeling and rolling, blasting up storms of dust. Noting that the left brake was rather weak, he edged the throttle forward to blast the Spit around into position behind and to the left of Art's plane. He squeezed the hand brake to halt the Spit and swiveled his head to look at the rest of the three squadron formations lined up, noses pointing down the great field, thirty-six Spitfires in all. Jim was on the left outside rear of the middle squadron.

"I should have looked this crate over," Jim told himself, spooking at an unfamiliar beat in the motor. He'd only taken off once before without inspecting the airplane he was to fly, and that time he had discovered at twelve thousand feet that the oxygen valve behind the seat's armor plate hadn't been turned on.

Ahead, at the point of the center vic, the dark brown figure of Colonel Proffer raised an arm, pointing straight up from the open cockpit. The colonel's plane was lettered JDP, the initials of his own name, James Dana Proffer.

He'd sure like to get hold of my plane, Jim thought with pride of MSV, out for an engine change. Colonel Proffer had already tried a few tricks to get it after Jim had fixed it up, but Jim had so far been able to insist on ownership on the grounds of having labored to improve it.

The ailerons of the colonel's plane began wiggling. Jim moved the spade grip of his stick from side to side, and the ailerons of all thirty-six Spitfires in the three formations wiggled, signaling that everyone was ready. Abruptly, the lead ship began to roll forward followed by the others. Jim focused his eyes on Art's ship ahead and to the right, palming the throttle forward skillfully with his left hand to take off in close formation. The yellow stubble of the field blurred, racing behind, and falling away as the thirty-six fighters became airborne as one. Climbing rapidly, Jim switched hands on the stick to work the landing-gear lever with his right, and banked the Spit into line astern behind Art, listening to the horn blow until the wheels slapped up into the wings.

"Ah-h-h," Jim sighed, looking to the right and left at the sleek beauty of climbing, sun-bathed Spitfires as he reached up to pull the plexiglass canopy bubble forward to cut out the slipstream. Mission after mission the thrill and the pride were renewed each time he climbed shooting into the blue, destination glory or death or both. Strapped into his tiny crowded office, the sun beating through the crystal-clear canopy, he felt free and clean and alive, his troubles left below, far down there with the yellow-brown flatness of the earth.

He switched on the VHF radio, just in front of the throttle, and listened to the radio silence maintained on the outward flight of a mission. He reached up and flicked the switch which lighted up the gold ring of his reflector sight, and with his thumb he flicked off the safety beneath the teat triggers mounted in the spade grip of the control column. And as they climbed above the B-25's, which were now heading east by north toward the enemy sky, he began rocking the stick, gracefully weaving the Spitfire behind the three weaving Spitfires flying line astern ahead in blue flight. He noted that the wings seemed unusually light, but the boost indicator showed that Ace's old plane needed far more power to maintain speed than Jim's own.

"La Fauconnerie." Jim talked to himself above the motor's throb as he looked down at the wicked-looking formation of B-25's. They were pink in camouflage, indicating they had originally been used in the Middle East. "La Fauconnerie," he said again into his oxygen mask, thinking of Barney. "I hope they clobber it good."

This was the third day they were bombing the four Luftwaffe bases at La Fauconnerie in Air Marshal Tedder's all-out effort to destroy the Luftwaffe on the ground and in the air.

"Flak. Two o'clock," an undistinguishable voice popped in the earphones. Some damned fool was always calling out "Flak," as if that did any good. Jim watched the small white puffs ahead and to the right of the middle-cover squadron formation, little white puffs that suddenly appeared in rows, unheard above the roaring throb of the motor. "Light stuff," Jim analyzed. "Twenty-millimeter stuff." With that he dismissed the flak and began the automatic routine of scanning the clear blue, sun-glaring sky: fifty seconds above, behind, to each side, thumb against the ball of the sun; below, behind, above, both sides, and ten seconds forward, weaving beneath and behind the tail wheel of the plane ahead. He widened the weave, holding the steep bank from side to side briefly to look below for any specks that might be Messerschmitts or Focke-Wulfs in the sky below the B-25's and their close cover of twelve Spitfires fifteen hundred feet down.

Suddenly his Spitfire bumped with a tinny spanking sound, and he looked back to see a black octopus-shaped formation of smoke.

"Flak." The undistinguishable voice crackled in the phones.

Jim reached with his left hand and pressed the transmitter lever. "No kidding," he said, and released the lever.

The formation began to dive and climb in a loose zigzagging pattern among the large black flak bursts as Colonel Proffer took evasive action.

God, I'm getting good! Jim thought ecstatically as the Spitfire banked, turned, followed his every whim. No more than the thought was necessary any more, and the Spitfire always obeyed. What if I roll over? he thought, and the Spitfire rolled slowly, gracefully, over on its back, giving him an unobstructed view of the bombers below and the yellow ground far beyond them.

"On the button," he observed, marveling at the luck that had made him roll over just in time to see the thick orchard of bomb bursts spring up magically among the lighter yellow squares that were the Luftwaffe airfields of La Fauconnerie. The Spit righted itself smoothly, and he continued weaving among black and white flak bursts as the formation circled toward the homeward course.

"Give me a Hun today," he prayed, scanning the vastness of the glowing sky. "Please give me a Hun." The whole armada—the bombers and close cover at about fifteen thousand feet, the middle cover, of which he was a member, at seventeen thousand feet, and the top cover at twenty thousand feet—were heading home now, the early morning sun at their backs. Jim noted that the chronometer on the instrument panel read 8:01 o'clock.

"Hello. Cobra red leader," the earphones suddenly popped. "Bandits, one o'clock low coming in on our friends."

Jim's eyes darted ahead and past the inner starboard wing. He saw them, four of them, blue Focke-Wulfs streaking down toward the B-25's.

"Roger," came Colonel Proffer's voice in the helmet phones. "Cobra Squadron, tallyho, now. Let's get 'em!"

The colonel's plane up ahead in the center flight rolled over on its back and began a wide graceful split-S dive, followed by the other planes behind him and red and yellow flights on both sides.

"This is no way to get them," Jim snorted angrily into his oxygen mask as he rolled over, starting to follow Art's Spitfire in the gentle fast arc, watching below the Focke-Wulfs diving through the bomber formation. With a sudden jerk he hauled back on the stick, flattening himself against the seat with pressure, hauling his own arc short so that he was headed for two of the Focke-Wulfs, but losing sight of the gentler arcing formation.

"Haul it in tight, Art," he crackled into the transmitter as the Spitfire gained speed heading straight down. "I'm already inside of you and will take the first one. You take the second. Over."

"O.K., Jim, I'm with you," came Art's reply as Jim pulled up slightly, aiming at the first Focke-Wulf, which was rapidly growing larger, but losing the second Jerry beneath his own nose and wings.

"This is Jim again," he called. "Don't miss that second one, Art. He'll be right behind me."

Jim held the throttle wide open, and the roaring, forward-diving Spit closed up the gap between him and the first blue Focke-Wulf. He sneaked a quick glance into the concave mirror mounted atop the windscreen and saw the second Focke-Wulf behind him, and a smaller silhouette gleaming behind that.

"Now," he told himself as the wings of the enemy ahead grew larger, almost fitting the crossbars of the cold reflector sight. He let go of the throttle, leaving it open, placed both hands on the ring of the spade grip to hold it steady, pulled the yellow dot at the center of the sight up through the plane ahead, steadied it, and pressed the cannon teat with both thumbs. The twenty-millimeter cannon in both wings coughed and bucked for two seconds. He looked in the mirror, saw nothing, sighted again, and pressed the button for another two seconds, noting that somehow the Focke-Wulf was pulling away from him. Suddenly the Focke-Wulf began spewing white smoke which streamed back from its engine cowling, enveloping the fuselage.

"Enough," Jim said to himself, pulling the Spitfire up out of the dive and leaving the enemy out of sight. "A probable. Run away and live to fight another day."

Turning as he pulled out of the dive, he looked around and reached for the throttle. To his sudden horror, he found it had slipped closed while he had been using both hands on the trigger teat. A frightened glance at the airspeed indicator exploded sweat all over his body. It indicated 240 miles per hour.

"Christ! I should be doing 500!" he cursed, pointing the nose up toward the formation which was now a group of tiny specks away up and far ahead in the direction from which he had attacked. Automatically, he pushed the boost teat for emergency power and switched on the transmitter.

"Hello, Cobra red leader. Blue Four calling." He spoke levelly into his mouth mike. "Mechanical trouble. I'm climbing up slowly from six o'clock. Slow down for me, will you?" As he spoke he watched the airspeed of the trembling, overtaxed, climbing Spitfire roll back to 180 miles per hour, its most efficient rate of climb. Still ringing sweat, he looked out to one side and saw tiny white puffs of smoke appearing suddenly. He looked back and saw the Focke-Wulf, still streaming smoke, climbing rapidly on his tail now.

"He's supposed to be dead," Jim cried to himself, jerking the Spit into a turn. But the airspeed was too slow for the sudden evasion, and instead the Spit snapped into a spin. At the half-turn he dumped the stick, kicked the rudder, recovered, and swooped out immediately into a clean-flying formation of planes. He was in the middle, and they were in line astern, four on each side, dead level with him. They bore black crosses on their blue and gray fuselages.

"Cobra, come on down. I got eight of 'em here at ten thousand feet: two Focke-Wulf's and six Messerschmitts. It's a field day!" he barked excitedly into the transmitter, and banked quickly behind one of the Messerschmitts and pressed the cannon teat. The sleek blue fighter, not fifty yards ahead, instantly became a ball of yellow flames; and Jim followed through the bank, kicking down rudder in instinctive decision to take the fight to the deck.

"God! They didn't see me coming," he decided as he wound the Spitfire toward the desert ten thousand feet below in a corkscrewing aileron dive, which he knew the German planes were unable to follow well enough to sight and shoot. "Boy, oh, boy! Not a bad morning's work," he chortled. "One destroyed and one probable, and when the rest of the boys get here it'll be a field day. We'll get every one of them."

As he dove, constantly turning, toward the deck, he looked back at the rotating vision of the German planes trying futilely to get inside the turns for the kill, but he knew nothing could out-turn a Spitfire. He switched on the radio.

"Hello, Cobra leader. I'm taking it right down to the deck. There are only seven of 'em now. So come and get 'em, boys!"

The winding desert, its scrub foliage now distinct, rushed rapidly up at him. Just as he pulled out he heard Colonel Proffer's voice in the earphones.

"Close up the formation, boys," the colonel calmly said. "We're going home."

As Jim leveled off in a tight turn, his starboard wingtip just a few feet from the sand and weeds, a Messerschmitt shot past him. Jim instinctively pressed the teat as the enemy flew into his sight not more than seventy-five yards ahead. The Messerschmitt tore into the ground, throwing up a cloud of sand, weeds, and plane parts. Jim stayed in the turn, raging.

"That son of a bitch!" Jim cursed. He tightened the turning as the Spitfire lost some of its dive velocity. He edged the right wing down to within a few inches of the blurring sand and dry bushes, knowing the Germans could not out-turn him, and knowing that as long as he kept turning close to the ground they could not make passes through him. His anger was not for the Germans, whose four remaining Messerschmitts and two Focke-Wulfs were making futile level passes as Jim tried to figure some way out. The tracers that had streamed whitely from his cannon at the end of his last burst into the second Messerschmitt had told him he was out of twenty-millimeter ammunition. MSO's cannon were fed by drum magazines which only allowed eleven seconds of total firing, not twenty-one seconds as did the belt-fed guns in MSV, his own plane.

I still have my machine guns, Jim remembered with relief. He had long ago made it a habit to save his thirty-calibers to fly home with after a fight. Jim wondered where he was, and studied the revolving desert landscape trying to orient himself, ignoring the enemy planes which could not hit him as long as he kept turning. He reasoned that the highest ridge of yellow-brown hills that he could see must be to the west, and that somewhere over there was Faid Pass and the American lines. Suddenly a blue Focke-Wulf breezed by slowly, its black-helmeted pilot plainly visible looking back over his shoulder in the cockpit, and Jim straightened out for the opportunity.

"Now it's your turn," he gritted, pressing the lower teat on the spade grip. His wings spat too light a song, like a kid blowing beans through his teeth. Jim cursed, but saw the white bullet strike on the wings and fuselage of the Focke-Wulf, which kept on flying straight ahead, trailing white vapor, as Jim hauled the Spit back into the tight turn.

"Only two thirties," Jim said, in a new sweat. "No wonder the wings felt light. Ace took two of the machine guns out for maneuverability."

Pulling around in the tight 180 degrees, Jim observed with satisfaction that the Focke-Wulf he had just hit was small in the distance, leaving the fight; but the remaining five enemy planes were circling about, waiting for him to make one mistake.

"About thirty miles to our lines," Jim estimated, eyeing the ridge of low mountains. "If I get that far I don't care if they do shoot me down." Jim decided he'd better do something positive. When the Spit was pointed east in the next turn, he suddenly straightened out and headed straight up and head on at the remaining Focke-Wulf, squeezing the machine gun teat as the two ships came together. The Focke-Wulf veered off, sky-blue belly exposed; but Jim didn't see any strikes. Instead, he watched with hope the remaining four Messerschmitts, two on each side, turning to follow him east. Abruptly he hauled the Spit into a tight turn and headed west toward the mountains, looking back to watch the slower turning German planes crisscrossing one another to catch up. He knew that both Messerschmitts and Focke-Wulfs at low altitude could fly faster, climb faster, and dive faster than a Spitfire. By bringing the fight to the deck he had eliminated two of those advantages. Now they couldn't dive without hitting the ground, and there was no point in their climbing. The Spit could out-turn them. All they could do was fly faster. But that was quite an advantage.

"Might as well take it easy," Jim told himself, looking back over his tail to watch the five German planes rapidly catching up. He sighed, the first charge of combat adrenalin wearing off. "It's going to be either an awfully short fight or an awfully long one."

He waited until the leading Messerschmitt's nose and wing cannon started flashing and smoking before he pulled into another turn. This time, in turning, he noticed that the entire instrument panel was shaking, and remembered that his emergency boost power teat was still pushed forward. He thumbed the teat back, and the instruments stopped jumping. Once again there was nothing to do but keep turning and wait for an opening. All five of the Germans were to the west of him now, between him and the mountains, as if to herd him back. Jim began to feel sleepy. His feet tingled, full of blood forced down from his head and upper body by the pressure of the constant turning.

"Jesus, they'll keep me turning here until I'm out of gas!" But he waited, turning, his wingtip inches from the sand and brush. Suddenly he saw all five of the Germans diving slightly toward him from the west. It was better than he had hoped for. Sleepily, he knew what to do. He pointed the Spit straight at them, and once more pushed the boost teat. The motor bounced with power. He lined his sight on the black propeller hub of a Messerschmitt and pressed the trigger. The two machine guns hissed like a deck of cards being riffled. He saw a white tracer shoot out, strike the propeller blur of the black-nosed ME, and ricochet off at a sharp angle. Tracers. The guns stopped firing. The last five rounds were tracers to let the pilot know he was out of ammunition. Jim gritted his teeth with sudden decision to collide with the German. The ME rolled over on its back, and the two ships passed inches apart. Jim could make out a black numeral 2 on its side, and for a split second as the canopies passed, top to top, he found himself looking straight into the goggled eyes of the enemy pilot.

"What a damned fool stunt that was!" Jim raged at himself, and instantly the rage turned to panic and the sweat turned frigid against his body. "Oh, God, I've had it! I've had it! They're going to kill me now! I'm going to die!" And then a calm followed, whispering: "So what? So what? You're going to die. That's all. Die."

Jim shook his head to clear the mist that was blurring his vision.

A nice day for flying, he thought calmly, watching the mountains ahead turn to purple beneath a big white billowing passing cloud. And then he looked back and saw the Germans. There were only four of them now, rapidly closing up the distance he had gained.

I must have put that Black Two out of action, he thought, smiling. Boy, wait until they hear this report. Two destroyed. One probable. Two damaged. I'll get a couple more medals. And this time, maybe, I'll take a leave.

He watched curiously, shaking his head every couple of seconds to clear the mist, as two of the Messerschmitts climbed up to the right, and one climbed up to the left. The Focke-Wulf started down the corridor of sky in between, headed straight for the line drawn by Jim's tail fin.

They're getting organized now, Jim thought. When the wing and cowl guns of the Focke-Wulf began to blink light, Jim rolled easily into a tight turn.

This could go on forever, Jim thought, lazily, watching the instrument panel jump with the overtaxed motor, and seeing how close he could keep his starboard wingtip to the ground without hitting it. Suddenly he saw a blue lake on the desert and began to widen his circle on that side so that he edged toward it. He reached down and switched on the transmitter.

"Hello, up there," he tried. "Hello, any friends flying east of Faid

Pass. I'm down by the blue lake with four bandits. Come down and help me, if you hear me. Down by the lake northeast of Faid Pass. Over?"

There was no answer. He tried again.

"Hello, any friends near Faid Pass," he yawned, sleepily watching his wingtip just missing the desert brush. "Come and take care of these Jerries for me. They ain't so tough. Down by the lake. You can see it for miles." He yawned again, and let go of the switch, his left hand dropping back to the throttle. Completely relaxed, he watched the gray clumps of desert brush whipping back from his turning, almost perpendicular wingtip.

I'll bet I could hit one of those, he thought idly, and yawned, and fell fast asleep. Blackness brought the peace of oblivion.

Seconds, perhaps minutes, later came the languid awakening. Where was he? he wondered with mild curiosity. In the new sleeping bag on the air mattress at Thélepte? In a hammock aboard a crowded rolling troopship? What was the steady thunder in his ears? He must be dreaming. He began to force himself from the half-memory of a fading nightmare. Then he remembered!

"I blacked out turning!" his brain told itself. "Gotta wake up!" He began struggling, eyes wide open but seeing only a red mist. He numbly felt the stick's spade grip in his right hand and the throttle ball in his left. He began shaking them forward and back, rapidly, shaking himself awake with the whole plane. For a minute he thought himself coming out of a practice maneuver high above the low clouds of England.

"No. No!" screamed his memory. "You're right down on the deck. Wake up! Wake up!"

He shook the throttle and stick violently, back and forth, back and forth, in a panic, helplessly waiting until the terrible red curtain in his brain began to clear, and the nightmarish roar of the engine settled down to fluctuating blasts jazzed by the throttle. In his fogged memory Jim once again saw his right wingtip skimming the desert brush.

"I'm alive," he marveled. "I didn't crash." Automatically, his clearing vision struck out toward the hazy dial of the airspeed indicator: 280. He shook his head violently and looked out over the side through the bubble of the canopy. Blue water and a desert shore beyond. He was climbing slightly, wings level.

"Level! Level!" his instincts screamed. "Turn! Get back into the turn!" His reviving muscles twitched as if to obey.

Something slammed into the armor plate behind him like a sledge hammer. A shell exploded like a thunderclap inside the cockpit by his left thigh. Instantly the cockpit was full of bitter-smelling white smoke. Another shell crashed into the motor up ahead, and black smoke came billowing back around the fire wall.

"Fire!" Jim sobbed hysterically, but his left hand automatically jammed the throttle open and reached forward in the same motion to turn off the magneto switches. Red and yellow flames joined the black smoke welling back around the fire wall. The flames licked at his boots as he drew back the stick to climb for altitude so that he could bail out. Automatically he watched the altimeter climb and the airspeed hand sway back to 140.

"Now," he decided, and reached up to grab the canopy emergency ejector. He pulled the little dangling rubber ball and it came away in his hand. But the canopy remained locked in place above him.

"No! No!" he screamed, horrified by the flames at his feet and the canopy that held the thick black smoke and himself in the cockpit. He dumped the stick forward and tried to look out the side, but he was blinded by the smoke. He could see neither sky nor ground. Panic shocked through every nerve of his body.

"I'm going to die. I'm going to die," he told himself. "And by fire. I'm going to burn!"

Just as suddenly as it had come, the panic vanished and was replaced by a great calm.

"I'm trapped. The canopy won't open," he reasoned. "Well, I'm ready. Now I'll know what happens when you die. Now at last I'll know everything. Well, I'm ready."

But instinctively his eyes peered through the smoke at the artificial horizon on the instrument panel, and his hands and feet, at no conscious bidding, held the wings level and the nose sightly down. He could hear the propeller swishing around up ahead, and the muted roar of the burning oil tank.

"Try opening it the regular way," came a whisper from deep in his brain.

"Jesus Christ, yes!" he roared into the oxygen mask, and with his left hand he reached up and forward for the ordinary handle of the canopy. The canopy slid easily back, admitting the slapping slipstream to fan the flames at his feet. The smoke was still too thick for him to see the ground.

I ought to hit pretty soon, he thought, holding the airspeed at 160 miles per hour. With his left hand he reached up and grasped the rear-view mirror above the windscreen and propped himself stiffly. In that position, flying blind by the artificial horizon, he waited while flames scorched the leather of his boots.

Finally it came. Jim felt the mighty jolt as the propeller and nose plowed into the unseen earth. The first shock slammed the canopy forward so that its metal frame dug into his left forearm. He was slapped forward against the straps of his Sutton harness as the plane bounced and ground along to the sounds of breaking, ripping metal. There came a mighty wrenching of metal behind him, and suddenly the jolting stopped and the only sounds were the licking of the flames at Jim's feet and the whistle of planes overhead.

"Now!" Jim yelled, jamming the canopy back open with his bleeding forearm. "One," he counted aloud as he ripped his helmet and mask forward and off over his head and face. "Two." He pulled the pin unlocking the Sutton harness. "Three." He twisted the metal lock of his parachute and smacked it, releasing the straps. "Four." He dove head first out of the smoking cockpit, landing shoulder down on the Spitfire's starboard wing and rolling on down to the ground. When he looked up, roaring flames were shooting twenty feet straight up in a furious column of red and yellow from the cockpit. Black smoke climbed up toward the blue and gray German planes circling overhead. . . .

Chapter Eleven

No wind. No snow. Feet plodding in the first hour of darkness of the early new day. Fred Wolkowski glanced sideways past his blanket cowl at Jim.

He's had it, Fred thought, hating the thought as he listened to the rasp of Jim's moans. With each step Jim's groaning grated in nearer loudness. It's that canary he's packing, Fred reasoned, exhausted, angry, and faced forward again with the march, unable to maintain his bleary focus on the hunched, plodding shape of Jim. "It's that stupid pack," he muttered, unaware that he was muttering. "It killed Fritz, and now it's going to kill Jim."

"What time is it?" Jim's voice interrupted his own anguished pulsing just enough to ask.

"I dunno," Fred answered, turning his head awkwardly in muscular pain again. "Twelve-thirty, one, maybe. You O.K., Jim?"

Jim stopped moaning suddenly. Fore and aft in the ghostlike formation sounded many moans of others, blending with the shuffling beat of boots.

"They can't stop me!" Jim grated. "They can't stop me! They'll never stop me!" Something about the way Jim hissed it out made Fred want to grin, but he was too exhausted to lift the corners of his mouth. After a bit Jim hissed again: "They can't stop me! I've got to buy a Mass."

It was easy for Fred to scowl. "Buy a Mass?" Fred wondered, without realization that he was talking to himself. "What's he mean by that? Jim ain't no Catholic." Jim was still, dark-shaped, plodding ahead, and no longer moaning with each step.

"Christ!" Jim swore angrily, but not aloud, as the heavy pack on his back pounded with each step like a sledge hammer against foot bones that felt like pumice filled with raw nerves. "I was groaning out loud. That must've sounded great to the boys. That'll do them a lot of good."

Then Jim, pushing each foot forward one by one in real pain, became aware that ahead and behind and to both sides throughout the formation nearly every man was making audible vocal noises, ranging from low muttering to terrible groans, and all blending together with the pressing shuffle of boots against the ice into a low, rotten, unholy chorus. He tried to lift his arms so that he could press his mittens over the blanket cowl against his ears to shut out the hellish sounds of the murmuring, moaning mass of men. But the brain refused to send the message down through the molten weariness of the neck, and the arms continued to dangle as the feet kept shuffling forward, one, two, one, two.

"Throw the pack away," some weak, distant echo in the brain said. But the arms dangled and the feet kept shuffling, bruising, bruising, onward.

"Throw the pack away, Jim." It was Fred's voice. Once again Jim became aware that he was moaning, that the moans were coming out of him unbidden in cadence with the forward shuffling of his own hurt feet. Think of home, he ordered himself, and he tried. Seattle—there were hills, but they jumbled together—he couldn't see more than a blur. With a terrible effort he raised his eyes. What was there about Seattle? He tried to make his mind focus on some aspect, some picture of his home, but his mind wasn't working that way. And then he remembered the Mountain. Yes, there it was, white and rising, rounded at the majestic peak, above the heads of the men. But the Mountain faded rapidly and in its place was the reality, dreamlike but there. It was only snow clinging to the branches of but one of the forest of trees through which the road wound. Jim's heavy eyes, lowering as they passed under the dull white branches that had looked like the Mountain, saw, but failed to register, a cowled figure falling back in the formation.

"Havin' a rough go?" Major Smith's voice broke into the fog of Jim's brain.

"Yeah . . . I guess so," Jim sighed with difficulty.

"You and me both," the major sighed, turning his head. "I'm too old for this. But I just picked up some good gen from the formation

164

ahead. The word is being passed back that we're bivouacking soon for the night."

Beyond Major Smith, Tom Howard jutted his head forward, letting his blanket cowl fall back. "Huh?" he said. "What's that, Major?"

"If it's pukka gen, we're stopping for some sleep in a town not far ahead. Pukka or bad, we might as well pass the gen on back."

"How far ahead?" Jim asked weakly.

"Not far, they say. One thing bothers me, though. They say the name of the place is Moscow. That's what they say. Moscow."

"Aw, for Christ's sake!" Fred gasped to Jim's right as they marched. "Moscow? What a hell of a time for a gag!"

"Well, might as well pass it on back, men," Major Smith said. "Only, better leave the Moscow part out of it." He started to pick up his pace to catch up forward again.

"Wait, Major," Jim cried with new energy. The major fell back again, eyes questioning through the darkness.

"That sounds pukka!" Jim exclaimed, panting slightly. "It's not Moscow. It's Muskau. M-u-s-k-a-u. It's a town on the Reichsbahn— the railroad line from Sagan to Berlin. It figures. I remember it from X briefings."

"Hot damn!" Fred gurgled excitedly to Jim's right.

The major raised a mittened finger to rub at the ice of his lower lip. "Muskau, huh? Well, now it makes sense. Pass it on back. And take it easy." He patted Jim's sore left shoulder. "Now we know where we're going."

As Major Smith edged forward again Bob's voice came from behind. "Hey, what's the gen?" Fred fell back to pass it along. Jim marched on, pushing his bruised feet ahead willingly now, but no less painfully.

"I've been saved again," he marvelled to himself. "Once again my mind gave up, but my body kept on working. I wonder why?" He looked up into the darkness between the walls of snow-hung trees. "Who's there?" he asked silently. "Who moves in when I quit. And why?" There was no answer in the low drifting black clouds above. Yet Jim, despite himself, felt an awe, a mysterious satisfaction. "Gott mit uns," it said on the belt buckle of every German soldier. "God is with us." What a hell of a thing for every Nazi to claim! And yet Jim realized that now again he felt a strange security in his misery. The black clouds stirred above the dark canyon of trees. "I'm ready," Jim whispered. "I've been ready for a long, long time. . . ." The treetops rustled slightly beneath the black ceiling of clouds.

"Dead . . . dead . . . dead . . ." the weary chorus seemed to intone as devils jabbed at his feet, his legs, his back, his neck, squeezing the individual organs inside his body, as he trudged on and on through the frozen level of hell.

"Muskau, Muskau, Muskau!" he wanted to cry back as the familiar dizziness of unreality made his vision real. "How can I be here?" the old question, that had been recurring in his mind time and time again through almost two years of drab monotony caged within rusted barbed wire, slipped easily into his exhausted brain. Ahead the cowled column wriggled slowly up the curving, slightly climbing road through the darkness like a bulbous, dying centipede. "Maybe this is hell and we don't know it." He lifted his aching eyes again toward the gently swirling black ceiling of clouds. "Gott mit uns." The damned Nazis.

There had been religious arguments in Room 8, Block 162, at Stalag Luft III, just as there had been arguments about everything else during the long days and nights.

"Sure they will!" Al Koczeck had once vehemently declared with conviction that primitive savages would go to hell, even if they never heard of the Catholic Church. But later, Al, after reading some Catechism, admitted that he had been wrong. "But just the same," he assured, "if you know about it, and refuse to accept it, then you go to hell."

"You'd better read some more of that stuff," Jim had suggested, knowing nothing at all about it. "Maybe you'll find the rest of us ain't doomed yet either."

The superstitious momentary horror of the sight of hooded figures writhing ahead in the dark column relaxed a bit as Jim thought: Well, if this is hell, what are good Catholics like Al and Fred doing here? And the miserable moaning of the men mocked him back.

"I'm not a bad Christian," Jim assured himself as if to ward off the punishment of the aches in his tooth and body, and the drilling torture of the cold. "I know the Twenty-third Psalm. 'The Lord is my Shepherd; I shall not want. . . .' I know the Lord's Prayer. 'Our Father which art in Heaven, Hallowed be thy name. . . .' I went to Sunday school. . . ."

He had attended kindergarten and the first grade in a convent just off San Francisco's Chinatown. He had gone to interdenominational Sunday school in Los Angeles, and as a small boy had seen Aimee Semple McPherson persuade the lame to throw away their crutches in Angeles Temple. In Seattle he had attended Sunday school at the First Baptist Church, at the same time singing for five dollars a week across the street in the choir of the Episcopal St. Mark's Cathedral, while his mother studied the power of metaphysical thought downtown at the Truth Center and Dad slept off his Saturday night beer and bathtub gin. Dad, whose farmer parents had wanted him to be a priest.

"I believe in God." Jim knew it, even through the pain and fatigue fighting each other in every fiber of his body as he jolted along and looked up through darkness at the blackness of the clouds. Now he had flown the last of his many missions. Once again he relived every breath, every action, every thrill of his last moments of combat.

"Yeah, I was good then," he recalled, suddenly conscious that the memory of that vivid action had for a time, and for the first time, carried his thinking away from the misery of the cold, the grating joint ends, the failing muscles, and the march across this lonely frozen stretch of a German winter's night. And he realized with a sudden, dull indication of a start that he was moaning again, the sounds rasping forth independently of his brain with each endless step forward. I was ready then, he thought miserably, for the adventure of death, but not for these adventures of unexpectedly continued life. With all the will power left him, he tried to stop moaning as he slogged on. But he could no more stop the moaning now than he could stop the pain pounding up from his feet.

". . . looks like it." Jim heard a fragment of Fred's speech alongside. ". . . Muskau . . . must be."

Jim, watching the filmy blur of the ice passing back beneath the black blobs of his feet, tried to speak. "How much—How much—" was all that came out.

"Yeah . . . must be." He heard Tom's voice on the other side.

"How much—How much—" Jim tried again. "To Muskau—how much farther?"

"Look, Jim." Fred's voice sounded faint above Jim's own moans. "We're here. Houses . . ."

Jim raised his swimming head enough to see, as if through a film, the dark shapes of buildings on both sides of the writhing black mass of the column.

"Muskau," he sobbed softly. "Muskau, Muskau . . ." He staggered weakly into the man ahead as the column came to a halt. Jim sank with a long groan onto his knees. The tin pack continued downward until it too rested against the ice. Its shoulder straps pulled Jim's shoulders back and down so that his head dangled backward, face pointing up toward the restless black sky.

"Thank you," Jim whispered with half open mouth sucking in lung-freezing gulps of air. "Thank you. Thank you."

"Hey, fella, what's the gen?"

Tom was calling to a bundled figure, seated, face buried in arms on its knees, before a dark house at the side of the road.

"Hey, fella," Tom called again, from a position on one knee. "This Muskau?"

The head of the figure raised, eyes dull white spots in a dark face.

"It's Thunderbird," Bob Montgomery's voice twanged behind Tom. Bob scrambled wearily to his feet and limped over to the sitting Negro ace. "What you sittin' here for, Thunderbird?"

"Hello B-Bob," Thunderbird chattered weakly, looking up from between hunched, blanket-draped shoulders.

"I don't savvy," Bob said, when the shivering ace remained silent after the first greeting. "What you sitting here for? Your bunch was way ahead somewhere, wasn't it?"

"Outa gas—outa bullets," Thunderbird said softly. "Had it. . . . Couldn't go on. Had to bail out of this."

Bob reached down and shook his colored friend's shoulder. It moved forward and back unresisting. "Jesus, Thunderbird!" Bob cried, the space between his front teeth revealed in open-mouthed bewilderment. "What's the matter with you?"

Thunderbird's mouth lightened in a weary half-smile. "Let me rest, Bob," he muttered softly. "I could never make another four kilometers."

Tom, standing now beside Bob, clipped: "Four kilometers? This is Muskau, ain't it? This is where we bed down."

Thunderbird silently shook his head.

"What do you mean?" Bob cried.

Thunderbird's eyes rolled slowly from Tom back to Bob. "That's just it," he said softly. "This isn't Muskau. Muskau's four kilometers ahead yet."

"Oh, Jesus," Tom sighed, his thin poker face reduced to sagging, lined despair. He turned and walked slowly back into the formation. "This isn't Muskau," he told Fred, who was lying flat on the ice, head resting on his blanket roll. "It's four kilos yet."

"You know," Fred said casually, propping his cheek up on one fist and elbow, "I kind of had an idea this couldn't be that place. It looks kind of small to billet ten thousand men—or what's left of them."

"Well, men," the major's voice, tired but still firm, came back over the crumpled length of the formation, "we've got to keep going. So let's get started." Figures reclining, sitting, and kneeling on the ice stirred. "Let's go!" Major Smith bawled. "Now!"

Fred sat up and looked at the strangely sprawled form of Jim, who appeared to be asleep, strapped backward around the tin pack. Fred reached over and began to work the shirtsleeve pack straps off Jim's inert shoulders.

"C'm' on, men!" Major Smith roared. "Up and at it!"

Bob, by the side of the icy road, looked down at the unmoving Thunderbird.

"Get up, Thunderbird," he said. "Let's get marching. Four kilometers isn't so far."

"Too far for me," muttered the colored pilot.

"Too far, hell!" Bob snorted. "I never heard before that you were yellow."

Thunderbird smiled gently upward. "You can't make me mad, Bob. Go on and let me rest."

"Jesus Christ, you can't stay here! You know what German civilians might do to a nig—a Negro, if they got ahold of you?"

"That's my boy," Thunderbird smiled back. "Goodbye, Bob. You can't scare me, either. I know."

Bob looked down painfully at his former roommate. With sudden decision he sat down beside Thunderbird. "Move over," Bob said with determination.

Thunderbird's eyes whitened as he turned to look at Bob. "What you doin', Bob?"

"I'm staying, too."

"What's the idea?"

"You coming? Or am I staying?"

Thunderbird reached over and gave Bob a weak shove. "Go on, man," he said. "Leave me alone."

Bob lay back in the snowbank, jaw set, hands clasped behind his head.

"You kiddin' me?" Thunderbird asked in a louder voice.

"Not kiddin'," Bob grated, a faint whistle hissing through his clenched teeth.

Slowly Thunderbird climbed to his feet. "Here," he said, and held out a mittened hand. Bob took the hand and was pulled to his feet. Together, the two men limped back into the slowly rising formation.

"Jesus Christ, let's go, men!" the major hollered again at the head of the formation.

"C'm' on. Gotta wake up. Wakey, wakey, wakey," Fred Wolkowski called into the sagging face of Jim. Fred slapped him twice. "Gimme a hand," he called to Tom Howard. Together, one on each side, they hauled Jim to his feet.

" 'S matter? Time is 't?" mumbled Jim, slowly returning to consciousness.

"Gotta go. On to Muskau." Wolkowski answered. "Here. Here's your pack." But instead of the large tin pack containing Jim's heavy manuscripts and the stolen radio, Fred slipped his own lighter blanket roll over Jim's head and shoulder.

"Yeah . . . Muskau," Jim said, shaking his head to clear it. "Thought . . ." But the memory was too much for him.

Fred reached down and picked up the heavy tin pack. He tested its weight, glancing thoughtfully toward the side of the road.

"Here we go!" Major Smith roared.

Fred shrugged his narrow, permanently hunched shoulders slightly, and swung the heavy pack around to slip his arms into them. As the column moved forward he looked around briefly to note that several still figures remained sitting or sprawling on the road. As they slogged on, passing other shapes of men who had dropped out from formations ahead, Fred wondered why he was now carrying the heavy radio that Jim had stolen. He glanced sideways at Jim, who had resumed his uncontrollable moaning with each step forward. Fred grinned slightly, thinking of the slick way Jim had stolen the radio.

As they passed on beyond the dark cluster of houses, Jim's vision began to clear slightly. He read a sign at the roadside: MUSKAU 4 KM.

I must have dreamed it, thought Jim. I thought we were there. . . .
Pain still jabbed upward through his bruising feet as the column
began climbing up the side of a snow-banked hill. Did I dream I
was flying? wondered Jim as the terrible cold began to needle through
his reviving body. As his frozen lungs throbbed, and the joint ends
grated throughout his aching bones, he looked ahead at the winding,
writhing column of blanket-shrouded backs. Am I awake now or
dreaming? he wondered. Am I alive? Or am I dead? He listened to
the moaning of the men, and heard his moans among the others. He
tried to stop moaning. But he still moaned as the column began
the last four kilometers toward Muskau.

Fred Wolkowski: "There I was. . . ."

Say, you know, it's kinda funny me packing the hot canary now for Jim, who's nearly out on his feet. The other guys in Room 8 always called me the Sack Time Kid from Chicago because I slept so much of the time. Well, my feet hurt, and my back aches, and I'm plenty corked. But, you know? I think I'm making out easier than the guys who made cracks about me sackin' down all the time. I started this march rested.

That's why I don't mind so much packin' this radio for the last four kilometers. Besides, I kind of admire the slick way Jim lifted it from right under the goons in that farmhouse. It was neat. And I ought to know.

It's kinda funny me being a prisoner now for almost two years, because I joined the army to keep out of prison. I'll never forget what a break I thought I was getting when the judge back in Chicago looked at me across his chamber desk and said:

"Fred, this is the third time you've been in trouble, and each time it's been a little more serious. But Father Ryan here insists that if I give you another chance, you'll show us that you've finally learned your lesson. What do you think?"

"Your Honor," I pleaded, "if you'll give me a break, sir, I promise you'll never see me again."

The judge sighed, looking back and forth from Father Ryan to me. "If you could only know," he said, "how many times I've heard that one, and how many times from the same people over and over again."

"But I mean it, Judge. Honest I do. I don't have to steal. I got a job. I just started this along with the rest of the guys, well—because I guess we were looking for adventure or something, I guess."

Father Ryan, his pink face serious, said softly: "Well, Fred, we all know there isn't much in the way of honest thrills for young men in Chicago, but you do realize now that looting parked cars isn't right, don't you?"

"Oh, yes, Father, I sure do."

"Hm-m-m," worried the judge, looking over the paper before him. "Picked up at the age of sixteen for window peeping. You don't do that any more, do you?"

"Gosh, no, your Honor. That's kid stuff." The judge grunted. I remembered how it all started. First we started sneaking around among the apartment houses shooting out back door lights with BB guns, or lighting firecrackers and tossing them into the hallways. Then we got to pouring kerosene along brick window sills, lighting it, and yelling fire. Boy, how the people moved inside when they looked out and saw the flames. Then one night one of the boys looked in a window and saw a peachy blonde undressing. The next night about the same time we all went around and watched her. Was it our fault she left her window shade up? Pretty soon we had a regular route every night. You'd be surprised how many people leave their window shades up. And, boy, what some people do when they don't know anybody is lookin'! We had it figured if we got caught in between a couple of buildings we could say we just stepped in to take a leak. But when they caught us, the cops didn't see it that way. Neither did the guy whose wife we were watching take a bath. He hit one of the guys over the head with a rock.

"At the age of seventeen," the judge went on, "caught stealing a crate of candy bars from a warehouse."

It wasn't long after they let us off for window peeking that we got to lifting stuff. Mostly it was magazines. One of the guys had a paper route, and we'd take turns wearing his delivery bag to look over magazine stands. Each time we'd leave, we'd have two or three Western story magazines in the bag. Once in a while we'd siphon a little gas or swipe a spare tire for somebody's jalopy. When we went into that warehouse after candy, we hadn't counted on a burglar alarm.

"After we let you off that time you did pretty well for a while," the judge went on. "Now you're twenty and ought to know better. Going through parked cars. Stealing radios, guns, cameras, flashlights, tennis rackets, clothing. How do you explain yourself?"

"I don't know, your Honor. I was just plain stupid, I guess. I got restless just working in the radio factory. I guess I was just looking for excitement."

Father Ryan cleared his throat. "He's been wanting to join the Air Corps for some time now, Judge. But his parents, especially his mother, have objected."

"I see." The judge frowned. "Why do they object, Fred?"

"They think flying's dangerous," I answered, "but they're wrong. They're just too old-fashioned to realize it's safer even than driving a car or crossing the street. I never could make them see it, and every time I talked about it they raised such a fuss I finally gave up."

The judge looked at Father Ryan, who nodded.

"Well, Fred," the judge said, "you've been in jail a week now. How do you like it in there?"

"I don't like it at all, your Honor."

"I'm going to send you back for another day," the judge said, turning to Father Ryan. "Meanwhile, can you bring Mr. and Mrs. Wolkowski to see me, Father?"

A policeman took me back up to the day tank in the precinct jail. When the barred door clanked shut behind me, I could see some of the prisoners slipping a burning newspaper under the steel bench where Con Tamborski, my night cellmate for the last few days, was sleeping. He was a parolee from the Federal pen who had been brought back for sticking up a post office. When the burning newspaper made the steel bench real hot, Tamborski jumped three feet in the air, yelling.

"You dumb greenhorn bastards," he shouted, rubbing his scorched back and looking around trying to figure out who set the fire. "Don't you crummy sons of bitches know better than to wake a man up when he's doing fast time?" He glowered around some more. "I've got eleven years to do," he said, still mad. "I'll kill the next two-bit punk who wakes me up."

Later that night, as we lay between itchy blankets in the darkness, Tamborski told me:

"The only way to do time, son, is to sleep it out. Let me sleep it out and I can do eleven years standing on my ear."

The next day, when a policeman took me to the judge's chambers, my parents were there with Father Ryan. Beneath his bald head, my dad's eyes were dark-ringed behind his glasses. My mother's face looked like the muscles were tight beneath the loose flesh, and her mouth was set thin and straight.

"Fred," the judge said as I sat stiff, "I'm going to give you another chance on one condition. That condition is that you enlist in any one of the armed services. I'm putting it that way in case the Air Corps turns you down on your physical or mental examination. They will not have access to your record here, for I am going to keep it in my office for one year. In effect, you will be on probation for that year. If at the end of the year Father Ryan reports to me that you are doing well in the service, then I shall destroy the record of this business and you will have a clean name. Do you understand?"

"Gee, yeah. Yes, sir, your Honor. Gee, thank you, your Honor." I felt like saying something stronger than "gee," but you don't to a judge.

"I hope you realize what a chance I'm taking on you," the judge said, rising and holding out his hand. "Now don't let me down. Don't let any of us, down."

As I shook the judge's hand, I felt like flying through the ceiling. I had won. It was a funny way to win an argument. But I had won. Now my folks had to let me go into the Air Corps!

Yet I must have known that some day it would happen. For when I wasn't out looting cars or working, I had been studying. I had always wanted to be a flying cadet, and it isn't easy without two years of college.

I guess my folks found out it wasn't so bad. They were real proud when I passed the test and the physical. And the only time they were ever prouder than when my appointment as an aviation cadet arrived, was the day I was commissioned a second lieutenant bombardier and got my wings. If anyone was prouder of those wings than they were, it was me.

But you know, funny things began happening after I received those wings. One night while I was asleep in the BOQ at Denver someone went through my things and stole forty dollars from my billfold. I always was a sound sleeper. I didn't report it. I lost a suitcase on the train from Denver to Boise. It just vanished from under my lower berth. In New York, just before we were ready to fly to England, I picked up two broads. They took me to a hotel room, gave me a drink, and I woke up in a crummy bar with an awful headache and minus more than $160. In England someone stole my camera and the wheel off an RAF bicycle that I had to pay to have replaced.

When my plane was shot down and I bailed out into Germany, one soldier held a gun on me while another took my watch, Air Force ring, and shirt insignia. When he started to grab my silver bombardier's wings, the soldier with the gun said, "Nein." They were superstitious about taking the wings. About a year later, in Stalag Luft III, I got a letter from home saying my personal belongings left in England had never been returned. Somebody must have looted them. All I had left were my silver wings.

One day last summer a Kriegie came into Room 8 and said: "We need some volunteers to build scenery for the Kriegie Theater. Any you guys want to help?"

I had been sleeping all morning, so I decided to donate my time. It was a hot day, so I took off my shirt and hung it on a nail backstage while I worked. When I went to get it, the silver wings were gone.

"That's a hell of a thing for one Kriegie to do to another," Jim said at the time.

Yeah, it's kinda funny me being here packing a radio that Jim swiped from the goons back there. I joined the army to keep from going to jail for stealing. Ever since I've been in the army, everything I've had has been stolen from me. Instead of going to a Chicago jail for a few months, I ended up in a German prison camp for nearly two years. And here I am packing the dead weight of a stolen radio on my back in forty degrees below zero.

Oh, well, it really doesn't seem like nearly two years. It was Con Tamborski, in for eleven years in Leavenworth, who taught me how to do fast time sleeping. I guess I've been doing it standing on my ear.

And I kinda get a kick out of the way Jim lifted this radio right from under the goons back there at Graustein. That was pretty slick, and I guess I know.

Chapter Twelve

The moaning column trudged on along the road high beside a valley. Bill Johnston panted as he looked toward an electrically lighted hole in the side of the hills across the dark snowy valley. "There's another one." But Ed Greenway didn't look. For more than an hour along the last four-kilometer lap toward Muskau, Bill had been commenting every time they passed yellow glaring mine tunnels far across the valley to their left.

Ed sobbed as he marched. "Mama . . . Mama . . . Mama . . ." The sound was lost in the greater sobbing about him as he sagged on and on in cadence with the tottering column. Muskau. . . . When would they reach Muskau?

Bill Johnston still watched the distant shaft of yellow light dissolve toward them from across the frozen valley. "Maybe they're salt mines." Far below, the black snake of a train rattled hollowly. Its whistle peeped and echoed. It passed on up the valley ahead of the column. Bill looked ahead at the lurching back of Thunderbird. He panted extra long and sniffed. He looked further at the whining dark shape of Jim. He sniffed again.

Jim's rasping moans of an hour before were reduced to weak whines. Between whines, Jim prayed. He prayed as a novice prays, hoping for something to be proved. Beside him Fred grunted: "Take it easy, Jim. We must be nearly to Muskau."

The prayers had to be answered. Major Peter Smith's voice filtered back, "There she is, men!"

Far ahead and down at the valley floor the crawling dark column met the blackness of an almost sleeping city. But to prove the place was alive the tall black silhouettes of smokestacks belched rosy billows of night-blending smoke.

Jim still whined with each breath, but remembered to thank God. They let bone-bruised feet slip gratefully down a long icy slope toward the speckled dark map of Muskau. Far ahead a night-hidden train peeped goodbye.

The blotch of the town spread out and became a street along which they stumbled between darkened houses. Al Koczeck threw back his blanket hood to peer at the buildings. "Jeez. Where they going to put us this time? I don't see no barns."

"It won't be the Ritz." Bob Montgomery breathed hard.

The column slowed. Dark-shuttered buildings on both sides of the street rose two and three stories high. The men passed the gilt signs of business firms, pensions, and beer halls. The town looked deserted or dead. Their feet clacked against the iced cobblestones and echoed between the buildings. Up ahead a single light waved back and forth.

It was Lieutenant Pieber with a flashlight. "Turn to za right 'ere, Major." Pieber's spectacles picked up a glint from his light. "Ve vill stop here for za night, zhentlemen." Pieber's accent was more German than usual. They turned down a street between large black warehouses and snow-crusted metal fences.

Every time they stopped, Ed Greenway swayed forward and backward and squeezed his thin thighs desperately. "We better get there preety quick," he repeated. "Preety damned queek." Nobody laughed.

Again a flashlight ahead jiggled sideways. It was Hohendahl once more, directing the column in a sharp left turn. Now they walked between high-fenced storage yards, acres of snow-mounded silence on both sides. Orange smoke burbled high above from three tall black smokestacks. Each time the men had to halt and wait, Greenway staggered around uncontrollably. He giggled. "Better get there preety quick. Preety damned quick."

Tom Howard's skinny frame shook in violent jerks. "Nuts. It's all nuts."

The column moved forward. They were again directed uphill past snow-covered railroad tracks. Jim whined again and heard Ed giggle behind. He looked up into the black sky. "Oh, God!"

Beside him Fred looked up into the biting air. "Huh?"

Ed's giggle came louder and higher pitched. His legs curled and he collapsed to the ice. Bill Johnston leaned frantically over him. "What's wrong with you, Ed?"

Ed's body sprawled on the ice. He giggled. "They're gone."

"What's gone?"

"My legs. Can't you see? They're gone."

Bill glared down frightened. "What do you mean they're gone?"

Ed put his arms over his shaking face. His terrified voice was muffled. "My legs. They're gone. My legs are gone!"

Bill clutched at the fallen man's shoulders and pleaded. "Get up, Ed. Please get up, fella."

"How can I get up without legs?" Ed began to cry softly.

Jim bent slowly to put a hand under one of Ed's shoulders. "Let's lift him up." Jim and Bill strained, but their hands fumbled. Jim gasped toward Al Koczeck and Bob Montgomery. "Help us." The four of them could not lift Ed Greenway. Jim pulled one of the sobbing man's hands away from his face. "What's the matter, Ed? Can you hear me?"

Ed cried weakly. "Yes."

"Tell me what's the matter?"

"My . . . legs."

Jim's voice was faint. "What about your legs?"

"They're gone. They're just not there."

"They're not gone, Ed." Jim pinched one of the fallen man's thighs. "There. Feel that?" Ed gave no sign he felt it. Jim pinched again, harder. Ed continued to sob into his hands. Jim slowly straightened up and turned away.

"What are we going to do?" asked Bill.

Jim shivered and shook his head. "Nothing to do."

Bill's voice was tired but defiant. "I ain't leaving a buddy." Jim shrugged and sighed mournfully. Bill glared. "Son of a bitch." He turned back toward the fallen man as the column began to move forward.

Ed's voice cried out weakly behind them, "They're gone!"

Just across the railroad tracks to their left appeared high wooden bins piled with coal and snow. Again the column halted.

Jim wailed softly. "I can't stand this. I can't stand it any more."

Fred said, panting, "We're all in the same boat."

Al Koczeck snorted behind them. "Look, men. There's where we're going to sleep. In them coal bins."

"You're crazy," Jack Noble whimpered. "We'd freeze."

"Listen to him," Koczeck jeered. "He expects a bridal suite."

"But there's no roofs."

Jim looked at the black coal jutting through the snow in the bins and swayed. "I can't stand any more." He moaned deep in his chest with each breath. "I'm going over and lay down."

The mumbling of ailing voices whined louder farther back in the formation. Men turned slowly to look.

"I don't know," a deep drawling voice complained. "They just give out. That's all."

It was Tex speaking. His huge body was curled up on the ground. "Jesus!" someone back there pleaded. "Can't you move 'em at all?"

Tex's puzzled voice answered louder. "I tell you I can't move 'em. I can't even feel 'em. I can't feel anything from my ass down."

"The same as Ed," Tom whispered softly beside Fred and Jim.

An eternity of cold filled each long second of waiting. Jim moaned weakly and long. A hand fell on his shoulder. Slowly he saw the icy black beard of Major Smith.

"What's going on back there?" the major asked.

Jim's eyes shut. "Tex . . . Legs gone. Like Ed's." The cold darkness of the night oozed into his brain. His whine changed to a whisper. "God. Got to lay down. . . ." Arms held him and he tried weakly to push them away.

Major Smith's voice rasped very close. "No. Don't." Jim opened his eyes close to the ice of Smith's black beard. "Don't, Jim. Not you. Stay on your feet."

His eyes moved. Three men were holding him up. A worried grin lit up Fred's dark stubbled face. Jim's body straightened slightly from shame. He spoke with a trace of force. "I'm all right." Then he mumbled. "I'm O.K. Leggo." They let go, and he swayed as he watched Tom's mouth curl up on one side while steam floated from the major's white teeth. Jim smiled sheepishly. "In grade school they called me sissy."

Major Smith turned and walked forward through the blur of unreal dark figures in the cold night. Jim looked toward the coal bins. They looked lumpy and lonely and cold.

The column slowly moved toward the vast black bulk of a factory. Obergefreiter Glimlitz stood at the first corner of the building. Beside him the smaller figure of Captain Daniels called out.

"Anybody from you guys drop out near back?"

Fred answered first in a tired voice. "Yeah. Two. One just back down the hill a ways and one two turns back in town."

Daniels nodded his wool-capped head. "We'll get 'em."

Jim stirred himself, glad to recognize Danny in the dark. "You know Tex. It's Tex, Danny. And another good guy—a really good guy, Danny, from my room. Name's Ed Greenway. Their legs gave out. Like they were paralyzed."

The dark shape of Captain Daniels's head nodded wisely. "Don't worry, Jim. I'll get 'em."

They moved on between the factory and a long building to their left. Fred sighed a wondering sound. "That's funny, y'know. Guys' legs getting paralyzed."

Jim breathed faintly. "But they got here."

Indistinct shouts echoed back between the buildings. From the big black building on the right a feather of yellow light drooped across the crowded narrow street.

"Hubba, hubba, hubba!" Al Koczeck rubbed his mittened hands together in exhausted enthusiasm. "They're bedding us in the factory."

Up ahead ragged men turned out of the darkness into the light. Their breaths sparkled white as they passed into the large building.

"Even the light looks warm." Tom shivered and stumbled.

After a few more steps Fred answered. "It'll be better than a barn. Maybe there's heat."

They stopped. A bundled-up German officer closed the door. "Ja. Kommen sie mit, bitte."

Jim sleepily identified the fat German's uniform. "Wehrmacht."

The Wehrmacht officer pushed open a wide door that creaked. "Hier." His flashlight beam darted in toward the darkness.

Fred groaned. "Shifted again!" Major Smith followed the German.

"Ach so." A faint glow from high up inside filled the doorway.

"Let's go!" called Major Smith.

They surged in through the doorway. Jim called, "We got to stick together." All inside was velvet black except for four light globes which dangled from a vast black ceiling. Their feet kicked up small black swirls from inch-deep soot.

The crowding men came to a stop and stared at the soot-lined cavern. "What is it?" asked Fred. Footfalls and voices echoed from the black walls. Small lumps of rubble and large bulks of machinery dotted the huge floor. Men swarmed around them. Hank pointed wearily up toward a barely distinguishable ledge about twenty feet up one black wall. "It might be cleaner up there."

Jim swayed without looking up. Fred shifted the big tin pack on his own shoulders. "Come on. Heat goes up. So lets us." He gave Jim a shove to lead the way. Jim lurched forward in slow motion, and instinctively his night-adjusted eyes found a metal ladder as black as the wall. He looked up its soot-runged height and whimpered in doubt.

Koczeck slipped past Jim. "Let's go." Koczeck grabbed two rungs of the ladder. His brown wool mittens turned instantly black as he hauled his squat frame slowly upward. Jim numbly followed. Halfway up, gobs of fine soot showered down on his face. He clung to the ladder for a moment, then jerked his way up and crawled onto the ledge. He lay on his belly in soot and breathed desperately as the others grunted and thudded down beside him.

Fifteen feet back from the ledge Al Koczeck dangled his arms against the final black wall. He sounded satisfied. "It ain't cleaner, but it's privater."

Tom kneeled in the soot beside Jim and swore. "Jesus! Ever see anything like it?"

The black floor below was hidden by a squirming mat of men. Prisoners crawled over one another. Their voices babbled through loud ripping reports of breaking wood. A dozen small fires glowed. Men foraged among boxes and rubble for fuel. Close below, at the foot of the ladder, Fred waved his arms and shouted unheard. Someone flipped down a length of greasy black rope to haul up the tin pack containing the radio. Fred followed it up the ladder.

"Two on the bottom enough?" Jack Noble yelled as he spread a blanket on the soot of the ledge.

On his knees Jim counted. Nine men. He sighed. "More on top the better." He fumblingly unfastened the lid of the tin pack and pulled out his own two blankets. Someone tapped his shoulder.

"C'm'ere," Bill Johnston beckoned. Jim dazedly got to his feet and followed down the now crowded ledge. Bill stopped and leaned close. "We all supposed to sleep under the same blankets? Together?"

Jim coughed weakly from the soot and the smoke of the fires beneath the ledge. "Sure," he finally managed. "We can keep warm." He started to turn away, but Bill stopped him.

"Him, too?"

Smoke made Jim's eyes smart and blur. "Who?"

"Thunderbird. That jig."

Jim groaned and coughed. "Christ's sake! Let's get some sleep."

Bill also coughed from the thickening smoke. "I ain't sleepin' with no smelly jig."

"Don't, then," Jim gasped softly. He shuffled back to where the rest were arranging the blankets.

Far below, the frantic prisoners tugged the entrance door down for firewood. The crash echoed over the uproar. Bill stood above the bed of blankets and smiled down with disgust. "I'm not stayin' in this smoke. I'm going to look for Ed Greenway." They wearily paused and looked up. "That guy Daniels must have picked him up in his wheelbarrow." Nobody agreed or disagreed. "Well, so long." He walked across the ledge and disappeared down the ladder in the rising smoke.

Bob stared at the top of the ladder. "What's eating him?"

Jim cleared his throat painfully. "Hell with 'im. Eight's enough anyhow."

"Eight what?"

"Men." .

Each man worked in a daze as the bed was built. A combination of shivering from the cold and hacking from the thickening smoke made Tom Howard stop before he could even speak. "Maybe heat rises," he gasped. "Smoke does, for sure."

Koczeck dumped a bundle of sooty wood at the foot of the wide blanket bed. "Burt scrounged some wood for a fire." It was bound in a loop of the black rope they had used to haul up Jim's tin pack. "We had a time getting it up."

Tom coughed and rasped. "That's what we need. More smoke." His stinging eyes shifted to watch Bob deal out eight cards face down on the blankets. "What for?" he rasped.

Bob finished the deal and looked up. "Two low men sleep on the outsides." Solemnly each picked up his card and placed it face up on the blankets. Bob's shaking finger indicated the two low cards. "Noble and Tom." Tom grunted and Noble groaned.

"They trying to smoke us out?" Thunderbird coughed as he fumbled with his bootlaces.

Tom fell coughing to his hands and knees on the blankets. "God-damned smoke. Jim? How you feel?"

"Not worth a damn." Jim swallowed painfully and loosened his boots with numb fingers. "Not a damn."

Koczeck's voice a few feet away sounded far off as he started to build a fire at the foot of the wide blanket spread. "Cut off some more small shavings for kindling." The smoke beyond the ledge flickered red. The shouting was replaced by a thick murmur and the crackling of fires.

An inexorable curiosity overcame the numb soreness of Jim's body. Dragging himself to his feet he swayed forward and looked down from the edge of the ledge on the unreal sight below.

At least thirty bonfires blazed red and orange amid the slowly writhing mass of men on the huge floor. A glow flickered over the smoke-hazy gulf. A fog of smoke bunched and balled upward, finding no escape through the high vaulted roof, so that it thickened and curled among the black rafters. The babble of voices, the splintering and thudding of wood bounced from wall to wall in a throbbing roar. "Hell," Jim whispered, and staggered back a half-step to keep from hurtling into the pit. He coughed weakly. Tears burned his eyes. The scattered fires fumed blood red in the murk. "Men do this." He sank to his knees in the soot to try a prayer. Instead he looked up in the shadow and asked a question. "You!" The shadow swirled slowly. "What's a man worth?" The drifting shadow of smoke did not answer.

When Jim returned, Bob was already a lump under his greatcoat spread over his portion of the blanket covering. Thunderbird spread his greatcoat and sighed deeply. "Man, I hope they never wake us." He pried his shoes off and crawled in close to Bob.

Fred squirmed in next to Tom. "How long we get here? If it's another four-hour deal they can shoot me." Two seconds later he began to snore long and low.

On hands and knees, midway at the long foot of the blanket bed, Burt and Al Koczeck blew desperately at the glowing shavings in the soot. "Blow," Burt rasped. "Blow!"

Jim used his left foot to force the shoe from his right. "They can't move us," he said.

Tom mumbled sleepily. "Seems to me . . . I've heard that before." Snug in the blankets, he eyed through slitted lids a fire built by others up the ledge.

Koczeck's voice rapped hoarsely. "Give me some small pieces!" Burt handed him some from the pile of dirty wood as the shavings puffed into flame.

Jim wriggled in between Fred and Thunderbird. He sighed ecstatically. "No . . . difference. We can't . . . be moved on."

Al Koczeck was the last to bed down. For a few minutes he stood proudly by the blazing fire. "Feel that heat?"

"Good night, Bob," Thunderbird whispered when all was quiet except the popping of many fires and the wheezing mass breath of the men.

"Good night, Thunderbird."

No one heard more.

Jim Weis: "There I was. . . ."

What is a man worth?

Sometimes I've felt worth a lot. I remember how valuable I felt I was when young, curly-headed Captain Hall, commander of the flying-cadet school at Santa Maria, stood before us all in a hangar one evening and said:

"I want you all to realize this is serious business. Before you've done with training it will cost Uncle Sam thirty thousand dollars apiece to make you military pilots."

It was serious business, all right. Only, whoever worked out the system didn't seem to know it. Standing in the sun-baked ranks of cadets, 73 per cent of us having been washed out and waiting for discharges, I used to wonder: How much does it cost to train a man just so far, teach him to love to fly, and then ground him before a long-faced washout board of officers?

How much did it cost to train Fritz Heine to navigate tons of metal, explosives, and men that he never was permitted to navigate? Perhaps Fritz was worth more as a four-grades teacher in a Wyoming school-house. And what is he worth now?

"Never in the field of human conflict was so much owed by so many to so few." Winston Churchill said it of the Battle of Britain fighter pilots, and the words hung framed back of every RAF bar in the world. But I never stood in one of the endless RAF pay parades waiting to draw my monthly $83 without hearing some shaggy mustachioed fighter pilot put it this way: "Never in the history of human conflict have so many waited so long for so little."

But you can depend upon Uncle Sam to make you feel worth something—worth something big. In the fall of 1942, still wearing the blue uniforms with Eagle shoulder patches, we were sworn back into the Air Force that had once washed us out. It was in a small room of a building called Pen Corner in London.

"Gentlemen," a white-haired colonel with a silver mustache matching his eagles, just like in the movies, said to us, "you are now the most valuable men in the United States Army Air Force. You're going to find yourselves among a bunch of hot pilots just coming over from the States who think they know it all." The colonel flashed his expensive dental work. "But you and I know they don't. They've got a lot to learn, and we expect you gentlemen to teach it to them. We expect to build the greatest Air Force the world has ever seen around you boys. I say right here, and I'm not exaggerating, there isn't a man in this room who won't be a captain within six months. And most of you will be majors and colonels."

That sounded good, especially to us second lieutenants.

"Hey, Jim," Barney said eagerly afterward, his spanking new green blouse glittering with British and American do-dads as he entered the Picadilly bar where we were treating the barmaids to extra clothing coupons, "did you hear what they're paying for us?"

"Who's paying for us?" I asked, motioning for another Scotch and water.

"Our country. Uncle Sam. They're paying the British twenty-eight thousand dollars for each non-combat transfer and thirty-five thousand smackeroos for each of us combat types."

"That's nice," I commented, grinning at the excited flush beneath Barney's red hair. "Now wouldn't it be a new theory of warfare if they paid each pilot thirty-five G's?"

But the only G's that came our way during the next six months were in the pull-outs and turns high and low over Algeria and Tunisia. Around 9 G's you black out, and at 5 or 6 G's if you turn inside the Huns long enough at one stretch. And then you're not worth a damn.

It was six months and six days after the silver-haired colonel told us we'd all be captains and majors and colonels that I found myself still a second lieutenant, crouched by the side of my broken Spitfire, watching the flames blast up from the cockpit toward the killer planes circling above. Six months and six days, and I hadn't been able to teach the West Pointer who led this last mission a thing. In the heat of my battle he'd coolly dropped me and gone home like a chicken rancher who has lost one egg.

Oozing sweat, I watched the three Messerschmitts and the Focke-Wulf each circle and dip for a look at me crouching there between smoking fuselage and shattered tail draped forward over the wing. Would they shoot? Would they strafe? Maybe, but the burning plane would certainly explode. So I sprang to my feet and started to run. I ran twenty feet and fell flat on my face in the sand and brush of the desert. I spit sand and looked down at my legs to see what had made me fall. There were jagged bloody holes in the brown khaki over my left thigh. A small round hole in my right calf oozed thick dark red. Crimson seeped through rents in the heavy dark leather sleeve of my jacket just over the forearm. I felt no pain—nothing.

The four killer planes passed, banking and rolling low overhead, each with a distinct whapping sound, and then whined off in the direction of the bright low morning sun. On hands and knees I faced the opposite direction. The mountain ridge I had failed to reach in the fight stretched yellow and brown, appearing very close on the horizon, and dipping slightly to the south. Gingerly, I stood up and tested my bleeding legs. There was still no pain, but they were stiff and clumsy. I began to limp toward the mountain ridge, scuffling through the desert brush. My left black RAF escape-type flying boot gaped open from shin buckle to scorched instep laces, its zipper broken.

There was the utter unreality of it. The it-can't-be-happening-to-me feeling combined with the immense stupefied joy and relief of being alive, of escaping the horror of death by flames. And there was the hope, the desperate hope, of crossing those mountains ahead to the American lines and safety—yes, and even glory. For it had been one hell of a fine show, one to report to intelligence with pride. Two destroyed. One probably destroyed. Two damaged. That would prove my worth to a West Point hot pilot who had more of a stomach for heading home than for the business at hand of killing Germans. I could see the smug young face of Colonel Proffer beneath carefully combed prematurely gray hair, and I began to grit my teeth as I limped across the hot sand. I could see him putting himself in for another Silver Star, or maybe even the DSC for leading a hundred-odd consecutive missions without ever firing a shot, except at some American tanks once.

"All right, boys. Close up the formation. We're going home."

God, what an ugly, disgusting thing that calm voice is when you hear it over and over again as you slowly limp on stiff, bleeding legs across the desert, alone and miles deep behind the enemy lines. A man puking sounds braver than that.

First the Arab shouted. He was a gesturing tassle of white rags approaching across the scrubby gray clumps of desert grass from the northwest. As he grew closer, still shouting unintelligibly, the white rags draped over his head and shoulders appeared raggeder and dirtier.

"Hola!" he seemed to shout, following it with the gibberish that is any language you don't understand. His face was the yellow-brown color of strong tea. Waving a primitive gnarled gray staff, he grinned, showing teeth like Limburger cheese.

"Allemand?" he shrilled excitedly. "Allemand?"

I looked back toward the smoke-spewing wreckage of my Spitfire, wishing I had saved the parachute so that I could bargain with its silk.

"American," I said, and repeated it when the incredibly tattered figure didn't seem to comprehend. "Ah-merr-eee-cannn." I squatted stiffly, forcing blood out of the holes in my legs, and drew a crude star in the sand with my finger. I straightened up and watched the idiotic yellow-brown face spew out more gibberish. If only I had something to trade. I remembered the red silk scarf I was wearing. I slid the long ends from the loop at my throat and pulled it from my jacket. It was double thickness, three yards long, handmade and monogrammed by my mother, my horoscope color. I handed it to the Arab.

"Merci, merci, merci," he jabbered, feeling the rich silk and jumping up and down so that each of the hundreds of dirty white tatters of his robe bobbled in the sun.

If only I had learned something in French other than Voulez vouz coucher avec moi and Ooey ley oofs. Ooey lay oofs. It might work for something beside eggs.

"Ooey lay Faid Pass?" I asked. "Ooey lay Faid?"

"Ah-h-h, Faid!" he marveled, draping the bright red scarf over the rags on his skinny shoulders. He pointed southwest toward the dip in the mountains and made noises like "guerre" and "boom-boom."

That made sense. I knew there was a ground battle going on at Faid Pass. Once more I squatted, oozing more blood, and drew the figures for five thousand francs in the sand.

"For you," I tried to explain, pointing from the figures in the sand to the peering-down face. "Take me," I pointed to myself, "to Faid." I pointed to the dip in the mountains.

"Ah-h-h, oui, oui." He grinned. The yellow-brown face became suddenly serious. He took a tattered rag of a shawl from over his head and placed it over mine. "Allemands," he explained, gesturing slowly in a wide circle all around us, and then pointing to his own head and jerking his thumb in unison with a "poop" sound from his rotting mouth. He handed me his staff and we started to walk toward the distant dip in the mountains.

A sudden heavy dull crump to the rear made us turn around in time to see a cloud of black smoke shooting skyward from the Spitfire, now a bulb of flame on the sunny desert a quarter of a mile back. The Arab grinned his rotting teeth at me. "Plooey!" he said, tossing his hands palms upward. I turned, holding the dirty white shreds of the shawl draped over my head tightly, hoping I looked like an Arab, and started forward again. My bottom was beginning to sting, and I guessed I'd been hit there, too. Ahead, between us and the long ridge of mountains, the desert was becoming suddenly alive. As if from nowhere, white and yellow figures had appeared, some walking toward us, some trotting. I couldn't figure out where they had come from.

My right calf began to throb with pain as I limped, blood still running slowly from its hole and soaking my torn pants leg. My left thigh started to burn from within as if it contained hot metal, which I figured it probably did. I had to limp slower and slower, the mountains beyond the scattered approaching Arabs seeming farther and farther away. I wondered where the Germans were, but could see no life other than the nearing figures of the Arabs on foot, and the rapidly approaching figure of a heavily robed rider on a pure white horse. A horse. If I could get to ride that horse.

There is nothing prettier than a pure white Arabian stallion. I watched its flanks quiver and twitch at the flies as its rider talked in gibberish, but authoritative gibberish, to the Arab whose dirty rag I wore draped over my head. The rider's purple cape contrasted with the clean cream-colored robes beneath it. Obviously he was a chieftain.

"Salaam aleikum," I said, touching my forehead, mouth, and chest, when the chieftain deigned to look down upon me. That was as near as I could remember what Intelligence told us to do in such a case.

I caught the word Faid several times, and each time the chieftain barked something at the ragged Arab and shook his head. With a swish of its white tail the stallion and its rider clopped off at a gallop. The Arab in rags looked at me mournfully, shook his head, gibbered sadly, and threw up his arms. I sat down on a large hot boulder. My legs were really beginning to hurt, and I couldn't walk any farther.

One by one the motley Arabs arrived and stood around my seat on the boulder. Some of them were women watching me with one eye from cowls held tightly before their faces. I began to think about cases I'd heard of what Arab women had done to fallen flyers before turning them loose to roam the desert. I drew a cigarette from my shirt pocket and lit it with a paper match.

"Cigarette. Cigarette," they all started jabbering, hands outstretched. I pulled forth the pack, ripped the top off, and passed cigarettes around to the dirty, greedy hands. I stood up, but it was no use. My bleeding legs were through walking, so I sat down on the boulder again. I studied the red oozing hole in my right calf and wondered if it was a bullet or a shell splinter. More and more Arabs were arriving by the minute. A woman's brown hand extended from a pillar of rags offering a tin cup. I took it and drank it down. It was goat's milk. An Arab man, face and hands erupting in sores, handed me an egg with holes punched in each end of the shell. I didn't want it, but I sucked it clean and gagged swallowing its slimy globule.

I heard a familiar sound and looked to the northeast. A high-winged monoplane was circling there, low over the desert.

"Go way!" I shouted at the Arab rabble surrounding me. "Get out of here!" I barked, gesturing violently with both my good right arm and my bleeding left arm. Their jabbering increased. "Go 'way!" I shouted again, standing. I didn't have a gun. Some Arab had sneaked into my foxhole back at Thélepte and stolen it. But I reached inside my jacket to my left armpit as if I did have one. The Arabs directly in front of me scurried backward, trying to hide behind one another. I turned slowly, hand still clutching nothing inside my jacket, and the whole crowd of Arabs backed up. They formed a respectful circle about forty feet out completely around me. I sat down on the hot boulder again and could hear that calm, collected voice.

"Close up the formation, boys. We're going home."

I looked around at the circle of dirty, ragged Arabs and tried to estimate how many there were. About three hundred of them. A gun would have done me a lot of good. From the air they must have formed quite a target. And I was the bull's-eye.

The small monoplane circled closer and closer, the white crosses on its sides clearly visible. I had studied pictures and silhouettes of it. It was a Fiesler Storch, the kind of defenseless crate a fighter pilot dreams about finding—in the air. It finally came close enough so that I had to look up at a high angle to see it. The Arab whose rag I was wearing over my head broke from the crowded ring and began waving the red silk scarf I had given him. The Storch dropped wide wing flaps and landed by the smoldering wreckage of my Spitfire.

"Got to get out of here," I said to myself, suddenly coming alive. As the Arab, still waving my scarf, started running toward the idling German plane, I started to try to run in the opposite direction toward the ridge of mountains. I fell to my hands and knees, struggled up again, and two brave Arab youths, jabbering hysterically, grabbed me by either arm. It wasn't much of a struggle. They held me as I watched the Arab with my scarf lead a German toward us from the Storch. The black peak of the German's cap flashed in the sun.

"Good morning," the slight, slender German greeted, motioning sharply for the Arab youths to release me. "You are wounded?"

"Yeah," I answered.

"Well, we will get you soon to a doctor," he said casually, as he patted my body and legs looking for a gun. "And how are the Brooklyn Dodgers making out this year?"

I didn't answer him.

"No pistol?" he asked, straightening up. "You wouldn't have one in your boot, would you?" He looked down at the zippered-up boot on my right leg. "No, I suppose not. Lower your trousers and I will give you first aid." He pulled a compress from a pouch on his belt. I lowered my pants and looked away quickly from the red splashes on my white shorts and the holes and lacerations in my legs. "I have only one bandage," he said. "This one looks the worst." He began wrapping the compress to my left thigh. The Arabs, men, women, and boys, crowded around watching. As he straightened up, a cowled Arab woman handed him a tin cup of goat's milk. He pretended to take a sip, and handed it back. "It's not good to drink," he explained to me. "Not pasteurized. Tuberculosis." He took me by the left elbow. "Shall we go? I will fly you to a doctor."

"Where did you learn English?" I asked him, as the Arab mob followed us toward the Storch and my burnt Spitfire.

"I used to live in Brooklyn," he answered. "It's a nice place." A humming roar grew in the air. We looked up and saw a formation of A-20's and the tiny specks of its thirty-six escorting P-40's heading toward the sun in the northeast. "Right on time," the German said, looking at his wrist watch. "Every hour they come. We will miss this one, but we will be in time for the next at ten o'clock."

We paused briefly by the hot, twisted metal that had been my Spitfire. "Not much left," the German smiled. "For you the war is over. How long have you been flying combat?"

"Long enough," I answered.

"I'm sure of that. They say you put up quite a fight. You killed one of my friends, you know, and burned another one badly."

"Only one," I snorted.

His mouth tightened. "It's war," he said, pointing due east. "One of yours died over there last night, about two miles away, just before sunset. He was a Spitfire pilot, too."

"Did he have red hair?" I asked quickly.

"I don't know." The German shrugged. "He burned."

Barney.

There was another German in the Storch. Together they helped me up into the cabin. "You Americans are just beginners," the first German called up to me from the ground. "You see these?" He tapped a medal ornament pinned to the lower right-hand front of his cotton tunic. "These are Spanish wings. I have been flying combat since 1937." He started to climb up into the cabin, but paused at the clamor of shouting Arabs behind him. "Oh, yes," he said, winking at me, "I almost forgot."

He turned, drew a billfold from an inside jacket pocket. The Arab I had given my red scarf to held out both hands greedily. The German drew forth a sheet of paper currency and handed it to him. The Arab straightened up from a bow, looked up at me and shrugged sympathetically, clutching the bill.

"Now, shall we go?" said the German pleasantly as he climbed into the tiny cabin and occupied the pilot's seat. As he started the motor I watched out through the cabin window. The twisted mass of my Spitfire had almost stopped smoldering. I figured it out. That had been a $20,000 airplane. Uncle Sam had paid $35,000 for me.

The three German planes I had destroyed that morning would have been worth at least another $60,000. That added up to $115,000 all gone to hell in twenty minutes.

As the Storch began to taxi, I looked back at the ragged mob huddled about the Arab wearing my red good-luck scarf. He was showing them the bill the German had given him. I could see it very clearly.

It was a thousand-franc note, German issue. One thousand francs. That's twenty dollars in our money. That's what I was worth now. Just twenty lousy bucks, Reichs cash on the line.

Chapter Thirteen

Major Smith was conscious that weary men in the doorways of buildings on either side of the loading yard of the Muskau glass factory watched him as he walked through. Though his shoulders felt welded together at the shoulder blades, he tried to hold them straight and conceal the misery of his lungs and weak feet. Frosted breath sparkled in his beard. His eyes watered as he stepped into the large smoke-saturated room in which so many had been bedded down for the night. Through deep soot he crossed to the men of Room 8 who had deserted their ledge for the draughty doorway.

"What block are you men? Oh, it's Nooky Nook. How are you boys getting along?"

Bob stopped touching his bare lacerated feet and looked up. "Need any raw hamburger, Major Smith?"

"Nope." Major Smith grinned and looked down at his own feet stirring in the soft soot. "Maybe we should have joined the infantry. Are all you men accounted for?"

Jim shrugged. "Fritz Heine is gone. Ed Greenway flopped out paralyzed. Bill Johnston left to see if Ed had been picked up."

Major Smith grated his teeth. "I don't want guesswork. Jim, you try and find them in this glass factory."

Jim stared up at him. Painfully he got to his feet. "Yes, sir." He inched his head around to peer through the smoke that blackened the huge room. "Jesus, Major. Last night Ed's legs wouldn't work any more. It happened maybe a block—maybe a mile from here. Do I look for him now in here?"

Major Smith nodded toward the north jet-black wall. "Try next door. Captain Daniels has set up some kind of hospital in there."

Jim lowered his voice. "Major, they're not marching us out of here today?"

"That's what they've got in mind. The Old Man is with them now." Major Smith led Jim a few steps toward the smoke-filled doorway. "We've got to keep track of every man from our old Block 162, Jim. The least we can do is remember where we left them."

"I'll never make it," Jim growled wearily. He looked toward the cold paleness of daylight beyond the smoky doorway. "How can they force us to go on?"

"Go find your two boys, Jim. That's all you've got to worry about right now. I've got to check with all the rest of the room Führers, if I can find them in this hole. Go find your two boys." Major Smith turned and walked away into the smoky depths of the huge room.

"You going to find Bill?" It was Jack Noble, his chubby face serious beside Jim.

"Yeah," Jim started limping toward the light.

"Well, he's carrying the salt. Get some from him, will you? Oatmeal is better with salt."

Jim turned away from Noble and stepped from the smoke out into the sharp cold of the fresh air. About to place his mittened hands over his instantly stinging ears, he suddenly stopped dead in his tracks on the trampled ice, his arms half lifted. He stayed, listening, trying to hear above the mumbling and shuffling of passing men in the factory yard.

"What's the matter, Jim?" Tom Howard came alongside carrying an empty glass flask, the product of the factory.

"Listen," Jim croaked hoarsely.

Tom listened a few seconds. "I don't hear anything."

Jim listened and cursed with low intensity. "Where are those Goddamned Russians?"

The only sounds were the crunching of boots of other prisoners wandering past and the low chatter of voices from a ragged queue of prisoners curving into the doorway of the next building ahead. The men in the line carried tin cans, glass beakers and flasks, buckets, tin canteens, and an assortment of other containers.

Tom's thin face pointed about experimentally like a dog's. "Can't hear any war going on around here today."

Jim's arms fell to his heavily padded sides. "What a hell of a time for them to stop! What kind of luck do we have, anyhow?"

Tom started forward. "C'm' on. I've got to get in that line for water. Maybe not such bad luck at that."

"How do you figure?"

Tom took a place at the rear of the line for water and looked fixedly ahead. "Suppose we had tried to make our escape back there the way we once planned it. If the Russians did stop, you and I would still be sitting and waiting in some snowbank. By now we'd be frozen as stiff as fish in a warehouse. I'll meet you inside if you're still in there by the time this line gets there."

Jim limped on up to the head of the line and tried to squeeze through a press of men at the doorway.

"Hey," someone in the line snarled, "wait in line like the rest of us for water!"

Jim turned and snapped back. "Who's getting water? What do you think I got? A rubber pocket?" Still grumpy, he faced one of two men obviously blocking the doorway and controlling the water queue. "Let me in, will you, Brownie? It's official business."

The big man named Brownie wore a stubborn face. "Everybody's got official business in here. It's the only place with decent heat. What's your business, Jim?"

"Major Smith sent me to look for two missing men."

"So what?" Brownie retorted. "There are lots of men missing on this trip."

Jim let go a big sigh, fighting down prickling irritation. "Look," he pleaded calmly, "the major ordered me to come over here and see if Danny has these guys. Is Captain Daniels in there?"

Brownie stepped aside to let five men out of the doorway carrying steaming containers of water. The other doorkeeper counted five men from the line in. "What's Major Smith so anxious to find these guys for?"

"How the hell do I know?" lied Jim. "I don't ask questions when Little X orders me to do something, do you?"

"Oh. Well, why didn't you say it was that kind of business?" The big red-faced officer pulled Jim through the doorway by an arm. "We can't let everybody in here, Jim. It's already too crowded, and those sick guys up there need room."

"Thanks, Brownie." Jim looked across the huge crowded room. Electric light sparkled against white tiled walls. "Where's Danny?"

"Up there."

Jim followed the five men who had been admitted to fetch water. Their way wound in a slow zigzag course between tightly packed squatting prisoners. A large white tile and chrome furnace rose out of a steel framework and platform in the middle of the mass of men. The din of hundreds of voices echoed back and forth between the tile walls. The air was hot, moist, and stifling. It smelled overwhelmingly of sweating bodies. The huge furnace towered monstrously above Jim in the glare and sound of the room. He pulled the thawing mittens from his hands and with fumbling weak fingers unbuttoned the front of his greatcoat.

"Where's Captain Daniels?" he shouted, leaning over a pack of men who sat with their backs pressed against the tile side of the room's center platform. One of the men cupped a hand about his ear. Jim leaned closer and shouted again. "Captain Daniels?" The seated prisoner pointed a finger straight up. Jim turned toward a short stairway, but looked down again at a tug on his greatcoat. The man pointed at the crowded platform and shook his head. He then pointed higher toward a wide metal catwalk which wound around the furnace twenty feet above. Jim nodded. "Thanks," he shouted. Men made grudging way for him as he picked his way up the stairway to the platform. He stood there a moment sucking great draughts of hot foul air into his sore lungs. He looked down at men filling their containers from the steaming sinks round the base of the round platform. The calves of his legs touched the closely seated prisoners. He felt dizzy from the heat. Once more he moved slowly, stepping gingerly between the packed bodies until he reached a steep ladder winding upward. Painfully, he pulled himself hand over hand up the corkscrew ladder.

"Off limits!" The speaker's face was close as Jim's eyes came level with the wide steel catwalk which curved around the great furnace.

"I want to see— Oh, hello, Mort." He recognized the librarian from Stalag Luft III and pulled himself up to sit on the warm hard surface of the steel catwalk.

"Hello, Jim," Mort answered. His short body stretched out naked from the waist down. His bare feet pointed toward the curving furnace wall. "This is off limits up here, Jim."

Jim looked to the right and left. In comparison to the rug of humanity which writhed down below, the catwalk was empty. Yet, side by side, like spokes of a wheel, men lay on the catwalk, their bare legs pointing in toward the smooth white wall of the furnace. "I'm looking for a couple of guys unaccounted for." He noticed the strange way the small librarian was cocking his head. "What's the matter, Mort? Something wrong with your neck?"

"No. Move over on this side of the hole, will you?"

Jim slid around the opening through which he had climbed to the catwalk.

"It's my legs," Mort said, grinning sheepishly from flat on his back. "I can't move them. Silly, isn't it?"

Jim stared at Mort's naked thighs until he became embarrassed. He looked ahead and back at the line of men stretched out nude from the waist down out of sight in both directions around the curve of the furnace. Most of them seemed to be asleep. Others stared wide-eyed toward the glare of the ceiling.

"It's some kind of paralysis," Mort explained self-consciously. "It's a funny thing. It hit a lot of us. Just after we got here last night. We just fell down and couldn't move our legs. Did you ever heaι of anything like that, Jim?"

Jim looked back at Mort's naked legs glowing healthily enough in the light. "Can't move 'em at all?"

"Can't even feel anything in them." Mort looked away from Jim's stare, chewing a lower lip. "Ever hear of anything like it before, Jim?"

Jim watched the kneeling figure of a prisoner who had come into view around the bend of the furnace. The kneeling prisoner began to massage one of the paralyzed men's bare legs. "It happened to one of the men from my room," Jim said. "I'm looking for him. Do you know Ed Greenway?"

"He may be around here somewhere," Mort answered. "It all seemed to happen just as we got here. You've done a lot of reading, Jim. What do you think caused it?"

"Gee, I don't know, Mort. But it won't last long. A thing like that couldn't."

Mort reached down and slapped his right thigh. "Absolutely dead, Jim." He chewed his lip again before going on. "I read a lot, too. I figure it's psychosis."

Jim tried to grin. "Aw, bullshit."

"No," the paralyzed man argued sincerely, "it's some kind of psychosis, all right. How'd you make out on that last stretch last night?"

"I almost didn't," Jim admitted.

"Something just seemed to keep you going in spite of yourself? That it?"

"Something like that. I almost didn't make it."

Mort's head nodded against the steel surface of the catwalk. "Your conscious mind keeps telling you you can't go on, that your legs can't march another step. But something else—your unconscious mind, it must be—makes your legs keep moving on and on and on, one step after another, because if they don't keep going you'll die. And then when you've reached where you are going, the unconscious mind says, "O.K., legs, you've made it. You can stop working. So they just stop. Just like that. That's the way I figure it."

Jim looked beyond Mort at the men lying peacefully upon the catwalk, silent in the roar of sound rising from the mob below. He spoke softly, almost unheard. "Maybe the unconscious mind is a lot wiser than the mind we control."

"It's all in the mind. I know that, Jim." Tears of quiet rage made the little librarian's eyes glisten softly. "And yet even knowing that—even knowing it's just in my mind—I can't seem to do a thing about it." Once again he slapped his bare thigh so that it quivered. "They're dead, Jim. They're absolutely dead. Just as dead as the rest of me will ever be."

Jim got awkwardly to his knees and placed a hand on the tormented man's arm. "They're not dead, Mort. You'll be all right. I'd better be looking for Greenway." He managed to get to his feet and stand in the heat waves from the furnace that shimmered all along the catwalk.

"Jim."

Jim looked inquiringly down at Mort, who was smiling slightly now.

"Don't forget what I told you," Mort said, looking up. "Be sure to hurry up with that Hemingway novel. There's a big list of guys waiting."

Jim grinned back. "I'll see you later, Mort. Take it easy."

Mort nodded, and Jim walked along the curving catwalk, holding onto an outer railing as he passed the ring of faces. He studied them one by one. Some of them he recognized, but he hurried past, embarrassed at the sight of these men lying helpless, limply nude from their hips down. He came abreast of the prisoner who was kneeling and massaging the legs of one of the stricken men. He paused to watch. The masseur, olive-drab shirtsleeves rolled up over long-sleeved underwear, continued to knead the unresisting thigh of the patient.

"Doing any good?" Jim asked cautiously.

"I just started," said the masseur. "Ask Captain Daniels. He's been doing this all night."

"All night!"

"Yeah," said the masseur, shrugging without ceasing his work. "How can you figure a guy like that? He rounded all these guys up, got 'em up here himself somehow. Oh, I guess a few guys helped him set this up. But Captain Daniels has been working ever since. Now me. I wasn't good for nothing last night. How about you?"

Jim remembered with horror and awe. "He must have had some sleep."

"Nope. Not a wink. First thing he did when the rest of us were corking out nine-tenths dead was get ahold of a wheelbarrow some-place and go out and gather up most of these guys where they dropped. How you feeling, son?" he asked the patient.

Jim moved on, the monotonous rumble from below the catwalk echoing over him like a weight. He passed several men who were rubbing the legs of others, and then he saw Ed Greenway. Somehow they all looked alike, Ed like the rest. Ed's short-cropped blond head rested on a folded blanket and his eyes were shut in sleep. His naked legs forked toward the furnace wall, rosy from recent rubbing and motionless.

Mission accomplished, Jim thought, looking down at his room-mate.

"Better let him sleep. Friend of yours, Jim?"

Captain Daniels stood there, short, stocky, eyes red but alert.

"From my room," Jim answered dully. "What's the score, Danny?"

"Shock, I think. All they need is rest." He moved past Jim on the catwalk. "C'm' on. I've got to keep busy."

Jim followed and squatted with Danny by another patient. "What if the goons march us on?"

Danny shrugged. "You can lead the horse to water." He pinched the leg of the patient. It jerked slightly in response. "You're coming around," he told the patient. "The nerves and muscles are beginning to revive."

"Not me," said the man, looking mildly belligerent. "I'm going to be one of those horses this time."

Jim stood up with Danny. "Danny, I hear you haven't had any sleep yourself."

Danny smiled. "We'll all get all the sleep we want someday. How's the tooth, Jim?"

Jim stared at the shorter man. "Oh, hell. You need any more help here?"

Danny motioned with his head toward the men who were kneeling from place to place along the catwalk. "We can handle it. These fellows know a little about the muscles and nerves. They learned it running the heat therapy room we set up back at the camp. We're getting along all right now, but thanks, Jim. Here." He brought a jar from a musette bag slung over his shoulder and poured some aspirin tablets into Jim's hand.

"I didn't come after aspirins."

"A toothache can ruin a man," Danny smiled. "That's just in case I get left here. You might have a hard time finding some."

Jim caught up with him; he was already kneeling down beside the next patient. "Why would you be left here?"

Danny poked carefully at various spots on a pair of thighs. "Somebody's got to stay with these fellows. They're my patients: Excuse me, will you now, Jim? I'm awfully busy."

Jim shoved the aspirins in his right greatcoat pocket, started to turn away, and turned back. "You figuring on setting up a practice in Spokane when you get back?"

Danny looked up from bending a limp leg at the knee with his hands. "If I ever get through medical school. That's my home."

"Well, that's only about three hundred miles from my home," Jim said seriously, "and if you ever need any business, Danny, you can yank my appendix out any time."

Danny bent over his patient. Jim walked somehow more easily, forgetting the stiffness, soreness, and weakness of his body. Starting down the spiral ladder through the hole in the steel floor he smiled through the grime on his beard stubble and gave a thumbs-up sign to Mort, who nodded.

Tom Howard waited at the bottom of the ladder holding the glass beaker now full of steaming water. He leaned close to Jim's ear and spoke loudly. "Find Greenway?" When Jim nodded, Tom called again over the noise of the huge throng. "Johnston is over there."

Jim, followed by Tom, began to work his way through the undergrowth of prisoners. Bill Johnston, face rosy and clean-shaven, was seated on the platform floor with his back pressed against the radiating side of the furnace.

"Howdy, Jim!" Bill called, looking up with lively brown eyes. "How'd you make out in the Black Hole last night?" He turned his head from side to side toward the men sitting next to him. "Fellas, this here is Jim Weis and Tom Howard, two of my former roommates."

"Former?" Jim shouted down.

"Yeah. I like it in here. We got steam heat. I've joined a new combo."

Jim looked down at the mocking face a moment. Then he shrugged. "Good enough. Who's your block commander now?"

Bill lifted his shoulders and pointed. "There he is over there."

Jim and Tom looked over toward the edge of the crowded platform where a black-haired, dark-complexioned officer wearing an overseas cap with a silver oak leaf pinned on it stood gazing over the multitude like Napoleon looking out from Elba. Jim grinned slightly. "Colonel Condon?"

"I guess that's his name."

Jim held out his hand toward the sitting former roommate. "You'll know it soon enough. Gimme some salt."

The sitting man winked sideways at his new companions. "Seems like everybody forgot to bring salt, don't it, fellas? What you got to trade for it, Jim?"

Jim's face lengthened. "We didn't forget. You volunteered to carry it for the room."

Bill put a hand to an ear. "What's that? I can't hear you?"

Stubbed face set grimly, Jim turned away. "C'm' on," he shouted above the babble. Tom followed.

Bill yelled after them as they started to pick their way through the press on the floor. "You still got that boogie with you?"

Tom held the flask of water ahead. "Here, you carry this, Jim." Jim took the flask and continued stepping ahead without looking back. Tom turned, reached Bill in two awkward but precise steps and bent over. There were cans, chocolate bars, soap, cigarettes, and two small open paper bags on the floor beneath Bill's propped-up knees. "Is this salt or sugar?" Tom asked loudly but calmly as he straightened up with one of the bags in his hand.

Bill started to get up. "Hey, you leave—"

Tom's right foot swung in a short arc landing just below Bill's ribs. Bill sat down, grasping his solar plexus, choked, coughed, and groaned. His rosy face turned violet. Tom dipped a finger in the paper bag and tasted it. "It's salt," he said, not loud enough to be heard over the tumultuous background.

The surrounding prisoners watched attentively. The man sitting on Bill's left put a hand on the kicked man's racking back and looked up accusingly. "That's a hell of a thing to do. Kick a man while he's sitting down."

"Yeah," called Tom, pouring a small quantity of the salt into his hand. "With feet as sore as mine it's hell." He handed the sack to the man next to Bill, turned, and walked away.

Jim waited at the top of the steps leading down from the platform into the mass of humanity on the main floor. "Where you been?" he shouted.

Tom took the flask of warm water from Jim and emptied his handful of salt into it. "Talked him out of some salt," he yelled back.

They started down through the press of men sitting on the steps. Halfway down they halted and listened to a change in the noise about them. There were almost imperceptible staccatos in the sounds tumbling from the gleaming walls. Yet they were enough to make them pause and look questioningly about. Jim saw a pointing arm in the wriggling lake of men before them. His eyes followed the arm's direction. Then he, too, pointed.

"Colonel Baker!" he yelled into Tom's ear. "And Pieber!"

The staccatos were shouts for quiet originating near the doorway where Lieutenant Pieber stood stiff and small beside Colonel Baker, who stood with arms raised.

"Quiet!" Jim yelled along with many others barely heard in the din of the place.

"Quiet! Quiet!" boomed out other voices just above the noise of the room.

"Quiet! Quiet! Aw, for Christ's sake, shut up, you guys!"

The stronger voices shut the weaker ones up. It became very quiet, like an empty swimming pool. The hundreds of listening exhausted men waited for Colonel Baker to speak.

"The order is!" He paused as though it were the end of a sentence. "We march on—" A great simultaneous groaning interrupted. The colonel lifted his long arms again, his hands waggling like semaphores for silence. The crisp voice clipped through the hot, smelly room and bounced around the gleaming walls. "We march in about one hour!"

Somebody broke the absolute silence that followed by starting to boo. It was slowly but magnificently picked up. The white room shook with the pressure of that terrible bellow of protest. It was a sickening sound that subsided only after Colonel Baker and Herr Pieber had turned and disappeared.

"Well," shouted Tom over the confusion of the lesser noises that followed, "here we go again."

"Yeah," murmured Jim, not loud enough for Tom to hear. Then he spoke louder. "Let's go back to the Black Hole and cook that oatmeal."

Together they picked their way toward the distant doorway. Jim glanced back once, not at Tom, who was following with the flask of warm water, but up above at the steel catwalk around the huge womb-shaped furnace.

Both men limped through the doorway.

Captain Daniels: "There I was. . . ."

Maybe it was from seeing *Men in White* or too many Doctor Kildare pictures, or maybe it was from reading *Magnificent Obsession*, but whatever it was, when I entered Washington State College I knew what I wanted to be. I had a magnificent obsession to be a doctor.

Instead I became a professional boxer.

That seems like an awful big difference, doesn't it? Instead of saying, "Calling Dr. Daniels!" it ended up, "Introducing . . . at 158½ pounds . . . the winnah of foahteen straight bouts by knock-outs . . . the outstahnding contender foah middleweight honahas . . . from Spokane, Wahhshingtonnn . . . Doc Daniels!"

The crowd in the American Legion stadium would roar. I'd wave at the movie stars and the directors and the agents at ringside, and dip my shoes in the resin box, and the bookies and tourists and the rainbow-clad mob of Los Angeles behind them would howl.

"Go get him, Doc!"

"Kill him tonight!"

"Slaughter him, Danny! We're with you!"

They were with me, all right, in their Palm Beach dinner jackets, race track sport coats and mink capes to protect them from the air conditioning system. And I was with them, right in the squared middle of nowhere just because I happened to take a P.E. course in boxing at W.S.C. and end up West Coast intercollegiate champ.

That and the money.

"Look at it this way, Doc," Harry Evers said to me across a steak-covered table at the Brown Derby the day after I took the title from U.S.C. "Here you are beating your brains out—oh, yes, you can do it with the eleven-ounce gloves—and for what? All you get out of it

206

is that big red W on your chest. Who pays your bills, kid? The alumni?"

"No," I told the silver-haired nice-mannered fight manager. "I pay my own bills, and I get free meals where I work."

"What kind of work, son?" Harry's teeth and twinkling eyes contrasted against his suntan.

"I clean off the tables and stack up the dishes. It's not so bad. I'm making out all right."

"Sure you are. You've got what it takes. But you know something, Doc? It takes cash to pay your way through medical school. Lots of cash. With me you can make that cash. What do you do in the summertime?"

"I get jobs picking fruit."

Harry pulled the cellophane from a big cigar. It had his name printed on it. "Doc, when is school let out? 'Bout two or three weeks? I'll tell you what you do. You come and spend the summer with me. I'll send you a plane ticket. I've got a place up at Big Bear Lake. We'll go up there, and I'll see to it you get the best of everything. Good food. Red meat. And training. We'll show you how to use the eight-ounce gloves. I'll get you a few fights when you're ready. Not right away, and not hard ones at first. You can see for yourself how you like it. I'll guarantee one thing, though. At the end of the summer you'll have more money than you'd ever save up picking fruit. All you'll have to pick up this summer is lettuce. The kind you can spend. What do you say?"

I looked at the easy smile and thought I saw easy money. "Well, I don't know. I want to be a doctor, not a fighter."

"Well"—he shrugged good-naturedly—"I don't want you to do anything you don't want to do yourself. But you think it over. Write to me." He pulled a card from inside his gabardine jacket and handed it across the table. "If you decide to come down, I'll show you how to pay your way through medical school in style. It's all up to you, Doc."

I went back to Pullman with the boxing squad, but Harry won. I flew back down to L.A. after school let out in two weeks. And Harry had told me the truth. We went up to his summer home at Big Bear Lake. It was nice. Everything was nice. The food was wonderful. The training wasn't easy, but I enjoyed it. I like to train, and pretty soon I felt better than I ever had before in my life.

Then came the registration for the draft. I was classified 1-A.

"This is the only way to beat it, Doc," Harry told me as we drove up in his convertible to the box-shaped ultramodern administration building of a big aircraft factory just south of L.A. "Now, don't you get in any lines in there. You just walk right up to the receptionist, give her my card, and tell her to call Mr. Wherrey. I've got it all fixed. It'll be some kind of job you like; it'll get you a deferment; and it won't interfere with your training."

They gave me a job taking the blood pressures for routine physical examinations of new employees. A lot of them even called me Doc. I was billed as Doc Daniels for my fights, too. One sports writer tagged me the Spokane Anesthetist. I put 'em to sleep in El Centro, Bakersfield, Tia Juana, and finally in the Legion Stadium in Hollywood.

But I wasn't getting much closer to becoming a doctor.

"Now look, Doc," Harry argued reasonably when I wanted to go back to Pullman for the fall quarter with even more money in my bank account than I had expected, "you're going over great now. The movie gang is going for you. They like a fighter with brains. And you're just beginning to make real money. I can get you main events pretty quick now, and picture work on the side."

"I've got to get back to school, Harry. It takes eight years of school to become a doctor and I've still got a long way to go, so I can't waste time."

"Now, Danny, I've got an idea. Why don't you go part time to U.S.C. or U.C.L.A.? They're good schools, and you can afford 'em. While you're going you can earn bigger and bigger purses at the Stadium and put away lots of that long green to pay your way into the best medical school in the country. Johns Hopkins, maybe. And besides"—he rocked the boat we were sitting in, casting his trout line into the rippling blue of Big Bear—"if you go back to Washington now, you'll not only be giving up all this easy scratch; you'll be quitting that defense job you have. That means you'll be 1-A again. Did you ever think how much time you can waste in the army?"

Harry won again. I stayed. I made a down payment on a second-hand yellow convertible with red leather seats so I could travel quickly between my apartment, the aircraft factory, night classes in Westwood, Big Bear Lake, the gym down on Main Street and the Legion Stadium on fight nights. Life was getting kind of complicated, but I kept winning fights, and I wore a gold wrist watch engraved from Jack Oakie.

"Danny," my pre-med adviser at U.C.L.A. said to me one evening when we were working out my schedule for a second semester of night classes, "I don't suppose this would interest you, but I'll tell you about it anyway. The Army Air Force has asked us to advise promising pre-medical majors of its new program. They are looking for qualified men to train as technicians in flight medicine. It's a comparatively new field and quite interesting. At least it is to me. Does it interest you?"

"I don't know," I answered truthfully. "Tell me about it, Doctor."

"Well, I really don't know a great deal about it myself, Danny." The professor smiled. "As I say, it's a comparatively new field, this flight medicine . . . a whole new science of specialized medicine growing up with the tremendous advance in aviation. The applicant, if accepted, would enlist as an aviation cadet and receive seventy-five dollars a month for one year's training. At the end of the training he would be commissioned as a second lieutenant and receive the pay for that grade. But what I thought you might be interested in, Danny, is that those who show promise during the one year's training will be eligible to apply for further medical training in flight surgery. In other words, the Air Force will put you through medical school, paying all your expenses plus an officer's salary. Well, I just thought I'd mention it. Here, you take this circular and look it over. Now, let's get at that schedule. . . ."

Look it over, he said. I looked it over and thought it over. It showed up in my training.

"What's the matter with you, Doc?" Harry asked me after a sparring partner almost floored me down at the gym one day. "You need a rest or something?"

I didn't tell Harry I had driven to March Field that afternoon and filled out all the forms to apply for aviation cadet flight-medicine technician training.

"Flight-medicine technician training," a red-faced lieutenant said, looking through a classification index. "Now what in hell would that be? Oh, yeah. Here it is. One-oh-six-four." He closed the book and called over to a sergeant typing out the forms. "Ten forty-six, Sergeant."

"Ten forty-six. Yes, sir."

They wished me good luck and told me I would be notified by mail. A whole month went by. I got through two more fights at the Stadium, both by knockouts.

"You're getting smooth, Doc," Harry told me in the dressing room. "You want to be champion? How'd you like to travel east with me? You want to be champ, Doc?"

I wanted to be a doctor. I didn't tell Harry when I received notice to report to March Field for a physical. It was November 8th. Election day.

"That's quite a build you got there," one of the doctors commented as he was about to give me a Schneider test. "You ought to be a prize fighter."

I didn't answer him, but it took my mind off of what he was saying as he instructed me how to step up and down on the chair for the Schneider test. He took my pulse and I started hopping up and down onto the chair.

"Hold it!" the doctor barked. "That's not what I told you to do. My God, you're stupid! I'll bet you voted for Roosevelt today. If you can't follow simple directions like that, how do you ever expect to be a pilot?"

"I don't," I answered. "I expect to be a doctor."

"Then what in hell are you doing taking a six-four?" he demanded, picking up my papers and squinting at them. "It says here 'aviation cadet.'"

"That's right." I felt embarrassed standing there in my skin. "Aviation cadet flight-medicine technician training."

"Oh." The doctor sighed. "That's a new one on me. Well, it probably doesn't take as many brains for that as for flying, so listen carefully while I tell you how to climb that chair again."

Once again I was told I'd be notified by mail. I waited and waited and waited. Christmas came, and I went home to Spokane to see my mom, leaving my address with the landlady so she could wire me if the appointment arrived. It didn't, and I went back to L.A., my defense job, night classes, and the Legion Stadium. I wasn't fighting so often now, but they were main events and brought in bigger money.

"This will be your last one in the Stadium," Harry told me, puffing his cigar while my hands were being taped. It was March 4th, Roosevelt's third inauguration day. "At least for a while. I'm laying you off, Doc, boy, until we get a fight back in the Big Garden. I'm working on it now, and it's almost set. What do you think of that?" He squeezed the muscles of my right shoulder.

"Harry," I said, looking down at the floor from my seat on the rubbing table, "you've been very good to me, and I don't want to hurt you. I wasn't going to tell you until after the fight, but I think I'd better now. Go over to my locker and take the envelope out of my inside pocket."

"What's the matter?" he asked, chewing the cigar as he crossed to the locker. "You in trouble, kid? If you are, don't worry about it. I can fix it—anything. What's the matter, Doc?"

"Look in the envelope, Harry."

I watched over my shoulder as he unfolded the paper and looked at it. He took the cigar from his tanned face, dropped it and stepped on it. He was looking at my orders to report to March Field for enlistment on March 13th. He shoved his hat back and scratched at his silver hair in bewilderment.

"Why? Danny. What is this? I don't understand how—how—" He looked right at me, a hurt look on his face. "Explain it to me, Danny."

"I should have told you before, Harry, but I wasn't sure I'd get the appointment. I didn't want you to talk me out of it, and I know you probably would have."

"But no, Doc. No." I thought his eyes blurred, or maybe mine. "I wouldn't talk you out of anything you want to do. But the air force. Aviation cadet training. I just don't understand it. I thought you wanted to be a doctor, not a pilot. I thought you were saving all your dough to go through medical school."

"It's not pilot training, Harry. It's flight medicine. If I do good I can get to be a flight surgeon, and Uncle Sam will pay for it."

"Oh, that's it." Harry absently reached out and placed the unfolded orders on the top shelf of my locker. "Well, Doc"—he crossed over and placed a hand on the towel at the back of my neck—"if you want it . . . I want it, too." He crossed to the door, spat thoughtfully on the floor and turned around. "Then this is our last fight. Make it a good one." He ran his fingers through his hair and set his hat on straight. "I'm going over to . . . out to get a cigar." He left, the door swinging slowly behind him and the noises from the arena rolling down the concrete corridor.

The main event was delayed while some movie star whose draft number was about due made a speech about national defense and got sworn into the Marine Corps in the middle of the ring. After that I climbed in and won the last fight by a knockout. Before I could climb out again I had to wait while the referee, who had been tipped off by Harry, announced that I, too, had joined up. I finally climbed out through the ropes with another gold wrist watch while the P.A. system bleated out "Off We Go into the Wild Blue Yonder" above the howling of the standing fight-night mob. It was a sendoff I hadn't counted on, and I guess I cried a little and had to get into the shower fast.

"Go in that room over there and strip for a six-four," a medical corps corporal directed at March Field.

"But I already had a six-four here four months ago," I explained.

"Go in that room and strip down," the corporal repeated. "You fly boys will be taking six-fours the rest of your lives, if you live that long."

"I'm not a fly boy," I insisted. "I'm for flight-medicine technician training."

"It says here you are an aviation cadet. Go strip down for the six-four."

This time I did the Schneider test without any mistakes. I received exactly the same treatment as all the other men reporting for duty even though they were all signed up for pilot training.

"Don't ask me, mister," one sergeant said to me. "If you're sent here, I just run you through. Better ask the major, if you get a chance."

"How do I get to see him?"

"Make an appointment. Next?"

Talk about an assembly line. The aircraft factory I had just left could have learned something from that one.

"Who's had previous service?" a fat master sergeant bawled at us, lined up outside the headquarters building.

"Here!" one of the men barked back.

"Rank?"

"Buck sergeant."

"All right, you're in charge of these civilians." The master sergeant handed the former buck sergeant a bulging manila envelope full of papers. "You'll board this bus here and proceed to the depot at

Riverside where your train passes through in about fifteen minutes, so step lively. Tallest men to the upper berths, two men to each lower berth. Food chits are in the envelope with the travel orders. Now move."

"Sergeant," I said, as the flashily attired flying cadets moved with their suitcases, "are you sure I'm supposed to be with these guys? They're for pilot training and I'm for flight-medicine training."

"What's your name?" he grunted looking at a list attached to a pinch board.

"Daniels."

"You're on the list. Get aboard."

"Could there be any mistake?"

"Mister"—he grinned—"one thing you may as well learn right now is that the army *don't make mistakes!*"

I got aboard. Fifteen minutes later I was sitting in a first class Pullman car well on my way at last to becoming a doctor.

Just after dark the next day the train stopped to let us off somewhere in the middle of nowhere in the middle of Texas.

"Pick 'em up, misters!" a cadet in blue uniform snapped. "On the double to that bus over there. On the double! That means run!"

We picked up our suitcases and ran. As the bus rolled along a straight highway across a moonlit flat land, the cadet in blue stood up beside the civilian driver and faced us.

"Now get this, you dodos. You're all dodos from now on. Remember that. You are dodos!"

"What's a dodo?" somebody asked.

"Sir!"

"Sir, what's a dodo?"

"A dodo is an extinct bird that flies in ever decreasing concentric circles until it disappears up its own asshole. Remember that! Until you dodos solo you are all *dodos!*"

The cadet officer sat down and started talking to the bus driver. I got up and made my way forward between piled-up suitcases until I got to him.

"Excuse me, I'd like to—"

"Sir!"

"Excuse me, sir—"

"Sir! Excuse me. You always say 'sir' first. Remember that!"

"Sir, I want to ask—"

"And underclassmen, especially dodos, don't speak until they're spoken to. *Remember that!*"

"But I—"

"Down, Dodo. Down, or I'll have to gig you."

The bus drove along a mile or so of high mesh fence bordering a dark airfield. The jumping and running, picking up and setting down of suitcases, and mercilessly barked orders picked up in tempo just as soon as we had piled out of the bus inside a guarded gate.

"Look," I started to say when I finally stood before an infantry major seated behind a desk in a room labeled Adjutant's Office.

"Mister Daniels," the tan-faced major admonished, looking down at my travel orders, "don't you even know enough yet to say 'sir' when addressing an officer?"

"Sir, I beg your pardon. But all I want to do is make sure I'm at the right place."

The major looked up with his mouth hanging open a few seconds before he spoke. Then he winked at the cadet standing near the door and laughed.

"Mister Daniels," he said. "You're in the right place all right. You're in the army now."

"Sir, what I mean is—well, all these other fellows are for flying training. Do you have a flight-medicine technician school here, too."

The major stopped laughing. "A what, mister?"

"I signed up for flight-medicine technician training."

The major's face seemed to pale beneath its tan. He sighed and leaned his forehead against the palm of his left hand. Then, very carefully, he lifted back the stapled pages of my orders, studying each one. Finally he looked up.

"Mister, you are a flying cadet. It says so right here. This is a primary flight training school, and you are assigned here for pilot training. It says that here, too."

"But, sir, I—"

"Yeah, don't tell me. Flight technical medical—what was it again?"

"Flight-medicine technician training."

"That's fine. That's just great." He stood up and turned to look out of a window into darkness. He turned again and rapped the sheaf of orders on the desk with his knuckles. "Mister Daniels, these orders say you are a flying cadet here for primary flight training. I'm assigning you a billet with the rest of the dodos. We may be able to straighten this out in the morning. But in the meantime, you had better act just like a dodo should or the upperclassmen will have your ass from hell to breakfast. Remember that. That's all."

An upperclassman ran us on the double with our suitcases and overcoats through the biting night between rows of barracks.

"Halt!" he roared. "You're going right past it. Barracks C. Get your heads out of your asses!"

I learned inside how to pop to and sound off and how to sing "The Eyes of Texas Are upon You" and a lot of other violent foolishness. After I finally climbed into cot Number 13 I didn't get much sleep that night. I felt like I had gotten myself into an awful mess.

"Captain Clark," the major said, walking ahead of me into the C.O.'s office the next morning. "This is the Mister Daniels who said he signed up for flight-medicine technician training and got sent here instead."

"Sit down," the young pilot wearing a leather jacket with silver wings stitched to it said. "I've been trying to figure out what could have happened. I think I've got it. It's quite simple, really." His freckled face broke into a grin. He was looking at a sheaf of mimeographed paper. "Here it is. Flight-medicine technician school. Classification number one-oh-six-four. Ten sixty-four." He picked up another sheaf of papers. "Now here are your orders, copies of your application, medical examinations and everything. They all read one-oh-four-six. Ten forty-six. That's flight training. Mister Daniels, whoever typed out your original application got the last two numbers of your classification turned around. Right from the start you have been processed for flight training."

"Well, I'll be damned!" commented the major.

I leaned forward in my chair. "Well, gee, then it's just a big mistake. Thank gosh. I was beginning to think I had been Shanghaied."

The major cleared his throat noisily.

"Mister," the captain said, "do you have any idea how hard it is to get an appointment for flight training?"

"No—sir."

"Well, let me tell you. After the two years of college requirement is taken care of, only one man in seven can pass the six-four physical."

"Yes, sir, but I want to be a doctor."

The whining of airplane engines starting up came through the open window.

"Look," the captain said patiently. "All your orders, records— even the original application—say ten forty-six. That's flight training. Aren't you interested in flying at all?"

"But, Captain, it's all just a mistake. They got the last two numbers twisted around. That's all."

The captain looked at the major. "That's all, he says. Just two numbers twisted around. At the recruiting office in Los Angeles. At March Field. At Air Force Headquarters in San Francisco. At this Air Force Headquarters at Randolph Field. At Air Force Headquarters in Washington. And right here." He turned to me. "Don't you understand, mister? You're in the army, and every record the army has of you in this great big world says exactly the same thing, and one thing only. Mister, you are now a flying cadet, and you are here for flight training! That's all there is to it."

"But I want to be a doctor. That's what I signed up for." I stood up in sort of a panic. "I've got to get out of here. How can I get out of here?"

The captain stood up too, and looked right into my face. "Mister, there's only one way any cadet leaves here without learning how to fly. That's to wash out. You've got a good chance at that, too. About half of the cadets do wash out."

I calmed down and heaved a big sigh. "What happens if I wash out?"

"Discharge. You'll be a civilian again. Then you can start all over again and apply for flight medicine or whatever it is." He looked at me sympathetically for a minute, while my mind was completely fogged up. "Don't take it so hard, Mr. Daniels. Flying isn't so bad. You might like it."

When the major and I got outside and were walking in the bright morning sun, I thought about the campus way up in Pullman, and I thought about Harry's hurt look in the dressing room at the Legion Stadium, and I remembered the roaring sendoff the crowd had given me just a few days before.

"All my life I've wanted to be a doctor," I complained to the major. "How could anyone make such a mistake? Getting two numbers twisted around."

"Son"—the major put an arm over my shoulders—"there's one

216

thing I think you have learned this morning. It'll stand you in good stead. And that is this: *The Army doesn't make mistakes!*"

And so I became a pilot. The captain was right. I liked it. I got to be a pretty good pilot. When the big fracas started I was in on the ground floor. I was a long way from being a doctor. I was a flight leader instead. But a bullet that hit my oxygen bottle and exploded it to blow my tail off over Malta put me back on the right track.

My flying and fighting days are over now. I've learned a lot about medicine practicing without a license in Stalag Luft III. Maybe I've done some good for others as well as myself.

Did you ever see a doctor with so many patients?

Maybe the major was right. *The Army doesn't make mistakes!*

Chapter Fourteen

The rebellion was quiet. Even the ordinary babble of voices quieted during the hour. For the most part the men simply stopped talking and sat around the bonfires. The rebellion was surly, born within fatigue-racked bodies. Among the seven remaining men of Room 8 dazedly eating watery oatmeal from tin cups, Bob Montgomery was the first to express the general decision.

"I'm not going," the Texan said, looking down past his tin cup at his broken-blistered feet.

Al Koczeck grunted, pouring more of the oatmeal from the fire-darkened flask into his cup. Jim set down his cup in the powdery layer of black soot on the floor beside him and stared into the red and black swirl of the fire. Occasional terse voices throughout the room blended into a murmur, but it was an oppressive sound, a noise of fear, disgust, and hate.

"I'll be damned if I will," Bob Montgomery continued. "I can't."

"They're crazy," Burt Salem said softly, his short body hunched on a seat of dirty bricks. "Crazy . . ."

Tom Howard stirred the thin oatmeal in his cup, carefully spat into it and poured the mixture over the ashes at the edge of the bonfire. "That was terrible," he said as he looked at the sickening slop. "Why didn't you make it a little thicker?"

Al Koczeck grunted. "Had to be thin to pour it out of the jug. What time is it?"

" 'Bout that time," answered Bob, "but I'm not going."

Koczeck gazed wearily about at a few figures moving from place to place in the gloom. "Some guys are getting their blanket rolls ready."

Fred Wolkowski kept his fingers wrapped around the warmth of his cup and swore. "Them God-damned eager beavers. You'd think they was working for the bastards."

Thunderbird peered thoughtfully through the haze at the few figures moving among the mass of unmoving men. He shut his eyes, shook his head slowly, and spoke in almost a whisper. He sighed. "I can't go on either."

Jim's bad tooth began to ache from the sugar in the oatmeal. He started to reach into his pocket for some aspirin, but gave it up.

Jack Noble looked morosely down at a small pile of boards beside the grimy bricks he was sitting on. His voice was raised in complaint. "If only they'd let us have enough time to make a sled."

The eight huddled in a circle. The smoke and the soft surly sounds of the weary floated over them toward the dull glow of the doorway and the terrible cold beyond. They sat and stared hopelessly into the fire or looked down at the soot. Major Smith limped up and lowered himself with difficulty beside them.

"Well, what do you think?" he asked slowly, his bearded face moving slowly as he looked at each in turn.

Koczeck grunted.

The major let his eyes rest on Jim's grimy downcast face. "There's going to be trouble this time."

Jim nodded dejectedly and spoke in a tired low voice. "There's always trouble."

Smith picked at a brick with a mittened forefinger. "The Old Man says everyone should try to go on—if possible."

Jim looked up, wrinkling his dirty forehead. "What's that mean?"

The major shrugged. "Yeah. Not many seem to think it's possible." He turned the brick over on its side in the soot.

"The goons will make it possible," Jim said bitterly. "They'll goose us out of here with guns."

"Not me, they won't," snarled Bob Montgomery. "I don't care if they shoot me."

"They will," Jim said seriously.

"Let 'em." Bob's lips remained tautly open, revealing tightly clenched teeth.

"Who cares?" wearily added Thunderbird from across the fire.

Major Smith picked up the brick and hefted it experimentally in his mittened hand. "You men all feel that way?"

Jim stared at the brick. "Aw, for Christ's sake, Major."

Major Smith's beard pointed one by one at each of the men in the circle. "How about you, Koczeck? You got a wife and son, haven't you?"

Koczeck paled beneath his dirty stubble. "If everybody goes on, I'll try, but it won't do any good. We won't last long out there." "Howard?"

Tom's thin face broke in a slight artificial smile, then he reached down and picked up a brick. One by one the circle slid bricks into place beside their throwing arms. Jack Noble looked wildly around the room, his lips quivering.

"There's no place to hide, Noble." Major Smith rose grunting in discomfort. "Personally, I'd rather take my chances in the cold, but this is a free country. Majority rules." He looked around at the smoke-laden crowd in the great room. "You can lead a horse to water . . . or slaughter." He looked down at the brick in his hand. "At least these make better ammunition than the rock gardens we set up back at Sagan."

"Crazy," Burt Salem muttered in awe. "Everybody's crazy."

Jim rose to his feet, ignoring the pain. "Major, surely not everybody wants this!"

The major shrugged. "Almost everybody. They say they can't march. They won't march. The Germans say we will. Do you think anyone is bluffing?"

"I say let's march on." Jim looked at the brick he had instinctively picked up when he rose. "Maybe we can't make it, but, Christ! it's a better shake than having a go at them with these."

The major shrugged again. "Any way you look at it, it's murder. When they come in that door and order us out, it's every man for himself. You can go out if you want to. You're in a good spot for it here." He nodded toward the smoky opening of the doorway and limped off through the sprawled pack of prisoners.

Smoke burned into Jim's eyes, and the hazy scene through his tears of frustration became even more blurred. "He doesn't mean that," he said loudly. "He's just trying to egg us into marching."

Bob, over his raw sore feet, muttered. "He ain't egging me into marching."

Jim wiped his eyes, leaving smears in the soot on his face, and looked down at the circle of men. Tom Howard and Al Koczeck looked thoughtful. Bob was openly defiant. Thunderbird sat with eyes closed, head drooping. Jack Noble stared back at Jim with bloodshot frightened eyes. Jim's toothache throbbed into his right ear, and he shook his head a little, biting the scab off his chapped lower lip so that blood ran down onto the stubble of his chin.

"I'm going to get my stuff in shape," Jim said, letting the brick fall from his hand with a thud. "I'm not counting on any bluff of a sit-down strike working here any more than it did back at Sagan."

Bob looked up with a sneer. "Who's bluffing?"

Jim turned and limped through the pack of prisoners sitting grimly about the fires across the great floor.

It was a wild idea back at Sagan and it won't work here, he thought bitterly to himself, remembering how they had all trimmed their vegetable gardens with rocks so that if the Germans ever decided to liquidate the prisoners, there would be something to fight back with. With a rage that burned through his exhaustion, he noticed as he zigzagged between the throng that each man had two or three bricks piled handily. It wasn't really putting up a fight. It was giving up. The accumulated sound of many voices was oppressive as he leaned against the rusted steel ladder leading up to the shelf where his blankets were. He looked up the ladder to where it disappeared over the ledge.

"Don't forget your artillery." Tom Howard nudged Jim with a brick.

Fred stood behind Tom. "You guys both go up the ladder a ways," he suggested, grinning strangely. "I'll pass some up and we can relay 'em over the top."

Jim grunted, hand over hand, one aching step at a time, up the rungs and passed his brick onto the ledge. Twisting painfully he reached down for the next brick passed up by Tom, who was half-way up the ladder. The three clung to the ladder until they had passed up eight bricks.

"Go up," Tom gasped, his thin dirty face twisted in torture. "I've . . . had it. . . ."

Jim nodded and pulled the throbbing hulk of pain that was his body up and over into the deep soot of the ledge. Tom and Fred followed, and they lay there on their bellies looking out over the crowded inferno beneath them.

"Now," Fred panted, "if it comes we can throw down on them."

"How about—" Jim sucked in a great burning lungful of smoke and warm air. "How about when we run out of bricks?"

Fred snorted amongst his panting. "We can piss on 'em."

They lay gasping and dizzy from their efforts. Other figures stirred on the crowded ledge.

After a bit, Jim wriggled to his feet, swayed slightly, and staggered past the charred black debris of last night's fire. He flopped on the spread-out blankets, and buried his face in his arms. He heard Tom and Fred flop down on either side.

"Going to make up our blanket rolls?" Tom asked discouragingly.

Jim's voice was muffled by the blankets and his sleeves. "What's the use?"

They lay silent in the smoke and the pressure of the constant grumble of the room. Jim's face pressed against the rough comfort of the blanket. Fred, with chin resting on overlapping fists, stared blankly at the nearby black wall backing the ledge. Tom, on his back, gazed up into the slowly churning smoke above. "What a place to end up," Tom said softly after a while. "A black hole in Muskau. No wild blue yonder, no bands playing, no soft music and sad songs, no . . ."

Tom sighed deeply. "Why don't they come?"

"Hey." Fred scowled at the wall. "Look over there."

Tom twisted slightly and looked disinterestedly toward the wall. "Isn't that an outlet?"

"What?" asked Tom, straining to make out anything against the sooty blackness of the wall.

"Looks like an electric outlet." Fred wriggled up onto his knees and moved on all fours through the soot. "I'll be damned. It is an outlet."

Fred shuffled back on all fours and turned around. "It is an outlet." He spoke softly. "If it works, what's to stop us from getting some use out of that canary we been packing?"

The three men looked at one another, new interest in their faces.

"What have we got to lose?" Fred asked. "You've been listening to the canary every night in camp, Jim. But, Christ! I haven't heard anything but goon radio in nearly two years. What have we got to lose?"

Jim bit at the wet scab of his lower lip and then got to his hands and knees. "Not a God-damned thing. Come on."

Sprawled prisoners on both sides watched as the three men knelt about the pack. Jim carefully brought out his manuscripts and personal belongings and handed them to Tom. "Put 'em over on the blanket. I knew I packed this thing all this way for some good reason."

"What do you mean?" Fred grinned. "I packed it the last few hours last night."

"You did?"

"I didn't think you'd remember."

"The hell you did!" Jim frowned in surprise and pulled the end of the cord out of the pack. "We can play it in the pack. Plug it in."

"Hey," a nearby Kriegie called, watching Fred plug in the cord, "you guys got a radio there?"

"Forget it," Jim snapped in a low voice. The Kriegie moved closer and squatted, watching.

"I hope it'll pick up BBC." Tom watched over Jim's shoulder as he fumbled with his hands inside the tin pack at the knobs of the set.

"If it works it'll get BBC." Jim twisted the dial knob slowly. Other prisoners moved up to form a silent kneeling semicircle about the operation.

"Where'd you get it?" a prisoner asked.

Fred grinned at the man wryly. "Swiped it."

"I didn't think you built it."

"Sh-h-h." Faint music came from the tin pack. Jim cautiously turned it up. It was a waltz, heavy on strings and crude on the beat. The men listened for a moment.

"What is it?" Tom asked.

"Goon music." Jim twisted the dial. The music faded to be replaced by a voice speaking a strange language. "That must be Czech or Magyar." He turned on past those stations, picked up static which crackled as the men listened attentively. More prisoners joined the curious circle. They bent forward when the radio suddenly blared out a series of rich chime notes. Jim quickly turned it down.

"What the hell is that?" asked Tom, kneeling close beside Jim. The pattern of the chimes repeated itself over and over: three quick notes of one pitch followed by an equally quick lower tone.

"Dit-dit-dit-dah!" Jim intoned in rhythm with the chime beats. "Dit-dit-dit-dah!"

The circling prisoners uttered sounds of excitement.

"V," Jim explained simply. "V for Victory. It's BBC."

"Dit-dit-dit-dah . . . dit-dit-dit-dah . . ." They listened to the chime pattern repeating itself monotonously.

Tom frowned, looking at the composed face of Jim. "Is that all they put out? Don't we get anything else?"

Jim shrugged and sighed. "It's between programs. They just play that when there's a lull to let you know they are still on the air. There'll be something else in a minute."

"Dit-dit-dit-dah . . . dit-dit-dit-dah . . ." It continued resonantly over and over.

"Get something else," Tom suggested impatiently. "Get another English station."

Jim crawled back from the pack and sat on the blankets. "You just have to wait, that's all. BBC is all there is out of England. They don't time their programs like American shows. When one ends you just have to wait until the next one starts."

"Dit-dit-dit-dah . . ."

Fred lay down beside Jim on the blankets and softly snorted. "V for Victory!" He made a gesture with the middle finger of his right hand. "I for Invasion."

Tom sprawled wearily on the blankets. The other prisoners remained kneeling. The chimes continued to beat, giving a pulse to the fatigued and eerie murmur that echoed throughout the great black room. The three friends lay there, their eyes focused on the door—far below beyond the ledge.

"Maybe they've changed their minds," Tom's voice was casual. "Maybe they're not coming."

Jim's voice was as casual. "They'll come."

Suddenly the V for Victory chimes stopped. The three rolled over onto their stomachs and fixed their gazes on the tin pack. A clear British voice spoke.

"This is BBC, the British Broadcasting Corporation. Before resuming our regular schedule of broadcasts here is a bulletin just received from the House of Commons.

"A few moments ago, in an address before the House, Foreign Secretary Anthony Eden issued a warning to the families and relatives of all prisoners of war being held in prison camps located in eastern Germany and Poland to be prepared for bad news.

"Mr. Eden told the House of Commons that Allied Intelligence has learned that P.O.W.'s in camps about to be liberated by the advancing Red Army are at this moment being force-marched westward across Germany. An estimated sixty thousand Allied soldiers and airmen are involved in the mass march, according to the report.

"These men have been on half-rations for nearly a year and are undernourished, Mr. Eden said. They are being forced to evacuate on foot through the coldest parts of Poland and Germany at the coldest time of the year. There will be casualties, Mr. Eden warned the relatives of prisoners. . . ."

Jim snorted and started to say something, but the men crowding around the pack hushed him. The voice went on:

"These men are being brutally marched on foot while Nazi railroad cars are traveling west from the east front empty, the Foreign Secretary said. Mr. Eden branded the Nazi officials responsible for the forced march as war criminals and said they will be held accountable for this terrible atrocity upon helpless unequipped and undernourished thousands of our captured forces. He charged that such treatment of prisoners of war is in direct violation of the Geneva Convention and said that protests have been forwarded to the Nazi government through the protecting powers in Switzerland and Sweden.

"Mr. Eden warned the relatives of prisoners who were being held in the areas of Breslau, Shubin, and in the Silesian concentration of prison camps about Sagan to be prepared for very bad news. The exact whereabouts of these men are not now known.

"For further details of Mr. Eden's message to the House of Commons listen to the next complete BBC news report in just fifty-five minutes. Now we present, by transcription, a portion of last night's concert by the London Symphony Orchestra playing . . ."

An explosion of voices drowned out the announcer. Fred yelled at Jim and Tom as they rolled over to sit on the blankets. "Jesus, they know about us!"

Jim smiled. Tom wrinkled his forehead in puzzlement. "How'd they find out so quick? Spies?"

Jim nodded. "Yeah, sixty thousand of them. Some canaries work both ways."

Fred, lying on his back, began to laugh.

"What's eating you?" asked Jim.

Fred stopped laughing, but grinned as he answered. "I don't hear a thing but goon radio for a year and a half, and then the first thing I get is V for Victory and some Limey son of a bitch telling me I'm bad off and unaccounted for. Prepare yourself for bad news, Ma. Your kid is in trouble again." The grin curled itself a little strangely and a globule of moisture rolled from the corner of his eye, washing a furrow through the soot.

They lay silent, waiting. Jim thoughtfully drew two aspirin tablets from his pocket, popped them into his mouth, and tried to swallow them before they disintegrated in his dry throat. He cleared it and swallowed twice before he spoke. "That does seem like a dumb thing to do."

"What?" Tom asked the question disinterestedly.

"Get our folks all upset. What's the point in that?"

Tom didn't answer for a while. Then he changed the subject. "Well, anyway, we got soft music." Eyes fixed on the doorway, he listened to the symphony behind him. "Funny thing. I never went for that kind of stuff before, but now it sounds better than Glenn Miller." Suddenly he stiffened and jerked forward onto his hands and knees facing the ledge. "Here it is!" His voice snapped Fred and Jim to sitting positions.

The three men and hundreds of others throughout the room below saw Lieutenant Pieber enter, followed by Colonel Akron and Colonel Baker.

Fred spoke quickly out of the side of his mouth. "Don't see any guards!"

Tom hurried forward on hands and knees through the soot toward the bricks they had left near the ladder.

The babble lessened abruptly but did not stop.

Jim spoke bitterly. "They'll be there."

Tom tossed a brick toward them. Jim grabbed it and passed it to Fred.

"Attention, men!" Colonel Baker's voice clipped out clearly, silencing the voices in the huge room.

Tom tossed another brick to Jim. Only the sound of moving men came up from below the ledge. The symphony music suddenly sounded loud behind them. Tom tossed another brick onto the blanket.

Colonel Baker's voice mumbled something down below, and the shorter figure of Colonel Akron stepped farther into the room.

Tom tossed two more bricks back and followed them onto the blanket with two more in his hands.

"Gentlemen." The senior American officer's voice rolled resonantly over the hushed room. The symphony music sounded clearly in the pause. Behind him, Lieutenant Pieber cocked his head sharply at the ledge.

Jim muttered between his clenched teeth. "Get in front of me while I turn that damned thing off!" Tom and Fred closed in as

Jim backed from between them and reached into the tin pack. The music stopped with a click.

The colonel's voice continued. "Please listen to what I have to say very closely." Pieber, one hand placed to the leather peak of his Luftwaffe cap, still peered upward toward the ledge as the colonel spoke. "I have told the Kommandant that most of us are in no condition to march on today. I have given the Kommandant my personal word that if we are allowed to stay over here and rest for one more night we will cooperate fully by all of us marching on willingly tomorrow!"

A buzz of chatter welled up into the smoke of the room. Colonel Baker, behind Colonel Akron, held his arms up for silence. The colonel continued. "Remember that I have given my word and am depending upon you, for the Kommandant has agreed!"

A brief instant of silence was followed by a sudden roar of disbelief. The colonel shouted above the noise: "The Kommandant has promised me that there will be no more marching at night and that after we get a good night's sleep tonight, we will proceed tomorrow in short easy daylight stages!"

Someone started the cheering which instantly exploded, filling the huge room with a roaring blast of noise. Prisoners, so exhausted they could scarcely move a moment before, suddenly screamed a great discord of relief at the tops of their aching lungs, pinched one another's sore arms, and slapped their weary backs.

Fred had hold of Tom's shoulder and was laughing with tears streaming down his dirty stubbled face. Jim slapped the thin unmoving back of Tom and yelled, "They're human, Tom!"

Tom turned calmly, leaned very close to Jim's face, and shouted, "Pieber heard the canary but he's leaving."

In turn with many others they squeezed down the ladder into the bedlam below and made their way to one of the fires near the doorway. There they collapsed in the soot. Major Smith motioned for silence.

"Hey, how about you guys shutting your tater traps for a minute? I am about to speak!"

Somebody deep in the throbbing mass shouted, "You tell 'em, Major!"

The major made a great business of noisily clearing his throat while the noise subsided. "Men! What I want to tell you is this. If your feet are awfully bad—by that I mean if they are blistered and broken-blistered and if you have blisters on the broken blisters— the Germans have given us adhesive tape. We can patch up the blisters. The line is forming outside the laboratory at the north end of the buildings. But don't go for it unless your feet are really bad. You will have to stand outside in the cold until we can take care of you." Major Smith turned and kept on going through the smoke-misty doorway.

Al Koczeck sprang weakly to his feet and followed the major.

Bob Montgomery grinned at Tom, Jim, and Fred around the fire. "Pieber is looking for you." He winced, pulling a heavy wool olive-drab sock up over the red bony bumps of his foot and ankle. "Wouldn't you know? To get sore feet fixed you got to stand in line!"

Thunderbird slowly stood up. "I'll walk up there with you." He turned and looked seriously down at the faces in the circle. "I'll see you Room 8 fellows again."

Little Burt Salem peered up at the large Negro. "You leavin' us permanent?"

Thunderbird nodded. "I've found my buddies. I'm going back with them."

Burt Salem drawled, "Hell, Thunderbird, you're welcome to stay with us!"

"Thanks. But they're my buddies. We've been together a long time now. But thanks, anyway." Thunderbird's teeth gleamed in a warm, sweeping smile. "I'll see you chaps later." Thunderbird helped Bob to his feet and together they limped away through the doorway. Another figure entered and approached the circle. It was Junior Jones, who kneeled in the soot facing Jim.

"I just left Shorty." Junior spoke breathlessly. "I've got some gen."

"Yeah," Jim answered, sighing. "Our people know we're marching. We heard it, too."

"Shorty picked that up, but that's not what I mean. It's the Russians. They've stopped!"

"What?" Jim leaned forward from his seat on the tin pack. "Pukka gen?"

"Pukka as it comes." Junior shrugged, unbearded face flushed. "Stalin's Order of the Day. Halted for regrouping, the communiqué called it. Jiggers, here comes Pieber." Junior sat back on his haunches.

Pieber's slight, stiff form loomed above them as he stepped out of the swirl of smoke, sound, and packed humanity. "Lieutenant Weis," he clipped downward, red flames reflecting in his spectacles, "what were you doing up on top of the brick ovens?"

Jim looked back up steadily from his seat on the tin pack. "Slept up there last night. By the way, Herr Pieber, I thought I heard a radio up there. Did you find it?"

Pieber glared down stiffly. The other men in the circle watched Jim and the German. After a moment Pieber made a gesture of petty annoyance with his gloved right hand. "Enjoy your rest, zhentlemen. You see? We are treating you well." He turned and walked briskly with a stream of limping Kriegies out through the doorway.

Jim sighed, slid his rump down off the tin pack into the soot, and leaned back. Junior, knowing nothing about the radio in the pack, bent forward to continue his report. "Yeah, they're regrouping back of the Oder River. They haven't advanced since three nights ago— since before we started to march." He noticed the utter weariness of Jim's face and looked down at the tin pack. "Kind of heavy, ain't it?"

Jim nodded. Beside him Fred grinned crookedly. "Getting heavier all the time. Guess we better help Noble build a sled."

Noble looked up from the assortment of boards he was fiddling with at his feet. "You're doggoned right. It's a good thing the Germans gave us time."

Junior Jones laughed. "The Germans didn't give us time. I got it straight from a guard. Blue Boy told me. You know why they're really letting us rest over?"

Jim lifted his head. "Because the Russians stopped coming?"

"Nope." Junior looked around. "The German guards gave out. The goons themselves are pooped! They couldn't march a mile! So we rest."

Tom hefted a brick thoughtfully in his right hand. He spoke softly. "It's a good thing." There was just a trace of a smile on his thin face. "People who live in glass factories shouldn't throw bricks." He tossed the brick. It landed in a puff of black soot near the edge of the fire.

Jim watched the soot settling over and around the brick. He grunted. "For a while I thought they were suddenly getting human." Idly he threw a handful of soot into the fire and watched it go up with the smoke.

Jim Weis: "There I was. . . ."

"He may be an ace, but he's no good," Barney once said in the operations hut of an RAF base in England. "I don't care if he is a Pole and hates the Germans. He had no business shooting that Jerry while he was dangling in his chute."

"He was absolutely right in killing him," I argued. "I don't hate the Jerries. Hell, I've been there. They're not so bad. But now they happen to be our enemies. Any way you can kill 'em is the right way. That free Pole did the right thing."

The argument got hot, with others taking sides. "There's an unwritten law among pilots of all lands," Barney argued. "It's a sort of Knighthood of the Air. You just don't shoot each other in parachutes."

I thought I had him. "Would you shoot a man in a chute if he was a Jap?"

"Aw, hell. That's different. A Jap ain't a man. At least a German is human."

We finally took the argument to Squadron Leader Haviland-Keith, the oldest fighter pilot around. "How do you mean?" the Yorkshire ace asked. "You mean over England or over enemy territory?"

"What difference does that make?" asked Barney.

"All the difference," the older man explained. "If it's over England, why shoot him in his parachute? He'll land and be captured, and maybe Intelligence can learn something from him. But if it's over occupied land or Germany, why certainly. Go ahead. Shoot the bastard. If you don't, he'll only be up after you again the next day—and he'll be a harder Jerry to deal with. Why give him a second chance to kill you?"

"But, sir," Barney pleaded, "wouldn't that just make the Jerries madder at us? Shooting them down helpless like that?"

"Not at all. If you didn't do it when you had the chance—without exposing your own tail—the Jerry would just laugh at you and say you were weak. No, chappies, don't ever give Jerry a second chance if you can get him without getting killed yourself."

That was one way of thinking of the enemy. He would laugh at you and think you were weak if you didn't kill him in his chute. But there were lots of opinions about Jerry. For instance, I really believed all the talk about concentration camps was just propaganda to make us fight. I really had quite a high regard for the enemy. One day, still in England, a bunch of us were down at the pistol range getting some practice in with our side arms.

"What in hell do you expect to do with that?" I asked, laughing, when Barney started firing a tiny .22 caliber automatic you could hardly see in his big hand.

"This may come in handy," Barney answered, grinning. "It fits in my boot. If I ever get shot down and captured, I might be able to use this to escape."

"You're dreaming," I sneered. "What do you think the Germans are? Stupid? They'd look in your boot right off."

"It doesn't hurt to carry it," Barney said, as the little automatic kept popping at the target. "It may come in handy, and it doesn't weigh much." He had to move much closer and try again because the target was out of range.

That was another way of looking at the enemy. Either you thought he was stupid, or you thought he wasn't. Once I saw a shot-down German pilot brought under guard up some stairs to be interrogated by a British intelligence officer.

"Heil Hitler," snapped the cocky German.

Whap! The British officer smacked his fist into the German's jaw and knocked him bouncing and tumbling all the way back down the stairs. "Now, come back up here, you bastardly Hun," roared the Limey, "and don't you ever say that dirty word in England!"

You could think of the German as a Hun, or you could feel sorry for him. Neither Barney nor I ever got to feeling about the enemy as the Poles and the British did, but then they had never dropped bombs on our homes or burned our cities or imprisoned our relatives or pushed us bleeding into the sea.

"By golly," Barney said one day while we were holding shaking cigarettes beside his Spitfire on an airfield in North Africa, "you can say one thing for the Jerries. They sure got guts." A whole squadron of us had just been sent wheeling and dodging in high pandemonium by one lone Messerschmitt which attacked from below and then casually climbed off up into the sun.

"They sure have," I agreed.

You think and imagine all sorts of things about the enemy as you approach the day of acquaintance.

"Did you see Barney?" I asked one night, interrupting Kenworth as he was telling a group of boys how he got his fifth victory a few moments before.

He lowered his hands for a moment, thinking carefully. "No, Jim, I didn't." He raised his hands and continued. "I was right behind this Focke-Wulf. I knew I had him because he was smoking like mad, and I was close enough behind to see flames coming out of his cowl. I was just starting to give him another burst, when I had to stop. The pilot was climbing out of the cockpit to bail out. But when he starts to sink back into the cockpit, I push the teat again. This time he really gets out, and I stop shooting to give him a chance to jump. Jeez, I'd have felt bad if I'd have hit him."

"Why?" I wanted to know. "Why let him bail out over his own airport?"

"I'd have felt bad, that's all. Jeez, I wouldn't want to shoot a poor devil who was trying to bail out. What good would that do? I got the victory anyway."

Mark up one score for Kenworth, and one score for the enemy. Nobody saw Barney.

I thought a lot about Barney next morning, sitting behind a German gunner and a German pilot in the Fiesler Storch. I sat there on the floor of the small sunny glass-enclosed cabin looking at the back of the pilot's head and the side of the head of the gunner who was absorbed in scanning the blazing morning sky for any sign of his enemies, my friends. I kept looking from those unsuspecting heads, the dark one of the pilot looking straight ahead on its skinny neck and the blond red-cheeked one of the gunner staring far out, anywhere but at me. And I kept looking down at my black right flying boot with my blood coloring the sheepskin bulging at its top.

Did I think the enemy was stupid? They hadn't looked in my

boots! Why, oh, why didn't I have a little .25-caliber gun hidden in my boot? I could pull it out now. Neither the pilot nor gunner was watching. I could pull it out, put it up toward the head of the gunner, and pull the trigger. Then I could move forward two yards, jam it against the hollow just above that pilot's skinny neck, reach forward to grab the stick, and pull the trigger. Then I could sit on the pilot's lap and fly a captured German plane back across our lines and land it with two German corpses in it.

Wouldn't that be something? Two destroyed. Two damaged. One probably destroyed. One Fiesler Storch captured, its crew killed. All in one morning's work. Only, I didn't have a gun in my boot. I hadn't thought the enemy stupid enough not to look in a captured man's boots. I wondered about Barney, missing, same area, just last night. What had he done with the gun in his boot?

The German with the skinny neck guided his Storch low over the desert, twice zooming to pass over pole-strung power lines.

"Do you always fly out after shot-down planes?" I asked as he and the gunner helped me limping across the short dirt strip upon which he had landed the Storch.

"Ja," he said cockily. "It is what you call a rest for me. I am a Jaeger. A fighter pilot."

The gunner and the pilot still supported me by my arms as they stiffened to attention and snapped a salute to a khaki-clad German officer sitting in a folding chair beneath a canvas umbrella. Other Germans sprawled in chairs about the handsome dark officer, who was wearing a Maltese cross snug beneath his tanned chin, suspended by a red, white, and black ribbon. The Storch pilot reported in rapid German, too rapid for me. The important German regarded me and asked a question in German. An interpreter standing beside him put the question to me.

"Hauptmann Baedel congratulates you on your fight and wishes to know if you are an American ace."

I looked down at the swarthy confident set of the handsome officer's face. "Tell him I can only tell my name, rank, and serial number."

The Hauptmann nodded when relayed this, and motioned for a chair to be brought up. I sat down while the Hauptmann put another question to the interpreter. "And who is your leading ace now?"

"Sailor Malan."

"How many victories, please?"

"Thirty-two . . . not counting probables." I looked over my shoulder toward the field and the sleek blue-mottled Messerschmitt 109G's and Focke-Wulf 190's carefully dispersed, with tan coveralled group crews peacefully working on them. The Hauptmann chuckled.

"Hauptmann Baedel has shot down twice that many," the interpreter offered. "He has shot down sixty-five planes." The Hauptmann shrugged modestly and said something. The interpreter reflected his modesty. "Of course, that includes Russian planes on the Ostfront. You will notice he has been decorated with the Ritterkreuz—Knight's Cross and Oak Leaf."

"Perhaps you will join us for lunch."

I could hardly believe my eyes. An orderly with a tray was passing out plates full of food. Real china plates with real knives, forks, and spoons. When they handed one to me, I found it heaped with chicken and rice, steaming and delicious, and we were served fresh lemonade in clear glasses. Those Germans were living in style.

"You remember me, ja?" A square-faced grinning German with wide-spaced teeth and wearing a canvas cap stood before me, eating from a plate in his hand. "Schwarz Zwei? Ve almost go boomp up da?"

Schwarz Zwei. I remembered my high-school German. Black Two. "Yeah, I remember you." The shape of his mouth was actually familiar from that goggled head in the cockpit that had shot past mine inches away.

"Vy you do dot? Vas war you doing so near?"

I leered up at the grinning face. "I was trying to ram you."

"Was?" He looked over to the interpreter, who explained it back to him in German. "Aha!" he grinned evilly. "But you don't did it? Vy you don't boomp me? I let you!"

"I changed my mind."

"Aha! I sink so. Ja, I sink so."

I had lost my flying helmet in the crash. The noontime African sun was beating down on me. Blood was still oozing slowly out of holes in my legs and rear end. In spite of the numbing sting of my butt, I could feel that my shorts were wet with blood.

This can't be true, I kept thinking to myself, gazing round at the half curious cluster of the enemy munching chicken and rice. It could happen to a lot of other guys, but not to me. But it was happening.

"You should have kept turning," another nice looking sun-tanned youth said to me with only a slight pleasant accent. "You almost got away from us. If you had kept turning we would never have got you."

I should have kept turning. I should have carried a pistol in my boot. I should have checked the throttle before take-off. I should have gone home after fifty missions.

Somebody took the empty plate from me, and the Hauptmann with the Ritterkreuz was saying something. "Here comes one of the gentlemen you shot down," the interpreter told me. "He wanted to have a look at you."

He came limping toward me across the yellow ground, half supported, half carried by two straining tan-clad soldiers. His hands, swathed hugely in white bandages, dangled from supported forearms. His face, bright violet from some coating of medicine, grimaced horribly from pain. Brought and held up before me, he looked down out of eyes rimmed with white where his goggles had been. "Which one was he?" I asked looking up into the brightly colored distorted face.

"The Focke-Wulf you attacked first," said the interpreter. "You set him afire, but he flew back here and landed just the same. He is a very good pilot."

I snorted a little. This was the enemy I had gotten into trouble over, the one I had left smoking to fight another day, the one who had turned around and, still smoking, taken a shot at me. Suddenly the injured German began to quiver there in his blue and white striped hospital robe. Sounds blasted from his cracked and purple mouth. He was cursing. I don't know what he was saying, but he was cursing, spit foaming on his lips. He cursed and cursed, and spat into my lap.

"Achtung!" The decorated Hauptmann barked the order from his folding chair. Instantly the injured German stood stiffly at attention, bandaged hands at his sides, the two soldiers still supporting him. The Hauptmann let fly with a stream of guttural rage. The purple-faced German stood there, taking it. Eventually the Hauptmann snorted out an order and dismissed the three men with a wave of the hand.

"We apologize for that man's conduct," the interpreter said to me. "You see, he is quite badly burned and in pain, and is not responsible for what he was saying to you."

"What was he saying?"

The interpreter smiled. "It was not very gentlemanlike. Hauptmann Baedel has placed him under arrest."

How about that? He tried his damnedest upstairs to kill me after I tried my damnedest to kill him. He was the one responsible for getting me into this mess—Christ knows how long I'll be a prisoner before the war ends—and now he gets put under arrest for spitting in my lap. A strange breed of cats, these Germans.

I heard a sudden sharp report, like a cannon cracker. I looked around in time to see two white balls of fire arching with tails of black smoke into the bright sunny air. The interpreter looked at a watch on his brown wrist. "Your friends are coming again. Right on time. This time you will enjoy the bombing with us from down here, nicht?"

I didn't like the idea a bit. I'd been through bombings in England and Algiers, but not the kind we were delivering every hour on the hour on La Fauconnerie. It's one thing to be sitting at ten, fifteen, or twenty thousand feet looking down at tiny red and yellow flashes that instantly become a small orchard of little smoke puffs, and another thing to be waiting down below to find out just how big that orchard of high explosives and hot piercing steel really is.

"The Kommandant wants to meet you," the interpreter told me, as the enemy pilots came alive, dashing across the field, scrambling for their fighter planes to meet their enemies, my friends. "So we are going to send you upstairs to fly you over to the other field."

"What other field?"

"Ach, there are four airfields here at La Fauconnerie. Didn't you know that?" I had forgotten. "This time you will be upstairs where it is safe. Next hour you can enjoy the bombing that will surely come."

They helped me to limp across a corner of the field, blond young enemies patiently and considerately supporting me by my arms.

"Kom. Ve hef time. I show you vot you do vis me." Schwarz Zwei, grinning out of his square face, said something to the Germans holding me up and we vectored slightly toward a parked Messerschmitt, its engine exposed because the cowling had been removed. "Looking," he said, pointing at a neat little hole in the top blade of three propeller blades. "Here is wo you shooted me. It is much besser zat ve didn't boomp, nichtwahr?"

236

I looked at the black propeller blade with its .30-caliber hole, at the big black 2 on the side of the beautiful fighter plane, at a small black wolf's head painted beneath the removed cowling, a wolf with forked tongue of red jagged lightning over the small numbers 77. I also saw three tiny white stars and five red stars painted under the edge of the opened cockpit.

"You should haf continued to turning." Schwarz Zwei clucked his tongue admonishingly. "Nun. Aufwiedersehen. I must go op so die boombs won't to get my Messerschmitt." Schwarz Zwei climbed into the cockpit of the cowl-less fighter and we passed on. Planes were roaring up from the ground now, retracting wheels slapping into place, fine desert sand burbling back in thick yellow clouds. Energizers whined, motors coughed to life. I saw Schwarz Zwei taxi by, the innards of his motor still exposed. Everything that could fly was taking off. The Fiesler Storch was already up, circling the field at about three hundred feet. The idea seemed to be to get everything in the air, fully repaired or not, as long as it would fly. They lifted me into the cabin of a yellow camouflaged Focke-Wulf twin-engined trainer, and quickly we were airborne, airfield and desert wheeling slowly below. The pilot, a youth in his teens, grinned impishly, pointing upward into the sun. "Nicht gut . . . wenn sie kommen."

A German sitting behind me and I peered up into the sun, seeing nothing, hoping nobody up there was seeing us. The pilot nudged me and pointed downward, grinning. There it was, closer than I had ever seen it before, just a few hundred feet straight below—an orchard of bomb bursts, full, jagged, and stationary, lights blinking yellow and red in the smoke puffs. The pilot banked us steeply over the sudden inferno below, cut the throttle, lowered wheels and flaps, and glided swiftly toward a runway which was reappearing beneath thinning smoke and dust. We touched and rolled crazily and recklessly along the bombed field. As the plane rumbled to a stop, a German appeared from out of a slit trench waving frantically for us to get the hell off his field, but the young pilot beside me just grinned some more, taxied between a couple of bomb craters toward the waving figure, slapped on the brakes hard enough to lift the tail a little, and switched off the engines.

There was a lot of chatter in German as they helped me down out of the trainer. Eventually a brown painted Ford V-8 sedan drove up in a swirl of dust. They put me in it and drove me off the field, which was beginning to come alive with men appearing from slit trenches.

"Have you had lunch?" one of three officers seated in a canvas-walled enclosure asked me pleasantly in perfect Oxford English. All three of the officers wore Ritterkreuze at their throats and were eating chicken and rice.

"Yes, I have. Just a few moments ago."

"Then sit down and have some lemonade." The speaker, a young dark handsome man wearing shorts, pulled a canvas-backed folding chair out from the table for me. "Are you wounded badly?"

"Not so bad."

"You are a Spitfire fighter." He smiled admiringly. "A fine airplane. I have engaged many of them—oh, I can't tell you how many Spitfires in combat. See?" He pulled his shirt tail out of his khaki shorts to show a deep scar in his waist. "A Spitfire did that to me. Lieutenant Weis, this is our Kommandant, Colonel Wermuth, and Colonel Nokoli." The two older officers, who apparently did not speak English, nodded and continued with their eating. "And my name is Major Fillip. You may have heard of me. Do you have an American cigarette?"

I passed Chesterfields around. The two older officers laid theirs carefully beside their plates. Fillip produced a rope lighter for his and mine. One wall of the small open enclosure was formed by the back of a camouflaged trailer, the roof of which supported radio and radar antennae. A face appeared at a small window, and some words were exchanged with the officers sitting with me at the table.

"You need not feel too badly." Fillip smiled at me. "It has just been confirmed that you were shot down by Reinert, our leading ace in North Africa. You are his 135th victory."

I set my glass of lemonade down to keep from spilling it. "One hundred and thirty-fifth!"

"Does that surprise you? It is not unusual in the Luftwaffe. I have a cousin who has shot down more than that. He is up in France now. We are not amateurs, my friend. Our aces have been much more successful, I think, than yours."

"Sure," I said. "That's why you are losing."

"Oh, but we are not losing. We are winning." He broke into a radiant smile and shrugged. "But have you not noticed? Both sides always think they are winning. Otherwise they would stop fighting and there would be no more war. Perhaps you are lucky."

"How do you mean?"

"For you, the war is over."

For more than a year you try to kill Germans and they try to kill you. Then you find yourself sitting in the sunshine, sipping lemonade with them and making small talk. What do you think of the German now? Is he an idiot landing an airplane on a field still smoking and pock-marked with bomb craters? Is he a vain strutter still proud of his Spanish wings won six years before? Is he a hot-tempered man unable to control himself before the man who burned him in fair combat? Is he the arrogant leader eager to match his score with that of his enemy? Or is he the confident, pleasant fellow, hospitable to his conquered foe and exchanging the philosophy of war?

"You will not attempt to escape?" Fillip asked me as he aided me limping toward a slit trench for the next on-the-hour bombing raid. "If you do, we will simply have to shoot you, and that would be a pity. It would be quite useless, you know." He and an enlisted German lowered me carefully into the seven-foot-deep slit trench.

"Where did you learn to speak English?" I asked him as he slid down into the dusty trench with me.

"In England." A far-away look came into his dark eyes. "I went to a university there. I have an English fiancée, a nurse . . . but then I suppose that is all over now. What do you think? Would an English girl wait for me?"

"No."

"No, I suppose not. War is a bad thing. But then I think she has heard of me. The English pilots were very much afraid of me, I think, last year and the year before. Fillip was a name well known to the English. Have you heard of me, perhaps?"

"How many did you shoot down?" I countered.

"One hundred and seven. Mostly Spitfires." He smiled. "I think perhaps my fiancée has been hearing of me."

About that time the flak guns around the slit trench began going off, spitting their puff balls high up over our heads.

"There they are." The German ace pointed up toward the specks of the formation approaching from the southwest. The roar filled the sky and pressed down into the slit trench. The fighters were tiny weaving gnats round the larger, closer formation of the bombers. They came on relentlessly through the sky full of flak bursts. "Keep your head down!" He didn't have to tell me. The ground jiggled with the tremendous surrounding blast of bombs. One blast . . . two blasts . . . three blasts . . . four blasts . . . somewhere outside the slit trench, thank Christ! Then all was quiet except for the fading moan of the squadrons, and the tinkle of flak fragments returning to earth. "How did you like that?" Fillip asked, smiling. "I'd like it a hell of a lot better up there than down here." "Yes." He nodded sadly. "I can no longer fly." He tapped the part of his shirt that covered the scar he showed me earlier. "I am grounded because of what a Spitfire did to me last year."

They took me to a field hospital in a cool grove of orange trees. The doctor, after he had tended minor wounds of Germans injured in the bombing, placed a dressing on my left thigh and pinned a tag to my jacket instructing the Luftwaffe hospital in Tunis to remove the splinters. They opened up an army cot for me in front of the main entrance of a mansion in another orchard. It was the headquarters building for the four airfields of La Fauconnerie.

"This is the pilot who shot you down," Fillip told me, leading closer a slim, serious-looking fellow who had been watching me from a distance. "Obergefreiter Reinert. Lieutenant Weis." My nemesis nodded coolly.

"He is not an officer?" I asked from flat upon my back.

Fillip laughed and said something to Reinert before turning back to me. "No. He is what you would call a sergeant."

"Well, tell him that in my army if he had knocked down 135 planes he would be a general."

Fillip obviously enjoyed relaying the message. Reinert looked embarrassed, saluted casually, and walked off. "He is not a professional soldier," Fillip explained. "When there is no war, he works in business. However, soon he may be given a commission. It is different with us, you see. Our military is quite different."

Quite. The air raids came every hour. Each time now they would help me limp over under the branches of a nearby tree for protection from falling flak pieces. At dinnertime I was sitting in the darkness on my cot, eating open-face corned deermeat sandwiches and drinking hot spiced wine when Fillip came out of the headquarters wearing a white calfskin jacket. "We may have some company for you. Another American Spitfire was shot down on that last raid."

I felt I could use a little American company, but I wasn't to get it. A few minutes later Fillip came out again. "It's too bad. He was killed. I have been asked to invite you. Would you like to come in and join us for a little wine?"

It was getting pretty cold outside. As Fillip carefully helped me toward the door he explained the invitation. "The wine is being bought by the pilot who just shot down this last Spitfire. He feels grateful toward Americans. Last night some American stopped shooting long enough to let him parachute out. He is very grateful."

We went in and drank wine. Germans are just like anybody else when they're drinking wine.

Chapter Fifteen

The Germans had told the truth. They kept their promise. For a day and a half the survivors of Stalag Luft III had marched in short easy stages across frozen Germany from Muskau in the general direction of Berlin. It had been easy the night before to tell in which direction Berlin lay.

"Holy smoke! Listen to that!" Tom had said close to Jim's ear where they lay bundled up together in the luxurious dusty straw of a village barn the first night beyond Muskau. Hundreds of prisoners jammed together in the loft and on the ground floor of the tiny barn listened in silent awe to the hour-long pounding Berlin was taking. It made the wooden walls of the barn creak and the earth tremble.

It was the second night of complete rest. The first was the night of reprieve at Muskau when most of the prisoners turned in early, thankful to God for another night of shelter in the great black smoke-filled room, while others sat around comfortable bonfires on the main floor chatting and mumbling to the popping of burning wood. Jack Noble had been the hero of Room 8, for Noble had located bales of cottony fiber-glass insulation somewhere in the maze of the glass factory and it had made a downy mattress upon which the seven survivors of the combine found sorely needed comfort. They had become used to the smoke of the black room. It was Noble, too, who became the hero of the next day.

"Come on out in the yard," he had invited them just a couple of hours before the march from Muskau was to begin again. "Bring your stuff and I'll show you how it works."

Outside, they piled their belongings on the sled that Noble had designed. They found to their delight that two men could pull the heavily loaded sled over the ice with ease.

"It sure beats the hell out of toting it on our backs," Fred Wolkowski said happily a few miles out of Muskau when he and Jim took their turn at the hauling rope.

"Yeah." Jim was thinking about the catwalk high up on the furnace in the tiled room back at Muskau and the men still stretched out helplessly around it when the time came to march on.

"You don't have to stay, do you, Danny?" he had asked when paying his farewell visit to Ed Greenway.

"We'll be all right," Danny said softly so that his patients wouldn't overhear. "I'm afraid of what the Germans might do to these guys if somebody didn't stay to take care of them. I don't think the Germans want to fool with them."

"You think the goons might—"

Danny smiled and interrupted. " 'Liquidate' is the word. Yes, I think they might if we just leave them here helpless. They were pretty sore when we told them these guys couldn't go on. But if I stay to take care of them and maybe put up an argument—"

"But, Jesus! Danny. They're liable to—"

"Sh-h-h. One man on his feet can reason with them better than three hundred flat on their backs."

"Three hundred?"

"That's about how many there are."

So they had left Danny and his three hundred patients high up on the catwalk and formed into line once again in the gray midmorning light. They had wound slowly, an endless snake of ragged but rested men, out of the sprawling factory district of Muskau. The column twisted over hills and along the banks of frozen streams, past white-shrouded country estates and even a castle where they had waved and shouted to English prisoners, billeted in the neat cobblestoned horse stables. Once a shock rippled like cold lightning through the column.

"That's what they say. Twenty-seven hundred. It couldn't be!"

But the cold lightning shock twisted through the chilled breasts of the marchers for many a kilometer onward after the shouted news that twenty-seven hundred men were lost in the blizzard before Muskau.

Major Peter Smith: "There I was. . ."

What now?

I think that was the first question I asked, looking around the breakfast table at my wife and two little girls in our home in Texas when the news came over the radio that Sunday morning toward the end of 1941.

"Ladies and gentlemen"—the announcer's voice was quivering with excitement—"we interrupt the program to bring you a bulletin from Washington. The Japanese have attacked Pearl Harbor. President Roosevelt announced a few moments ago that a large force of Japanese aircraft is bombing . . ."

I looked at Meg, and Meg looked back at me with big frightened eyes. Three-year-old Janey and one-and-a-half-year-old Cindy kept right on messing with their food.

"Oh, Peter. What will happen to us now?" My wife asked the question, too. It was a good question for a first lieutenant with a family secure in the comforts of a peacetime Air Corps. The B-25 was a nice safe plane to be flying around on routine practice flights from an air base in Texas. It was new and had two engines and we seldom flew in bad weather.

I jumped up from the table and hollered at Meg: "Help me get my uniform together! I've got to get out to the post!"

Little Janey began to cry. "Daddy, don't go work. Mommy, Daddy don't go work."

But off to work I went . . . off to see what could be done about winning the war before sunset of December 7, 1941. Do you know what it was like at an Air Force base on Pearl Harbor Day? Sentries were posted like mad. Pistols and ammunition were issued to everybody. Pass words were set up. People ran about trying to think up something that hadn't been thought up. Airplanes were dispersed all over the field. And after every precaution had been made for the defense against a Japanese attack in the middle of Texas, everyone stood around chain smoking, listening to the radio, and asking each other the same question. What do we do now?

It took weeks for someone in Washington to figure the answer to that question. Finally, it was posted on the ops bulletin board.

ATTENTION ALL PILOTS

The following officers will report to the Group Adjutant's Office for reassignment and travel orders:

The group was split in half. My name wasn't on the list, so I was left behind. My old friends who were on the list were shipped off to form a new group in Oklahoma. When they took off for Australia weeks later, we were still sitting in Texas asking each other the same question. What happens to us?

"You act like you want to leave us," Meg accused me one night after the children were asleep.

I stopped pacing and sat down beside her on the davenport. "No, honey. I don't want to leave you. I just want to know what's next."

Next, they turned us into an Operational Training Unit for B-25's. We got the kids fresh out of flying school and let 'em risk our necks day after day and night after night while we were trying to teach them how to keep from killing us. Some of the old boys liked it. Some of us didn't. We kept asking each other the same question: How long can this keep up?

"Gentlemen." The colonel addressed a few of us who had been called to his office one day. "What I have to say to you is probably as much Greek to me as it will be to you. Someone in Washington has picked your names out of the files to give you a chance to volunteer for special training." The colonel turned and looked out of the window at something.

"What kind of training, sir?" someone asked.

The colonel turned back. "That's the hell of it. I don't know. I don't even know where. All the order says is that I am to tell you it's vitally important—and dangerous—duty. You may volunteer or not. It's up to you."

I looked around at the other fellows. They were the best pilots, bombardiers, and navigators on the post. I volunteered.

"Secrecy." My wife sniffed while we were packing my things a few nights later. "I think it's silly." She was peeved because I couldn't tell her where I was going.

"Don't worry, honey. You'll be able to join me soon."

It was really mysterious. I lay awake on the train speeding toward the secret destination asking myself the same question over and over. What gives?

"First Lieutenant Peter Smith reporting as ordered, sir," I said, saluting the new adjutant.

"Sit down, Captain." He motioned toward a chair.

"Captain?"

"Congratulations." He smiled. "I have your promotion orders right here."

Nothing happened all the next day. A lot of my old classmates were at the new field, and we looked over the new B-25's and kept asking each other the same question over and over. What's the score?

"Gentlemen"—the adjutant addressed us all assembled in a briefing room the second day—"your new commanding officer, Colonel James H. Doolittle."

Colonel Jimmy Doolittle. The last time I had heard of him, he was a major and breaking speed records or something. You couldn't help liking the Old Man right from the start. He didn't tell us much that first meeting. One thing he said started up a buzzing in the room.

"You fellows are the best B-25 pilots in the Air Force. That's why you were selected to volunteer for this job." His Kewpie-doll face grinned widely when he said that. "But here you are going to learn to fly the B-25 like you never knew it could be flown before. For instance, you are going to learn to take off with flaps from a short field. . . ."

That gave us something to talk about. Why would you want to take off with flaps?

"What's it all about? What are you doing here?" Meg asked in the apartment the Air Force had provided for us.

"Honey," I told her, "even if I knew, I couldn't tell you. We don't know what we are doing ourselves, but we are doing it."

We flew low. My bombardier developed a bombsight out of a couple of pieces of wood that worked fine if you were flying under two hundred feet. We took off over and over again, each time shortening the take-off distance until we were practically taking off straight up. Why? Why?

"You know what it looks like to me?" one of the pilots said as we looked at the oblong chalked-out area we were supposed to take off from one morning. "It looks like the stuff those Navy boys do. That could be the outline of a carrier deck."

"All right, men," the Old Man said before us late one afternoon. "You've guessed it and mastered it. You've learned how to take a fully loaded B-25 off from the deck of an aircraft carrier. Don't forget how to do it. But forget you ever heard of it. In a day or so, we'll have flying orders. Say nothing to your wives. I repeat. Say nothing to your wives!"

Hell, it had been that way for a long time. When you were at home all you could talk about was the children and the housework and women's clothes. You couldn't talk about your work. But you couldn't stop your wife from asking the same question over and over again, even if you couldn't answer it. Where do we go from here?

It was a far day from the times when I joined the Cavalry with an ROTC commission from Oregon State College and from when I went through flying cadet training in grade as a second lieutenant and fell in love with my Texas girl. We planned things then. My God, how we planned! And the plans worked out fine for a while. We had each other and little Janey and Cindy to prove it. There was nothing could stop little Janey from asking a question on the night after our last day of special training when we were packing a single flight bag.

"Where Daddy going, Mommy?"

"Daddy is going away, dear. He's just going away for a while."

A good wife would tell a three-year-old the same thing if Daddy were going to the electric chair.

"There it is," my bombardier said, excitedly looking over my shoulder in the cockpit of Meg, my new B-25, as we crossed over the Oakland Bay Bridge. He was talking about the blue-gray flat top of the Navy aircraft carrier slotted into a dock down below. "What do you suppose we're going to do from off that thing?"

Questions. Questions. I had one. We now could take off from an aircraft carrier, but we couldn't land on one. No. It may sound like a statement, but it was a question to me.

We got on it and rode in it and slept in bunks pressing from the steel floor to the steel ceiling. And then one day the Old Man made a quite stirring speech. All I can remember of it was one word.

"Tokyo!"

Now we knew where we were going. But a Jap ship the carrier's guns set afire and sank in a choppy gray sea fixed that.

"They saw us and radioed to Japan!" That was the general opinion. So where do we go from here?

We take off with enough gas to get us to Tokyo and no farther. That was an easy question. Where do we go from Tokyo? Nowhere.

"Where Daddy going, Momma?"

Nowhere.

But sometimes it's a long trip to nowhere. We took off from the swaying carrier loaded with high potency bombs and just enough gas to get us to Tokyo. But Someone lent a hand. A tailwind came up. When we swept in low over the edge of Tokyo, and the plane lurched as the bombardier yelled, "Bombs away!" we still had some gas. We headed east with Jap guns firing at us from the ridge to our right and their shells exploding among the houses in the valley to our left . . . east on out over the darkened China Sea.

"Where we headin', Captain?" the crew chief asked as the B-25 bucked into the rain and blackness of a storm.

I pointed at the blue glow of the instruments. "East, son . . . to China if we're in a tailwind. To hell if we're not."

We still didn't know if we had made it when we found ourselves bobbing and dropping through the black rain in our parachutes. When I hit the wet ground I had a natural question. Where am I? It was one hell of a lot of Chinamen later before I found out. But all those Chinamen managed to smuggle me through the Jap lines to Chungking.

A medal from the Generalissimo. A piece of lucky jade from the Madamissimo. A chance to send a cable: "Meg, darling, I'm healthy and coming home to you." And three of my air crew were missing.

Thank that tailwind. I found myself, a hero, Meg looking with proud upturned face at me standing on the steps of the Capitol at Washington, D.C., and F.D.R. pinning a D.F.C. on me.

"I hereby, in the name of the Toyko raiders, turn these gracious gifts of the American people over to a most worthy cause," I speeched behind my new medal. "I give it gladly to the American Red Cross in the name of my comrades throughout the armed forces who are fighting everywhere and being helped everywhere by the Red Cross. May you all do the same. Money, I mean. Thank you."

Man alive. There was more than a hundred thousand dollars in that envelope that military regulations forbade us to split up and keep.

I also sold bonds. I really saw the country before I saw Africa. But I didn't see much of Africa. I had time to write one V-mail to Meg. "Darling, I'm well and happy. This will be over soon, and I'll be home with you and Janey and Cindy again soon. . . ." It was over before I knew it. Before I knew it I was on the ground at the wrong end of my second combat mission with a goon officer wearing glasses smiling enviously at me and popping off with the thing every prisoner of war hears until he wants to spit. "For you the war is over."

Well, I've had two years since then, and it isn't over yet. "Meg, darling, I don't want to alarm you, but things will get a hell of a lot worse before they get better. Love, Tokyo Pete."

Oh, almighty Tailwind. Why don't you blow?

Chapter Sixteen

The column bent over the top of the hill and the dripping woods dropped away to the right.

"Hubba, hubba, hubba!"

The rest looked at Koczeck in amazement. "What's eating you?" Bob asked. "Going round the bend?"

"I know where we're going. Don't you get it? Remember the railroad we crossed? We're going to the railroad."

"And ride?"

"That's it."

Bob sneered. "You optimist."

Koczeck handed his part of the sled rein to Bob. "You pessimist." He did a little jig, like an Indian war dance, rubbing his mittened hands together. "We're going to travel by rail. We're going to ride!" His voice was high-pitched with glee.

The rest looked at the stocky Minnesotan, "You're nuts."

"Wait and see. Wait and see. You'll see."

Jim edged toward Fred Wolkowski and muttered out of the side of his mouth. "Jesus Christ." He was serious. "I'm not doing so good. I've lost Fritz Heine. And Ed Greenway. Sort of lost Bill Johnston, although that son of a bitch is all right, as wrong as he can get. But, God, we can't let Koczeck go!"

Fred grinned warmly, nice but uneven teeth flashing yellowly in the dusk. "Aw, hell, Jim. Al is all right. You know Al. We're all going to make it if anybody does. The only one I have any worries about is Noble."

Jim looked at the pudgy Noble plodding along pulling his side of the sled, unaware of any conversation. A tug at Jim's sleeve pulled him around to look into the dancing face of Al Koczeck.

"There, you see?" he bubbled, pointing frantically ahead across the wooded gully dropping steeply to the right of the trudging column. "It's the railroad! We're going to ride!"

The men stared open-mouthed at the railroad tracks, four pairs of double tracks stretching east and west ahead and far below the road upon which the long mass of prisoners marched. Bob snorted. "What makes you think so? We've crossed railroad tracks before."

"I feel it in my bones."

Gradually, a rise of trees and snow across the gully to the right gave way, to expose a long line of coupled boxcars standing on a siding beyond the main railroad tracks. The road dipped steeply toward the tracks.

"There she is. Hubba, hubba, hubba."

Fred looked into Jim's frowning face and grinned, chuckling. It was becoming darker and darker. Water gurgled from the slush of the road down the steep wooded bank to the right. "I hope he's right," Fred commented. "I bet you could get some sleep in one of those things."

The tempo of the march picked up going downhill. Jim grunted. "You pick up a big hope, and then when we cross the tracks and keep right on marching on the other side you have a big letdown."

Al Koczeck, still rubbing his hands together enthusiastically, started to sing in tempo with the march. " 'I've been working on the railroad, all the livelong day. I've been working on the railroad . . .' "

A prisoner back farther in the formation called ahead, interrupting the song! "Hey, Koczeck. Did you ever hear how Smitty here got shot down?"

"Huh?" Al looked back over his shoulder at the man, a recently arrived prisoner. "No. Who cares?"

"Tell 'im, Smitty. Tell Koczeck how you got shot down."

Smitty, a small man, spoke in a deep Southern voice. "Shootin' up a railroad, son. That's all they is to shoot up these days for us fighter men. I don't want no choo choo ride. No, suh. No choo choo for me. I'd leave as soon walk."

Through the dusk ahead the shadow of the column leveled out and crossed a bridge over the railroad tracks. Jim muttered sideways to Fred. "What'd I tell you? We're crossing the tracks."

A Luftwaffe guard passed through the formation from the left side of the road to get a better look ahead. Faint shouting up ahead grew louder and louder as it welled backward along the column. There were sudden cheers in the formation ahead of Block 162. Major Smith turned around, walking rapidly backward as his voice boomed out. "We're catching a train, men! From now on we travel by train!"

"Yipeeee!"

Koczeck turned and playfully punched Jim. "Was I right? Or was I right? Anything else you'd like to know?"

"Yeah. Where we going?"

Water dripped down from icicles hanging from the steel sides of the bridge as they passed over the tracks. Burt spoke above the booming sound of many feet. "I heard if you march across a bridge in step, it will collapse."

"That's right," Tom agreed.

Bob laughed good-humoredly. "How the hell do you know?"

"It's a fact," Tom said calmly.

Lights glowed and bobbed on the right of the long line of cars as the column of men turned down toward the siding. A signal light hooded for the blackout glowed green atop its pole. The column halted and started forward and halted again as prisoners far ahead were assigned to the cars. Eventually Block 162 came abreast of the rearmost boxcar. It was faintly lighted by a lantern held by a trainman standing quietly beside the tracks.

"Forty Männer, eight Pferde," Fred said slowly, trying to read the words painted in white on the dirty red side of the boxcar. "What does that mean?"

"Forty men or eight horses," Jim translated. "After this you'll be eligible to join the American Legion."

Burt Salem stared up at the undersized car. "You mean they can get forty men into one of those?"

Tom grunted. "They must use a shoehorn."

They moved slowly along the line of cars over the cinders of the siding bed. A faint smell of animals came across the distance from the empty boxcars. During one of the halts, Major Smith turned and raised his voice. "Men, it looks like when we get aboard these Pullman cars Block 162 is going to be split. That is, if they don't put us all into one car." There was cold laughter. "There's no telling where we are going or how long it will take to get there, but we've got to keep organized. It'll be up to the men in each car to find out among themselves who is the senior officer. And the senior officer will be in command." The major looked over the heads of his men for a moment. "Anybody got anything to say?"

"Yeah, Major," a voice called out. "Which way is the club car?"

They moved ahead shivering. Up ahead they could see groups of men being cut out of the column and herded into the cars. Jim squatted beside the sled and began unfastening the ropes which held the bundles. "We'd better get our packs off. We can't take this thing along."

Tom and Al Koczeck squatted down to help. Jack Noble looked on in dismay. "Hey, can't we take the sled? We may need it again."

"Relax." Bob Montgomery motioned toward the boxcars with a mittened thumb. "With forty men in each of those things there won't be hardly enough room for us people."

The melting snow trickled down the sides of the cars. It was dark now except for the lanterns swaying in the hands of the trainmen. Lieutenant Pieber's voice could be heard counting prisoners into a boxcar ahead. Jim felt the soup he had drunk at Spremberg press with a slight tingle into his bladder.

". . . vierzehn . . . sechzehn . . . achtzehn . . . zwanzig . . . zwei und zwanzig . . . vier und zwanzig . . ." Pieber's voice droned on above the murmur and shuffle of the men.

Koczeck rubbed his palms together excitedly. "It won't be long now."

Fred grinned, shivering happily in the darkness. "I'm going to log some sack time. Don't nobody ever wake me up."

". . . sechs und dreizig . . . acht und dreizig . . . vierzig . . ."

Tom peered up the long line of cars. "They're headed west." His voice was flat calm. "That lets the Russians out of the picture for good." He sighed.

"Hey!"

The men stared at Jim, who had pushed the scarf back from his ears.

"Listen!"

". . . sechs und vierzig . . . acht und vierzig . . . fünfzig. Jawohl!"

A groan went up from some of the listening men. Noble looked wide-eyed at Jim. "What's the matter?"

"Fünfzig. These are forty-and-eight cars, but they're putting fifty into each car!"

Bob gasped disbelieving. "Fifty! Into one of those?"

"Listen."

Pieber was counting off the men directly ahead of them now. As the Luftwaffe officer tallied them off by twos, the men scrambled up into the square black door space of the next car ahead. The listening became intense when Pieber started into the thirties.

". . . zwei und dreizig . . . vier und dreizig . . ."

"So long, Major!" Major Smith waved a long arm and vaulted up to disappear within the blackness of the car.

". . . acht und dreizig . . . vierzig . . . zwei und vierzig . . ."

The groan went up again. "Jesus!" Bob groaned. "In Texas we wouldn't even put eight horses into a little thing like that."

". . . funfzig. Jawohl!" The last of the fifty counted vanished inside the small boxcar.

"Next truck, please, zhentlemen." Pieber pointed the beam of his torch at another square black maw. ". . . zwei . . . vier . . . sechs . . . acht . . . zehn . . . zwölf . . ."

Tom and Jim tossed their blanket roll and tin pack into the car and clambered up into the blacker darkness within. "Phew!" Tom grabbed his nose in disgust. Jim began to sneeze at the instant overpowering smell. Behind him, Bob scooped up a handful of the moist crumbly stuff that formed a thin layer on the floor of the car. He cursed. "Jesus Christ! Horse shit!"

Two by two, in rapid succession, the prisoners scrambled in, groaning, grunting, coughing, and cursing at the first overwhelming blow of the stink. Jim controlled his sneezing but could not stop the burning flow of tears from his eyes. Feet boomed against the floor as the men packed closer and closer together, invisible to one another as more and more jammed in. They stepped on one another's feet, coughed into one another's faces, stumbled over their bundles, and would have fallen had they not been held up by the press of bodies.

"Tom, where the hell are you?"

"Right here," a voice clipped close to Jim's ear. "Don't flap, men. Don't flap."

Suddenly the door rolled clattering shut, increasing the stink of manure. The men stopped cursing and calling to listen to the rattle and thud of the crossbar outside locking them in.

A voice called out. "What do we do now?"

"Somebody light a match," another voice suggested.

There was the sound of shuffling throughout the solid blackness. A match flared and cast a flickering pallor from an arm held high. Two more matches in other parts of the car added to the soft yellow light which revealed men jammed together clutching packs and blanket rolls, an oblong of wretched life pressed closely on four sides by dark dirty brown walls, frightened eyes glinting in the glow which faded to utter blackness as one by one the matches went out.

"Stay there!"

"Room 10 over here!"

Cries rang through the blackness.

"This way, Room 8!"

"Is that you, Jim?"

"Yeah, Room 8 over here!"

Men groped their way, squirming and squeezing past one another "God damn this smell!"

One by one friends found friends. Matches flickered, burned, and went out, providing intermittent light, causing shadows to leap and cower blackly over the ribs and crossbeams of the walls.

"We've got to have a better light than that," Jim said as Tom lighted a match from one in Bob's hand just before it burned down to his thumb. Jim turned and called, "Anybody got any candles?"

"Oh, yeah . . . sure!" Jeers met the question.

"I got a Kriegie lamp," a voice called out from the other end of the press, "if I can find it."

"Help him," Jim yelled.

Several men held lighted matches while the volunteer dug in a pack held by two others. Soon he produced an empty tin of liver paste with a rope wick protruding from a hole in its top. A slight cheer came from a few throats. A pair of eager matches reached to light the rope, which flickered for a few seconds and then blossomed into a two-inch orange and yellow flame sending up oily black smoke.

"Stick it up on one of those two by fours," Jim suggested, "and let's get organized."

The steady low light of the Kriegie lamp showed many of the men holding dirty handkerchiefs or scarfs to their noses.

"Like what, Jim?" a heavily accented voice from near the lamp called back. "Organize what?"

"Well, we ought to do something about this horse shit. There's no telling how long we'll be in here."

"Now you're talking.'
"Let's get at it."
"What'll we do abou   Jim?"
Jim scratched his he   .rowning. "I don't know. Maybe we can
figure out some way to   .p it."
"Sweep it where?"
Koczeck managed, in   .e of the press of men around him, to clap
his hands together and ru) his palms briskly. "We could sweep it up
to the other end."
Voices exploded at the other end.
"Oh, no!"
"No, by God!"
"I got a better idea. Let's sweep it to *that* end!"
Jim looked disgustedly at Koczeck, who shrugged and dropped his
hands to his sides. Jim turned back to the problem of organization.
"I guess we'd better do what the major told us to do. Find out who
the senior officer is and let him handle everything."
"They ain't nobody here but us lootenants, Jim."
"No captains?" Nobody answered. Jim sighed, snorting out the
stink he sucked in by doing so. "Then it's got to be the senior first
lieutenant. Who's the senior first lieutenant by date of promotion?"
When nobody answered, Jim sighed again, getting a lungful of stench.
"Well, Jesus Christ! Anybody here made first looey in 1941 or earlier?"
No response. "1942?" Men looked about at one another, but no one
answered. "Then who got it before June of 1943?"
Several voices popped up.
"June, '43."
"June 1st, 1943."
"Mike here made it in May."
Jim looked about. "Any earlier?" Everyone looked about but no
one spoke up. Suddenly Jim faced Bob. "Say, Montgomery. What was
your date of promotion to first lieutenant?"
Bob stiffened. His mouth opened slowly. "God damn it." He
cursed without separating his teeth. "April, 1943."
Jim shrugged and turned away. "Then you're it."
When they saw who the senior officer was, a mumble started at
the other end of the car. Koczeck managed to bend over and slap his
own knee. The mumble at the other end grew until one voice boomed
out for all. "Oh, no! You ain't agoin' to sweep it up to this end! Not
any lousy first lieutenant. You ain't asweeping it up here!"
256

Bob reached over to grab Jim's shoulder and turn him slowly around. The Texan looked deliberately into Jim's eyes over the handkerchief he was holding over his mouth. Bob spoke coldly and deliberately. "Thanks, pal."

Jim's shoulders were shaking slightly in rhythm with the shadows on the narrow walls of the boxcar.

"Well, Montgomery," a voice called from somewhere within the shadowy mass, "what do we do about the horse shit? Or do we just stand here like a bunch of vertical sardines for the rest of the war?"

Bob spoke carefully, trying to cover the confusion of his sudden authority. "How do I know? I'm no West Pointer."

"If you were, you'd know how to handle it!"

"He knows anyhow. He's from Texas."

Tom Howard spoke up calmly. "I've got an idea."

Bob turned slowly but tensely belligerent. "All right. Let's hear it."

"Don't let's flap, men. Each of us has at least two blankets. A little bit of horse shit isn't going to hurt us unless we have to lie in it. Why don't we each spread one blanket down. That way there'll be plenty of overlapping and we can cover the floor completely and everything that's on it. That's all."

Bob looked around in the flickering gloom. "Anybody got a better idea?"

Jim took the handkerchief from his face. "That's the best deal."

Bob made his decision. "O.K., men. Start spreading."

The fractional light of the Kriegie lamp flickered down over the seething concentration of bent backs. The men opened packs and waited, coughing and gasping, to spread their blankets over the manure on the floor. When they had done so, and the overlapping blankets were trampled by soaking wet boots, half of the men sat down clutching what was left of their personal goods between their knees and disinterestedly regarding the baggy trousers of those who had moved too late to find room to sit.

"Jesus," Bob pleaded to Jim who had also been too busy supervising the laying of blankets to flop into a sitting position, "now what do we do?"

Jim leaned close to the boxcar commander's ear and whispered louder than normal speech above the din of the squalling men. "Make me your adjutant. Make it official."

Bob grunted and sounded off. "Quiet!" The smell had been only slightly lessened by the blankets. "Quiet, you guys! Since I'm stuck with this stupid job, which I want no part of, I guess you'll have to take orders from me. I hereby name Jim Weis here as my adjutant and second in command. Weis is an Old Kriegie, so do what he says."

"Bad deal!"

"Atta boy, Jim!"

Jim surveyed the half seated, half standing mob and self-consciously cleared his throat. "In the first place, we need nails. Who's got any nails?"

Nobody answered.

"Come on, God damn it! I'm not fooling. This is no time for hoarding. Unless we want to keep half standing and half sitting for God knows how long, we've got to nail our packs and stuff to the walls. Now, who's got nails? You can have 'em back whenever we get wherever we're going."

Men both seated and standing stirred into movement.

"I've got some."

"I got a couple."

Jim looked straight down between greatcoats and legs at Jack Noble.

"I've got a few." Noble began fishing in the pocket of his great-coat.

Jim, holding the large tin pack by its slings, let it down to rest on Tom's narrow shoulders. "All right. Now get out the prangers and start nailing stuff to the walls."

Rusty strips of steel and iron and small rocks followed the assortment of discolored nails from the packs of the men. Bundles, blankets, and packs were passed to the outer edges and with a great clattering were nailed to the walls of the car. Jim passed the tin pack to Bob, who passed it to Fred, who helped Koczeck hold it while Noble, wielding a short steel bar with a hole in one end, pranged two bent but hefty nails into the rear wall near the packed left-hand corner of the boxcar.

"Hey!" Noble cried, as Koczeck and Fred hung the pack on the nails by its shoulder strap. "Looky here. A window!" Noble lifted a hinged board head high on the left-hand-side corner wall. Cold air shot in through an opening two and a half feet wide and nine inches high. "Gee, we could have passed the manure out here."

Jim headed for the slit of fresh air. "Let it ride," he gritted at Noble. Then he opened his mouth and sucked cold air from the blackness beyond the slit of the window. Immediately, his bad tooth began to throb with pain.

"Anybody want to donate some margarine to the lighting system?" Someone else was organizing that, and Jim was grateful. Behind him and his throbbing molar, most of the men were now sitting, leaning into each other's chests, backs, groins, and faces. "Jesus!" Jim gasped at Noble, "nail it open."

"I haven't got many nails left."

"Nail it open."

Noble pranged the board shutter permanently open. Outside, guards stood shivering in the slush, faintly and uncertainly lighted by distant moving lanterns. Jim wondered what had become of the dogs. Somehow he missed those ferocious brutes of the night. He could visualize them jerking and straining at the leash in tempo with the hot searing throb of his tooth. But they weren't there, and only the barely visible guards, the smell, the pack of humans at his back, and the toothache remained. Jim kicked his way back through the press of resentful men. He squeezed himself down until he had claimed a place between the buttocks of Bob, Fred, and Al Koczeck. He heard Fred ask, "How's a man going to log any sack time all jammed together like this?"

"What I'd like to know," Koczeck answered, "is how long we got to stay like this? How long is this trip going to last?"

"What trip?" Bob jeered. "I don't feel us moving no place."

Tom leaned back between Jim's legs and held up a pack of cigarettes. "Smoke?"

"No." Jim wriggled his left hand down between his own and Koczeck's hip to get at the aspirins in his greatcoat pocket. His elbow ground into Bob just above the groin. Finally swallowing one tablet and grinding the other against his gum below the bad tooth, he shut his eyes and waited for the burning drug to numb the pain.

"Who's got a can? A big can."

"What in hell you want a can for?" another voice asked.

"What in hell do you suppose for? I got to go."

"Oh."

After a while the distressed voice spoke again. "Thanks."

Jim listened to the tinny sound of rapidly running water, and it sent a signal to his own full bladder. He began to tingle again within his groin.

"Here," said the same voice, much relieved.

"Don't give it to me. I don't want it."

"Well, for gosh sakes pass it over to the window, will you, please? You don't expect me to carry it in my lap for the rest of my life, do you?"

"Oh, all right. Here. Pass it along, friend."

"I'm next on that thing," a voice rang out.

Jim shouted, "I'm number two after you!"

Other voices clipped in. "Number three!"

"Number four, here!"

Over by the window, Jack Noble accepted the German meat tin and poured it quickly out of the window slit.

"I'm number five!"

"Six!"

"Seven!"

"Now wait a minute!" Noble cried. "I'm not going to stand here and pour out pee all night. Take it easy, will you?" He passed the can along on its way to number one.

"Jim." Bob spoke softly close to his ear. "This is going to have to be organized. What'll we do?"

"Number eight after Smitty," the game went on.

"Number nine!"

"Nine! No, ten!"

Jim spoke between nervously clicking teeth. "I don't know. All I want is that God-damned tin can!"

"Eleven."

"I'm twelve!"

Noble cried out from the window. "Aw, cut it out, for crying out loud. How many can there be?"

Tom answered, sharply and dryly, "Fifty. That's all."

"Thirteen, here."

Bob started to his feet by pressing his hands hard into Jim's shoulders and kneeing Jim's back. "Now, hold it! Wait a minute!" The counting built up to seventeen. "Pipe down and pop to."

The counting stopped to be replaced by a deep booming voice from the other end of the car. "Quiet, sirs. It's the Senior American First Lieutenant speaking."

Bob looked disgustedly toward the speaker and kept his voice icy and calm. "Thank you, balls'-eyes." He looked around over the mob from which the only sound was the rapid beat of the can filling up for the second time. "Now, look here. Jack Noble isn't going to be the only man in this car who does the dirty work. I'm going to set up tours of duty. After half an hour, he's going to be relieved by somebody else."

Another voice rang out. "Jesus Christ! Hurry up with that can so we can all be relieved."

The noise in the can stopped, and the user handed it carefully over two heads in the direction of Noble and the window slit.

"I'm going to get out a deck of cards in a minute," Bob continued in a frozen drawl, "and every man is going to draw one card. We'll start with the aces. . . ."

Tom handed the heavy can to Jim, who looked into it. It was only half full, so he decided to save a journey of the can.

". . . and we'll go by suits. Hearts high. Diamonds next. Then clubs. Then spades. Aces are high, too."

The people around Jim bent and shoved and grunted to keep out of his way, while he made burbling use of the can.

"Whoever draws the deuce of diamonds will relieve Noble in exactly half an hour, which will be"—he looked at his chronograph —"about seven-fourteen. Make it seven-thirty."

"Hey!" protested Noble from the window.

"That's the way it's going to be."

Jim watched the surface of the liquid rise until it made him nervous. But he stopped just in time. The quality of leadership, he thought as Bob Montgomery's words slowly sank through the relief in his brain. When you have to assume it, anybody's got it. He carefully handed the brimming can to Koczeck. "Be careful," he warned, ashamed of himself. "It's full."

"I'll say it is," Koczeck said gravely, as he gingerly balanced it and passed it on. Heads strained away from the precarious burden passed toward Noble and the window slit.

"Jeez," Koczeck protested as Bob brought out the grimy communal deck of cards, "that's the only deck we got."

Tom spoke calmly. "I got another deck."

Jim drew the first card from the down-turned deck and lifted it up. "Just to show you there's nothing crooked. I've got the deuce of spades." He passed on the deck to Tom, who drew the ace of hearts.

The deck passed from hand to hand bringing out curses of luck and ill luck.

"God damn!"

"Hot damn! Four of spades!"

The can kept traveling about through the smelly air. Once it partly spilled, and if there had been room there might have been a fight. But the uproar subsided and the can passed on its way to and from the window. Jim shut out the flickering light of the lamps at either end of the car by letting his eyelids drop. Soon he slid off into a doze. He was awakened by a dream. The train had started with a jerk, and the two lamps had fallen down. Men were screaming, jammed together in rapidly spreading white and red flames. Jim was caught in a press of flame roaring quickly closer at him over backs and heads like the tongues licking back from the fire wall of a burning Spitfire. He awoke with a smothered yell.

"Take it easy," Tom mumbled, also dozing.

Jim's legs were asleep. He had to use his hands and arms to pull his dead legs from the mass of legs, arms, and bodies in which they were entangled. The car was still standing motionless. Men stood smoking here and there in the tiny space. Beside him Bob sat fast asleep. Jim lifted the sleeping man's arm and looked at the Air Force watch on his wrist. Then he stepped carefully, forcing his feet down between unyielding men, until he reached the corner where the window was. Noble was huddled fast asleep, his back against the wall beneath the window, the empty can held between his propped knees. He looked up sleepily when Jim shook him.

"Wha—"

"It's time for me to relieve you."

Noble handed the can to Jim and struggled slowly to his feet.

"Have you got any more nails?"

"A couple. Why?"

Jim nodded toward the nearest Kriegie lamp. "We'd better nail those lamps to the wall. They'll fall if this train ever starts."

"Somebody already nailed 'em." Noble moved off into the center of the pack and squatted, pressing his body into the tangled mass.

Jim sat down beneath the window and pulled his blanket up over his knees and shoulders. A head adjusted itself to use Jim's feet for a pillow. Someone's leg slid smoothly into place beneath his drawn knees. Jim shut his eyes and fell into fitful sleep. Some time later he awoke with a nervous twitch. The boxcar was vibrating and rattling. The train was moving. Jim let the click-click, click-click, of the wheels beneath the floor lull him back to sleep.

Jim Weis: "There I was. . . ."

My father was in the transportation business for more than twenty years. He represented American steamship lines, British steamship lines, the French lines, all of the railroads of the world, and several air lines. Pop is an expert on transportation. But I can teach him a thing or two. For instance, when crossing the Atlantic in a ship, it's nice to have twenty-two or more troop transports and freighters zigzag through great waves and swells. It's nice if two of the ships are the Queen Mary and Queen Elizabeth. That way you will have two rings of forty destroyers and corvettes, a banana boat aircraft carrier, and maybe a blimp halfway. Even so, it's best that your sea hotel be decked out in latest style camouflage paint.

Do you know what happens when a sea armada like that starts the dodging dash across the cold sea? It's something like this:

"This is where a munitions ship blew up in the first war and flattened the city, killing twenty thousand or so people," Don Gentile, a fellow sergeant pilot headed for the Eagle Squadron, tells you as you look out from the jam-packed deck of the Orchades at the soup bowl harbor of Halifax.

"Jesus," you comment, looking over the pond filled with ships swarming like bees with troops, and long low tubs with de-winged airplanes and rondel-sided heavy tanks parked on the upper decks holding them close to the water, "there's bound to be some of these carrying munitions."

"They're the ones in the middle, mate," a Cockney voice volunteers in the breeze. He is wearing a blue turtle-neck sweater tight under a pea jacket, and you wonder what a civilian is doing riding on a troop transport, so you ask him. "I'm a distressed British seaman.

I lost my ship three days ago out there." He points out toward the sunlit low mist beyond the channel through which the convoy is parading out of Halifax.

"Lost your ship?" Don Gentile asks.

"She was sunk by a bloody torpedo squirted into her by a bloody U-boat just an hour and a harf out of Halifax here."

You gaze about you at the convoy. The low easy swells of green-tinted gold as you slide onto the Atlantic make you think of prewar crossings . . . of the big white-topped *Bremen* with its sun-deck restaurant, gypsy orchestra, dressing for dinner, and the headwaiter who knew the right kind of pill to cure seasickness or hangover.

Whooorhahhhmppff-f-sh-sh-sh!

Brought suddenly to reality, you gaze between the pitching and gently rolling gray shapes of the convoy to see a great wall of water tumbling slowly back into the sea behind a darting corvette.

"Practicing, huh?" you ask.

"Practicing, my arse, mate," the seagoing refugee beside you says. "We're under attack. Not harf an hour out and they're onto us already."

Whoruuuuumph-r-r-r-r-r!

Whoooomf-f-f-sh-h-h!

Other great white masses of jagged-topped water boil up out of the sea beyond the suddenly darting and zigzagging ships of the convoy.

"They'll be waiting for us in packs all the way across," the Limey predicts. "We'll be attacked every dawn and dusk until we reach Blighty."

The Limey is right. You listen for it evenings after eating standing up to make way for the troops behind you. It wakes you up every morning as you lie packed on the bunks and floor of what once was a stateroom. Sometimes it's invisible at the outer circle of destroyers. Then it's near and shakes the ship like an earthquake, and next morning the ground troops billeted below, far down in the bowels of the ship, show off rusty rivets blown in out of the steel sides during the night. And all the time you never see the submarines, but you know they are trying to kill you. Then after six days of traveling, packed together like soldiers, through wind and fog, rain and sunshine, pitching and rolling, zigzagging and darting—after twelve sunset and sunrise U-boat attacks—the convoy winds one morning out of the Irish Channel into Gourock. The Tannoy loudspeaker announces the score. "Three U-boats sunk. None of our convoy is missing."

Then begins your next lesson in transportation—the British troop train. You find yourself in an open-seated car, like those on an American train, filled with eager airmen: Scotch airmen, Australian flyers, Canadians, New Zealanders, four slope-eyed pilots of the Royal Burmese Air Force, South Africans. And the most eager of all are the Eagle Squadron volunteers peering out through dirty windows at meadows staked out with rusty steel rods to prevent a German landing, squinting up into the sky for glimpses of what you have been dreaming of.

"Look, there's one. A Miles Master!"

"How do you know?"

"See the gull wing?"

"Look over there. What's that?"

"Aw, hell. That's just a Tiger Moth."

In the first day you see Wellington Wimpy, Short Stirling, Lancaster, Oxford, and finally Hurricane. But you have to wait until the next to catch a glimpse of Spitfires darting in a graceful vic of three over the crawling train.

"Man! Look at 'em go!"

"It won't be long now, boys!"

But it's longer than you think. The troop train chugs along two days and nights from Gourock to Bournemouth. When you get off the train in the cold darkness of the third day, you have learned something else about transportation. If you are in a hurry, never take a British troop train.

Now my dad in his transportation business always advised tourists to travel light. I can tell him something about that. By luxury liner and air liner he sent many a person to where I went when I learned about traveling light. Here's the way it goes:

Immediately after your transfer from the RAF you learn all operations have been halted, not because your new group has suffered horribly high losses lately (which it has—that's why you are there as a replacement along with fourteen other former RAF Americans), but because the group has been alerted to be ready to move out of England.

"Out of England?" you ask amazed. "You mean to Scotland or someplace for a rest?"

"No, no," Barney, who arrived a couple of days ahead of you tells you. "I mean out of the British Isles altogether."

"But where, for Chris'sake? Russia? The Pacific? We're not going home, are we?"

"No," Barney shrugs. "I don't think so. I don't get it."

The next day, in the intelligence briefing hall, Colonel Stubby Larkin, the group C.O., is standing with a regulation musette bag dangling by its straps from his right hand.

"Gentlemen," he starts out, "I don't know where we are going. All I know is that we are ordered to take no more with us than we can carry in a Spitfire."

Barney and I look at each other. "Norway?" he whispers.

The colonel goes on. "I made several flights today, checking to see what our Spits will carry. There's no place except the cockpit to stow baggage, and we've got to have room for full maneuverability. We don't know whether we will have to fight or not, but I think you'll agree that we had better be ready for it."

Not have to fight? Where can you fly to from England with a Spitfire and not have to fight? Even in Ireland they'd fight.

"This is what can be carried." The colonel held up the musette bag. "Just one musette bag full of belongings. I tried it doing aerobatics—slow rolls, loops, Immellmanns, and spins. You can fasten one musette bag down in the cockpit with you and that's all. That means extra underwear, extra socks, extra shirt, two towels, shaving equipment, soap, and tooth-brushing equipment. All your other belongings you are to pack in two parts, one to follow us and the other to be stored. Don't worry about your airplanes. We're leaving these here and picking up some new ones someplace else. Any questions?"

"Yes, sir," someone answers. "When are we leaving, Colonel?"

"Soon. I don't have to warn you about maintaining absolute security. If you have any business to clear up in England, apply to your squadron adjutant for twenty-four hours' leave."

Twenty-four hours. To say goodbye to your girls. Only, you are forbidden to say goodbye. Absolute security. You pick out your best girl in London—one you would probably marry if you stuck around long enough. You go into London for one last night.

"My God," she breathes, gleaming in the red glow from the fireplace of the suite they always gave you in a hotel near Hyde Park, "you are wonderful tonight. Did you shoot down another Jerry?"

What a girl!

"No, dear," she says frankly when you propose. "Unless you are willing to become an Englishman. I'm not a poor girl looking for free passage to America. I'm English and I'll always be English. This is my home."

She cries during the last soft warm wet embrace just before you have to hop out of her compartment in her commuter train.

"Darling, I wish . . ."

She puts a wonderful finger on your lips. "I think I know. Don't tell me. Goodbye, love. Be careful."

She knows the rules. The train chugs and toots off in the blackout. She is the daughter of a Scotland Yard inspector.

"You start out with the thrill of going abroad," my pop used to tell his prospects. "There is the last farewell aboard ship and the trumpet pealing 'All ashore that's going ashore.' Serpentine streams from your hands, and the colored streamers slowly part while the orchestra plays and you start out on your adventure."

One day, wearing our forty-fives and our musette bags slung over our shoulders, we piled into trucks for the nearest railroad. We clambered aboard a troop train. Hours later we stood shivering on the platform of a village depot in the chill sun of English autumn.

"Gents," the squadron C.O. suggested to relieve the wait, "better check to see that your guns are loaded. No use packing them if they won't shoot."

What a lot of damned nonsense! You stand there feeling silly, pointing your forty-five at the platform boards like the rest, pulling the breech back, letting the hammer down to safety, and then sliding the clip out to replace the ejected bullet. What kind of damned fool would be carrying an unloaded gun?

You pile into another troop train and ride for hours.

"I don't get it," Barney keeps saying. "We're vectoring westward. Where do we go from there?"

"Maybe we're going to invade Canada," someone suggests.

It gets dark. Finally the troop train stops for the last time. You get out shivering in your fur-lined flying jacket, stamping your fur-lined flying boots to keep your feet warm.

"This way, gentlemen."

An English flight sergeant without wings leads the column of seventy-five American pilots down a dirt road to a wired-in compound.

"What in hell are we doing here?" voices from the rear demand. "Where are the Spitfires?"

"It's a personnel depot," voices from the front explain.

You bed down for the night in a Nissen hut.

"We're not going anywhere," Barney complains from the cot next to yours just before you drop off to sleep. "We're in the American army now. We're just being shoved around."

"Wakey, wakey, wakey," the Limey sergeant orderly yells gaily, barging through the barracks pouring tea into cups held by a corporal. "Wakey, wakey, wakey!" and a cup of warm tea is thrust into your face. It is still dark. Well, now! Maybe this is it. Maybe now is the big day and they are going to give you a Spitfire, maybe even a new Spit IX, and tell you where to point it, and you can strap this damned musette bag in the driver's seat and get going.

Nup.

Up before dawn for a breakfast of kidneys on toast, it is past noon before the colonel passes the word around that you can take a bus in to see the sights of a nearby Welsh city. The sights you see are in foamless pint mugs of bitters until the pubs close, and then rather blearily an American movie, *Son of Fury*, with Gene Tierney in a sarong and Frances Farmer in a string of pearls. Back to the personnel depot for a meal of kidney pie as only the Limeys concoct it.

"Well, I guess there's nothing to do now but hit the sack," Barney suggests. "Looks like we're here for the duration."

But at about 11:00 P.M., when you are trying to decide whether or not to read one more chapter of *The Passionate Witch* from a borrowed Pocketbook, the door flies open and a British officer walks in. "Pack up, gentlemen. Pack up and fall out front."

It doesn't take much time to pack up. You're traveling light. A half-hour later you are marching along the wooden platform of the railway station. You pile into the granddaddies of all railroad coaches. They are third-class rural coaches with separate compartments opening from the outside and hard wooden benches for seats. After a while the troop train starts to rattle and clatter through the night, which you spend snoozing and smoking and snoozing again, periodically slapping your own rear end, which keeps getting numb. At the end of this, you figure, surely there'll be Spitfires.

Nup.

"The way I figure it," Barney says, checking a map from his boot against the names of passing stations in the cold gray of dawn, "is that we're headed for Glasgow and we're almost there."

Glasgow! Sure enough. The troop train breaks out onto the bank of a firth filled with ships, large and small, passenger, cargo, and naval, at anchor and in docks, their sides heavy with landing barges.

"By God," you say, recognizing the scene, "it's Gourock again! But, man, what a convoy!" It stretches across the wide mouth of the Clyde, ships swarming with men and bristling with guns, nestled beneath the calm blobs of barrage balloons, here and there among the larger gray shapes, tiny tugboats and landing barges darting to and fro.

"It must be Norway," somebody breathes, and you start remembering the fiasco of Dieppe not long before. Only, that day you were upstairs. This time it looks like you're going to ride one of those floating targets with landing barges hanging all over the sides.

"Naw," Barney disagrees. "We're not going anyplace by boat. We're going to fly. Else why would we be bringing only one extra shirt?"

So you shrug one of the two shirts you now own as you file up the gangway of an incredibly small ship almost like a ferry boat. It is a ferry boat. An Irish Channel boat with benches for sightseers in rows on the narrow decks already crowded with American troops and grinning RAF types.

"Oh, well," you say to Barney, "we couldn't be going far in this little tub."

"First lieutenants, flying officers and above, this way!" an army transportation corps major yells.

"Second lieutenants, pilot officers, and flight officers, follow me, please," bellows a sergeant.

As you surge into a small bay from the deck, a British merchant seaman thrusts a canvas and rope bundle into your arms while another sergeant counts you through. "A hundred and fifty. That's all. The rest of you gentlemen over on the port side, please."

"What do we do with these?" someone yells, hefting the bundle in his arms.

"Sling 'em up, sir. Instructions on the wall."

You jam around the framed yellowed diagram screwed to the white wooden wall. You read: "Plan for emergency accommodations forward starboard section C-2. Fifty hammocks."

Only, there are a hundred and fifty of you. An hour or so later, when you've gotten your hammock suspended from pipes along the low ceiling, it is one of a maze of interlapping contraptions jammed together, each hammock scraping four others in the stuffy air. You peer under the maze toward the unventilated wall which curves with the bow of the little ship. You are glad you don't get seasick at sea, and hope you can count on that. Your musette bag stowed in your hammock, you go out on deck. Right in front of you a jeep is dangling in midair being loaded by a winch. A long line of solemn-looking men, all dressed alike in grayish olive drab, is filing steadily up the gangplank below.

"Rangers," somebody says. "Looks like we're in for a show."

But where? All day long, as more and more men and equipment are piled into the little ship, everybody keeps trying to figure it out. That evening you stand with a huddle of American and British officers of all ranks and attire before the curtained glass doors of the dining room. A dining room? Can you imagine that? Maybe this isn't going to be so bad after all.

"What rank is that?" Barney asks, nudging and nodding toward a large man with a short haircut, properly dressed in Class A green blouse and slacks, but wearing absolutely no insignia. "Warrant officer or something?"

It's something to talk about, so you do for a while, and then you decide to ask him. "Pardon me. We were just wondering. Would you mind telling us? You're not wearing any insignia. What are you in?"

The fellow grins. "War correspondent. Associated Press. My name's Wes Gallagher."

You introduce yourself and Barney and a couple of other guys and in turn are introduced to Chris Cunningham of UP, Bob Nixon of INS, and a Reuters man. "Say," you get around to it, "you guys must have some idea where we're going."

"Well," Wes grins, "we brought along plenty of furs. Our guess is around Norway to Russia."

Plenty of furs! Aside from your field flying jacket, all you've got is an extra shirt and some underwear.

"Who're all these guys?" You nod around at a lot of other fully uniformed army officers waiting for the dining room to open.

"Eisenhower's staff . . . all the lower echelons. They've brought furs, too."

But when the convoy rolls out through the neck of Glasgow's harbor into choppy seas late that night, it doesn't head for Norwegian seas. It skirts around North Ireland. In the salty sunlight of next morning the great stretched-out convoy is steaming west in the direction of New York.

"Excuse me," Wes says in the lightly populated dining room after breakfast. "I'm going to work on the captain."

No matter how many times the correspondents climb up that swaying ladder to the bridge of the channel steamer Leinster during the next two days, the answer is always the same. "Sealed orders. The captain doesn't even know. If he does, he's not telling."

The other ships in the convoy, except the banana boat carrier Biter, don't look like they are rocking much. But the Leinster, designed for the short dash across the Irish Channel, bobs and weaves, shudders, rolls, and rears to plunge again hour after hour. You make for the little barroom, a Godsend on all British troop ships, and inoculate yourself with quadruple shots of good Scotch at a shilling a throw. Most of the boys don't do that, and it gets quite messy on the floor beneath the hammock maze. But the dining room isn't crowded and neither is the barroom, and between treatments there is poker in the correspondents' staterooms. For three days the Leinster tosses and groans its way toward New York. Then suddenly the convoy heads south.

"Well." Wes looks at the other newsmen after tossing his ante in for a third hand one afternoon. "I can't file the story, so I may as well tell you. We're going to North Africa."

"North Africa! What's in North Africa?"

"I dunno. It's Vichy French. Maybe it's the back door to Berlin."

It's very drunk in the barroom that night. Most of the men have ridden out their seasickness. "I can tell you boysh now," a colonel of one of the other fighter groups beams after the usual dirty songs. "We're goin' into Morocco, an' we're fightin' our waysh in! We're pickin' up our planesh on the Rock." But in one place in the ship it is not so gay. Before hitting your hammock you stagger through a lower deck where four hundred Rangers are silently oiling their rifles.

But D-day is not quite yet. Next day one ship in the convoy drops anchor in the middle of the Atlantic. The convoy begins slowly to circle around and around the anchored ship. Signs are posted above all fresh water taps.

Attention. Due to the large numbers of troops aboard the *Leinster* it has become absolutely necessary to conserve fresh water. Proceeding immediately, all fresh water will be turned off except between 0900 hours and 0930 hours and between 1730 hours and 1800 hours. By order of the Captain.

For three days in tropical waters the convoy wheels slowly about the anchored ship. You wash your double set of shirts, underwear, socks, and yourself in salt water. With Scotch you drink soda water, which costs more than the Scotch but is easier to get than fresh water.

"Hey," Barney calls, waking you up in your hammock, "wake up!"

"Whassa matter?"

"We're heading east."

Under cover of darkness, within sight of the miraculously glowing lights of Tangier to the south, the little *Leinster* sneaks away from the creeping convoy and warps into the crowded, lighted harbor of Gibraltar. It wends its way between anchored ships and cluttered floating docks, swiftly disgorges that part of its cargo made up of fighter pilots, war correspondents, and Eisenhower's headquarters personnel. You are conjured safely in trucks away from the sight of Spain to the Governor's Cottage on the seaward side of the Rock. Twelve days at sea with a musette bag for luggage. I'll bet my pop would call that traveling light.

"Gentlemen, we take off at dawn tomorrow," an intelligence officer briefs the assembled pilots in a large Nissen hut theater after you have all been hiding out for two days. "Two groups to Casablanca. Two groups to Oran. Two groups to Algiers. Our forces will hit the beaches at exactly nine o'clock. We should arrive about noon." You are issued new, strange maps. You are given a cellophane escape kit containing gold-sealed American occupation money, French francs, silk maps, a compass, Benzedrine in case you get tired, sulfa tablets in case you get wounded, and plastic gloves filled with sulfa powder in case your hands get burned. "You gentlemen," he addresses your group, "will fly to Oran and land at Tafaraoui at about noon. That's twenty-seven miles inland, but if everything goes according to schedule paratroopers and fast-moving mechanized units should have captured the field by then. With belly tanks you have only enough gas to fly one way. You could never make it back to Gibraltar. So in the event Tafaraoui is not held by us, your orders are to bail out. Is that clear?"

"Too damned clear," someone groans beside you. "Twenty-seven miles inland, and our dogfaces are supposed to have it in three hours."

In the misty sun of dawn you taxi your new Spitfire in single file from the hiding place under the lee of the Rock through streets of the blocked-off part of town to the airstrip separating a bit of England from a lot of Spain. Mushing spookily from the weight of a belly tank that does not contain enough fuel to bring you back again, you point with the sky full of planes for Morocco and an invasion that will not begin until you are halfway across the vast flat Mediterranean below. And you pray for the dogfaces on all those ships, and the Rangers oiling their rifles for maybe the last time on the little Leinster now back with the convoys lying somewhere out there just off Arzew. And praying for them you are praying for yourself, for unless they can invade twenty-seven miles inland in three hours you'll have no place to land.

That's what I call traveling light. I can tell my dad about a one-way passage. I can tell him about riding on troopships, troop trains, invasion ships, fighter planes, camels, Nazi planes, traveling on foot, and now about a horse car. I used to think pop was a transportation expert. I'm the expert now.

Chapter Seventeen

It was a black night. The close-packed men squirmed constantly against each other, rousing occasionally to mumble dirty words.

One of the countless cries in the sticky blackness came from Fred Wolkowski. "Let me go!" He peered around to remember where he was sleeping. He prayed. "Let me go."

Dawn oozed in through the flat slit of the boxcar window. The only man asleep was Fred.

Jim squeezed through to the slit and rubbed his seedy eyes. "Boy, she really is a thaw."

"We're heading south," a prisoner standing at the window announced.

Al Koczeck nodded. "Yeah, but not very fast. Train kept stopping all night."

Jim looked mildly surprised. "Say, I thought it did, but I wasn't sure."

Koczeck shrugged and smiled. "Jesus Christ! Didn't you hear it?"

"Hear what?"

"Bombs away! Some place up ahead took an hour-long pasting."

Jim snorted. "Hell, I'm getting so I can sleep any place through anything."

Tom pointed toward the grotesquely curled-up figure of Fred. "He's still got you beat. Anybody got any water?"

Nearby, Bob Montgomery growled: "How could anybody have any water? Yesterday it was too cold to carry it without it freezing. Today, when it's warm enough, we haven't got any. Pass that can over here. I'll give you some water."

"Take it easy." Tom Howard lumbered to his feet, pressed through to the window slit, and stuck his skinny arm through, fumbling about at the eave's edge. Soon he brought in a tiny icicle about four inches long and sat down sucking it. He called after Jack Noble, who was crossing to the slit. "Be sure you reach forward into the slipstream. That ain't all melted snow behind."

Fred Wolkowski straightened out, pushing a foot into someone's stomach, and slowly sat up, blinking at the bilious light in the crowded car. Burt Salem chuckled good-naturedly. "Sleeping Beauty!"

"Hey!" someone called from the slit window. "We're coming into a town!"

"Yow! Look at that!" someone up at the slit shouted, starting off a burst of excitement among those who could see. "What's up?" Koczeck shouted, trying to jump up in the air in the cramped space he was occupying. "What's up? Jim!"

A flushed red face close by turned back and shouted. "Boy! Has this place been blasted! Wrecked cars and twisted-up tracks everywhere!"

The train rolled slower and slower.

"Great day in the mornin'," the red face continued to shout. "We're now passing what is left of hundreds of boxcars. Peppered with holes, roofs smashed in, chopped into kindlin' wood, burned right down to the wheels, turned over on their sides, upside down and—I tell you, I never seen anythin' like it!"

Jim strained high to get a general impression of a jagged shamble of train wreckage, much of it still smoldering. The scene of destruction stopped slipping past as the prison train came to a halt. Outside, men bundled up in olive-drab rags moved about dragging twisted rails and other debris.

"Hey!" a prisoner in the boxcar shouted at a nearby worker. "What are you guys? Limeys?"

A yellow-whiskered face peered up at the slit. "We're furkin' well not. We're Aussies." The light whiskers divided into a gold-toothed grin. "You cobbers are Yanks, ain'tcher?"

"Not all of us!" a Southern accent boomed.

"Hey, what's going on here, Aussie?"

"Not much. It was a bit thick last night, though. Furkin' thick!"

"RAF?"

"It wasn't the furkin' Luftwaffe!"

Bob Montgomery had managed to work over and get up to the

slit by using his elbows and new-found rank. "What's the matter, Aussie? You sound mad at the Lancaster drivers."

"Look, Yank." The Aussie prisoner's big, suddenly serious eyes didn't show up as white as his blond whiskers. "Maybe you don't comprende." He nodded about him at the other Aussies bent over and working hard clearing the smoking, twisted rubble. "This is my home now. We live here. How would you like to have a visitor like them Lancs every couple of nights?"

Burt's voice exploded mournfully from his perch on Koczeck's back. "Live here!"

The blond beard nodded solemnly toward some boxcars standing at the edge of the maze of tracks. "We were billeted there last night. The front truck is still a bit messy."

"Jesus . . ."

Three of the four camouflaged freight cars bore a few scratches and holes. The roof and walls of the front car were caved in on its wheels like a smashed cracker box. A score of men who might have been sleeping lay alongside the ruined car. But sleeping men move, and these were motionless.

"Kom an, Mach. Get to vurruck." A good-natured Wehrmacht Feldwebel appeared beyond the slit talking to the Aussie. "Vat are you furkin' off for?"

The Aussie winked at the men in the car and bent over to tie his shoe. The German shrugged and walked on. It was silent in the boxcar, with those who could see gazing across the marshaling yard toward the smashed freight car and the silent forms beside it. Jim was the first to speak.

"What's the idea, old man? Why are the goons making you sleep in a place like this?"

The Aussie straightened up and patiently explained in a weary voice. "Because this is the main target. This is the marshaling yards. Here is where most of the work is every bloody mornin'. We ain't furkin' orficers. We harve ter work. Where else they going to put us? In the houses? Three-fourths of the furkin' houses in Leipzig are clobbered to the ground this fine mornin'."

"Leipzig! Oh, is that where we are?"

"It ain't Sydney!"

Another voice boomed out. "Where we headin', Aussie? Any Luftwaffe camps around here?"

Before the Aussie could answer, the Feldwebel returned. "Ach, kom an, Mach. Quvit furkin' off. Get busy to vurruck vunce now. Stop furkin' off."

The men in the jam-packed space just within the window slit grinned. Jim chuckled. "Which one picked it up from which?"

The Aussie picked up a charred railroad tie and walked over the tracks to drop it onto a pile of railroad garbage. The men watched sympathetically until the Aussie returned and looked up and down the track. He shook his head decisively. "Yanks, there ain't no Luftwaffe camps near here. There's but four kinds of camps south of Leipzig: enlisted men's camps, slave-labor camps, concentration camps, and extermination camps. If you're lucky, you'll end up in a slave-labor camp."

"Why?" Bob wanted to know. "What's so good about your set up? This is slave labor, isn't it?"

One of the Australian's eyes winked above his beard. "We may get bombed, Yank, but we eat. When we get this marshaling yeard cleaned up, then we'll be taken uptown to clean up, and as yer no doubt know there's lots of ways ta clean up."

Tom's voice came out brittlely. "Like what?"

The Aussie's gold teeth gleamed darkly through a shrewd grin. "Ye're orficers, ain'tcher? How long has it been since ye've seen a nice fresh white cackleberry like this one." The men in the boxcar gasped as the prisoner from down under held out an egg! "Now, who'll give me five cigarettes for it? You can have it scrambled, boiled, fried, poached on toast. . . ."

Bob had difficulty in speaking through the sudden saliva in his mouth. "I'll give you ten cigarettes for it!"

Fred grinned gleefully. "Make it fifteen!"

"Twenty!" shouted another voice.

The Aussie looked startled. "Twenty! Why, I can buy a whole horse and wagon for that. I've done it!"

"Thirty!" someone yelled quickly.

Bob followed it up desperately. "I'll give you two packs! Forty American!"

The Aussie's mouth gaped in his beard.

"I'll pay three packs!" an unseen speaker in the next car down the line yelled.

The Aussie looked toward the sound, spat, and snorted disgustedly.

"Oh, don't be a bloody fool!" He handed the egg up to Bob. "Just give me one furkin' pack. There's more cackleberries around here than there is people." Lighting one of the cigarettes, the Aussie suddenly stiffened and listened, looking up into the gray sky. Other prisoner laborers and German guards in the railroad shambles stood paralyzed by the same shock. The Aussie beat sparks out of his blond beard. "Oh, my aunt-furkin' uncle! Here they come again!"

Then the men in the boxcars heard it. Like the squall of the devil's baby, sirens began to moan and wail, up and down, in mournful, terrorizing warning. Near and far their howl, overlapping and rising and dying, pierced through shuddering eardrums. Someone started pounding on the door.

"Open up! Open up, for Christ's sake! You sons of bitches, where are you? Open up!"

Someone started to whimper, and Jim's voice grated out as hard and as menacing as granite. "Shut up! Shut that man up! Shut yourselves up!" Suddenly he grinned at the little mob, each member of which was trying to back into the very center of the locked boxcar. "I'm telling you to use your furkin' heads and keep your bowels for something better than thinking." He turned his back on the tense pack and looked out the slit. Strangely, he noticed that the sun cast sudden golden light on the twisted railroad tracks and wreckage jutting into the sky. "Hey, Limey! You still out there?"

A muffled voice came up from beneath the boxcar. "Don't call me a Limey, you furkin' Yank!"

"You furkin' Aussie!" Jim yelled back, and laughed out loud. "What are you doing down there? Drilling for oil?" Other men in the boxcar began to grin, some of them forgetting their terror. There was no answer, then a blond bearded face followed a pair of rag-clad forearms up into the window slit. The Aussie grinned.

"I just wanted to make sure I was right. There are enough fat asses in here to make under the truck the safest bomb shelter in the world." The arms and face dropped away along with the laughter. Jim stared out through the slit at the last of the laborers, guards, and civilian trainmen hurdling the debris to get to the ditches and slit trenches at the edge of the marshaling yard.

"Let us out! Let us out, for God's sake!" Cries of the prisoners in other boxcars sounded through the wailing of the sirens. One by one, the men behind Jim in the car slowly crouched down, a maze of intertwined bodies pressing hard against the floor and one another. Koczeck, clutching a rosary out of sight in his pocket, moved up beside Jim, who was gazing into the sun-goldened haze.

"Watch out!" Bob Montgomery crouched in the mass on the floor and cupped his fresh egg to his chest. "I'll brain any bastard who busts it!"

Suddenly the sirens stopped howling. Jim held a thumb up to the sky and carefully scanned it. Tom spoke calmly behind him. "What do you see?"

"Nothing—yet."

Pressed against the floor and into a corner of the car, Jack Noble breathed deeply the foul scent of the place. Tears trickled unhindered down his plump face. The Aussie's muffled voice came from beneath the floor. "Here they come, Yanks!"

Koczeck brought the rosary from his pocket and, letting it dangle at his side, stared up at the casually approaching swarm of silver-winged specks high in the hazy west. "They're Messerschmitts!"

Tom grunted disagreement. Jim, moving his thumb and, slowly sighting the formation, laughed. "You bomber driver! They're P-51's."

Huddled in the middle of the car, the P-51 pilot who had talked the day before of shooting up trains spoke briefly and bitterly. "We've had it."

Jim sighed and waited patiently. Is this it? he wondered to himself. Will it be this time? He almost hoped it finally, once for all, would be. At the same time some other unit of his brain was analyzing the formation. About ten thousand feet. Three o'clock high. Four, eight, sixteen, twenty-four friends. Friends! He smiled a little and noted curiously the formation they were flying. Four vics of four. Not three flights of four line astern the way it used to be done. These Mustangs weren't even weaving. Suddenly he heard the moan of the Rolls-Royce engines. The fresh air coming through the slit into the stink began to smell clean and distinct. Jim's ears began to jingle and he could hear a buzzing that was not the aircraft now almost on the target. Without looking around he saw the packed, dirty, shivering mob steaming in the locked coffin of the boxcar. He gritted his teeth. This is not it, he ground into his soul. I'll not die in here! The planes had almost arrived. He noted the unspoiled silver of the Dural wings, and his vision flashed back for a moment to the mottled camouflage required earlier in the war. He could see the white star insignia under the wings and the little vaporous whirl of the twenty-four propellers.

"Pretty! Ain't they?"

Jim jerked his eyes down with a start to see the blond-bearded Aussie casually standing outside the slit and looking upward. By the time Jim got his eyes up again, the twenty-four P-51's had passed over. He looked back at the smiling Aussie. "What the hell? They didn't—they didn't. Christ, they're gone!"

The Aussie picked up a shovel and leaned it over his shoulder. "Right enough, Yank. Those were fighters, not Forts."

Jim sighed. "Does this sort of thing happen often here?" he asked the Aussie.

"Sometimes twice a day. The fighters are looking around for trains right enough, but not in a flak nest like this marshaling yard. They'll get you later when you're out in the open."

Someone took the can off its nail. There were many demands for it. Prisoners, guards, and civilians were popping up from their shelters and walking back through the wreckage of the marshaling yard. Jim looked up at the empty blue of the sky. "I didn't see any flak."

"They don't shoot unless they have to. They don't want to make them mad. Oh, oh. Here comes the old goon. I guess I been furkin' off long enough." Grinning wide and golden, the Aussie made a grand thumbs-up sign. "So long, Yanks. Godspeed." He turned and stepped away over damaged and undamaged tracks, the tatters of his ragged and scorched greatcoat fluttering gently.

"What's going on out there?" someone not curious enough to go to the now accessible slit called from the pack. "What's holding us up?" In reply, the boxcar jerked and the train rattled forward, gradually picking up speed as it left the graveyard of the Leipzig railroad yards.

Jack Noble: "There I was...."

I studied nights to keep away from the dirt of the steel mills. I made a lot less money than the other fellows who went to high school with me, but, gee, they were going to spend the rest of their lives in the mills just like my dad. I couldn't stand the dirt and the smoke and the heat. I'd die before I would come home all greasy and sooty and pooped out the way dad did every night. Steel men are tough when they're not too tired or when they are drunk. I don't want to be tough and dirty. I want to respect myself and be clean and married and have children that go to a nice school and someday to college.

I don't drink. I don't swear much. I had my first cigarette just the other day. And the sight of blood . . . Excuse me. I can't stand it.

"Give me your first-aid kit, Lieutenant," the crew chief yelled at me one day, sticking his head up into the nose compartment. "Ted has been hit very bad. Better pray for him."

I prayed. I wasn't good for much else that day. They had been shooting at us with flak, and the 109's, 190's, and 110's had been diving in and shooting at us for half an hour. Ted was the tail gunner. I prayed.

"Two o'clock high," Phil the bombardier yelled before me into the intercom, and started shooting the twin fifties.

I buried my face and oxygen mask in my arms and prayed. That's all I was good for. I couldn't make myself use either of the two thirty calibers pointing out through the rubber sockets on both sides of the nose blister. They weren't using me to navigate. I might have been able to do that, but someone a hundred forts ahead was doing that. I prayed, and when we got back they lifted some pieces of Ted out of the tail. The rest they washed out with a hose.

Phil wasn't mad at me. He never told the others or said anything about it to me. I couldn't help it. The same thing happened every time. When the shooting started I would cover up my head and pray. I should have told the C.O. or the doc or the padre, but that's awfully hard to do.

"Why worry?" Phil said to me when I mentioned it one day. "Another nine missions and we'll go home. You'll be with that filly of yours in Pittsburgh and, if you like, I'll be your best man."

"But why am I going out every mission?" I asked him. "They don't need a navigator. I'm no soldier at all. I'm no good to anybody."

Phil roughed up my hair. "Look," he said, "they don't need a bombardier either. We're just along for the ride. I'll do the shooting because I'd go nuts if I didn't have anything to do. If anything happens to me, you push the toggle button when, up ahead, you see the bombs away. That's why you're along. Those thirties couldn't hurt anybody anyhow. They're too small. You just press the toggle button in case I've bought it."

All the way through the next two missions I wondered if I could do just that. Gee, I didn't want it to ever happen. Phil was a swell guy. But I couldn't help wondering if I could pick up the toggle switch and watch the planes ahead for bombs away if we were being shot at. That wouldn't be much to do for the war. The next mission it happened.

Without looking up I could hear the terrible noise of Phil's new fifties. I was praying. All of a sudden there was an awful loud noise, and then I couldn't hear anything. Nothing at all. I couldn't even hear the motors. I looked up. Phil was flat on his back. A stream of blood was squirting straight up from his chest at least two feet and splashing back down over him onto the floor of the compartment. I still couldn't hear anything. I yelled but couldn't hear myself. "Phil!" I yelled, but my lips just moved. The fountain of blood squirting up from his chest grew shorter and shorter. "Phil!" I kept yelling, and just barely began to hear myself. The nose was full of wind coming in through a blown-out panel of plexiglass. It must have been a rocket. I looked ahead, past the glow of the gunsight and the tipped-up breeches of the fifties. The forts ahead were flying through a pattern of black, white, and yellow flak bursts, and German fighters were knifing in from both sides. Tracer smoke crisscrossed like a spider web. We were almost at the target—Berlin. I still couldn't hear much. I felt very sick, but I looked down for the toggle switch. Then I saw it.

My flak suit was torn open at the waist. Part of me was hanging out of the hole. Liver, like you see at a butcher shop, and some intestines. Blood was oozing in a red flood down over my stomach and hip. I stared at my own organs. Then I screamed. I hardly heard myself. Nobody else did. I screamed again. I flicked the intercom switch and screamed. Away off in the distance I barely heard a voice. "Who's that, for God's sake?" it crackled. "Identify yourself."

"Jack and Phil!" I cried into the intercom. "We're dying. We're dying!" The nose compartment went round and round. I vomited and clutched at what was falling out of my middle. I began to feel and hear. It hurt and I sounded awful. I fainted into my own blood and vomit.

When I woke up I was lying on the floor by a waist gun. One of the crew was holding a bottle of plasma that was running down a tube into my arm. "How you doing, Lieutenant?" he asked, looking down at me over his oxygen mask.

"Oh, Christ!" I heard the crew chief say. "Why did he have to wake up now?"

My whole middle burned like red-hot fire. I screamed again.

"Give me that morphine," the crew chief said, and I calmed down waiting for it. I didn't even feel them stick it into me; but suddenly I was dreamy and it didn't hurt so much down around my middle.

"Phil?" I was able to ask.

I didn't care. Somebody was tying a silk cord to the ripcord ring. "Shall I give him another shot of dope?" the waist gunner asked.

"Put it in his pocket," the crew chief ordered. "He'd better not be too doped up when he lands. He'll have to yell or something to get found."

The waist gun on the other side started shooting. "Christ!" the other waist gunner yelled. "Let's get him out of here and get back to fighting."

They carried me on a stretcher and laid me on one of the bomb bay doors. The crew chief leaned down and kissed me on the forehead. "Good luck, fella," he said, and pulled his hand out of mine. They tied the silk cord to an empty bomb rack and left me alone. My eyes were just half open, but I remember watching the empty bomb racks jiggle with vibration. Then the bomb bay doors started to open. I rolled down the one they had placed me on, hit the parting crack, and dropped away. The tail wheel whipped over my head. The chute cracked open with a jerk that just about killed me in my hurt middle. I swayed and swayed and looked down at the sunny ground. It was quiet. Blood was running down my legs. It dripped from my dangling shoe toes. It was awfully red in the sunshine. It fell away from my shoes going down in big drops far faster than I was falling. I stared at it and felt the wet slick of my bandaged stomach. I went to sleep at about ten thousand feet.

When I woke up again it was ten days later and I was in a German army hospital in a big ward with a lot of hurt Germans. They told me that whoever cut the steel out of my liver saved my life. They said whoever pushed me out of the plane saved my life. You know? I can't even remember that crew chief's name.

I never pushed that toggle switch.

Chapter Eighteen

The train clattered through the city. In the boxcar a few curious prisoners pressed their foreheads against the top of the slit and soberly noted the bomb holes which had pricked out tons of earth and, casually crossing in file over the long sheds of factories, had made similar holes in them. "Hell," Jim remarked with the cold breeze wiping his nose, "look at 'em. Ninety-nine per cent of 'em didn't hit anything but the ground."

"Yeah," Bob said, concentrating more on the egg he was cupping against his chest than upon the occasional ragged grooves in the long camouflaged sheds that whipped past, "that's RAF stick bombing. It ain't as good as daylight with the Norden."

Jim looked at the hands cupped over the egg. "What you going to do with that? You can't cook it."

"I'll cook it or hatch it. Man! Aren't eggs wonderful? We used to have a million of 'em on hand all the time back home."

A series of bomb craters peppering the green and white earth outside held their attention for a few seconds. In the middle of the chain of holes a green and white painted shed stood cloven in the middle, broken glass sparkling in the dirty half melted snow. "There's the only kind of eggs that count now," Jim said.

Bob shivered, stepped over about ten men, and sat down, studying his egg. At the same time Fred stood up in the mass of men. "What you going to do with that? Suck it?"

Bob looked up belligerently. "It's my business, isn't it? It's my egg."

Fred looked studiously at the rough ribbed walls and ceiling of the boxcar. With thumb and forefinger he agitated the dark stubble of his chin. He sighed a single word. "Say . . ." Then he bent down, picked up a blanket, and stepped over dodging prisoners to where Noble was sitting Sphinx-like against the vibrating front wall of the car. "You got any more nails? And some wire?"

Noble looked up, irritated. "No nails. I've got wire. Why don't you get your own stuff and keep it?"

Fred stood relaxed, bobbing with the motion of the car and studying the walls and ceiling. "Let me have some wire, will you, Jack? I've got an idea of how to log some sack time."

Fred folded his blanket double, put his teeth to it, and bit holes in the heavy wool. Spitting out the lint, he strung wire through the holes. Ignoring both complaints and advice, he tied the wires of each end of the blanket to the nails already supporting packs and other gear at the end walls of the boxcar.

"It won't work."

"Say, that's not a bad idea."

Opinions of the prisoners below the makeshift hammock were divided. Fred pulled down on the olive-drab wool sling and nodded. He looked down at Noble and at Koczeck. "Give me a boost, will you?"

Somebody in the pack offered an opinion. "It'll smell worse up there, Wolkowski. Heat makes it rise."

Fred's teeth gleamed in the natural dusk of the boxcar. "You don't smell anything when you're asleep. You don't taste, you don't feel, and you don't worry."

Jim looked up, grinning as Noble handed Fred some more wire. "You'll waste your life away sleeping all the time. What's the use of living if you don't know what you're living through?"

There was a great deal of grunting as Noble and Koczeck boosted Fred up by both wiry legs. Then Fred gingerly poked his dark flashing face over the edge of the taut blanket to look down at the still grinning Jim. "The worst that could happen to me up here is a wet dream. And that wouldn't be so bad, would it? Good night, men." The face disappeared and the downward-bulging blanket jiggled a couple of times.

Koczeck and Noble sat down beside Jim directly under the blanket bulge. Jim shook his head. "That guy could sleep in a boiler factory."

Down at the other end of the car someone else was improvising a hammock diagonally across a corner. The conversation was just a mumble in the louder rhythm and rattle of the rolling train. Lighting a cigarette and inhaling deeply, Jim blew out a stream of gray smoke and reflected that they were almost used to the smell. It had long since passed from an overpowering stench to simply an atmosphere. It was warm from body heat and from body contact. It beats walking, Jim thought. We must be over the hump. Now things will get better. Noble whined slightly. "I'm awfully thirsty. Hungry, too. Aren't they ever going to feed us? And I got to do number two." Bob glared at the younger man. "Who doesn't? It's because we're thawed out. But you can't do it in here." Tom smiled dryly, puffing on a cigarette. Koczeck relaxed, leaning back between Noble's soft thighs. Burt Salem, hemmed in by other bodies, nodded drowsily in rhythm with the train. Jim, huddled over a pocket notebook, tried vainly to think up verse to scribble with the stub of a pencil. The murmur and cough of the men mingled with the clatter and rattle of the crawling southward train.

At Chemnitz they halted in the main station. Jim and Bob, who was now free of his egg, which was carefully wrapped in a handkerchief and stored within easy vision in a tin can nailed to the wall, led the press to the window slit.

"S.S.!" the men whispered to each other. "S.S.!"

Across a jam-packed platform, under the bomb-shattered skeleton of what had once been a glass and steel arcade, stood a troop train filled with the black-uniformed élite of the S.S. soldiers. They wore the forked lightning insignia on their lapels and white skulls embroidered on the points of their caps. The ruined station was a bedlam of shouting. Wide-eyed civilian refugees and the handsome, brown-faced S.S. milled about on the platform.

"Herr Knabe!" Jim shouted at a boy who was ladling out ersatz coffee into the plastic canteen cups of several of the black-uniformed Germans. "Bitte, Herr Knabe! Wollen Sie hier kommen?" The boy looked curiously at the faces filling the slit of the boxcar, but continued serving the Germans until they turned away satisfied. They had paid him nothing. Jim tried again. "Herr Knabe!" He held out a pack of cigarettes. "Wollen Sie ein Packet zwanzig Zigaretten für eine Flasche Kaffee nehmen?" Jim poked the neck of the Muskau flask through the slit.

"Zigaretten?" the boy inquired quaveringly, pushing his large three-wheeled urn halfway toward them. "Für mich?"

"Jawohl!" Jim offered the pack violently. "Amerikanische Zigaretten. Für nur eine Flasche Kaffee."

The boy looked around bewildered, and then suddenly pushed the urn up close under the slit. Jim thrust the pack into the boy's hands and tapped the neck of the flask. Quickly the boy began to ladle out the ersatz and to pour it into the large flask. From within the car other cups and containers were passed up. The boy worked rapidly, nervously spilling some of the liquid.

"Jesus, Weis," somebody behind complained, "give someone else a chance. You got enough."

Jim calmly let the boy continue until the flask was about two-thirds full of the brown steaming stuff. Just as he was pulling the flask away to make way for some of the hands thrusting cigarettes, cigars, and chocolate bars over his shoulder, a black back blotted out the boy.

"Kerl! Schwein!" was all that Jim was able to make out. The black back turned, revealing a tall blond S.S. trooper gripping the boy fiercely by the shoulder. The S.S. man shouted an unintelligible volley of dialect, shaking the terrorized boy so violently that his chin kept striking his chest and knocking his teeth together. With a roar and a shake of a large brown hand, the S.S. trooper sent the youth sliding along the cement floor. He kicked the boy's thigh with a shiny hobnailed boot, crossed to the urn, picked up the ladle, and slopped the hot stuff violently over the sobbing boy. After three ladles, he scooped up a fourth and turned toward the slit. "Kaffee für Amerikaner!" His arm made a violent sweep, and coffee flew into the faces of the cowering prisoners.

When Jim stood up, wiping the sticky liquid from his face with his sleeve, the S.S. man was gone. His comrades in the crowded cars across the platform were laughing uproariously. Jim's forearms tingled, and he shivered as if he were awakening from a nightmare. Tom produced a second pack of cigarettes and started to toss it to the boy kneeling in the puddle of coffee. Jim caught Tom's arm. "Don't. You'll just get him in more trouble. He's still got my pack."

The boy scrambled in a panic to his feet, and with S.S. troopers and civilian refugees alike howling derision after him ran pushing his coffee urn out of sight down the platform. Someone grunted and spat through the slit. "I wonder how brave they'd be fighting men."

Bob turned away. "They're brave enough."

"Well, anyway," Tom commented dryly as they squeezed into their regular positions in the wriggling mass on the floor, "you got something to drink."

Koczeck slapped his hands together and rubbed them. "Yeah. C'm' on. Let's have a slug."

Jim passed the lukewarm flask around. "Better take it light. Can't tell how long we'll be cooped up in here. We might get thirsty."

"If we don't get out for a bit pretty soon, we'll get dirty." Bob wiped his lips. "Whew. Never thought that stuff would ever taste good. It ain't coffee, but it's wet."

Koczeck took another sip and looked up toward the hammock. "Hey, Fred! You want a drink?" The bulging blanket moved slightly and became motionless. "Fred?"

Jim stretched to his feet and peered over the edge of the blanket. Fred's mouth was slightly open. He snored softly through a gentle smile. Jim shrugged. "He can have one when he wakes up."

"Hey, in there!" The call came from outside. Jim looked out and could see Junior Jones and another Kriegie pushing a baggage car piled high with large brown cans and dark gray loaves of Reich bread. "Be ready to divvy up rations when we stop out of town." A Wehrmacht guard stood patiently by while the message was delivered. "We get to climb out for a pee call. So be ready."

A small cheer went up in the car as Junior moved on. Jim took a last look at the black-uniformed giants snoozing against the steamy windows of their first-class railway car across the platform, and sat down in his own sticky quarters. "Well, we're sitting pretty now. We get food, drink, and a chance to relieve ourselves all at Chemnitz. We got cigarettes, we're warm, we're riding and"—he looked up at the hammock—"Fred Wolkowski's even got a bed. Ah, Chemnitz, you lovely place you . . . a place to remember."

The train started forward, splashing ersatz coffee from the tilted flask onto Noble's stubbled chin.

A couple of kilometers out of Chemnitz the long drab train slowed at a turn high on a banked-up roadbed. With a shudder of jamming couplings it came to a stop. Tom looked from the slit down the steep snow-covered bank and ahead at the curving train and steaming locomotive. He sniffed. "What a place to stop!"

Jim shrugged. "It's so they can pick you off easy if you make a break for it."

Behind them prisoners stood up eagerly. Some even joggled up and down, grunting a little with eagerness to get out of the car.

Bob Montgomery raised his voice above the chatter of the crowd. "Who'll volunteer to stay by the door and collect the rations?"

Tom Howard spoke calmly. "I'll stay."

Rifle-toting guards were walking toward the center of the train from both front and rear, pausing in the soft snow by each car to unlock the steel crossbars and release the sliding doors. Jim and Tom turned away from the sight of prisoners squirting like waves from the cars forward and behind. Tom remained by the slit, watching the swirling mass of men inside the car, while Jim elbowed his way toward the rest of the combine. "Give me some fodder." Noble was passing out paper from the roll he had packed from Sagan. Jim took a length and followed Bob up into the impatient press against the still closed door. There was a loud rattling at the door. Someone shouted above the others. "Stand back so we can open it!" The press leaned back in a single body. With a rolling sound the door slid open and the men jumped out.

Noble paused by the hammock, grabbed its edge, and shouted at the sleeping face of Fred. "Fred! Wolkowski!" Fred's eyes opened and the pupils rolled casually toward Noble, who continued. "We've stopped. They're letting us out for a bit. Don't you want to get out?" Fred smiled dreamily, shook his head gently, and closed his eyes again. Noble sat down on the floor's edge and dropped to the trodden snow.

A stiff breeze blew from the rear of the train toward the panting locomotive. Men squatted in a long line facing the entire length of the train, draped over the edge of the steep slope. Soiled paper, carried by the wind, whipped along the cringing, dodging line. Jim, ducking several crumpled lengths of paper, turned to Bob, who was trying to protect his face with a cocked elbow. "Come on. Let's go down the bank a ways where we won't get clobbered by this stuff." They broke through the line of men and joined others wading through the soft snow down the steep bank to less crowded positions. Side by side halfway down they set about their business. Jim suddenly had to lift a leg and lurch to dodge a cannonball-sized snowball which came hurtling down. He looked up the slope. "Jesus Christ! Look at that." The posterior view of the line of prisoners along the top of the bank was not what he was referring to. Both Jim and Bob gaped in amazement at the sight of hundreds of tiny snowballs rolling down from the top, gaining in speed and growing as they constantly picked up more snow and hurtled down toward them. The snowballs kept coming as more and more Kriegies took the places of those who stepped away from the ranks along the ledge.

Suddenly, with a mournful whir in the distance, a siren began the rising wail of an air-raid alarm. "Here we go again," Bob muttered, straightening up and hauling up many layers of clothing, as sirens in the direction of Chemnitz joined the warning. Jim stood up and, clutching at his unbuttoned clothing, slogged after Bob toward the thinning ranks by the train. The wind pierced through them like the mournful sobbing of the sirens. Guttural commands whipped along the ridge. As they reached the top, men scrambled back into the boxcars and shouting guards ran up and down the length of the train. A Wehrmacht officer in faded green breeches ran back and forth shouting. "Get in! Einsteigen! Get back inside, Gott tammitt!"

"But we're not through yet!"

"Give us a chance, will you?"

Jim and Bob passed the still squatting men just as the German officer whipped out a Luger and started waving it at those who were still lagging. "Gedt back in derr or dtie! I don'dt fool vidt you! Einsteigen! Righdt now!"

Jim and Bob were just ahead of the last men to clamber up into their car. After the air outside, the interior was overpowering. Instinctively each man shouldered and stumbled his way through the confusion to his own combine's bit of boxcar. Before they could see clearly in the gloom, the door rolled shut and the crossbar was dropped. Jim dropped beside Tom Howard, who was sitting calmly on five brown cans, protecting with his arm a stack of five loaves of Reich bread. "Is that all we get?" Jim wiped his eyes.

"One loaf and one can for each ten men. It's bullied deer meat."

Gradually the men settled down in the usual tangle of bodies. The muffled sirens were still chanting outside. The train was motionless except for the squirming of its cargo. The guards were shouting back and forth distantly outside. Bob looked at his watch. "You know how long we been here?"

"No."

"Five minutes."

"They sure gave us a lot of time," someone very nearby commented. "I bet some of the guys in the cars opened after us didn't even get to go."

Burt drawled. "What's all the rush about, anyways?"

Al Koczeck got slowly to his feet. "I'm going to have a look outside." He carefully stepped over and glanced upward through the slit. With a jerk he froze. "Oh, Jesus!" The specks he saw grew bigger as they swooped downward. He turned and cried in a whisper, "Lay down. . . . Lay down. . . . They're coming in."

The men dazedly watched Koczeck sink to his knees.

"A-a-a-hhh . . ."

"Oh-h-h . . ."

It was a convulsive movement. Men pressed, groaning and shivering, into one another and hid their faces and heads like ostriches under their arms and clasped hands. There were three quick crashes followed by a shocking explosion. Barely heard were the coughing noises outside followed immediately by a quick series of bursts above. Jim was the first man to sit up. He gazed over the cowering backs.

"Anybody hit?" he asked matter-of-factly. Slowly the men lifted their heads and looked first at themselves and then at one another. Noble's teeth were chattering. Bob Montgomery started whistling "Wabash Cannon Ball" between his front teeth.

Once again Jim called out. "Nobody hit?" His eyes spotted three holes high on the wooden side of the boxcar.

"Hey!" Noble called, tossing something hot from hand to hand. "Look at this!"

German voices began shouting authoritatively outside. "Will they come back?" a quavering voice inquired.

"Naw," the voice of the Southern fighter pilot drawled with conviction. "Never strike twice at the same target."

"Lemme see that." Tom took the cooling object from Noble and studied it. "Fifty-caliber ball." Jim and Burt leaned close to look at the flattened piece of metal that had apparently ricocheted off some metal part of the car.

Koczeck suddenly spoke up in surprise. "Say. I think I am."

Bob glanced at him. "What?"

"Hit. My back is beginning to sting."

Jim twisted toward Koczeck, who was busily pawing his back. "Get off some clothes and let's have a look."

The car was suddenly a storm of noise as the prisoners began outdoing each other in describing their recent terror.

"Man. man, man! I thought I'd give birth to turnips!"

"You did? I wanted to crawl into my socks!"

"God! Did you hear those devils come down?"

Jim and Tom helped peel several final T-shirts over Koczeck's head. Curious prisoners leaned close to look at a small pattern of black spots near the right shoulder blade of Koczeck's thick white back. Jim ran a finger over them. "Shell splinters. That loud one was an H.E. You'll be all right if they don't get infected. My rear end is full of them."

Tom turned around and called into the pack. "Anybody got any iodine or anything like that?"

"Is it bad?" someone called back in the sudden quiet.

"No. Any kind of disinfectant will do. Somebody must have some." After waiting long enough to search all of the blank faces, Tom shrugged. "No dice."

"Does it hurt?" Jim asked.

"No. Just stings a little."

"Well, put on a clean undershirt. You got one, haven't you?"

"Hey!" a prisoner by the slit yelled. "They got the engine!"

Men scrambled toward the slit. Jim stayed where he was, along with Tom and Koczeck. He sighed and cupped his face in his hands. "God, we're lucky! They must have been strays. Wonder how it is in the other cars."

"It was lousy shooting," Tom said. "You can't do much damage spray shooting."

"Boy, look at her spout steam!" someone by the slit shouted.

Koczeck poked his head through the neck hole of the T-shirt he was struggling into. "It wasn't so lousy. They got the engine."

Distantly, a siren began a long clear wail. Other sirens quickly joined in. Suddenly, with the piercing sound, Jim's bad tooth began to ache. He waited, hoping the pain would go away.

"Shut up!" someone by the slit yelled. "Listen!"

The silence was abrupt. Then they could hear faint words distorted by the stiff breeze. "Help! Help . . . wounded here . . . been killed . . . help us . . . dead man . . . please help . . ."

Noble came back from the press at the slit and sat down. "God. Someone's been killed."

The chatter resumed in the boxcar at a higher pitch. Jim grunted. Tom shrugged his scrawny shoulders. "What do you expect? There'll be more than one. Don't flap, Jack."

Noble shivered. Jim thought: All we can do is sit here and wait. It's just like always. Major Smith is right. Things will get worse before they get better. We've got to make the best of it. He smiled slightly at the vision the thought of that expression brought up so quickly. The green grass of an RAF fighter base in England. The delicately painted camouflaged Spitfires parked colorfully in the sunlight. The blue-clothed men casually bicycling around the taxi strips. And a big bosomed WAAF who at any mention of the lovely hardships of war in England would always say, "We've got to make the best of it, Willy Nilly." And Jim would crack back: "Don't call me Willy Nilly, honey. My name is Jim Weis." Jim noted the still shuddering Noble. "Say," he said seriously, "did I ever tell you what the lady said who called up the light company?"

"No," answered Tom, acting the straight man. "What did she say?"

"She said: 'Send a man out. I've been using a candle all night.' "

Tom and the now fully clothed Koczeck chuckled appreciatively. Noble frowned. "I don't get it." But he had stopped shivering.

Jim looked up in amused wonder at Fred's bulging hammock. It had not even stirred. Tom smiled broadly. "That's the way to fight a war."

"Hey, Oberleutnant!" someone shouted at the window slit. "When do we move out of here?"

"Ven ve get a new lokomotiff," the voice of the pistol-waving officer came back. "How you like your own medicine, eh? Id's not so fugging goot down here, eh? Now you know vod id iss aboudt."

"How many are hurt?"

"Only several American pigs. Only, unfortunately you haff killed the lokomotiff Führer and vounded za ozzer man in za lokomotiff, and zey verr goot Zhermans. So! Now you suffer a little. Eh?"

Noble began to shiver again. Tom looked at him sympathetically. "Don't flap, Jack. A bullet is no worse, maybe even better, than the snow. At least we're warm, and the rest of us are still alive."

A drop of moisture fell on Noble's forehead. He wiped it off with his hand. "What's it all about?" he asked softly, no longer shivering. "When's it going to end?"

Jim spoke up sharply. "It's about that moron out there who just called us pigs! It's about that black S.S. gorilla who knocked down a young punk who will grow up to be just like him! It's about ninety million gangsters trying to take over the whole world so they can be ninety million bosses! It's about ninety million monsters who consider themselves super-civilized while they gas and cremate thousands of old men and women and children. For Christ's sake, don't sit there shuddering about what's happening to us! If there's a God, this is supposed to be what we are here for! If there's no God, then we've got to be here for ourselves! Jesus! God! Stop it!"

Tom put a hand on Jim's sleeve. "What's the matter with you, Jim?"

Another drop of moisture splattered against Noble's forehead. He wiped it off and complained, "Now the roof is leaking."

Jim stared at the black smear left on Noble's forehead. He jerked to his knees and leaned forward. "Let me see your hand," he demanded, rubbing the smear on Noble's forehead with a forefinger.

"What . . ." Noble lifted his right hand. Jim looked up. They all looked up. The downward bulge of the blanket hammock had a dark spot at its lowest curve. Already the dark moisture was gathering into a drop.

"Oh-o-o-o." Jim jumped to his feet and grabbed the edge of the blanket. It was a good army blanket holding a man half bathed in blood.

In final sleep Fred's eyes were shut, and his mouth, slightly open, revealed his delicate teeth.

Chapter Nineteen

Fred's blood was scattered along many kilometers of enemy soil.

Al Koczeck first put the question in a weak voice. "What are we going to do with him?" The train clattered unconcernedly southward. "We can't leave him up there. He's dripping all over us."

Tom, standing beside Jim, spoke calmly. "Pass the can over. We'd better try and catch it. If we lower him down it'll spread over everything."

At the window slit a prisoner was screaming uselessly into the wind rushing past. "Help! Stop the train! Stop, for God's sake! There's a man dead in here! God damn it! Stop the train!"

As Tom placed the can under the fast-dripping bulge of the blanket, Jim reached in and unbuttoned the shirts beneath the still smiling blue-stubbled face. He turned away. "Who's got a knife?"

Koczeck reached into the helplessly shuddering Noble's coat pocket, pulled out a sheathed, sharpened table knife and handed it to Jim.

"Aw, cut it out," someone complained toward the man who was screaming out of the window. "Nobody can hear you."

The prisoner stopped screaming. Jim grasped Fred's dog tags, both his USAAF tag and his P.O.W. tag, and cut the cord that held them. The carful of prisoners was silent. Jim looked at the metal tags briefly and put them in his pocket. Noble let out a moan. Jim looked harshly down at him. "What's the matter with you?" Noble held out a shaking hand, its cupped palm holding the smashed and spent fifty-caliber bullet he had found just after the strafing. He let his arm sag, and the bullet thudded to the blanket-strewn floor.

Tom's voice brought the men's eyes away from the bullet. "Round up another can. We'll have to relay them." A clean can was immediately passed up from somewhere in the rear of the car. Jim took the first full can. His hand shook so that he was afraid he would spill it. He handed the can to Bob, who made his way easily between the prisoners to the window. The contents streamed out into the wind in a bright red sheet.

It was a silent routine process: filling up one can, then the other, then the first again, and pouring the red splash out toward the disappearing snow and slush and mud. Jim sat down because his nerves kept him from going on with it. Burt Salem, his face sheet-white, took his place. The train rattled on and on. . . .

The bleeding had long since stopped when the train came to a halt in a village. Five Wehrmacht guards with slung rifles waited shivering beneath the opened door while Bob, Tom, Burt, and Koczeck unfastened and lowered the dead-weighted blanket sling. Jim stood at the window slit, his hand thrust out and down toward the Wehrmacht officer. "Here are his tags."

The Wehrmacht officer bent over to blow his nose between his fingers and then stood up to finish the job with a white handkerchief. "Vadt I vandt dem for? I haff no need of dem."

Jim squinted his eyebrows together. "But aren't you going to notify the Red Cross?"

The German snorted. "You keep dem. You let dem know ven you gedt vere you are gedting."

Jim sighed angrily, but controlled his voice. "Jawohl. Wohin gehen wir, bitte?"

"Vadt care you? You gedt der sometime."

"Well, where are we, then, so I can tell the Red Cross?"

The German smiled scornfully. "Vadt care you?" He pulled out his handkerchief and wiped his thin red nose again. "You don't gedt out hier." He nodded sideways toward the blanket bundle being passed carefully down from the boxcar to the Wehrmacht guards. "He gedts out. Nodt you." The German turned, barked something very rapidly to the guards, and strutted away, grinding slush beneath his bootheels.

Jim turned around in time to see Noble vomit. Someone stuck a blood-lined can under the heaving youth's face before the mess got much worse than it was.

The door rattled shut. It was not opened again for thirty-nine hours.

When the train ground slowly to a stop early in the morning of the third night out of Spremberg, smelly moisture dripped from the ceiling and rolled in rivulets down the crossbeams of the walls. The sour stench of urine, vomit, and unwiped men welled up from the sweating mass packed together on the floor. Here and there, dazed, semi-conscious men groaned or snored gratingly, as though in a death rattle. Two men were unconscious; one had been so for a day past, the other for several hours. Others played gin, pinochle, or poker, using their knees for tables under the flickering light of the improvised lamps.

"I'll raise you a thousand."

"I'll raise you ten thousand."

"All right, you shoe clerks. I'll raise you both fifty thousand dollars! How does that suit you?"

"I'll call you."

Some of the men slept. Jim wriggled his knees in Tom Howard's back. "Tom. Lift up, will you?"

Tom sighed, disturbed but not moving. "Where you going?"

"Over to the window."

"Ah, just tell 'em to pass it over here."

"I want to look out and see where we are."

Tom arched his skinny back painfully forward. "Nuts. We're probably in another tunnel sweating out a raid up ahead."

Jim labored to his feet. He picked his way carefully around a Kriegie who was curled up clutching his stomach. Tom followed him. Jim picked a can off its nail beside the slit and passed it back toward the constricted Kriegie. The wet misty air slapped Jim in the face like a cold towel.

Tom spoke dryly. "What do you expect to see?"

Jim said, "This is it." He peered out through a dark night across several sets of railroad tracks, which, like the mist itself, glistened at intervals with a strangely remote light.

"What do you mean?"

Jim spoke softly, not knowing himself why he did not want anyone else to hear. "This is a prison camp. It's damned close, probably on the other side of the train. Look at those reflections. Goon-box lights. Wherever we are, this is it."

Tom looked out at the dark mist lighted at periods as if from a Stateside navigation beacon. "Maybe you're right."

"Look over there, and there and there . . . and there." Jim pointed across the gravel of the railroad yard. Sentries paced back and forth in the faint roving light.

Tom grunted once.

Jim put his chin up to the lower edge of the slit and called to one of the guard. "Wo sind wir?"

The guard lumbered through the mist. "Bitte?"

"Sprechen Sie English?"

"Nein."

"Wo sind wir?"

"Mooseburg. Stalag sieben ah."

"Stalag Luft sieben ah?"

"Nein. Stammlager sieben ah. Es ist ein Wehrmachts Kriegsgefangenenlager. Nicht Luftwaffe."

Bob nudged Jim from the press that was forming behind. "What's he saying?"

Jim spoke rapidly over his shoulder. "This is Stalag VIIA. Not a Luftwaffe camp. Army." He turned quickly forward to talk through the slit. "Wissen Sie? Bleiben wir hier?"

The German cleared his throat hoarsely and grinned, blowing breath vapor. "Jawohl. Für dich der Krieg ist zu ende." He stamped his feet against the wet gravel, the rifle bobbing on his back.

"Yeah," Jim announced calmly, "this is it, all right."

"Mooseburg," someone repeated thoughtfully. "We're right near Landshut—where they make the jets."

Jim licked his lips and whispered to Tom. "Get the jug." He turned back to the slit. "Haben Sie Wasser?"

The German cleared his throat again. "Nein. Es ist verboten."

"Für zigaretten?" Jim felt the flask passed hurriedly into his hands. The German looked steadily around, then placed a finger to his lips. Jim passed the flask down. The German hurried off into the misty darkness. Jim turned around and spoke to Bob. "Give him a couple of cigarettes for it. He'll make more trips. He's a tame goon."

Bob grinned sourly in the flickering light. "How tame?"

Jim snorted. "Plenty tame. If he starts anything, just make a lot of noise. Once the goon officers find he's accepted a bribe, they'll hang his hide on a fence."

Jim picked a spot between Koczeck and Burt and squeezed down against the floor. Koczeck looked at him. "Well, kid, what do we do now?"

"Just what we usually do. We wait."

Against a crowded wall, Noble wheezed in restless sleep.

Stalag VIIA was a vast maze of a prison camp as they walked along dragging their blanket bundles. There was a weary gray mist. The road was black top worn by many feet. The fences were a beehive ghost pattern of barbed rust. The buildings were everywhere the same long dirty prison-block shape except for two, white with large red crosses painted on their unshingled roofs. The straggling column moved along. Green-clad nervous sentries with long rifles moved faster, back and forth. Nothing else moved. Big dogs howled and yapped deeply in the dawn. The men filed through a simple single barbed-wire gate. A green-coated sentry stamping briskly along the thin north fence suddenly stopped, reversed himself, threw his long rifle to his shoulder and yelled, "Halt!" all in one movement. Jim looked wearily through the maze at the steadily aimed rifle barrel. "Hmff. What's eating him?"

Tom grunted, looking down along the thin dripping fence. "This fish net couldn't hold a fish. Let's take off out of here, Jim. It's a cinch."

Jim sighed. He looked ahead and saw two long low buildings, black with age, stall after stall gaping blackly without benefit of doors. "What the hell kind of a hole is this?"

Tom gritted his slim jaw firmly. "It's stables. Let's get out of here first chance we get. This place can't hold us."

Squalling Germans ordered them around the larger barn and finally into it. As the survivors from Room 8 arranged their dirty blankets to form a bed for the six of them in the turmoil of a surprisingly clean loft, Tom's teeth chattered from the cold. "What say, Jim? This place couldn't hold crackers."

Jim said nothing until they had crawled under the blankets and his shoulder blades pressed against the hardness of the loft floor. He nudged Tom's bony back. "Let's sleep on it."

Chapter Twenty

Halfway through the second night a shot cracked sharply somewhere outside the crowded barn. Only a few of the men heard it, and then rolled back to sleep. Tom Howard lay awake for quite a while, staring up toward the large beams supporting the roof.

Across the slit trenches beyond a high barbed-wire fence, fire logs were stacked in long rows. Skinny ragged Russian prisoners worked between the rows, weakly sawing or chopping at the logs. Beyond the wood yard and another high fence loomed the slanting roofs of prison block after block. Tom nodded beyond a group of Russians who were scrambling for cigarettes thrown across the fence to them by Americans. "Once we get in that mess we'll never get out. I say we better make our break now."

A Kriegie walked up and halted near Jim and Tom to watch the Russians. Jim nudged Tom, and they began walking down past the lines by the cisterns. "We're not in shape, Tom. We've got no X-food and we're already hungry. Skinny, too. I bet I don't weight 140, and you—you look like about 100. We'd poop out. You can't store up any energy on this diet of sausage and potatoes once a day. That damned sausage. I don't think there's any food in it at all."

Tom shrugged his skinny shoulders as they headed down between two of the stables. The babble of voices from the open stalls was endless. "What's there to lose? We may as well starve outside as starve in here."

Jim shook his head. "I don't think I could walk ten miles, and it's several hundred to the Rhine. Then you got to get across that."

Tom kicked a lump of straw and dung out of his path. "I got an idea last night. We head for Switzerland and go in short easy stages. There's supposed to be French slave-labor camps every few miles. Instead of hard-assing at night and holing up daytime, we steal some shovels or pitchforks or something and just stroll along the roads in the daylight, like we belong there. At night we sneak into slave-labor camps. The French will feed us, and they're not guarded much."

"Sneak into camps?"

"Sure. Who'd ever think of looking for an escaped Kriegie in a slave-labor camp?"

They rounded the end of one of the stables and started up the other side. Jim frowned thoughtfully. "You know, that's screwy enough it might work."

The two wandered in silence around the end of the stable near the cisterns and down between the stables.

"Hallo there, Jim!"

They stopped and peered into the dark straw-floored stall. Jim recognized the longest form stretched out among the others on the straw, hands clasped behind his head. Jim ducked in through the rotting wood opening. "I guess you're the man we want to see, Major." The smell was slightly cleaner than that in the boxcar.

Major Smith grinned. His beard jutted over the blanket wrapped around him. "How do you like my billet?"

Jim and Tom looked around the dark stall. On the muddy straw, blanket folds were scattered in disorder. At a nudge from Tom, Jim squatted down at the major's feet. "Major, we want to try something."

The major propped himself up on elbows hidden beneath his tight blanket. "Talk to Colonel Condon. He's taken over."

"Hell." Jim took a deep evil-smelling breath. "To hell with him."

"Who's Condon?" asked Tom.

"Don't you remember," said Jim. "He's that clean-shaven bastard Bill Johnston got in with back at Muskau. When Johnston was too proud to bunk with Thunderbird."

"How did he suddenly get so important?"

"Search me."

Major Smith sat up, letting his long arms out to hug the blanket around him. His eyes flashed like his teeth. "Men. Get up. Leave us talk some high-level strategy, will you? Junior, stand security."

One of the six men who lumbered to their feet spoke in a complaining voice. "Good gosh. In and out. In and out. Why did we have to get bunked with the X Committee?"

Junior followed the others through the doorway. "Aw, tell it to the padre."

Jim sat down on a blanket. "What's the latest gen?"

Major Smith shrugged. "Maybe it's good. Maybe it's bad. They're moving us into one of the regular compounds this afternoon."

Tom snapped his bony fingers. "That's it! We got to get out of here today."

The major smiled seriously. "You men still got X-itis, eh?"

Jim nodded. "I guess so. But I don't see how we can pull a wire job in broad daylight."

The smile vanished. "You'd better think it over. Curly Mathews got shot last night."

Tom spoke calmly. "I heard the shot."

Jim's head jerked. "Dead?"

"Just through the shoulder."

"Gee, that's bad."

"Not too bad. His side kick Burns made a run for it and got away."

"The hell he did." Jim grinned. "You mean they actually cut through the fence?"

Major Smith unfolded his blanket and pulled his long body to its feet. "Right over there." He stood in the doorway pointing between the stables toward the outer fence. A bearded Sikh wearing a faded, carefully wound blue turban was restringing new wire where the old had been cut. The Indian was working outside the fence. A guard marched briskly past the Sikh, long rifle barrel slanted toward the gray sky. The major spoke softly. "That's the fourth hole in two nights. We're keeping those Hindu prisoners busy fixing the fences."

Tom stared thoughtfully at the stoically working Indian. "Four holes, Major? How many have got out?"

Major Smith whispered. "Eight. One is in the cooler. One is in the hospital. Six got away and are not caught yet."

Once again the green-uniformed guard toting the long rifle passed the Sikh beyond the stables. Major Smith spoke softly. "You've got to watch out for those boys. Once they were the crack Wehrmacht Alpine division. They've retreated fighting, all the way back from the Crimea. There's only a few of them left, so they put them on guard duty. They're tougher than paratroops, and can shoot those long-range rifles straighter than most men can see."

Tom's thin face slowly tightened. "If only they'd leave us here tonight. I'd take my chances on their shooting at night."

The major nodded and grinned. "A little briefing and a little thought never do any harm. You don't lose much by calling off a mission."

Jim furrowed his bushy eyebrows together, staring at the faded blue turban of the Sikh working on the fence. Suddenly he turned his back on the Indian prisoner as if it was dangerous to look at him. He whispered hoarsely. "Take a look at that guy's hat and come inside!"

Junior Jones, his face flushed with eager curiosity, started to follow them in. Jim looked up. "God, Junior. Stay out there with your eyes peeled." Jim sat down on the major's discarded blanket, slapped his thigh once sharply, and then rubbed his forehead. "All the fence mending is done by Hindu prisoners. Right?"

Major Smith, squatting down before Jim, nodded. "It looks that way—at least so far."

Jim looked up seriously. "They all wear turbans?"

Major Smith frowned. "I guess so. It's religion or something."

Tom frowned, too. He spoke calmly. "You must have an idea, Jim. What is it?"

"No screwier than yours about what we do when we get out. Listen. What would that guard do if a couple more Hindus casually joined in on that job out there? You know. People like us, only wearing turbans?"

Tom whistled low. The major stared at Jim in amazement. He breathed out his reaction. "Jesus . . ."

"Sure, all we got to do is to get some blue cloth—those RAF issue shirts ought to do—and make turbans. Then we sidle up and help that Hindu joker fix the fence. Only, we work from the inside out."

Tom's voice was decisive. "All right. Let's do it. Only, we got to get cracking."

Major Smith straightened to his feet ahead of Jim. "Wait. It sounds like a fair idea, but I'm not Little X any more. You'll have to clear it through Colonel Condon."

Jim frowned impatiently. "Why Condon? You've always been the man before."

The major shrugged. "He ranks me, and he's decided he wants to be Little X in the new camp. So that's that."

"Well, Jesus, Major. We've got to get moving if we're going to get ready in time. To hell with Condon. We'll do it without him."

Major Smith sighed. "After nearly two years of waiting you're suddenly in a hurry. All right. Get your stuff ready. I'll talk to Colonel Condon for you."

"Thanks." They started out the door.

The major called after them. "Wait." He rummaged in his pile of belongings in the straw. "You may need this." He handed Jim a Kriegie-built wire cutter made of two lengths of steel joined at one end. "Condon's holding the loot now. I'll get some for you. Where are you billeted?"

Jim motioned through the wall of the stall. "In the loft of the big barn."

Major Smith wrapped a scarf around under his whiskers. "I'll bring it to you if Colonel Condon approves."

The three stepped out into the trampled mud between the long stables. They gazed briefly at the turbaned Sikh working lazily at the fence. Then the major walked one way, and Jim and Tom hurried the other against the tide of strolling prisoners.

In the crowded low-ceilinged loft Jack Noble begrudgingly handed Tom a chocolate bar. "You should have saved some of your own if you were going to try something," he complained.

Tom took the bar and stuffed it into his pants pocket. "You wouldn't have had this if I hadn't won it back at Sagan."

Jim sat cross-legged in a tangle of blankets sewing the last of a set of black buttons on his greatcoat. He turned the coat over on his lap and with a razor blade carefully cut away the military back belt. "There, that finished them. They ain't too civilian, but they'll have to do."

Burt Salem sat eagerly crouched forward. "Where you fellows heading after you get out?"

Tom smiled wryly. "Home."

Jim began to wrap an RAF blue shirt about his head. Koczeck grinned. "What's that for? To keep your ears warm?"

Jim mumbled irritably, fumbling with a drooping shirt sleeve. "Keep it down, for Christ's sake!"

"Jim." They looked toward the call. Junior Jones, his face flushed from climbing the ladder, motioned with his head sticking up through the trap opening. "Both of you."

Tom and Jim crawled on hands and knees to the opening. Tom got there first. "What's up?"

Junior was panting with excitement. "Colonel Condon wants to see you. Come on."

They followed Junior down the ladder, across the cluttered floor below, and out into the crowded air of the stockade. Jim hurried to keep up with Junior as they strode along the barn wall. "Where is he? He's not lousing us up, is he?"

"Naw. He wants to brief you in his office."

"Office!"

Junior grinned. "You said it. This Condon is really a rackets guy. He's got an office and a staff, too. One of your guys is on it. Here it is." Junior knocked on a cardboard makeshift door at the end of the barn nearest the fence.

"Come in." The voice was deep and powerful.

Junior pushed open the cardboard door which swung on rope hinges, and ducked into what had probably been a small harness room. Colonel Condon sat in an impossible position, darkly handsome, uniform freshly pressed, his legs relaxed gracefully, his ankles crossed on a desk made out of two boxes and a piece of dirty plywood.

"Well," he said with amusement, "so here are two brave men." He held out a strong cleanly manicured hand without shifting. "Whichever one of you is Lieutenant Weis, shake hands. We're both from the same home town."

Jim blinked, spotting Bill Johnston sitting with drawn-up knees between two other grinning prisoners against the wall of the tiny office. "You must be mistaken, Colonel. I'm from Seattle."

Colonel Condon casually brought his legs down from their uncomfortable position on the makeshift desk. "That's right. So am I." He smiled with polished white teeth. "Now, Major Smith told me about your little idea and I want to congratulate you for it. I think it's a good one."

Jim looked at the shaven face and felt uneasy. "Then we may as well get started. We need some loot, Colonel."

Condon reached in his pocket and handed Jim a small crumple of bills. Jim slid them apart, counting them. He looked up surprised.

"There's only sixty-five Marks here."

Condon smiled, and behind him Bill Johnston and the other two members of his staff smiled too. "That's the proper amount for a second lieutenant. We've got some order now that this X business is properly organized. First lieutenants get 85, captains 125, and so on, according to rank and rate of pay. It's a sound system."

Jim stared. Tom reached up and squeezed his shoulder before interrupting. "But, Colonel, there are two of us. Aren't we entitled to twice as much?"

Condon's face flushed. "Yes, of course. I guess I was thinking only of Lieutenant Weis." He looked mockingly at Jim. "Did you know you're a hero back home?"

Jim looked back at the colonel, muscles moving in his stubbled jaw between each sentence. "Sure, I know it. But what are we talking about that for? What the hell are you bringing that up for?"

Condon looked up grimly under his dark wavy hair. "I just wanted to be sure you knew you were a legend already before you pulled any more heroics, that's all." He went on without stopping. "Johnston! Give 'em sixty-five more Marks. Yes, you're a legend, Weis. And what have you done?" He smirked. "All you've done is write letters. Two of them are framed and hanging on a wall in the Library of Congress. Hooray for you!"

Jim looked helplessly at Condon. His voice quavered. "Colonel, what's the matter? Why are you mad at me? I don't even know you." Suddenly Jim flushed and drew up his clenched fists. "God damn you! You've got no right to talk to me like this!"

Condon stood up to his full slim height and stared coldly down at Jim. "Weis, you don't talk to a superior officer like that. Now pipe down and listen. I've thought up a few things for your little break you haven't even thought of in your young mind. First, this break will take place at exactly 1400 hours. Get that. At one half-minute before 1400 hours, or as near to it as we can get when the sentry is at the west end of the north fence, two men will start a fist fight down there to divert the sentry. Then you go to work." Condon cleared his throat. "While you are working and the fist fight is keeping the sentry looking at it, you will have to work very fast. When you get the wire cut and are ready to go out, you, Weis, lift your hand up, providing the sentry isn't looking your way. Then we'll have a man run out with flaming torches of burning paper

307

in his hands screaming that he is on fire. Then you can go and be a hero again. You got that straight?"

Tom spoke up calmly. "We've got it, Colonel. Thank you, sir." Tom saluted and turned to walk out. He had to turn back again to grab Jim's biceps. "Come on. We've got to get cracking."

Jim stopped his eyes from shifting back and forth from the faces of Colonel Condon and Johnston grinning on the bunk. Guided by Tom he went out into the moist air of the crowded outside. "That son of a bitch!"

Tom shrugged his narrow shoulders. "So he is. So what? He's worked up a good diversion for us. Once outside that wire we won't have to fool around with him any longer."

The flush still showed under the blond stubble of Jim's cheeks as they walked toward the barn. Suddenly he stopped. "I'll see you in a minute."

Tom looked suspicious. "Where you going?"

"I've got to see Major Smith. I forgot something. The canary."

"Oh. Well, make it pronto. We've got to study some maps and we've only got about forty-five minutes."

Jim nodded and headed down the crowded space between the stables toward where the Sikh prisoner was still lazily working on the fence. The major was sitting on his blanket. He looked up and shook his head slightly. Jim looked at the other Kriegies lounging miserably on the hard dirt floor and nodded. He squatted down close to the major and spoke softly. "You remember what's in my tin pack?"

The major whistled slightly and nodded.

Jim put his face close to the black beard. "Take care of that, will you?" He looked down at the blanket briefly and then back into the major's face. "And take care of my manuscripts, too, will you, Major? There's a good year's work there, and the goons wouldn't like it if they started to read it."

Major Smith nodded again. "We'll take care of it." He reached out and fumbled for Jim's hand. "Good show, Jim. Drop us a postcard from Paris."

Jim grinned rigidly. "Thanks." He straightened up and walked out of the stall, feeling Junior's hand squeeze his shoulder on the way. His empty stomach quivered slightly as he walked south between the stables. He paused for a second to look back over his shoulder. The Sikh was still working on the fence. Jim turned his head forward, sighed, and made his way steadily toward the barn.

Bob Montgomery knocked on the cardboard door of Colonel Condon's office. "Come in." Bob pushed the door on its rope hinges and entered. Condon sat erect on his box. "What can I do for you?"

Bob arched his eyebrows. "You sent for me, Colonel. At least that's what Johnston said."

Colonel Condon nodded. "Oh, yes. You're one of Lieutenant Weis's friends, and you have a watch."

"Yes, that's right."

Condon frowned. "What time do you have?"

Bob pushed the sleeve back from his wrist. "Thirteen fifty-two."

"I want you to cue Weis and Howard for their break. You'll have to be synchronized with mine. Get set for a hack."

Bob pulled the stem of his watch. "All set."

"In fifteen seconds it will be exactly 1350. Ten seconds . . . five, four, three, two, Woof!"

Bob snapped the stem down. "Got it."

Condon looked up, his olive face frowning. "How long have you been in the army, Lieutenant?"

"About three and a half years."

"Didn't anybody ever teach you to say 'sir'?"

Bob's mouth dropped slightly open. "Yes, sir."

"All right. Now, at exactly 1400 hours on the second, you start Weis and Howard toward the fence. The diversion will start immediately, so be on time. Don't snafu the works."

"Yes, sir. No, sir."

"Well, get started, Lieutenant. Get organized. This isn't coming off next week."

Bob turned and ducked through the doorway. Condon sniffed and spoke toward one of two members of his staff seated on the floor. "Damned civilian army. Farmers in uniform."

The cardboard door opened and Bill Johnston ducked in. "It's all set, Colonel. I found a guy with a watch to start it off on the second. These first two guys are ex-fighters. They'll make it look like a real fight."

"What about the third man?"

"He's got enough paper and margarine to look like a haystack afire. He'll put on a good show."

Condon smiled contentedly. "Then there's nothing to do but wait eight minutes. That man on fire diversion is a good one even if I do say so myself." He turned to see who was entering the office without knocking. It was Colonel Akron.

Colonel Akron squeezed his portly frame up against the door, holding it open. "Would you gentlemen mind waiting outside, please?" His flushed face was serious. "I want to talk to Colonel Condon."

Johnston sprang to his feet, joining Condon. "Yes, sir." Johnston and the other two staff members filed out.

The senior American officer shut the door. "What's this I hear about a wire job this afternoon?"

"That's right, Colonel. Lieutenant Weis and Lieutenant Howard are going to try it. It's all set up. Diversions and all."

"Call it off."

Condon stared at the older man. "I beg your pardon, Colonel."

"I said call it off. We've had one man shot already, and that was in the dark. I'm not permitting any fence jobs in broad daylight."

"But, Colonel . . ."

"God damn it!" The S.A.O.'s face was lined with real worry. "Those guards out there are completely punch drunk from fighting Russians. They're trigger happy. Now call this thing off before somebody gets killed. And in the future there'll be no more breaks without consulting me. If you're going to be Little X you may as well get used to that." Without another glance, Colonel Akron turned, slapped the cardboard door open, and strode out.

Condon stood staring out the doorway, the muscles of his face twitching beneath his neat cap. Suddenly he looked at his watch and shouted. "Johnston!"

Johnston appeared in the doorway immediately. "Yes, Colonel?"

"Colonel Akron and I have talked it over and decided to call this break off. A wire job is too dangerous in daylight."

Bill looked at the watch on his wrist. "Jesus, Colonel, there's only about two minutes left, and the diversion is all ready to go!"

Condon's eyes flashed and he spoke with authority. "That's what I called you for, Johnston. Get on over there and tell the diversion it's all off. We don't want a fist fight and a man on fire for nothing, do we? Call off the diversion!"

"Yes, sir." Bill moved away on the run. Condon sat slowly down on his box, placed an elbow on his makeshift desk and, with chin resting in the palm of his hand, stared frowning at the dirty wall.

In the shadow of a stable stall nearest the spot where the Sikh was innocently lacing new strands into the barbed-wire fence, Bob Montgomery stood tense behind Jim and Tom. Both were turbaned in faded blue. Thirty seconds before, the sun had suddenly popped out and glared down on the trampled mud between the end of the stable and the fence. Bob spoke quietly. "Get set." Jim felt the uncomfortable bulge of food, soap, and shaving supplies wound in a shirt beneath the clothing about his waist. "Ten seconds." Tom patted his turban to make sure it was still in place. "Five seconds, four . . . three . . . two. Go."

Tom and Jim strode forward casually, picking their way between the strolling prisoners until they stood at the fence looking through at the Sikh. Jim spoke out of the side of his mouth. "Where's that diversion?"

Tom took the Kriegie-built wire cutters from his right coat pocket and spoke coolly. "They'll be there. We might as well get started." He reached, levering the tool with both hands.

A strand of wire snapped. The Sikh, inches away, looked up, eyes widened over his beard. Tom snipped another strand of wire. The Sikh whispered hoarsely. "No, no, Sahib. No."

"Shh-h-h!" Jim warned, pressing against the fence to shield Tom's actions from the guard marching toward them from the west end of the fence. "The goon's coming. Where's that God-damned diversion?"

Tom slipped the wire cutters in his pocket. "Take it easy. You too, Mr. Hindu."

As the guard with his long rifle slung steadily approached, Jim was hazily aware of prisoners stopping curiously to watch. They were nudged on by more experienced prisoners. The Sikh, his eyes darting whitely, began again to twist at the wire. The tall green-clad guard passed inches away without giving them a glance. Jim looked wildly from the guard's retreating back toward the north corner of the stockade. "God damn it. Diversion. Diversion. Diversion!"

Tom, quickly snipping through strand after strand, cautioned, "Don't flap, Jim. Don't flap."

The Sikh, looking in terror after the German, pleaded in whispers. "No, Sahib. No. Pliss. No. Sahib."

"Look, Mr. Hindu," Tom said to the frightened prisoner, grunting between words from cutting wire, "we're cutting out of here. You might as well help us."

"No Ingliss. Spik no Ingliss. Pliss, no, Sahib."

Tom reached through with his heavy cutters and tapped the German plier cutters in the Sikh's hand. "Cut," he ordered, pantomiming.

Jim moved around to Tom's other side and pressed against the barbs of the fence. "The guard's turning around and coming back. Where in hell is that diversion?"

Tom continued cutting wire. The gap was growing. "It's up at the other end. They just didn't get started in time. That's all. They'll catch him this time."

The Sikh pressed his belly up to the fence to hide the slit from the nearing sentry. Jim could feel the eyes between the stables and up and down the strolling area watching them. "Can it," he whispered. "Here he comes."

Tom slipped the wire cutters into his left pocket. Jim could hear the Sikh breathing in jerks. The guard's boots sounded above the hundreds of Kriegie boots. Out of the corner of his eye, Jim saw the guard's rosy face go past close enough to reach out and pinch. Tom and the Sikh began cutting wire furiously now. The sounds of strands parting sounded like shots. Tom whispered to Jim. "It's big enough. Lift your hand for the man on fire diversion just before the goon gets there. I'm going through."

The Sikh, panting like an exhausted runner, but for some reason, grinning, helped pull the slit apart. Tom started through. "Unhook me." Jim took his eyes off the back of the guard and pulled the wire loose that had caught on Tom's coat. Jim looked up. The guard was almost at the turning point at the other end. Jim lifted his arm and waved it violently.

Nothing happened.

Jim continued to wave. Tom was all the way through and standing on the other side, helping the Sikh hold the wire apart. "Come on!"

The guard turned and saw Jim waving his arm. Jim stared back down the fence at the guard. "I can't now. He's spotted us."

They stood there helplessly while the guard stared. Suddenly the guard moved, slipping the rifle in one jerk from his shoulder. "Run, for Christ's sake!" Jim whispered.

Tom started to move. The German fired. A bullet slapped into the side of the Sikh's head, just below the turban. The Sikh flopped to the ground. Tom threw up his hands. "Nicht schiessen! Nicht schiessen!" The rifle barrel moved. Without reason, Jim sprang away from the fence and ran between the scattering prisoners. The rifle fired again. A bullet slammed into wood behind Jim as he dashed out of range, in between the stables toward the major's stall. He fell inside and tore the turban from his head, stuffing it into the dung and dirt beneath the major's blanket. Outside, the goon was shouting something unintelligible. Jim unbuttoned the altered greatcoat and stuffed it under the blanket, then sat on the blanket lump shivering. There was no one else in the shadowed stall.

A guard stood at the hole in the fence holding his rifle with trigger finger tucked in place. The corpse lay as it had sprawled, the blood black against the mud under the turbaned head. Major Smith spoke to Junior as they turned and walked away. "You sure you looked every place?"

"I can't find him, Major. I can't think of any place else to look."

They slouched along between the stables and turned into their stall. "What—" Major Smith stopped, and stared at Jim lying stiffly, his head protruding beyond the blanket in the dung.

Jim jerked into a stark sitting position. "Did he get Tom?"

"No. No thanks to you. What in hell did you run for?"

Jim gritted his teeth. "I don't know. Did you ever hear a bullet go into a man's head, Major?"

Junior squirmed slightly as he stood. Major Smith grunted. "Well, Tom has been taken off to the cooler. He's all right."

Jim nodded dully and huddled grabbing his knees. He spoke lo and bitterly. "What happened to the diversion?"

The major grunted again and slowly sat down in the dirt before Jim. "What kind of a temper have you got, Jim?"

"What happened to the diversion?"

Major Smith scratched the dirt with a forefinger. "The whole deal was called off. Colonel Akron decided it wasn't safe."

Jim shot forward onto his hands and knees. "What the—"

"Now, wait a minute! It wasn't the Old Man's fault. He ordered the break stopped, that's all."

Jim's face showed purple in the gloom of the stall. "He what?"

Major Smith reached forward and put a hand on Jim's shoulder. "Hold it, Jim. It wasn't the Old Man's fault. He just didn't want you to get killed."

"What in hell are you talking about?"

The major sighed. "He just ordered it called off. Condon notified the diversions and the security men. He just forgot to tell you. That's all."

Jim got to his feet and staggered. Wordless sound grated out of his chest. "I'll kill him."

The major jumped up and hugged Jim's arms. "Hold it, Jim. Get control of yourself."

"I'll kill the dirty son of a bitch."

Behind the major, Junior spoke. "It'd be too good for him."

Still holding Jim, Major Smith called over his shoulder. "Junior, you get outside and keep a lookout. Don't let anyone in here."

Junior scuffed reluctantly toward the stall exit. "I still think he's right."

The major released Jim, who walked over to the board wall and pounded his forearms and fists against it. "The bastard. I'll kill him!"

The major cleared his throat and tugged at his beard so that it hurt. "Look, Jim. I know how you feel. But you've got to forget it. You can't go around killing lieutenant colonels in this man's army. You can't do anything to anybody. So forget it. Just say we all make mistakes, and forget it."

"Mistakes, hell!"

"If you could beat him up it might do you both some good, but you can't even do that. All you can do is forget it."

Jim turned from the wall, free of his temper but still hating. "All I can do is forget it, huh? I'll never forget it. Not any more than I'll forget that West Point bastard who flew home instead of coming down to help me. That's why I'm here. Because of another God-damned West Point lieutenant colonel!"

Major Smith crossed to the wall and leaned against it beside Jim. "Condon isn't a West Pointer."

"The hell he isn't!"

"No. He isn't. He just wants people to think he is. He never got through the Point."

Jim sniffed and relaxed. "A complete phony. How in hell did he get to be Little X?"

The major sighed. "He's not a phony. He flew 127 missions and got seven planes. He's got a yard of medals."

Jim snorted, walked toward the stall exit, and turned back. "So have I. I've flown 143 missions and I'm still a second lieutenant. I really admire Colonel Condon. He's destroyed seven Huns and one Hindu. He damned near got two Americans a little while ago. He's a great man. He thinks he is. I think he's a prick." Jim started to leave, then turned back again. "By the way. I got nothing against West Pointers. I just don't like pricks who act like West Pointers, whether they've been to the Point or not."

"Jim, you did a good job."

Jim stared at the grin showing through Pete's beard and the gloom of the stall. "How do you figure?"

"You got the goons in a flap. Now they're not moving us until tomorrow."

Jim walked out and sloshed past the staring prisoners toward the barn.

It was blacker than black in a nine by six cell in a cooler of Stalag VIIA. Tom Howard, one of two men in a solitary confinement cell, squirmed and rubbed the bones of his scrawny back against the handful of straw-filled tick which only emphasized the hard-edged boards of his bunk. He grunted and sat up; one of his buttocks caught between the boards. His voice was flat. "This is nuts. How could a man sleep up here?"

A voice answered from the pit of the unseen floor. "That's what I told you. You can't. I made my break first, so I've got the floor. Don't worry. I won't pull rank on you. Tomorrow night you take the floor and I'll take the grater. We'll take turns."

Tom stared up into the pitch blackness. It was a little hole that had appeared suddenly beneath the turban of the Hindu. Tom shivered and wondered what the other end of the hole looked like.

In the flickering light of the Kriegie lamps, Jim lay staring at the shimmering shadows of the roof. He heard no snores or mutterings. He saw a hole. It had suddenly appeared just below the turban. It was not a large hole, about the size of a quarter, and bits of bone flew out of it like rice at a wedding. "Poor bastard!" No one around him heard the oath. "Poor bastard!" Jim whispered it again in anger, as a term of love. He held a hand tightly to his head. He didn't know that Major Smith had picked his way across the swamp of bodies until the major squatted and spoke.

"Jim. Jim. How about it? You want to try a break in the dark?"

Jim raised himself on his elbows and stared into the grinning face. He shuddered and whispered hoarsely. "If Colonel Condon had a tunnel dug all the way to Seattle, I wouldn't enter one foot of it!"

Major Smith shook with silent laughter. "I'm not talking about Colonel Condon. I just want to see if you've got any nerve left. You want to make a break tonight?"

Jim stared at the major. "What do you mean?"

"Condon isn't Little X any more. I am."

Slowly Jim started to smile. Then he lay back and laughed, instinctively considerate enough of those around him not to do so aloud.

Major Smith was doing the same. "Well, you want to try a wire job?"

Jim controlled his suppressed giggling long enough to put up a finger. "Up your giggi."

Major Smith reached down, tousled the cap on Jim's head, creaked to his feet and left. Jim lay back, spasmodically smiling and then chuckling toward the flickering beams of the loft. It was the first time in hours he had smiled. He was happy enough to fall asleep some time soon.

Jim Weis: "There I was. . . ."

When they stuck me in the Luftwaffe hospital in Tunis, I escaped out of the lavatory window and had to walk back two blocks to captivity when my boots filled with blood. Though it failed, that was a good job because they had to assign a twenty-four-hour guard over me in the Torre Bianca Regia Marina Hospital up on the white cliff over Trapani in Sicily. That tied up three Eyties. I got to know them pretty well.

The guy in the other bed in the two-man room was a sergeant gunner from Brooklyn with a broken back he got by riding down in a wallowing B-25 which slapped the Med just off that rock island by Trapani.

"Are you Catholic?" he asks me as soon as he figures the guard can't speak English.

"No," I answer.

"Well, neither am I. But they think I am. This is a Catholic hospital in a Catholic country. You'd better be a Catholic, Lieutenant. You'll be treated better."

So I was a Catholic. The padre with a hole shaved in his hair blessed us with holy water for Palm Sunday and placed branches over the heads of our beds. I hope God didn't mind.

But I loused it up. The nuns were pretty sore about a lot of things. The hospital didn't have any anesthetics. They didn't even have sedatives and were damned short on bandages. The Germans had them, but they weren't giving any to the Eyties.

The nuns were sore about the bombs. The first time it happened was at night. The RAF boys were at work upstairs. There was a hell of a flap in the hospital. These old nuns were trying to get all the patients who could walk downstairs out of the way of anything that might drop while the sirens were still howling. All the lights went out. Have you ever heard a bunch of scared Italians shouting in the dark? Neither the sergeant nor I could walk, so we stayed in bed on the top floor of the hospital laughing ourselves silly. There were lots of bombs, but only one of them landed near enough to where we were perched on the cliff to put a big crack in the wall of the hospital.

The nuns didn't feed us for twenty-four hours.

They took me into the operating room. The mother superior held my ankles while the doctor pulled down my pants and yanked pus out of the hole in my left thigh with a thing like a shoe-button hook. Then they slapped the same original German field dressing back on the hole and wheeled me back with the guard walking alongside to the room.

"I didn't hear you yell," the sergeant grinned at me from the cast encasing his whole body.

I grinned back at him with teeth salty from the blood oozing out of my tongue.

We began to like the Italians. There was a Sicilian orderly who used to come in and whisper: "When Americano come? Soon? When Americano come? We ready to welcoma America!"

And there was a noncommissioned officer in the kitchen from Trieste who used to come up with fresh Sicilian lemons and oranges and once in a while with a urinal bottle full of wine. "Mein Offizier," he used to say, "wir von Trieste sind nicht Italiano, nicht Deutsche, nicht Feind. Die Amerikaner sind unsere einzige Hoffnung!" or something like that. I kind of gathered these guys wanted us to win. "Feind" means "enemy" and "nicht Feind" must mean "not enemy." At the time I was ready to be not enemy to anybody in the world. That's what I thought until the second time the boys paid a visit.

The sun was glaring in over the balcony that extended around the building. It cast heat over my bed and the sergeant's bed. There was a hell of a flap in the hospital. The sisters running up and down the halls yakkety-yakked hysterically, and the walking bed cases sounded in so that until they got off the floor and headed for the basement it sounded like Babel. The guard went down below, too. I started laughing again. Then I got so curious I had to get out of bed and have a look. I couldn't walk, so I crawled, leaving a stretch of bed sheet between me and the open window leading onto the hot sunny balcony which stretched all the way around the building. It hurt to crawl in the blue and white striped night shirt I was wearing, but I had to see them up there. There they were, silver Flying Fortresses gleaming so high in the blue that you couldn't see the fighter escort. They were above me, so I crawled down the smooth concrete of the balcony to look down at the blue camouflaged Trapani air base with its blue cracker-box buildings way down below under the edge of Torre Bianca. I wanted to see the bombs that had already been dropped fall. I did. I hung onto the lower rungs of a metal railing and laughed as the Luftwaffe air base down there in the sun changed into a grove of sudden gray bomb bursts. I mean sudden. One second there were the blue camouflaged buildings and the Messerschmitts parked like mosquitoes at the dispersal points where they were being repaired—the big X of the runways with deadly gnats taxiing along them ready to take off and try to kill—and the next second all was lost in a thick forest of stretching dust trees rooted in yellow flame. I was laughing and cheering at the same time. Talk about precision bombing! That was it. In the sun the bomb dust completely hid the airfield below. I hung onto the twisted iron rods of the balcony and cheered out loud. I didn't think anyone was listening. I was wrong.

All of a sudden the mother superior was there beating me over the head with an escarpa, which is a slipper. She was screaming at me I don't know what. Hell, I don't understand Italian. You can't swat back at a nun even if you have a leg to stand on. So I just took this webbed leather escarpa with my arms above my face, yelling things at her in English that didn't make any more sense to her than what she was yelling at me.

Down below the ledge the smoke and dust cleared away and drifted off in the sunshine. The buildings were still there, blue in their camouflage. The runways were still there, and the Messerschmitts like gnats were darting along them up into the air.

She stopped screeching and pounding and ran with swirling black robes back down the balcony.

The pounding didn't hurt much. I was too busy looking down at that airdrome. I suddenly realized that bombs don't do anywhere near as much damage as most people imagine.

I sure as hell wasn't trying to escape!

But the mother superior came whistling back along the balcony, shoving and clutching at the green-uniformed guard's shoulder, yelping faster than a machine gun. You didn't have to understand Italian to know she was accusing me of trying to escape. I lay wriggling on my bad leg while she actually wrestled with that guard, her hand over his on his pistol holster, trying to get the gun out to shoot me. God, how she yapped and snatched! It isn't a good feeling to find yourself lying in the sun with no place to go but straight down and a nun trying to kill you.

"No. No, no, no!" The struggling guard pleaded along with a lot of other Italian, and I agreed with him. Above, the flak had stopped, and behind me, far below, the Messerschmitts were whining up out over the blue sea. I prayed to the Crucifix bobbing and jerking before the outraged mother superior's black-robed belly. It worked. She quit struggling and strode off down the balcony with her black skirts flapping. The guard mopped his forehead with a dank white handkerchief. He looked down at me with serious brown eyes. "Tenente. You no trya escapa? No?"

"No," I answered, and he hauled me to my feet and gently limped me back to the room.

"What did it look like?" the sergeant grinned at me from his cast.

"Great." I sagged, sweating like a wet rag, onto the wrinkled dry sheet of my bed.

We weren't served any food for thirty hours. I think I know why. About an hour after the bombing a gurgling screaming approached from somewhere down the hall. It grew closer as the sergeant and I grew paler until it was deposited, still gurgling and screaming, in the next room to ours. It was still gurgling and screaming something like, "Mama! Mahmmaha! Mama-ah! Mama!" over and over again when, hours later, the noncom from Trieste sneaked two oranges in to us. "Wer ist das?" I asked in my lousy high-school German.

"Ein armes Knäbchen," answered the man with a home but no country. "Nur vierzehn Jahren alt. Er war . . ." And bit by bit I got the story that this screaming thing next door was a fourteen-year-old Sicilian boy employed by the Germans to help clear up the debris after the raids on the Luftwaffe base down below. While he was working away, he found a dud antipersonnel fragmentation bomb stuck nose down in the dirt. He leaned over and started to pull it out. Now he lay in the next room with his chest and face blown open and his eyes scrambled, screaming for his mother. And the Eyties had no morphine.

One by one the usual crop of Italian fans of American movies came into the room that night, just before lights out. They paid little attention to the screaming close by. "Clarka Gaybla?" one of them would recite, going down the list.

The sergeant would nod, and then they would all look at one another, smiling and gabbling in Italian.

"Carola Lombardi?" another would ask.

The sergeant would shake his head, and they would look at one another mournfully, whispering, "Morte. Morte."

"Tom Mix?"

"Morte. Morte."

Suddenly the screaming in the next room stopped. After a bit of silence the night guard stuck his head in the door and spoke solemnly, with relief. "Morte." Some of the Italian patients gathered around the foot of the beds crossed themselves. Then the game started again. "Roberto Taylor?"

I've faced death a number of ways, and each time I've somehow escaped. It makes no difference what you're trying to escape, whether it's a burning Spitfire, a troubled past, the attacking enemy in the air or on the ground, the boring misery of any man's prison, whether of the mind or of the body, the best escape of all is from death. As long as you can do that, there's still hope.

Chapter Twenty-one

A shadow flickered on the windows of the cement-floored washroom. Jim looked up in time to see a silver fighter plane with a red- and white-striped rudder flit across the bit of sky that was visible.

Junior ran up to Jim's side and stared at the now empty patch of sky. "What was it?"

Jim grinned with excitement. "It was a P-51. Jesus! He wasn't over two hundred feet. A P-51." He held up his hand. "Listen." Somewhere in the distance machine guns coughed for a few seconds.

Junior's nose was pressed flat against the windowpane. "Damn! Why weren't we outside? What's he shootin' at?"

Other prisoners were running up to the two windows. "What was it?" somebody called.

"A P-51. I just happened to be looking out the window. He must be shooting up the railroads." Jim turned to Junior. "Let's get dressed and find out what happened." They took clean underwear from nails on the wall and climbed into it. It hung loosely on their skinny figures as they fumbled with the buttons. Jim laughed. "Hot damn! When our boys can cruise around on rhubarbs this deep in Germany, the goons have had it."

"Where do you suppose they came from?"

"They must have come from Italy. God damn this shirt." Jim had buttoned it wrong and had to start over. Quickly they donned clean clothes and shoes, picked up their wet laundry, and entered the smoke-filled doorway of the kitchen. There they halted to get their bearings. The floor of the small room was covered with Kriegies and cooking blowers made of wood and tin cans. At each blower one man turned a little crank which operated a rope belt which in turn spun a tin fan forcing air up into a burner made out of a can. The other man fed wood shavings one by one into the flaming burner and steadied the pan on top of the burner. As they worked, tears streamed down their sooty faces.

Junior nudged Jim and pointed down at a square-shaped frying pan balanced in the smoke burbling up from one of the burners. He spoke up above the din of the cranks and fans. "Jeez, look! Spam! Honest-to-God Spam!"

"Well, I'll be damned!" Jim gazed down hungrily at the sizzling rectangles of meat.

Junior squatted down beside the man feeding shavings to the burner and shouted, "Hey, where did you guys get the Spam?"

The Kriegie looked up blinded by tears and smoke. "What?"

"I asked where did you get the Spam?"

The prisoner shrugged. "You got to be in the rackets. It's up to you to find out."

They stared at the Spam for a moment, their eyes filling with tears and their mouths with saliva. Jim shouted into Junior's ear: "He ain't talking. Let's get out of here."

Gingerly they picked their way between the Kriegies and their burners, most of which were heating water or frying pancakes made out of a paste concocted from the day's ration of three potatoes per man. They stepped from the kitchen into the large prison bay, now almost empty of prisoners. Golden sunshine slanted in through the windows of the east wall. Bunk tiers and tables cast a pattern of shadows on the floor.

Junior sneered grimly. "You got to be in the rackets, he says. Who the hell does he think he's talking to? I'll find out where he got that Spam."

Jim shook his head. "It's hard to figure. There hasn't been any Red Cross food brought into the camp since that so-called trading project weeks ago. Yet guys keep turning up with some."

A few minutes later Jim and Junior hung their laundry in the crowded sun-filled compound. Jim nodded dreamily. "It's funny about today."

"Why?"

"March 24th. Just a year ago today the big tunnel broke at Sagan."

Junior crowded someone else's clothes to one side on the line to make room for his own. "Jesus! that was no lucky day. You remember the date?"

"My birthday."

"No fooling? How old?"

Jim grinned. "Twenty-three."

"You're older than that. I'm almost twenty-three."

Jim nodded. "I suppose I'm twenty-five. But I don't count the past two years."

Junior grunted agreement.

Instead of twenty-five years, Jim thought of fifty men. Fifty prisoners of war who had left Stalag Luft III a year ago that night had been recaptured and returned. Their ashes had been sent back in fifty cremation urns.

They strolled down the crowded space between two of the prison blocks. Jim grunted. "Let's not talk about food. I wish I had a cigarette."

"Me too. I haven't had five butts since Condon cleaned us out, trading our cigarettes to the goons for food. All that food. What a smelly deal!"

Jim shrugged. "I quit helping after the first day. I couldn't stand handling all that food and never eating any of it."

Junior smacked his lips. "I traded for three days and never drew a lucky number. I'd have swiped some pretty soon if the cigarettes hadn't run out. Hey, what's going on up there?"

Shouting came down between the prison blocks from the south fence. Kriegies were running and walking quickly in that direction. Jim started striding briskly. "Come on! Maybe some Red Cross food trucks have arrived!"

"Hot damn!" Junior trotted on ahead.

Halfway along between the two prison blocks Jim stopped and looked down at Tom, who was sitting shirtless with skinny white shoulders hunched against the building. "What's up, Tom?"

Tom unwound slowly to his feet. "Nothing to flap about. Just a purge of American Kriegies arriving from some other camp. They must be trying to crowd all the prisoners in Germany into this ill-begotten place."

The first shouting of the men along the fence had died down when they got there. They stood looking over shoulders and between heads at the straggling parade of tattered Americans trudging with their bundles and packs along the prison-camp road. Jim tapped Junior on the shoulder. "Who are they?"

"From some camp near Frankfurt. They been marching two weeks."

"Air Force?"

"Naw. Paddle feet."

Occasionally someone would shout through the fence at the ragged column of bearded Americans.

"Bring any food with you?"

"Food? What's that?"

"You mean that stuff you're supposed to put in your mouth and swallow?"

Neither the men marching nor the men watching through the barbed wire laughed. Tom turned away. "I'm going to finish my sun bath. What's the use of standing around? It only uses up energy."

Jim fell in beside Tom. "I thought maybe it was those white trucks we been hearing about. Red Cross parcels would make a big difference around here."

Tom found his former place against the wall and sat down. "If the white trucks come, they come." His voice was listless. "If they don't come, we've had it. That's all. There's nothing to flap about." Tom closed his eyes and turned his face up to the weak warmth of the sun.

Jim sat down, his mind slipping dreamily from one thing to another. The tip of his raw tongue incessantly curled back against his aching tooth and his gums, which burned from too much aspirin.

Suddenly sirens to the north, east, south, and west wailed up and down, overlapping in their mournful melodies. Jim laughed. "Air raid! Hot damn! They're busy with that new bunch. This time they've got to leave us outside. We can watch it."

Tom held a thumb up to look into the sun. "If they come over this way. Let's take a circuit." They began walking the circuit, the well trampled path which every prisoner always walked counter clockwise around the parade ground. They didn't talk as their feet kicked up puffs of dust. When they came to the east guard rail they turned north, strolling parallel with the barbed-wire fences which thirty feet away separated them from the enlisted men's compound. When they reached the north guard rail they halted and gazed past the sentry tower there at a huge field which stretched for several acres before it reached the wall of the pine forest. Row after row of dirty mounds pimpled the field. Tom spoke with tight lips. "The sons of bitches. Storing all those potatoes right out there in plain sight for us to watch while we starve in here. What do you reckon they're saving all those spuds for?"

"Probably a stockpile for the next war. What potatoes we do get must have been grown during the last one."

One by one the sirens moaned down to silence. Jim started walking west. "Come on. It doesn't do any good to look at them. We can't eat them."

Tom patted his belly. "All my life I've been skinny. If we're ever liberated I'm going to eat enough to get fat."

A couple of hundred Kriegies were sitting in the dirt along the west side of the compound. Suddenly all conversation ceased and faces turned skyward. Jim put out a hand to stop Tom. "Listen." A growing roar filled the air. There was no way of telling from which direction it came.

Tom scanned the glaring sky with a fighter pilot's eye. "Where are they? I don't see them."

Jim sneezed from looking into the sun. "Search me. They must be around here somewhere." The roar steadily grew louder and louder until it seemed to come from the ground. Suddenly several prisoners pointed high up to the west. Jim followed their fingers and lifted his. "There they are! See 'em?"

"Yeah."

A host of tiny specks against the blue grew larger and sparkled silver in the sun. Tiny white puffs suddenly appeared, strung out along the formation like beads. Jim peered under his raised forearm. "B-17's. Must be a hundred of them. Look at the flak." The mass of planes was passing at high altitude north of the prison camp. White streamers of smoke darted downward one at a time from the lead planes. "They're checking the wind. Must be going to bomb Landshut over there."

"What makes you think so?"

"That's where they make those Messerschmitt jet jobs. It's just a few miles from here."

Tom shrugged. "I don't hear any bombs falling. All they're dropping is smoke." There were five white streamers now reaching from the sky to the ground, twisting and curving with the wind at various altitudes. The great cluster of Flying Fortresses were moving away from them, yet the heavy roar of hundreds of engines was growing louder and louder. Tom looked back toward the west. "Here come some more. God, look at them!" Another swarm of specks was crossing the sky following the course of the first.

"Hey! Look over there!" someone yelled, pointing southward. "B-24's!"

While all eyes had been concentrating on the squadrons of B-17's flying in from the west, three huge formations of Liberator bombers had approached high in the southern sky. Through the engine roar could be heard the chop-chopping of small flak guns and the sharp loud barking of heavy flak pieces. Jim took his eyes from the spectacle long enough to look at Tom. "Man, oh, man! Those must be from Italy." When he looked back, more great clusters of bombers had appeared as if from nowhere. "They must be joining up with the boys from France and England for a big one."

The prisoners all along the circuit, gazing at the planes, chattered and whistled with excitement. Tom looked again to the west where hundreds more of the huge planes had materialized, then east where the first formations were slowly wheeling into a course that would lead high over the prison camp. Tom spoke casually. "Well, there's no use putting cricks in our necks. Might as well watch it in comfort." He sat down in the dirt of the parade ground and lay back resting his head on his arms. "This is the way to look at it, Jim."

Jim lay down beside Tom and found that by moving his head only slightly he could see any part of the great cloudless sky. The first formation crawled slowly, steadily, across the blue directly above the camp, heading west by southwest. Formation after formation of Fortresses and Liberators from the south wheeled in great arcs to join the Fortresses from the west in the great queueing up of bomber squadrons. "Somebody is going to get it. Maybe they're heading for Augsburg. It's over that way someplace."

Tom propped himself up on his elbows, straining his eyes. "There's fighters up there too."

"Where?"

"Those little tiny spots. See them weaving?"

Jim stared hard straight up. "You got spots before you . . . Oh, yeah. I see them." He licked his lips, looking up at the sky. In every direction it was filled with the approaching squadrons. "You know? Whoever planned this mission must have picked this camp for a rendezvous point. I'll bet they know we're down here."

"I sure as hell hope so. How many of this crowd do you suppose those slit trenches would hold?" He motioned toward a narrow zigzagging trench over near the fence between them and the next compound.

"Not very damn' many. They'd cave in, anyway. All the supporting walls have been robbed for fuel." Jim suddenly sat up, staring upward. "Hey. What the hell is this?" A cloud of something like confetti was growing above them as it floated downward. It twinkled and undulated in the sunlight, growing larger and spreading as it fell. As they watched a few small pieces of metal thudded into the dirt nearby. Jim picked up one of the jagged pieces. "Spent flak." He looked bewildered up at the ever twinkling objects above. "My God! All that isn't falling flak, is it?"

"Flak!" someone in the growing crowd yelled. "Cover your heads, boys. It's flak!"

A few men dashed into the slit trenches. Others in panic pulled jackets and shirts up over their heads and stood waiting with eyes shut. Tom folded his skinny arms over his head. "I don't know. Maybe we'd have been better off in the block."

Though Jim folded his arms over his head, he still stared up at the objects which seemed to be twisting and dancing about as they floated nearer. "It can't be flak. There ain't that much flak in the world. Besides, you can't see flak pieces falling. They come back down like bullets."

"I still could use a roof right now."

Jim lowered his arms. "Here it comes. It's paper!"

"Whoooeeee!" somebody yelled. "It's only chaff!"

Long strips of silver and black paper were floating to earth all over the parade ground. Prisoners dashed around picking them up. Jim picked up one strip and Tom another. Tom turned his over. It was metal foil on one side and black on the other. "What the hell is it?"

Jim grinned. "Chaff. I never saw any before, but that's what it is." The strips were drifting, twisting to earth all around them. "It raises hell with their radar. Everytime the metal side turns it makes a blip on the radar screen. The bomber drivers carry it to throw off the aim of the flak guns."

On and on the bombers came, the sun glittering on the silver fuselages of the Flying Fortresses, the white and black flak puffs playing hide and seek among them, the tiny specks of escorting fighters weaving in and out. Some of the formations were flying lower than others, and the spellbound men below could make out the shapes of the engine cowlings and the twin booms of the P-38's. All at once the ground trembled and there was a distant thunderclap in the east, followed by another and another and another. Still the swarms of bombers came on, systematically wheeling into the great streaming corridor leading to the target. Jim had to speak loudly to make himself heard over the steady roar. "How long they been coming? How long since they started?" Tom shrugged, and Jim turned to look over the crowd of Kriegies. "There's Junior. He's got a watch."

They started walking toward where Junior and Major Smith stood gazing up at the show. A stark low whistle halted them and turned their heads southward. A gray shape like a bat swooped in low over the prison camp buildings, and the whistle grew into a shrieking roar as it streaked with swept-back wings over their heads. The crosses flashed for an instant on the lower side of its tapered wing tips as it vanished over the top of the wall of trees north of the camp.

"Jet job!" somebody cried.

Prisoners made all kinds of excited noises as they stared in the direction where the strange aircraft had disappeared. Jim whistled unheard in the sounds of the great squadrons overhead and the bombs crashing to earth in the distance. "Did you see that thing travel? Wonder if he's going up after them."

Tom spat into the dirt. "Probably flying around on the deck to keep from getting bombed. Even a jet couldn't do anything with that mob of planes."

Jim caught a piece of glittering chaff before it hit the ground as they came up to Major Smith and Junior. The major grinned. "Take a good look, men." He waved a long arm at the thousands of American planes speckling the whole German sky like an almighty pox. "You may never see that many planes in the sky at one time again as long as you live. There may never *be* that many planes in one sky again."

Jim looked at the formations and chuckled. "'Way back in 1940, when I read about the Luftwaffe, sending five hundred planes against London, I said, 'If I ever saw five hundred planes in the sky at one time I'd shit green apples!' Well, I'll bet I'm seeing five thousand right now—and no green apples!"

Pete brushed away a strip of descending chaff. "I think there's more than five thousand up there, and they're still coming. They must be using traffic cops."

Tom tapped Junior's sleeve-covered wrist. "How long they been coming now? Did you check the time when they started?"

Junior nodded. "Yeah. But I don't have a watch now." He bared his wrist and grinned.

Tom's thin face frowned. "You mean you've lost your watch since this raid started?"

Junior winked wisely. "Oh, I wouldn't say I've *lost* it exactly. Would you, Major?"

Major Smith sighed. "I don't know. I haven't made up my mind yet."

Junior leaned confidentially toward Jim. "You remember that joker we saw frying the Spam? Well, I said I'd find out where he got it, and I did. He was right. You got to be in on the rackets. I've traded my watch for ten units of food. I get it as soon as we get back to the block."

Jim spoke softly. "What do you mean, 'ten units'? And who are you getting it from?"

"You got to know the rackets. Ten units. Two loaves of bread. Three cans of meat. A pound of marge. Two chocolate bars and two pounds of dried fruit. Boy, am I going to bash tonight!"

"Jesus! Who's got that kind of food? I didn't think there was that much food in the whole camp."

Junior grinned wisely. "There is if you know the rackets and have a Rollex watch. Guess who's doing business."

"For Christ's sake, I haven't got a Rollex, but who?"

"Your old roommate. Bill Johnston."

"Bill Johnston!" Jim stared back toward the prison blocks. "Where the hell would Johnston get all that food?"

"There's the jet!"

"Look at 'im go!"

Frantic fingers pointed skyward. High above the camp, and slightly to the northwest, the jet was darting down directly into a formation of B-17's.

"Get him!"

"Get the bastard!"

The dark jet fighter drove through the middle of the formation, which quivered, spread apart, and hustled together again as the enemy whistled in an incredible dive to vanish in the southern distance. Immediately white smoke began to stream from the wing of one of the bombers.

"He's hit!"

"Oh, no! No! No!"

The fallen flyers held their breaths, feeling earth tremble with the blasts to the east, watching the bomber formation slowly cross the sky westward, the one bomber drawing out a long trail of white smoke from its burning engine like a skywriter.

"Get that fire out," low voices coaxed. "Get it out."

As if by order, the white stream puffed twice and stopped.

"He made it!"

A great welling cheer rang up. Men slapped each other on their backs and shook hands.

"The son of a bitch made it!"

"He got it out!"

"He can keep up on three fans!"

Junior shook his head. "Boy, I thought he'd had it. How come we don't have jets?"

Jim remained silent for a time, frowning, tonguing his aching tooth, staring blankly up into the plane-filled sky. Eventually he spoke. "How much of this food has Johnston got?"

"Huh? Oh. He must have quite a bit. He's picking up quite a few watches from different Kriegies. We're supposed to keep it hush."

"Ten of these units for each watch?"

"He only takes Rollexes."

"You gave him your Rollex?"

"Yep. I get the food when this appel is over."

Jim squinted thoughtfully. "Jesus! A Rollex watch will be worth more than a hundred dollars back home."

"So what? Ten dollars a pound isn't a bad price for food when there isn't any any place else."

Jim got to his feet and walked over to the major. Jim squatted down beside him. "Major, doesn't it strike you there's something funny about Johnston having all this food to trade for watches?"

The major stared down at a circular face he was drawing with his finger in the dirt. He took a careful breath and exhaled slowly before answering. "Well, yes. It does."

Jim held his voice low and spoke rapidly. "You know the way it looks to me? Johnston is Condon's man. Condon was in charge of all that food we had to kick in our cigarettes for. I never did think anywhere near all that food was passed out. I think Johnston is fronting for Condon and the sons of bitches are fixing to go back home with a suitcase full of hundred-dollar watches they traded for food stolen right out of our mouths."

Major Smith looked coolly into Jim's eyes. "Can you prove it?"

"Hell, no. All the food we scrounged was turned in to them. There was no record of it."

The major nodded solemnly. "Then you had better forget it."

"How the hell can I forget it? The son of a bitch stealing food from starving men to make money? He ought to be court-martialed."

The major started drawing a new face in the dirt and sighed: "Jim. No proof, no court-martial. You can't forget, no. But remember, Condon is a lieutenant colonel. You're in the army and he's your commanding officer right now. If I were you I'd be like me and say nothing more about it."

Jim gritted his teeth for a moment and then slapped his right fist into his left palm. "The dirty bastard! And he has to be from my home town!"

Major Smith unfolded and stretched, his black beard glossy in the sunshine. He gazed upward at the relentlessly continuing armada of bombers and fighters. "I'll tell you one thing. The Tokyo raid was nothing like this. I hear it's your birthday, Jim." Jim nodded, and Smith's teeth flashed in his whiskers. "Well, happy birthday. This is quite a party."

Jim glared down along the herd of prisoners in the circuit path to where Bill Johnston stood talking to a man apart from the rest. Not far away, Colonel Condon stood gazing casually into the sky. The roar of engines was growing steadily fainter. The bombers were specks disappearing to the west and to the south toward France and Italy. Jim sighed. "They'll be eating good hot food tonight and sleeping in clean beds. You know? Flying combat ain't so bad. Not bad at all. Unless you get shot down."

Junior started walking. "Something's up. Let's go see."

Someone in the crowd across the field yelled something, but the distance drowned the words. All over the parade ground briskly walking Kriegies were angling toward the growing crowd at the southeast corner. Tom fell in beside Jim and Junior. "What's cooking, men?"

Junior's face glowed with curiosity. "Maybe there's a dame out there."

"They're here!" someone up ahead yelled. "They're here!"

They walked faster. Al Koczeck broke from the crowd and ran toward them. "They're here! They've come!" He playfully poked Jim's skinny arm. "They're here, Jim!"

"Who's here?"

Men in the crowd were laughing and shouting to one another, whooping and jostling one another with joy. As they came to the end of the Abort, Koczeck motioned southward. "The white trucks! Hubba, hubba, hubba!"

"Boy, look at those red crosses!"

"Them's American trucks! Them's GI trucks straight from home!"

Beyond the prison blocks and the compound's south fence, three white-painted and canvas-covered trucks stood parked on the road. Forward on the white canvas cover of the nearest truck, just back of the cab, was painted a red square containing a white cross. Koczeck poked Jim's arm again. "We eat tonight! We eat tonight!"

As they gazed, another white truck drove into view and parked abreast of the others beyond the barbed wire. A cheer went up. Two men got out of the truck and waved. Jim's eyes blurred with sudden tears. "There's my birthday present. God bless the Red Cross!"

Somebody called out to Major Smith, who was talking to a Wehrmacht noncom. "Major! Is it on the level? Are those things filled with food?"

The major laughed back. "That's the poop from group. This is to be the dispersal point for all the Kriegie camps in Germany."

Another cheer mounted, louder because everyone in the compound was crowding for a look at the trucks. Junior slapped his forehead. "Where's that Bill Johnston?"

Jim shrugged. "I dunno. Why?"

"I got to get my watch back." Junior darted off through the crowd.

Jim chuckled. "Remember this, Tom, the next time you hear somebody say the Red Cross is just a racket."

"I never said it was a racket."

Koczeck kept rubbing his palms together and making the same

sounds over and over. "Hubba, hubba, hubba. We eat tonight. Hubba, hubba, hubba. We eat tonight, men. We eat tonight."

The crowd of pinched faces wore smiles as they continued to gaze at the white trucks. Startlingly a siren began to moan, joined by another and another in the long eerie blast of an all-clear signal. Jim felt his stomach gurgle in anticipation of the Red Cross food. He felt slightly dizzy, as if hypnotized by the sirens' wail. Without saying anything he broke away from the crowd, walked a short way along the perimeter path, and sat down in the dirt. Jack Noble walked up from somewhere and stood over him. Noble's voice was high-pitched with excitement. "Did you see the white trucks, Jim? Did you see 'em right over there?"

Jim looked up and sighed. "Yeah. I saw them."

"I'm going back and take another look." Noble was off again, clothes flapping about his wasted frame as he walked.

Jim sat poking in the dirt with his finger for a while, conscious of the breath-consuming emptiness inside him. Absent-mindedly he reached one hand inside his shirt to an itchy spot on his chest and squashed a flea against his freshly washed skin. Briefly he fingered the stark ridges of his ribs.

"Hi y'all, Jim. Where's these white trucks we been hearing about?" Burt Salem and Bob Montgomery stood grinning down at Jim.

Jim motioned toward the nearby crowd. "They ain't standing there to see a parade."

Burt started walking. "Let's go see those trucks." They wandered off into the crowd.

Jim spotted Junior shuffling slowly across the parade ground and called out to him. "Hey, Junior. Did you get your watch?"

Junior crossed over and spat into the dirt. "The crummy bastard wouldn't give it back. He said a deal is a deal. He said it wasn't his fault the trucks arrived."

Men were leaving the south end of the parade ground and streaming toward the prison blocks. Jim got to his feet and dusted himself off. "That's a bum deal."

"Yeah. Colonel Condon was with him. He agreed with him."

"That figures." They crossed slowly toward the Abort and the prison blocks beyond it. "Well, you can always use the extra food."

Junior rubbed his belly thoughtfully. "Yeah. I'm throwing a big bash tonight. You're invited."

"Thanks. I can use it."

They automatically held their breaths as they passed the dark opening of the Abort. When they entered the prison block the bay was alive with sound.

The last of the American air armada roared away hardly noticed.

Noble entered the aisle and gloomily sat down on a lower bunk. He was followed by Koczeck. "It won't be long now, men. They're bringing 'em in through the gate now."

Noble looked up. "They're only giving us one parcel for each three men. Just third-rations."

Bob snorted. "How the hell do you know?"

Koczeck shrugged. "He's right. We were out at the gate. What the hell? A third of a parcel is better than none at all."

Jim started to climb up onto his bunk, but stopped when he saw Junior come into the aisle. Junior held up his left fist exposing his wrist watch. "If anybody wants to know what time it is, just ask me."

Jim's eyes widened. "You mean he let you back out of the deal after all?"

Junior was laughing so hard his whole body shook. He tried to talk at the same time. "He had to. The goons searched the block this morning and stole all of his food."

"No!"

"Yes! They took it all. You ought to see Colonel Condon. He's madder than a bull with its balls in a wringer." Junior doubled over slapping his bony knees.

Jim began to chuckle. The chuckle developed into a laugh.

"Food parcels!" someone yelled from the center of the prison bay. "Rations stooges front and center!"

Jim climbed up onto his bunk and lay there chuckling from time to time as all but he and Tom went out to look at the food parcels.

Tom pulled his skinny body up onto the bunk across the aisle from Jim's and looked over. "What's the matter, Jim. Don't you want to watch the unveiling of the grub?"

Jim grinned and closed his eyes. "All I want to do is lie here and think about food. I'll think about it hard right up—until somebody tells me it's all cooked and on the table. Then I'll stop thinking about it and eat it. I'm going to stuff my gut until food comes oozing out of my ears. There'll be cigarettes in the parcels. After I'm so full of food I can't jam another bite down, I'm going to light up a weed. I'm going to lie right here and smoke two in a row. Then I'm going to sleep not hungry for once and see what I dream about instead of food. Maybe it'll be a woman. Who knows? It's been a long time since I've dreamed about a woman."

Jim lay there thinking about the contents of a Red Cross food parcel. Powdered milk, Spam, corned beef, liver paste, salmon, cheese, margarine, K-ration biscuits, Nescafé, jam, prunes, sugar, chocolate, and cigarettes. As he waited for the food the unending murmur of the men throughout the prison bay sounded like the buzz of swarming bees.

Colonel Condon: "There I was. . . ."

The important thing is to be a man. Be a man that others look up to, even if you have to kick them in the face to make them do it.

West Point makes a man out of you. I guess I've had enough of the Point to make a man out of me. No, I never finished at the Point, but I got three years of it, and that's enough to make a man out of anybody.

It's funny how I happened to leave the Point. I suppose most of you characters would give up if you got washed out of West Point after three years of that kind of hell, wouldn't you? Well, not me. I spent three years at the Point, all right, and was doing fine. Then you know what happened? I couldn't pass French. What in hell does a soldier have to know French for? I went to the Point to become a soldier, not a God-damned linguist.

Well, when there's a will there's a way. That's how I got into the Point in the first place. The Congressman called on us at my dad's house on Capitol Hill.

"I'm sorry," he said. "The examination was fair and impartial. You just didn't score high enough. The only honorable thing I can do is to give the appointment to young Bill Stanley."

You can always tell when my dad is getting mad. He got up, spit into the fireplace, and said: "Who the hell is this Bill Stanley? Stanley. Stanley. What line is his old man in?"

The Congressman began to get nervous. "He's got no father," he says. "His mother works at Fielding and Nolan."

Dad turns around and runs his hand through his thin white hair, very casual. "Oh," he says mildly, "an executive? Buyer? What's she do?"

The Congressman looks at the carpet. "She's an accountant."

"Now look here," my dad roars, just like he was down in his junk yards. "You ain't going to pass over my boy for some snotty-nose son of some God-damned female accountant!"

"There's the examination," the Congressman pleads. "It's the only honorable thing I can do."

"Honorable shit," my dad spits back at him. He pulls out of his wallet the four one-thousand dollar bills he always carries. "There's your honor. Cash. What'd she give you? You're going to need all the cash you can get this fall. If my boy is in West Point this fall you may be back in Washington next year. If not, you couldn't get elected dog catcher. I'll ding you all down the line—and you know I can do it." Dad lowers his voice. "Now, look. We've been good friends for a long time. Why don't you go over to that phone and call up the newspapers? Tell them who gets the appointment."

It's the same thing at West Point. Only, at the Point it's rank that talks, not money. You've got upperclassmen kicking you around from the first year to the fourth year, and even then there's the regular brass hounding you. Sure, a fourth-year man caught me using crib notes in the French exam. What the hell? I couldn't have passed it without them, so I used them. They let me resign. The honor system, they call it.

I'd been getting P.O.'d anyway. West Point! What a hell of a place to fight a war! Several of my high-school mates had medals already, and my kid brother, just twenty-one years old, was already a lieutenant in the Air Force.

"Gentlemen," a colonel says to about sixteen of us who have washed out or resigned, "just because you haven't completed four years here is no sign the army doesn't need you. All of you have had good basic training and will be given an opportunity to apply for Officer Candidate School or the Aviation Cadet Training Program. There's no reason why you shouldn't all make good officers in the Army of the United States so that the Point can be proud of you."

From the West Point of the Ground to the West Point of the Air, Randolph Field. A condensed version of the same old shit all over again. But, as I say, three years at the Point is enough to make a man of you. I made Cadet Commander in primary, basic, and advanced. A man can get ahead in the Air Force.

The only thing that rankled me was my kid brother. He was already a major before I got my wings, and was getting too big for his britches. He had shot down seven Germans out of England and was already home on leave. We never wrote to each other, but I guess it was his idea of a joke to send me a clipping from the newspaper about this guy Bill Stanley. There was a picture and a story about how this guy was lost when a destroyer was sunk in the Pacific. Hell, he was only a seaman first class.

"Sit down, boys," a sloppy-looking lieutenant colonel tells us when we walk into a briefing room at Westover Field. He just sits that way with his feet up on the table reading a Sunday comic section until the room is full of pilots. Then he turns painfully, like his tail bone was hurting. "Boys," he says, "you may wonder about the record of this group. Well, it ain't got no record. This is a new outfit." He grins. "That means quick promotions if you don't buy it first." He motions toward some tired-looking guys sprawled in chairs against the wall. "We are all the experience this outfit has, so do what we tell you and maybe we'll get those promotions for you. If not, then the angels sing. Don't bother to unpack. We leave for England at 0300 hours."

"How are we going, Colonel?" someone asks.

The C.O. yawns. "We make like birds in P-47's. What's your name again, Sergeant?"

A master sergeant by the door popped to. "Smith, sir."

"Relax. Sergeant Smith Sir here will show you your Thunderbolts. Deal cards or something for first choice. Only, lay off the ones we've already picked out. Those are our babies."

Now I ask you. Isn't that a hell of a way to run an army? He stands up and tries to straighten out his wrinkled battle jacket. There's tarnished silver wings over the left pocket and miniature RAF wings over the right. He yawns again. "There's mail for some of you guys at the orderly room. After you've gone over your ships and checked your ground gear in at the tower, if anybody wants me I'll be at the bar in the Officers' Club."

When I picked up my mail it was the usual from my mother. A short letter telling me my kid brother was now a lieutenant colonel flying P-51's in Italy, and a thick sheaf of newspaper clippings. I picked up a beer at the club and sat down to look at the clippings. They're mostly about home-town boys getting decorated or promoted or killed. Then I open up a large one. It's a two-page spread in the magazine section. I don't even know this guy it's all about, but my mother has been sending me clippings about him ever since I was back at the Point. I'm getting sick of reading about him. A year or so ago one of the clippings says he has been killed in action, and I think that's the end of him. Then another comes saying he is a prisoner of the Italians, and I figure, well, we'll hear no more of him. Then another says he is a prisoner of the Germans, and I say so what? That's got to be the end. But, no, it isn't. The son of a bitch starts sending letters out, and every one of them gets printed in the paper. Just because he got into it a little earlier than anybody else he's a God-damned war hero. And here it is again, this double spread before me on the table at Westover. It's all about him again. There's a big picture of him sitting in the cockpit of a Spitfire.

"Say," the raunchy lieutenant colonel says, looking over my shoulder, "isn't that Jim Weis?"

"Yes, sir," I say, looking up at him swaying there from drink.

"Wahooo!" the guy yells like an Indian. "Hey, Micky! Speed! C'm'ere. Here's a write-up about Jim Weis." Then he looks down at me. "You know old Jim?"

I figure I'd better play it safe. "He's from my home town."

So the three of them, all raunchy types, move in with their drinks, passing the article around and jabbering. "Do you remember this? Do you remember that? There I was. . . . And old Jim gave him a burst of yours. Then I gave him a burst of yours."

That was the first and last time I ever fell for that one. "What's 'yours?' " I ask.

"Scotch and soda, thanks," they all chime in. "What's yours?"

When I've paid for the round and they've quit laughing, the lieutenant colonel leans across to me. "So you're a pal of old Jim Weis, huh? Same home town, huh? Say, how would you like to be my wing man?"

What a break! First day with a new outfit and I was wing man to the group C.O.

"We'll see what we can do with the tech orders," he promised me. "I think my wing man oughta be at least a captain."

You know, he was a drunken bum, but I never let him know I thought so. He couldn't go on forever the way he did in England,

and I knew it. You can't guzzle yourself blind every night and start flying those long missions early every morning the way he'd been doing for more than a hundred missions. Neither could those other second-tour boys. I figured all I had to do was be a nice wing man and wait. When the top men start getting knocked off, somebody further down moves up, see?

"We're going in to get 'em on the ground," he says one morning before dawn, raunchier and redder-eyed than ever in his flying clothes. "We just got the poop from Wing. From now on every plane destroyed on the ground counts as a full victory."

I liked that ruling. My kid brother had nine when he left Italy after his second tour. After forty-one missions I didn't have any yet. You don't get any, flying wing position.

"Tallyho!" he yells over the RT, and we peel off by flights four thousand feet over Lille. It doesn't take long until we are skimming over housetops through all the light flak and tracers in the world. It's kind of misty, but when the rooftops fall behind we are over the green grass of an airfield and parked Jerry planes are dispersed all over it. He takes one and starts pumping fifties into it. I spot one to the left and ease out of position to get me a score for a change. I got it. It exploded, sending up a plume of black smoke. I check to make sure my camera was working. Then I notice a Focke-Wulf 290 is on the C.O.'s tail. Before I can get back over there he slams smack into a house at the other end of the field. I take a shot at the 290, but I guess I missed. Anyhow, I got me one on the field, confirmed by my camera. I was on my way. We lost the group C.O. and a squadron C.O. Everybody on the ball moved up. I got the squadron. A month later I got the group. And I had four more destroyed on the ground. I was an ace with nine Air Medals and the D.F.C. That's all it takes if you are on the ball. Just one month and I was a lieutenant colonel and top man. I wrote a long letter home and told them to put that in the paper.

"Just remember one thing," I told my group exec. "Every fifteen missions put me in for the Silver Star." I got 'em, too. Silver Star with four Oak Leaf Clusters. D.F.C. with three Oak Leaf Clusters. Air Medal with thirteen Oak Leaf Clusters. The only thing where I got fouled up was the Distinguished Service Cross. In Normandy we were flying ground support, working by two-way radio with a tank battalion knocking out road blocks for them. I had a deal with the tank commander. I was going to recommend him for the D.S.C. and he was going to put me in for one for dive bombing, but the damned fool got killed. I put him in for his before I found out about it, so he got a D.S.C. posthumously. All I got was tough shit.

"Look," I told the group exec. "If I get shot down, do one last thing for me, will you? Put me in for the D.S.C. posthumously."

"Why don't you go home on rotation?" he asks me. "You're beginning to take too many chances. You've lost four wing men."

What an idea! Go home just before Paris is about to be liberated. I know damned well when Paris is taken there's going to be a hell of a lot of decorations, and a lot of 'em will be French. I could use a Croix de Guerre.

The big day comes. We've been out on one dive-bombing run and it looks like today Paris is going to be ours. While I'm waiting at headquarters squadron for a phone call from wing, the sergeant brings in the mail. I open mine and out falls a clipping, a column by Walter Jordan about this Jim Weis. How do you like that? A lousy second lieutenant who's been shot down a year and a half already, and he's getting more space in the papers than I am. I'm still thinking about that when I'm diving straight down from ten thousand feet on a road block in the outskirts of Paris. Automatically I pull the trigger and watch my tracers chasing each other down into the sandbag bunker. Automatically I press the toggle button and the ship jumps free of the bomb. Automatically I look in the rear-view mirror for my wing man. Only, something is wrong. That's no P-47 back there. It's a Focke-Wulf. My ship begins to buck. Pieces fly back off the wings. My engine cowl flies off. A hunk of my propeller splinters the glass in front of me. I cut the switches, pull down my goggles, and with my head sticking out in the slipstream manage to slow down enough to make a nice belly landing in the middle of a street on the wrong side of Paris—the German side.

"For you the war is over," a Jerry officer says to me in good English.

The hell it is. I got that posthumous DSC, and when I get back I'm really going to cash in on all those medals. Weis will be just another second looey; but I've got rank, and I'll cash in on that, too. It's kind of a joke on him when you think of it. If it hadn't been for that article about him I spread out on the table back at Westover, that lately lamented Group C.O. would never have made me his wing man and promoted me to captain. Without that head start I'd never have made lieutenant colonel so fast. Funny, isn't it?

I'd like to know where in hell that last son of a bitch went to that was supposed to be my wing man. If I could only get out of here, I'd have him court-martialed.

Chapter Twenty-two

It was dark in the prison bay, and tier after tier of food-filled men were trying to sleep. Yet there was constant motion. Here and there in the black maze of bunks cigarettes glowed, occasional Kriegies shuffled to and fro among the tiers bumming lights, and others made the longer trip along the hall to the crock in the front alcove. Jim lay awake on his bunk staring up into the darkness and listening to the rumbling in his abdominal organs. Ever since about an hour after the sudden big bash of Red Cross food, he had been fighting down nausea. He hoped the noises meant that the food was finally slipping down out of his stomach. He paid no attention to a Kriegie who suddenly ran down the dark floor of the bay and began to retch and vomit into the crock. Men had been doing that for hours, sickened from stuffing their weakened stomachs with unaccustomed food. Down near the floor Noble moaned softly in his bunk. Another dark shape traveled quickly along the bunk ends to the crock, and the sound of vomiting was replaced by the splash and splatter of a desperate bowel movement. That had been increasing in frequency throughout the long night. Across the aisle from Jim, Tom's thin face glowed ghostlike as he took a drag from a short cigarette held between his fingers.

"Tom?"

"Yeah?"

"Gimme a light."

Jim took the butt from Tom's extended hand and applied it to a cigarette of his own. He had to steady the tremor of his right hand by holding it with his left. There was a slight spasm of pain in his intestines. He handed the short butt back across to Tom. Nearby men were snoring, and somewhere in the darkness a man was coughing. Jim took a deep, deep drag on his cigarette and let it out slowly, enjoying the slight dizziness it caused. From time to time a bunk tier creaked as one of its twelve occupants stirred. The floor squeaked as the steady night traffic to and from the big crock in the alcove continued. A mumble of low conversation came from that direction. Tom whispered across the aisle. "How you feeling?"

"I think I've got the Gib. belly."

"The what?"

"The Gib. belly. That's what we called it at Gibraltar. It's the GI's."

Tom snuffed his butt out carefully and put it in a small tin can wedged in beside his pallet. "I know what you mean. I just hope it isn't dysentery."

Jim grunted, thinking what dysentery would mean in a crowded prison camp. "That'd be all we need."

A hoarse whisper came from somewhere nearby. "Hey, how about you guys piping down?"

Jim smoked on in silence, his cigarette glowing as he inhaled. His intestines stirred continually. A sharp gas pressure made him throw back his blankets and swing his legs over the side. With the cigarette's remains dangling from his lips and smoke curling up into his eyes he removed his shoes from where they hung on a nail and pulled them on, not bothering to tie the laces. He slid to the floor and smashed out the cigarette against the side of his bunk. Tom whispered softly. "Let me have the snipe for my pipe."

Jim dropped the butt in Tom's can and shuffled on out of the aisle.

A prisoner was vomiting into the evil mess which filled the stinking crock to the brim and ran down its sides onto the floor. Eight Kriegies waited impatiently in line behind him. Jim cursed toward a dim face near him. "Jesus! It's full to overflowing."

"You said it."

"But how can you sit on that thing?"

"You have to go down to the washroom after and douse yourself off with water."

Jim considered returning to his bunk, but the gripe in his guts wouldn't wait. He crossed to the front doors and opened one a crack. Cool air floated in to the rotten stench-filled alcove. The big black shape of the outside Abort loomed up against the glow of distant fence and tower lights. "Anybody heard the Hundeführer around here lately?"

"Christ, man!" somebody whispered. "You're not going out there, are you?"

The first man had stopped vomiting and was leaning weakly against a wall. Another in the line was trying to arrange some German newspaper on the wet filth of the crock's rim.

"Hurry, for God's sake!" someone in the line pleaded. "I can't wait."

Jim tore a couple of sheets of newspaper from a bunch nailed to the wall. He cracked the door open again and gazed across the empty dark toward the Abort. He listened carefully but could hear nothing. Nor could he see anything move beyond the Abort's black shape except an occasional probing searchlight. The gripe was unbearable, but so was the thought of climbing up onto the crock. "Don't let anybody lock these doors from the inside."

"Man, you're crazy!"

Jim stepped out and quickly closed the door behind him. Maybe I am crazy, he thought, and walked quickly but quietly down the prison-block steps. Surely and cautiously he strode with light footsteps across the distance toward the virulent odor coming from the entrance-way of the Abort. Looking to the left and to the right toward the fences of the neighboring compounds, he left the cold outside air and walked stealthily up the stone steps into the pitch-black cavern. "A dog would never be able to smell me in here," he reasoned as he reached the top of the steps and felt along the wall for the first cast-iron lavatory bowl. In final desperation he lowered the trap of his long underwear, sat down on the hard cold edge, and relieved himself into the great pit beneath the floor. Apart from the slight noise of his own breathing, the total darkness of the large room was absolutely silent. "How amazing!" he marveled. "I can see nothing and hear nothing. It's completely quiet. I'm all alone." He could even hear the light thumping of his heart in his fleshless chest. He had last been alone nearly two years before in the cooler at Dulag Luft, but there had been no darkness there. The light had burned all night. This was complete. Hear nothing, see nothing, a place to think. But he could bring his thoughts into no order. Maybe there's really nothing to think about, he thought. It was cold in the Abort, and he shivered a little. Finally he stood up, buttoning his clothes. Perhaps he could sleep now if he could get back without being caught. He bumped into another toilet bowl trying to pick his way toward the exit. Soon he found it, a lighter square of star-misted sky. Carefully he poked his head outside. Seeing nothing move, he walked out into the awesome

346

blackness. He started toward the dark squatting shape of the prison block.

Something clicked to the right! He froze. It clicked again, a sort of tinkling sound like a belt buckle. Then he heard the rapid patter of small feet. He saw it in the next compound. It was a sleek dark dog approaching the double barbed-wire fences at a furious lope! A Doberman pinscher! Jim started to run, watching the dog. In the other compound the Doberman left the ground in a mighty taut leap which made it soar up and over the barbed wire. Jim went up the block steps three at a time as the big black dog hit the ground at a run on his side of the fences. He turned the knob, jumped inside, and slammed the door just as the dog struck it a violent clawing blow on the outside, snarling in furious rage and biting at the door panel.

"Jesus!" somebody said. "Did he get any of you?"

Jim leaned against the door gasping great breaths of the alcove's foul air. "Will the door hold him? I want to get out of here."

"Let go of it a little bit and see."

Three men stood back a little from the door, listening to the fury of the beast attacking it.

"It'll hold. You had a close one. What were you doing out there?"

"He wanted privacy."

"Platz!" shouted a German voice somewhere outside. "Platz!" The dog ran off snorting.

Jim left the alcove and walked to his tier of bunks. Bob's voice came from one of them. "What happened over there?"

"I almost got et by a dog."

Jim leaned shaking against his bunk. He tried to pull himself up, but his arms were twitching and wouldn't sustain him. He took two deep breaths and tried again. This time he made it. With quivering fingers he removed his shoes and tried to tie them together so that he could hang them up by the laces. He gave up and jammed the shoes down in between the pallet and the bunk frame. Dizzy, he lay back and pulled the blankets over him. Tom's voice whispered from across the darkened aisle. "Good night, Jim."

"Good night, Tom." Gradually his breathing slowed to normal. Occasionally an arm or leg muscle twitched as with closed eyes he listened to the sighs and snores of many sleepers and the shuffles of those who could not sleep traveling back and forth along the hall. Already his guts were beginning to gurgle again.

Jim Weis: "There I was. . . ."

It's hard to tell when you're sick and when you're well when you're miserable all of the time. And every prisoner of war is miserable all of the time. Away back there in the Regia Marina hospital on Torre Bianca I began to think I was well again. I still had the eighteen-day-old field dressing around my left thigh, but I could walk again. With no trouble at all I could walk again, so I thought I was well. When two of the Afrika Korps came for me I put on my clothes and walked down the stairs to the Volkswagen which took me to the Luftwaffe base at Trapani. I even thought of making a run for one of the parked ME-109's dispersed along the patched-up runways. I just thought about it. I didn't do it.

"Kom," a soldier in Luftwaffe blue said to me, offering me a hand. "Ve go to Napoli."

I didn't take it. I walked under my own power and climbed up the ladder into the corrugated JU-52 that was sitting there with all three propellers turning over. And a couple of hours later, after we had flown over Capri and past the smoke hovering over Vesuvius, I walked under my own power past the bullet-holed Macchi fighter planes sitting like overstuffed birds on the Italian air base at Naples.

"Kom," the Jerry guard said, holding open the back door of a big brown open car. "Ve take you on a liddle zightzeeing trip an Napoli."

"I've seen it before," I said getting in.

"Ah, er war schon einmal hier," he told the driver.

And I had, less than six years before. It gives you a weird feeling traveling as a prisoner through streets and past landmarks where once you had traveled first class. And those landmarks were weird, too—

ornately fronted buildings piled high with sacks full of dirt and the streets nearly empty except for German and Italian soldiers walking seriously as if on business. We drove past the Arcade, from which most of the glass had been shattered, past the Cathedral, and rounded onto the bay front. I searched the hillside trying to guess which of the hundreds of hotels I had stayed in. A breeze was blowing off the bay from the direction of Capri, and I felt pretty well.

"Hier ve are." We got out of the car and he dismissed the driver. Then we walked into the marble lobby of a luxurious hotel that had obviously been taken over for a German headquarters. A sentry let us past him into an elevator, and we rode up three floors. I stood waiting while my guard handed some papers to a slicked-up Luftwaffe officer sitting at a desk.

"Nein! Nein!" the officer shouted looking up from the desk. Evidently my guard had made some kind of mistake. The officer shouted some more things, pointing to some print on the papers. He had made a mistake. We were in the wrong building. Not only that, we were in the wrong part of Naples.

"Ve hef lost the auto"—my guard shrugged after we were back out on the sidewalk—"zo ve must valk."

We headed east back toward town. "Where are we going?" I asked. He named some hotel. "Where's that?"

"By the Hauptbahnhof."

Jesus! I remembered. The main railway station was clear over on the other side of town. We walked and we walked along the bay front. At first I enjoyed it. Then my left thigh began to feel tired. Then it began to feel like it was going to sleep. After about a mile it started to ache in a numb sort of way. I noticed I was beginning to limp. We had a long way to go. We rounded a corner and started up a street that led to the main part of Naples. My leg hurt more and more. Italian girls sitting with and without German soldiers on the concrete edge of a park strip stared curiously at me as we passed. I could hear dirty little kids whispering things to one another and darting around to get a better look. I felt like a damned fool with one leg of my pants ragged with blood dried all over it and my right boot sagging open from a busted zipper and civilian women and kids staring at me like maybe I had snot all over my face. And all the time my leg was hurting more and more. I was really limping like the devil.

Another German officer put an end to it. It must have been quitting time when we got to the big open square in front of the Cathedral, because wops of all sizes and shapes, mostly women, came streaming down the street and from across the square like a tidal wave. This kraut officer walks past us, stops, and comes striding up behind and taps my guard on the shoulder with a glove. The guard jumps to attention and for the second time gets a beaut of a dressing down. I couldn't understand enough German to get much of it, but it was something like what the hell did he think he was doing walking an American prisoner down the main street of town. He called him a jackass, a dumbhead, and some other things that must have been worse, while passers-by grinned sideways at us. When the officer left us my guard was shaking in his black boots.

"Kom," he said, red in the face. "Ve take the Strassenbahn."

So we climbed onto the back step of a little streetcar so full of people they were sticking out the sides, with me hanging onto a steel handle for dear life, afraid my sore leg is going to give out and let me fall on the cobblestones that are whizzing past under us at about ninety miles an hour. At about the twentieth stop, with wops piling in and out all the way, we got off. I was beginning to feel weak.

"Kom," he said again, and we walked into a crowded hotel lobby just across the street from the square in front of the dirty black railway station. I remembered tipping a porter three lire for carrying my luggage up that street.

"Oh, ho!" says a hawk-faced German darting out of about thirty that were milling around in the lobby. "An American, eh? Glad to see you." I let him grab my hand. I didn't care. "From North Africa?" He didn't wait for me to answer. I was beginning to feel dizzy. "I've taken a lot of Americans up to where you're going. Frankfurt. You'll like it. It's a bloody good place. How are things going in Africa?"

"Not so good for you," I answered.

"Oh, ho," he says, laughing in a kind of loud, overconfident fashion. "You think you will win the war in Africa, do you? Well, all I do is take prisoners up to Frankfurt from Africa. I took two Aussies, an American, and a Limey up last time. We had a bloody good time on the way." You could tell by his vocabulary he'd been around too many Englishmen. "I'm on my way down to get some more now. And when I bring them up I go back and get some more. I keep making trip after trip until I've brought you all up and you've bloody well had it. You'll see."

"If you're going down now," I told him, "you'll be lucky to get back at all."

"Oh, ho! I'm not worried." He pumped my hand again. "Too bad I can't take you up. We'd have a bloody good time of it. So long, pal." He barged on out the door like he was going out to replace a full-back. You know what happened to that guy? Paddy Corrigan was in the next bunch that guy tried to bring back. It seems this joker forgot something, went back into Tunis to get it, and got his head blown off in the street fighting. Somebody else brought Paddy and the rest of the prisoners back.

Anyway, in this hotel they gave me a nice bed on the second floor. It belonged to some Kraut who was on leave. They fed me some of that weed soup they call vegetable stew. I got a good night's sleep, but when I woke up my leg was so sore and stiff I could hardly move it. My head ached. There were sore bumps on both sides of my groin and under my armpits. I definitely wasn't feeling well. At a breakfast of Reichs bread and jam and that glycerine stuff they call coffee, they turned me over to a German sergeant who was a tank commander to take me on to Rome. He spoke good English and was jolly enough, but he ate so much and so long that we almost missed the train. As crippled as I was, I had to run for it. He grabbed me by the hand and charged down the street to the railway station, dragging me like a stubborn dog through the station and onto the platform. He hauled me up the steps of a passenger car just as the train started to chug out of there. We ended up planted on wooden seats in a compartment with four other Krauts going home on leave. You know, it hurt even just sitting there? If they had wanted to fix me so I couldn't make a break for it, they couldn't have done a better job. I couldn't even walk to the can.

"Do you know what I like best about you Americans?" the tank sergeant asks me from his seat across the compartment. "It's your music. Jazz. I'm a musician. Of course, der Führer has made jazz verboten because it is written by Jews. But—well, you know. Sometimes when my band and I were rehearsing alone, we'd play a little jazz."

His eyes lighted up and he told me about jazz. Oh, he was real gone. I don't know how many hours it takes by train from Naples to Rome, but I had a fever, and pains in the glands of my neck, armpits, and groin, and my left thigh throbbed in jazz time until finally the train clanked to a stop in sunshine streaming through the shattered canopy of a passenger platform in Rome. The jazz addict had to hold me up as I slowly limped down the emptied corridor and onto the platform. I must have passed out on my feet, because the next thing I knew the tank sergeant was gone and a skinny civilian in a light gray suit and Homburg hat was holding me under my arms and walking me slowly through the ticket gate and into the station. "There is no hurry," he said in a soothing voice. "We take it slowly. There is plenty of time." Swarms of uniforms of all colors swirled around us as we crept through the station, which echoed like tom-toms and hyenas. "Do not hurry, Lieutenant. I am with the Red Cross. Soon we will be to a medical station. Take your time."

It took plenty of time. We got out onto a sun-baked sidewalk. Soldiers and civilians were dodging around us. We walked for about a block until I didn't think I could go on. "Now," the civilian guided me, holding me up at the same time, "just across the street. Just a little way farther." I let him worry about the trucks and cars bulling their way back and forth, and I guess he worried, too. I could feel him twitch and jerk, hurting my aching glands, as we dodged our way across. Then, with blotches dancing before my eyes, we were in some kind of shop converted into a medical station. I lay back on an examining table and didn't try to understand the German that was being spoken.

"Now don't faint," I remembered the man in the gray suit saying as they lowered my battered trousers and tried to pull the stuck bandage away from my leg. They did, and it burned like a hot poker. I looked down. The hole was red like a tomato, and bulging, and I lay back watching the cracked plaster ceiling spin round and round.

"I will try to get transport to take you to a surgeon this afternoon," the gray-suited man said as he eased me limping once more along the sidewalk. Then, around the corner, we entered a building and spent about twenty minutes climbing up a square staircase to the third floor. A Wehrmacht sentry there stiffened and saluted, heels clopping in the empty corridor. I noted that. Who ever heard of a soldier saluting a Red Cross worker? The soldier rapped on a white-painted iron door. A face appeared in a tiny window, like a speak-easy's, and the door clattered open. We walked past three small barred cells with German soldiers sitting in them and into a small office. Other Germans were walking about, and there were constant risings and fallings of many German voices. The gray-suited man eased me into a seat, sat down himself, and took a long form from the drawer of his small desk. "Now," he said, "we must complete this form for the Red Cross."

I must have looked like hell trying to grin at him. "Jim Weis," I reported. "0-885-360. Second Lieutenant."

He made notations on the form and spoke without looking up. "You are a fighter pilot?"

"You know that," I said. "Look. I've been through this three times before. Twice in Africa and once in Italy. All I tell is my name, rank, and serial number."

He stared at me for a minute and then shrugged. "I see," he said, like he didn't give a damn. "It will only delay the notification of your next of kin. Sooner or later we will find out anyway, so you might as well cooperate now." I shook my head and closed my eyes, trying to drift off into a fog that could stop the bitter aches in my bones. "Come along, then." I had a hell of a time getting to my feet, even with his help. My ass felt like it was a hell of a lot more full of lead than it was, and every piece burned inside somewhere. He motioned to the Germans in the cells as I limped past. "These chaps are not so lucky as you." He smiled. "Tomorrow morning you go to Germany. Tomorrow morning they will be shot."

I looked at the prisoners. Their eyes made me think of some guinea pigs I had seen once in a bacteriology lab. "Spies?" I asked him.

"No," he answered. "Deserters."

I had to climb two more sets of stairs. They left me alone in a room with four bunks in it, and open windows without panes. It was the first time I had been alone since getting shot down eighteen days before. They left me a couple of slices of bread like pressed sawdust and a slice of black soggy blood sausage. I nibbled on the bread but threw the blood sausage down at the street five floors below. It splattered on the hood of a German command car, and I ducked my head back and waited for something to happen. Nothing happened. I sat on a pallet looking out over Rome, thinking all the time that this couldn't be happening to me—it just couldn't be. I flew my last mission over a thousand times. If I'd only had more ammunition. If I'd only had more speed. If that God-damned colonel had only brought a squadron down to help me. If only I could have got the

Arabs to lend me a horse. If. If. If. It got dark outside and inside. The traffic noises down below lessened almost to a standstill. The air coming into the window grew cold. There were no blankets. I put two of the straw-filled pallets on one bunk and crawled in between them. All night I shivered and sweated and woke up hurtling through space in my Spitfire only to find myself in the cold of my own loneliness. A few times I tried to pray in the darkness, but I didn't know what to pray for. And I was out of the habit. A man could cry out in a night like that. I don't know whether I did or not.

"How are you feeling today?" the man in the gray suit asked me several hours after the sun had come up.

I could feel stuff clinging sourly to my lips. My eyes were caked and seared back to my ears. My left leg was a dull blob of pain hanging from one side of my inflamed groin. "When do I get to see a doctor?" I asked him.

He smiled kindly. "The attendant who examined you yesterday thinks you will be able to make it to Frankfurt," he told me. "There you will be placed in one of the finest hospitals in Germany."

"I don't know if I can make it," I complained.

"Oh," he scoffed, "you'll make it. Chin up, old man."

They gave me a cardboard box with a loaf of bread and a chunk of blood sausage in it and marched me even more slowly than the day before down the stairs, across the street, and up to the railway station. Two Luftwaffe soldiers were put in charge of me. They were elderly, and spoke neither English nor standard German. I don't remember much about that train ride except that we sat crowded into a compartment on wooden seats and that it lasted all that day and night and on until late the next afternoon . . . and all of it was hell. They kept trying to make me eat the bread and blood sausage. I'd just as soon have eaten a dead cat. I may have been out of my head. Either that or I slept some of the time, which seems impossible with the fever I had. Somewhere along the way a young telegraph operator sitting opposite me gave me one of the oranges he was taking back to Germany on leave and a box of German cigarettes. Sometimes I'd find my teeth chattering, and sometimes I'd be moaning in rhythm with the wheels. My head didn't ache any more than the rest of me, and my head ached like hell.

"Bitte, wo ist Durchlager Luft?" one of my guards asked the gray walrus-mustached ticket taker in the Hauptbahnhof at Frankfurt am Main.

Dulag Luft. I knew all about that place. In the RAF they used to show us movies about what would likely happen to you there—how they would ply you with women and liquor and soft treatment to get your guard down so that you would spill all the military secrets you knew. Believe it or not, they helped me out to the front of the Hauptbahnhof and we caught a streetcar. One of my guards tried to get me a seat on it, but a fat Frau spat something back about Luftgangster and stayed there on her broad ass. We rode standing on the back platform.

Through my fever I got that screwy feeling again about the streets I had strolled down as a sightseer before. I even spotted a Bavarian Bierhalle where I had got drunk and sniffed snuff over five years before. And there was that unreal sense you get the first time you see the Coca-Cola signs in the middle of Naziland. The only thing that wasn't outright nuts was the fever ache as I stood clinging to a pole in the rear of the swaying streetcar, the box with the untouched bread and blood sausage tucked under a throbbing armpit.

A mile or so outside town we got off the streetcar and followed the conductor's directions. We started a hike through the woods. It was a well worn path they limped me along, taking right angles around fenced fields. It was growing dark when we finally saw a little village ahead through the trees and the fenced-in prison blocks on its outskirts. Suddenly I wondered what I had been carrying the loaf of bread and chunk of blood sausage for all this time. I gave the box to my escorts. They were amazed that anyone would be giving away food.

"Nein," I protested generously in my high-school German. "Bald gehe ich ins Hospital. Es gibt vieles zu essen."

It was dark when we entered the orderly room of a long, seemingly endless building.

"Er ist verwundet," one of my traveling companions added, handing over the papers that went with me. Nobody offered me a seat, so I leaned weakly against a wall waiting to be taken to the hospital. The men who brought me were dismissed, and left. I let the conversation of those around me roll off me while a Luftwaffe private wearing a medical cross pulled the bandage from my thigh. The hole was puffed up, purple, and oozing white pus. Another private started going through the pockets of my lowered pants. I managed to slip the cigarettes and matches from my jacket pocket in under my shirt and hold them there unnoticed until I could get my pants fastened again.

The private went through my jacket pocket and found nothing. I was so tired I didn't even care where we were going when they walked me down a long low corridor lined on both sides by narrow doors with tiny square shutters bolted on our side.

"Wann gehe ich nach Hospital?" I asked the guard who opened one of the doors for me. He said nothing, just motioned with his blank face. I entered. It was quite a room, eight feet long and eight feet wide, painted white, with a ceiling light glaring over a small table and stool squeezed in with a single bunk, low to the floor. On the table was a tarnished metal washbasin. On the bunk was a fiber-cloth pallet that leaked wood shavings over five crossboards. The window was of dappled glass mounted in small squares between steel bars.

I sat down on the stool and waited, aching and throbbing, for them to come and take me to a hospital. The temperature was awfully high. I waited and waited, gasping for breath. Hot air poured in through a vent in the wall. No one came. I peeled off my jacket and opened my shirt. I pushed the empty basin back and laid my pounding head in my arms. No one came. I lay down on the rough pallet. The crossbars bit through into my back and neck. I perspired steadily. I struggled out of my heavy boots and managed to get my pants off. I rolled the pants around the boots and tried to make a pillow of them.

There I was, lying there with a fever, my leg and whole body aching like hell, sweating with the temperature God knows how high, over a hundred at least, with the light glaring down at me, and no one came. I thought maybe I was imagining it. Maybe I was going crazy. It just didn't make sense. It was silent. God, it was silent! All I could hear was my own breathing, or the creaking of the boards I was lying on. Sometimes the whiteness of the walls and ceiling and the pressure of the light above me would put me in a daze and I'd start to drop off to sleep only to wake up with my body jerking out stiff and sending a pain like a pickax shooting up from my infected thigh. I started counting my own breathing. It seemed too fast, and I'd concentrate on slowing it down, counting it in and out slowly as high as three and four hundred breaths. I felt my pulse. It seemed fast. There was no way of judging time. There was nothing but the whiteness, the heat, and the pain.

I may have finally fallen asleep, because once, when I opened my eyes, I suddenly realized it was morning. The light above me was out and the cell was dull gray instead of bright white. The steel bars of the window were silhouetted against the brown panes of glass which were filtering in some of the outside daylight. I had to take a leak. The parts of my body that were numb from pressing against the boards all night felt better than the live portions of me until the circulation started. There was nothing else to urinate in so I used the metal washbasin. The temperature was still stifling. I could hear faint sounds of footsteps through the thick door. Sometimes they were near and sometimes far away. I put on my pants and waited to be taken to the hospital.

You can imagine what it was like sitting there listening to the faint noises of feet moving on the other side of that thick wall and thick door. Sometimes they would seem far away, then closer. Then they would pass and go on into the distance. Never a sound of a voice. Just those footfalls, and I kept wondering when they would stop at my door, and hoping and praying they would stop while minutes, hours—who knows?—passed. And then, finally, they did stop by my door. I got to my feet. With a clatter the little square shutter at my eye level opened outward and a hand thrust in two dark brown slices of bread. Instinctively I took them and started to speak. "When do I—" But the little shutter clapped into place before I could even get started, and I heard the bolt jammed to.

The sawdust bread was spread thinly with margarine. I sat down on the tiny stool and ate it, and waited some more. It dried my mouth out. The heat and the fever made me thirsty. I smoked one of the smuggled cigarettes, and it made me so dizzy I had to lie down on the boards again. But I kept on smoking just to have something to do, watching the smoke, the ember of the tobacco, and thinking.

I thought a whole day had passed when the little shutter opened again and cupped hands thrust in four small potatoes. I took the warm potatoes and tried to speak in German. "Bitte, wann kann ich—" The shutter banged to. I tried to scrape off some of the dirt that had been boiled into the peelings, and ate the potatoes. No matter how much I concentrated I couldn't figure out what was happening to me, except that maybe I was going mad. The day wasn't over, after all, because it continued, hot, miserable, lonely, noiseless, light filtering gray through the brown window.

For what may have been hours I tried to keep myself occupied with my German safety matches. I placed them on the table in every fighter and bomber formation I knew. I plotted out air battles with them. I made designs with them. I built barricades with them and leaned them standing against one another in every manner I could think of. When I heard the bolt to my door clatter open, I scooped them up and jammed them into my pocket. A guard stood in the doorway pointing at the table and motioning with his head to follow him. I started to follow. He shook his head and pointed more violently. He was pointing at the washbasin with my urine in it.

"It's about time," I said, picking up the basin and following him into the hall. "Do I go to the hospital now?"

He walked on down the long corridor without answering. I limped terribly slowly behind, lightning jolts of pain shooting from my thigh up to my groin. "What's the score?" I called after his faded blue back. "Was geht hier?"

He stopped by a doorway without a door and motioned inward. I figured maybe he was a mute. It hurt so much to walk I hardly noticed how much cooler the corridor was than the cell I had just left. I entered the room he was indicating. It had a cement floor and was furnished with a washtub and tap against one wall and a toilet bowl without a seat against the other. I emptied the metal basin, turned on the tap, and started to bathe my face in the cold water. He pulled me up by one shoulder and pointed at the toilet bowl. I was too miserable for a bowel movement. I started to drink from the tap and he pulled me up again. He pointed into the bowl. "Can I take some back with me?" I asked him, pantomiming from the tap to the basin. He nodded. I filled the basin and picked it up. Dizzy with fever, desperate with fear, I limped step by step back down the silent corridor. "Look," I pleaded, maybe almost crying, "tell whoever is in charge here I've got to see a doctor. I'm in a bad way." He motioned me in and I went, still pleading. "Tell them I've got to see a doctor, will you? Please? Bitte, ich muss den Doktor sehen. Bitte?" He slammed the door shut. There was no handle on the inside. I set the basin down, took a long drink, bathed my face and dried it on my jacket. The cell seemed hotter than ever. The light was on again. Beyond the dappled squares of glass in the window it was getting dark. I wet my face again and lay down without drying it. A long time later the shutter of my door opened and a hand thrust in two more slices of bread. Fortunately, the heat kept me sweating almost as much as I kept drinking, and I didn't have to use the basin until the next morning. After that I couldn't drink again until the silent guard took me on another trip down the long corridor late in the afternoon.

A couple of days like that and you find yourself falling into dazes. You think about everything that's ever happened to you. You start playing games with yourself, like trying to remember all the teachers you ever had in school. When you get stuck for a name you just keep thinking until you get it. You try counting to a thousand, and then to two thousand, and then to ten thousand by fives and nine thousand by threes. You start remembering all the movies you've ever seen and the names of the players in them. You remember the faces and names of all the flyers you've known who have been killed. You try to get off that one, but it isn't easy until you start trying to remember the names, one by one, of all the women you've ever made and the circumstances. But the trouble is, the mind works too quickly and you slip back too easily out of the dazes and start worrying about how your folks are taking this and wondering if they know you're alive. And sometimes you wonder if you are alive after all. But the leg smells through its three-week-old bandage in the sticky heat of the cell, the dirt of the lukewarm potatoes grits in your teeth, and the electric light glares down into your eyeballs to tell you this is real enough. But try and try—you cannot understand why. Why are you here? Why are they keeping you like this, buried alive in an over-heated mausoleum? And along toward the end of the third day you don't care any more. All you want to do is to hear the sound of a human voice again, just any sound in any language. The absolute silence of the place is getting you, and you wonder and wonder with fanatical curiosity what is beyond the window.

It couldn't go on for ever. I learned later that some guys were left in that "cooler" as long as twenty-one days without ever hearing a human voice. In my case they came after me the morning after the fourth night. At first I couldn't believe it. I looked up dopey-eyed when the silent German opened the door. Another blue-uniformed German spoke to me.

"You will come with me, please?"

I didn't say anything. Somehow I managed to bend over far enough to pull on my flying boots. I slipped into my jacket.

"This way, please."

He walked beside me, not helping me, but keeping slowed down to my limping pace. "Where are we going?" I asked.

"This way, please," he said again, holding a door open.

We walked into the wonderful cold air of a courtyard formed by the wings of the building. The sun was shining. I could even hear birds singing. We reentered the building on the other side of the courtyard.

"This way, please," he said again, and held another door open for me. I walked into an office with rugs on the floor, a big desk, and pictures of Allied aircraft in frames on the walls. Orange and brown curtains hung down to hide two windows. I stood with my body aching like I had been doing hard labor instead of sitting for some eighty-odd hours in a hot cell.

"Please be seated, Mr. Weis," a smiling wavy-haired guy in a sports jacket said from behind the desk. I sat down in the chair before the desk and he held out a pack of cigarettes. "You're an American. Will you have an American cigarette?" I took one, and he held a lighter across the desk for me. It was an imitation American cigarette, the kind they made in France before the war for American tourists. "Now we will have a little talk," he said pleasantly. "We must have some more information in order to establish your identity."

I sighed. "Don't tell me you're a representative of the Red Cross."

He looked hurt. "But certainly. Now, when and where did you join your fighter group?"

I shrugged. "I can't answer that."

He acted like he never heard me. "How long have you been overseas?" I just smiled at him, or tried to, anyhow. "But, Mr. Weis, you must answer these simple questions. Everyone must answer these questions so we can process you and send you to a permanent camp where you will be more comfortable. Were you with your group when it left England last October 23rd?"

I did some rapid calculation. He had it about right.

"You see," he smiled. "We know everything about your group, so you may as well be sensible and answer a few questions to establish your identity. Look behind you."

I turned in my chair, and my breath stopped for a minute. Hanging on the wall behind me was a big board with tags hanging all over it. Across the top was printed the number of my group. Lower down were the numbers of the three squadrons. Each tag bore a man's name, rank, and position in the group. All the CO's names, group, exec, squadrons and flights, were there, and all the other names of the men I had been flying with. I looked back at him trying not to show any interest.

"We took your name down three weeks ago," he smiled, holding a tag before him. It had my name on it. "Now we must be sure you are really Lieutenant Weis, or if we don't ascertain that we may have to turn you over to the Gestapo. You have heard of the Gestapo?"

I nodded. "I've heard of them, but I'm not answering any questions. I would be court-martialed if I did."

He smiled patiently. "Just a few simple questions, then. You were flying Spitfires?"

"If you don't know what I was flying, I'm not going to tell you," I told him. "I was shot down behind your lines."

"Yes, of course." He nodded. "Now when were you expecting to receive your new P-51's?"

So that was it. I had been trying to figure out what I could possibly know that was important. "Look," I said, "I don't know anything. I need a doctor. I'm wounded. My leg is infected. Can't you get me to a doctor?"

He ignored that and reached over to pull a string that drew the curtains away from the window. Outside, beyond a double barbed-wire fence, I could see American and British prisoners strolling among stucco dormitories. Beyond the buildings several men in shorts were kicking a soccer ball around on a green field. "You see," he said, "we want to send you in among your friends where you will have plenty to eat and recreation. But we can't do that until you answer a few questions to prove who you are." He leaned toward me. "We are not like the Japanese," he said. "Do you know what has happened to American prisoners the past few days in Japan?"

"How would I know that?" I asked him.

"Those Tokyo raiders." He nodded sadly. "The Japanese have executed them—cut their heads off. But in Germany legitimate prisoners of war are treated with respect. We follow the rules of the Geneva Convention. But first you must prove you are a soldier by answering a few simple questions. When were you expecting to receive your new P-51 fighters?"

I kept my eyes focused on the men playing soccer on the green grass. "All I know is that I need medical attention," I said. "I was promised I'd be sent to a hospital here."

He pressed a button on his desk. "Very well," he sighed. "It's entirely up to you. We will give you a few more days in your room to think about it."

"I've got a fever," I complained.

The guard who had brought me entered. The interrogator motioned to me. "Take Mr. Weis back to his room."

"What about my leg?" I demanded.

He shrugged the shoulders of his sports jacket. "You were examined when you came here. The medical attendant reports that you are all right. He found nothing wrong with you."

"Nothing wrong, hell!"

"You're all right. While you are resting think over our little conversation. I'll see you again in a few days. I enjoy your company." He smiled like he really did.

"This way, please," the guard said politely. Slowly I limped back to my cell and heard the door slam shut behind me.

Nothing wrong with me, he said. I began to wonder if there was. Maybe I was exaggerating my own condition. I decided it was all right. I had just been babying myself. But it didn't do any good. I felt sick and sore. Periodically my teeth would begin to chatter, and then I'd start burning up again in the heat of the cell. Sometimes I couldn't eat the bread or potatoes that were thrust through the opening in the door and I'd leave them on the table. Then suddenly I'd become hungry and wolf the stuff down. I'd lie back on the ridiculous bunk and recite what few poems I knew aloud and sing all the songs I knew, the sounds coming out of my cracked throat so that I could hardly stand to listen to myself. I thought about all the things I had ever done and how I should have done them and how I should do all the things I wanted to do in the future. I couldn't make myself have a bowel movement on any of the daily trips to the can. The time passed more quickly because I seemed to fall into dreamless sleep. Perhaps it was delirium. Anyhow, whole stretches of time seemed to pass as perfect blanks. Once in a while I would bump my thigh against something, and the pain would burn red-hot for a long time afterward. The glands under my armpits were so sore I couldn't press my arms to my sides.

They left me in only two days the second time. Once again I found myself seated before the interrogator, but this time instead of a sports jacket he was wearing the tunic of a Luftwaffe lieutenant. "Would you like to make a radio broadcast to your family?" he asked me, pacing back and forth behind his chair.

"No," I answered.

"No?" He stopped pacing to register faked surprise. "You don't wish your family to know you are alive?"

"All I want," I told him, "is to get to see a doctor. My leg's in a bad way."

"You are all right," he said matter-of-factly. "Our medical orderly reported so. Why don't you wish to make a broadcast? We are listened to in America, you know."

"I don't want to help you get listened to," I said. "All I want is medical attention. You said you go by the Geneva Convention. Surely I'm entitled to medical attention."

"But you don't need it. Our doctors are very busy men. Now, this broadcast would save a lot of time." He stopped and stared at me. "What are you doing?"

I was taking down my pants. "Look," I gritted, pulling the bandage away from my thigh. "Does this look like I don't need a doctor?" I could hardly stand to look at it myself. The wound was swelled up like a giant blue, purple, red, and yellow boil, with yellow pus squishing up between the ragged distorted hole in the center. Immediately the smell filled the room. "Does this look like I'm all right? What are you tryng to do? Make me lose a leg?"

He stood staring at the wound, his pink cheeks turning white. "I'm sorry," he stammered. "I didn't realize—" He reached for the button on his desk and pushed it. "I will have you taken to the hospital in Frankfurt this morning."

I sat down faint from the sight of my own leg. It was worse than I had expected it to look. It was a foul-smelling volcano.

"Would you like something to read while you are waiting?" he asked me as I was being led out of the office back toward the cell. "I will send you a book. You may take it to the hospital with you."

And that's how I finally got medical attention under the rules of the Geneva Convention. When the colonel-physician at the Luftwaffe hospital in Frankfurt examined the leg, he wanted to amputate; but I talked him out of that. Even then I wasn't sure until I reached down and felt it when I was coming out of the anesthetic.

That's the way it is when you're a prisoner of war. One minute or one day you think you're all right. The next you're in trouble. You may feel fine when actually you're sick in the head. You never know whether you're coming or going. You can never be sure when you are miserable, and all prisoners of war are miserable—all of the time.

Chapter Twenty-three

The prison bay, identical in size and furniture to the last one, was stuffed with prisoners. Every bunk was piled with ragged bedding. Ticks and blankets were spread out over all the floor available between the bunk tiers. Even the tables had beds laid out on them. Jim looked down at his own trampled blankets on the floor between two bunk racks and shook his head. "I'd rather be in one of the tents than in here."

Tom looked around at the several hundred men lounging in the close quarters. "Jim, what say we move our beds outside?"

"What if it rains?"

"We can bank up dirt around the edges. There's high ground back of the Abort. With those tents out there, the goons have stopped turning those damn' dogs loose at night. What say?"

An air-raid siren began to blow, but the men paid no attention to it. Jim rubbed his chin thoughtfully. "Well . . . I suppose we could always come back inside if it did rain. Damn the goons anyway. Assigning us two men to every bunk."

Tom kneeled and began rolling up his blankets. "We might as well do it now before a lot of other people get the same idea and stake out all the best spots."

Al Koczeck entered the aisle and looked down at them. "You men going someplace?"

Tom nodded. "Yeah. How about giving us a hand with this stuff? We're camping out."

"Not for me. The ground is plenty hard."

"You drew a bunk. We didn't. The ground is no harder than this floor."

Koczeck kneeled and waited for them to get their belongings folded. "You heard the latest?" He waited for both men to shake their heads. "Patton advanced another ten miles yesterday. He's coming after us this time. I heard something else that isn't so good."

Jim looked up. "What's that?"

"I heard Roosevelt died."

Both men stared at Koczeck's serious face. "Where did you pick that up?"

"I just heard it . . . over in the Abort."

Jim sniffed and resumed packing. "That's a good place for a rumor like that. Let's pile one on top of the other." The three of them lifted the two pallets, and Jim shouted at the muddle of men between them and the doorway. "Gangway! We're coming through." Outside, they paused in the sunlight and stared ahead at the parade ground. Two long white barracks tents were already erected and six more lay spread out on the ground. Prisoners and guards alike were pounding stakes and hauling up the white canvases with ropes. Jim grinned back at Tom. "Just like the circus. Where to?"

Tom nodded toward the big square shape of the forty-holer. "Over behind the Abort. It doesn't smell so hot up close, but that'll give us some privacy."

Other prisoners dodged around them as they cut across toward the rear of the building. Men were everywhere walking or standing in clusters. Many squatted over smoking blowers cooking meager rations of Red Cross food. A steady flow of men moved in and out of the Abort. On top of a small smooth-worn slope beneath the Abort's rear wall Tom called for a halt. "This is a good spot. We can dig grooves to guide the water down around us if it rains."

They set the pallets down in the dirt. Koczeck turned and looked out over the sprawl of tents, men, barbed wire, and prison blocks. "How many men do you suppose are in here now?"

Jim shrugged. "Thousands. They're herding all the prisoners in Germany into this place."

Koczeck frowned. "Do you think there's anything to this gen that the goons are going to move us up into the Alps?"

Jim nodded solemnly. "I think they might try. The Nazis have had it and they know it. Their only chance is to withdraw into some mountain stronghold for a last stand. A redoubt, they call it. They figure with the SS élite corps they can dig in and hold off forever, or at least until the Allies and Russians get to fighting each other. Then they'd be in a position to bargain. But that's not all. They figure to have an ace in the hole. Us." Koczeck winced as Jim went on. "They've already got all the generals' and politicians' and millionaires' relatives who have been prisoners locked up someplace as hostages, probably already in the redoubt. Now they're gathering all the officers in one place here. It's only a fairly short march, several days at the most the way they march Kriegies, to Salzburg or Garmisch or wherever the redoubt is in the Alps. With all us officers as hostages they figure our planes won't bomb them out for fear of hitting us, too, and maybe our people will make a bargain to get us out."

Koczeck swept his arm at the sprawling maze of men, barbed wire, tents, and dirty gray buildings. "They'd never be able to march this many men."

Tom sniffed. "That's what we said when there were only ten thousand of us. But we marched. This time Jim and I are ready for them."

"What are you going to do?"

Tom sat down on the pallets. "Sit down. Jim, show Al the map."

They knelt down beside Tom. Jim rummaged in his blankets and produced a large blue paper-covered notebook that he had carried from Sagan. He riffled through the pages covered with finely printed verse until he came to one upon which was penciled in detail a map of southern Germany. Jim pointed to a small dot labeled Moosburg on a curving line marked the Isar River. "That's us here. Down here are the Alps. If the goons march us in this direction"—Jim's finger moved south toward the Alps—"Tom and I go this way." His finger moved westward. "We don't care if we get shot. If they march all these guys at once it'll take an army to guard us. There'll be chances to break away, and this time we're going to do it. I'll be God damned if I'm going to end up a hostage in any damned redoubt."

Koczeck studied the carefully scaled map. "You going to hard-ass it all the way to the front?"

"We're going to hard-ass it, but not to the front. We're going to hole up in a haystack or a barn or in the woods someplace and wait for Patton's army. He's moving a hell of a lot faster than we could, and I don't think he'll stop short on us the way the Russians did."

Koczeck nodded. "Can I come with you?"

Tom and Jim looked at each other. Tom turned to Koczeck. "No, Al. We figure this is a two-man proposition."

Worry lines crossed Koczeck's forehead. "But, Jesus! I've got a wife and I've got a kid I haven't even seen." He stared out over the busy panorama of the prison camp. "When the war is over I've got to get back. They've been waiting so long. I can't end up like that— a prisoner indefinitely up there in the mountains. I've just got to get back."

Jim kept his eyes turned down, his right forefinger scratching the edge of the map. "Three would be too many. Too hard to hide. We'd sure get caught."

Tom got to his feet. "Let's get this bed made."

The two partners worked in silence while Koczeck watched. They laid the two paillasses side by side and began spreading and over-lapping their meager blankets to make a double bed. When the blankets were tucked in as neatly as possible around three sides, Tom picked up two cans from the piles of personal effects on the blankets and handed one to Jim. With these they began gouging out a shallow groove in the hard-packed earth around the bed. Koczeck turned and started to walk listlessly away. Jim looked up. "Al?"

Koczeck turned back. "Yeah, Jim?"

Jim picked up the blue notebook and crossed over. "Take this map and make a copy of it. You can get one of the others to go with you, or you can go it alone."

Koczeck took the map and nodded gloomily. "Thanks." He walked off slowly and disappeared around a corner of the Abort.

When Jim turned back, Tom pointed up into the sky to the south-west. "Here come our boys again."

Jim shielded his eyes and looked. Three staggered formations of planes moved slowly across the white glare of a high wide cloud. "B-17's again."

"Yeah. Munich, maybe."

Throughout the camp men stopped what they were doing for a moment and watched the American bombers making their daily run across German skies. The bomber squadrons moved unhurried east-ward and headed gradually south. Junior Jones walked up the slight slope to where Jim and Tom were packing the loose dirt from the grooves they had scraped up against the sides of their blankets. "You guys seen Major Smith?"

Jim looked up. "No."

"I got to find him. Colonel Good wants to see him."

"Who's Colonel Good?"

"Tough-looking old guy. Infantry. Ranks Colonel Akron, so he's the senior American officer now."

"When did he get here?"

"I dunno. They're coming all the time. There's a steady stream of them coming in through the gates. A lot of 'em are paddle feet, but some of our people from Sagan got here a little while ago. The guys who couldn't march. The ones we left behind."

Jim stood up. "The hell you say." He turned and looked down at Tom. "Let's go see them." He whirled back on Junior. "Where are they?"

Junior motioned eastward. "In the next compound. There's only one fence between."

Tom spoke dryly from a squat. "Let's get this job over with first. They aren't going any place."

"I've still got to find Major Smith." Junior left them and walked quickly across the crowded ground to the prison block they had been assigned that morning and picked his way in. He stopped by Koczeck and Noble, who were seated on the bench. "You seen Major Smith?"

Koczeck looked up briefly. "Nope." He turned back to Noble, speaking in a low voice. "What have we got to lose? If they get us up to this redoubt place we're dead ducks. Our Air Force won't hesitate to bomb the place just because we're there."

Noble stared across at the next table where a Kriegie pudding was being guarded by a sleepy-looking prisoner. "Al, when will we have enough bread crusts saved for another pudding?"

"Not for another week. By that time we may not be here. Look, neither Burt or Bob is married. I am. That's why I've got to get back. I figured you're the nearest other man in our combine to being married. At least you're engaged. You don't want to leave her sweat it out while you sit in the middle of a Nazi last stand, do you?"

Noble licked his lips. "I wish we could get ahold of some bread and sugar."

"Christ! Jack. Don't you hear what I'm saying?" Koczeck had difficulty in keeping his voice low in the steady mumble of prisoners around them. "You're not going to let yourself be marched up into the Alps as a hostage, are you?"

Noble shrugged without taking his eyes from the pudding. "That's just a rumor."

"Well, maybe it is. But they're getting the German people ready for it. They're talking about the redoubt in the German papers. They're organizing the Hitler Jugend into Werewolf packs to fight the occupation from underground until the Nazis can make a comeback. That sounds like more than a rumor to me. What do you think they're crowding us all in here together for?"

Noble sighed. "I've saved all my cigarettes, but I can't get anyone to trade pudding for cigarettes."

Koczeck stared at him. "All you ever think about any more is your gut."

"Well, I'm hungry. I'm God-awful hungry. I can't stand it, I'm so hungry all the time."

Koczeck looked down for a place to spit and then swallowed it. "You don't say so." Then he walked over to his own tier and stepped over the beds on the aisle floor. He pushed aside the hanging clothing and crawled into his middle bunk. In the shaded light he lay back and looked long at the crease-cracked photographs of his wife and baby boy tacked to a worn and knife-whittled bunk post. After a while he opened the big limp blue notebook and began carefully to study the map.

With the first crash of bombs to the south, the men in the prison yard stopped what they were doing to look. There wasn't much to see. By straining the eyes the bombers could be made out, tiny specks cruising westward over about where Munich ought to be. Flak bursts made other tiny spots of different shapes among the first.

"There goes one," someone standing near Jim and Tom behind the Abort said casually. A thin stream of black smoke corkscrewed slowly earthward from the specks far to the south. "And another." Sunlight reflected briefly on distant wings flipping and twisting down from the sky. "Poor bastards."

Tom spoke out of the side of his mouth to Jim. "We'll be seeing some of those guys here today or tomorrow. There ain't no Dulag Luft now."

A sudden tiny ball of fire flashed in the sky and hurtled downward. Jim sniffed. "We won't be seeing any of that crew. Let's go see the guys who've just arrived." They turned their shoulders on the war to the south and walked eastward on ground that trembled intermittently. "I sure hope Danny and Ed are with them."

As they rounded the east end of the Abort, the earth ceased to tremble. Tom looked in the direction of the raid and could see nothing but a couple of columns of smoke climbing slowly upward into the sky. "That was a small one. Not more than three groups."

Across the fence from the last block in their compound another, smaller compound without a parade ground had been added some time earlier in the war. Tom and Jim walked up to the layer of Kriegies talking through the fence to the newly arrived Americans in the smaller compound.

Jim looked up and down the row of thin pale faces lining the other side of the fence. Finally he spotted Mervin Cahn, whom he had last seen standing in the snow before the Kriegie Theater at Stalag Luft III. "Hey, Merv! How's the boy?"

The skinny New Yorker came down the line, only the brown eyes lighting up in his beaked, chisel-chinned face. "Hello, Jim." He reached through a long skeleton of a hand. "How long have you been here? Excuse me." He stopped talking to cough into his sleeve.

"Oh, a couple of months. Longer, I guess. Ever since the march. What the hell did they do with you guys?"

The grin looked hideous in Merv's long face. "Nothing for five days. You should have been there. We had the whole camp to ourselves, not more than 150 of us. We had the run of the place. All the food you guys left behind. All the clothes. All the coal. We lived off the fat of the land. Meat and jam and chocolate five times a day if we wanted it. It was great. I wore a new shirt every day and then threw it away. Kriegies never had it so good."

Jim looked at the rags hanging on his fragile bones. "You don't look like you had it so good."

Merv smiled wryly. "That was at Sagan. Then they loaded us into boxcars. We picked up the boys you left at Muskau and rode on to Nuremberg. It wasn't so good at Nuremberg. There were several thousand of us. The camp was just on the outskirts. There were bombs every night. There was no coal. We whittled the bunks and the walls until there was practically nothing left, just trying to get enough wood to keep warm. And there was no food to speak of. For ten days once we didn't have anything. Red Cross parcels didn't get into us until about a week ago. Ever since then we've been marching down here."

A few places down the fence a Kriegie slipped a long pair of wire cutters from beneath his coat. It was so casual that Jim hardly noticed it. "You picked up the boys from Muskau? Is Captain Daniels with you?"

Merv nodded. "Yes. He's around here someplace, setting up an infirmary in one of the blocks. That guy never stops working, and some of our boys can use an infirmary."

The Kriegie with the wire cutters was nonchalantly clipping through the fence separating the two compounds. "Is Ed Greenway with you, do you know?" Tom asked.

Merv was grinning, staring at the wire cutter. "Don't know him. You got any coffee left? I'll be over for a brew in a few minutes."

Tom's eyes widened in the direction of the wire snipping. The man with the cutters grinned along the line without stopping his snipping. "Don't any of you guys go away until I'm done."

Tom and Jim looked at each other soberly and then up toward the goon box and the aged sentry standing beneath it. Tom licked his lips and muttered. "It ain't very healthy cutting wire around here. We know."

Merv shrugged. "We did the same thing at Nuremberg. These goons have had it and they know it. We're running the camp now."

On their side of the fence the new arrivals were in good humor, taking the wire cutting as a joke. The men on the west side of the fence became quiet and uneasy. Jim's eyes kept shifting from the machine gunner in the goon box to the old sentry standing beneath it. As if signaled by telepathy the old soldier's head turned and he saw what was going on. With a puzzled frown on his grizzled face, the old German walked along the fence toward them. Jim's voice fell to a whisper. "If he comes close enough, they won't open up with the machine gun."

Merv coughed into his arm, and then turned his smiling Jewish face toward the German. "Wie geht's, Grossvater? Bitte, kommen Sie hier?" He turned and whispered quickly to Jim. "If you've got any cigarettes, hand me a couple."

The old German approached warily, loosening the sling of his rifle on his shoulder. The Kriegie with the cutters cut through the last strand of wire, which twanged loudly and curled back upon itself. Merv waved his skinny long arm in a grand gesture toward the breached fence. "Sehen Sie? Das Staket war nicht gut. Nun ist es kaput. Freund ist mit Freund wieder."

In dismay the old man looked in through the outer fences at the damage. "Aber—" He slid the rifle on its sling halfway down his flabby arm. "Aber das ist verboten!"

Merv grinned wider. "Ach, nein. Nein. Nicht verboten! Aber vergessen. Wollen Sie rauchen?" Boldly Merv advanced across the forbidden area with his right hand extended offering two cigarettes. From the goon box the younger sentry looked down at them soberly, one hand resting on his machine gun. Merv thrust his arm through the inside fence. The old German looked over his shoulder toward the man in the tower. The machine gunner shrugged. The old German reached through, took the cigarettes, turned and walked sadly away. Merv came back from the outer fences grinning and coughing into his sleeve. Men laughed and began streaming back and forth between the two compounds.

Jim started to slap Merv on the back to help his coughing, and thought better of it. "You'll never live to be a hundred that way."

Merv stopped coughing and smiled wistfully. He tapped his hollow chest. "With what I've got in here I'll be lucky to live till I'm thirty."

A cry rang out somewhere behind them. "Return to your blawcks! Everybody inside! Return to your blawcks!"

Other voices picked up the cry. "Everybody back to your blocks! Report to your blocks!"

Tom sighed. "Now what?"

Merv shrugged his narrow shoulders. "Maybe the war is over. Well, see you later."

The ground shuddered as men streamed back and forth in every direction, crisscrossing their ways to and from the prison blocks and the great swollen white tents.

"What's it all about?"

"What's the gen?"

Nobody seemed to know. As they strode briskly along with the heavy traffic, Jim looked seriously at Tom. "First thing we'd better do is to get our map back from Al."

Tom nodded. "Yeah."

"This could be the march."

Four hundred men trying to squeeze into the center floor of the prison bay trampled as easily as they could on the floor beds laid from side to side between the two rows of bunk tiers. Colonel

Condon and Major Smith stood solemnly on one of the tables looking out over the pack of heads. The men stood in puzzled silence waiting for the last stragglers to press into the room. When all was silence except for the steady sound of four hundred men breathing, Colonel Condon looked at the wrist watch he was wearing and nodded at the major. The latter bit his lower lip before speaking.

"Men, we have received very bad news." His eyes glistened slightly as he looked down at the thin upturned faces. "Some time during last night, Franklin Delano Roosevelt, our Commander in Chief and President of the United States, died."

There was a sudden gasping of breath.

"President Roosevelt died of a cerebral hemorrhage. Vice President Truman has already taken his oath of office as the new President of the United States." Major Smith's head swiveled slightly as he looked about. "Well, that's all there is to say. It's official. At 1500 hours this afternoon memorial services will be held in the area directly south of this prison block."

The day remained the same. The news had no power apparently to alter or decently darken the afternoon sunshine. Ragged men from different nations stood erect in the rust fence compound, while chaplains from four nations and religions delivered their eulogies. The President of the United States was dead.

Chapter Twenty-four

Jim wasn't sure what had awakened him or what was keeping him awake. It could be the fleas, lice, and bedbugs that infested every bunk in the new prison block they had been assigned after the fences had been removed to add two more compounds to the great encampment. It could be the terrible ache of his jagged tooth against the raw tip of his tongue. It could be the tingling of his bladder filled with a nightcap of digested tea that wanted release. It could be all three. Or it could be the tension that gripped him more and more each day and night as Patton's Tenth Armored Division was reported ever advancing closer from the west.

One after the other Jim put three aspirin tablets into his mouth and swallowed them, hoping by a remote chance to stop the toothache. He could hear Tom breathing slowly and deeply in the next bunk of the lower tier. Jim felt lonely in the darkness filled with sleeping men and wished Tom would wake up. He would, some time during the night. Every one of the two hundred men in the prison bay would have to get up for a pee call at least once. That's what came from trying to fill empty guts with hot brew at bedtime in the hope that sleep would come before hunger. At any time during the night there were always plenty of shivering men in the big Abort buildings. Jim's kidneys twinged. Softly he whispered to himself. "Sonovabitch." With a creaking of chicken wire and wood he crawled from his blankets and reached under the bunk for his shoes. He shook them out carefully for bedbugs or cockroaches before putting them on. As he picked his way out of the aisle he slipped on his greatcoat. The Klim-tin cover of the lamp trickled a bare light over the bunk tiers. This prison bay was like the others. Moving from block to block provided no variety, for every block was the same mixture of twelve-man bunk racks and crowded men. As Jim passed the wooden wall of the infirmary Danny had set up in one corner of the block, another prisoner entered the front door and brushed past. Outside, it was cool and damp. Low clouds hid the stars, but the tiny fence lights and the sweeping shafts of the goon-box lights silhouetted the buildings of the camp. A white automobile stood parked just inside the compound gate. Jim glanced briefly at it and hurried on between the prison blocks to the Abort. Inside, he found a vacant toilet and stood over it. He spoke to any of the vague shadows who might care to answer him. "What's that white car doing out by the gate?"

"What white car? Where?"

"There's a white-painted car standing just inside the compound gate."

"Gee, I dunno. Maybe it's the Red Cross."

Jim left the building and, shivering slightly, hurried along between the buildings toward the white car. It was empty. It was a European Ford sedan. White paint had been brushed all over it, even the wheels and tires. Jim joined several other prisoners looking at the car. "What's the score?"

"Something going on in there." A prisoner nodded toward the next prison block. "The goon commandant and some of his staff are in there talking to Colonel Good and Colonel Akron and some other brass."

"Talking? At this time of night? What about?"

"Search me. Maybe the war is over."

A door opened in the building. Colonel Baker stepped out of the yellow oblong of light. Jim hurried over. "What's going on, Colonel?"

Colonel Baker peered down in the darkness. "Oh, hello, Jim." He bent nearer and lowered his voice. "Weis, how long have you been a Kriegie?"

"About twenty-five months."

"Well, you'll never be one another day. The commandant is surrendering the camp."

Every muscle in Jim's skinny body contracted as if he had been hit by a fist. "No!"

Colonel Baker grinned in the darkness. "Yes! That's the surrender car. He's going out in a few minutes to surrender Moosburg to an armored column that's waiting just a few miles west. This is it, Jim. This is what we've been waiting for."

Jim clenched his teeth, shaking with excitement. "Jesus, Colonel! Jesus!"

"Here they come!"

Grave-faced American, British, and German officers filed out of the lighted doorway. Jim found it difficult to breathe. Colonel von Munsing, the Kommandant, stiff-backed and wearing a gold-decorated sword, passed close by. Jim glared at him. This was the man who had let them starve with acres of potatoes stored in plain view beyond the fences. A Wehrmacht major stood stiffly holding the rear door of the white Ford. As a matter of habit von Munsing stood stiffly, waiting for inferior officers to enter the car first. An American colonel said something and motioned toward the car, reversing the protocol. The colonel bowed jerkily and got in, quickly followed by the American colonel and a British officer. The German major smartly slammed the door and slid into the front seat beside the driver. With a low meshing of gears the car slid forward through the opened gate and on down the dark prison road. The few watching prisoners spoke excitedly to one another in awed tones. Jim turned to Colonel Baker. "I can't believe it. I just can't believe it!"

Colonel Baker grinned down in the darkness and pressed Jim's hand in a firm shake. "It had to happen sooner or later, Jim. Congratulations on our new freedom."

"Same to you, Colonel."

A stocky figure stepped forward to address the small group of night-gathered Kriegies. It was Colonel Akron. "Gentlemen, I think we had best keep to ourselves anything we have seen here tonight. They won't be back for some time. There's no use starting a big flap in the camp at this time of night. So let us return to our beds and try to get to sleep. It'll be a great day when we wake up again."

Jim's chest and solar plexus felt like a wind tunnel, with great blasts of excitement blowing through. He had no thought of going back to bed. Instead he broke away from the group and began to wander dazedly about the damp darkness of the camp. He walked nervously along a blackly shuttered prison block, visualizing the sleeping men inside. Now he would inhale great gulps of the cool moist air; then he would be hardly able to breathe at all. He looked across a field of long gray silent tents toward the barbed-wire fences, like spider webs beneath their twinkling post lights. What would the goon in the box do with his machine gun now if he walked right up to the fence? How many hundreds of prisoners were sleeping on the ground in the tents as if this were any ordinary night in Stalag VIIA? His aching tooth throbbed and he could actually enjoy the misery of it. He passed other prisoners in the darkness unconcernedly heading for the various Aborts or returning to their blocks. He wanted to shout out to them. How could a man hold such a secret? He returned to the compound gates. They were closed again, but two American officers were posted there, waiting, looking down the dark road to the west. Jim walked up to them. "How long do you figure it will take?"

One of them shrugged. "Oh, couple, three hours, maybe. Why don't you grab some sleep? You can't get 'em back any faster."

"Yeah." Jim's heart beat hard against his ribs. "Might as well." He walked back toward his block. Maybe it would be easier that way, to wake up a free man. He entered the deeper darkness of the prison bay and walked slowly along between the rows of bunk tiers. He felt like jumping up and down. He must wake everybody up. This is it, chaps! This is it! That's what Paddy Finucane had radioed just before his Spitfire vanished, a puddle of oil on the English channel. All over! He felt his way into the aisle and down to his lower bunk. All over! It wasn't fair to hoard a joy like this. He whispered softly in the darkness, "Tom. Tom."

"What—whaz—huh?"

"Sh-h-h." He leaned close. "Tom, it's all over."

Tom's bunk creaked. "Who is it? Jim?"

"Yeah. Sh-h-h. Listen, Tom. I just saw it with my own eyes. In a couple of hours we'll be liberated."

"What are you talking about, Jim?"

Bob Montgomery's disgusted whisper came from the next bunk by Tom's head. "For Christ's sake, can't you guys can the chatter for at least one night and let a man sleep?"

"No, Bob. Listen. Just listen, but keep it quiet."

"I'm listening."

"Listen, men. I just happened to stumble into this. Hardly anybody else even knows about it, but I just had to tell somebody."

Bob's whisper calmed down. "What is it?"

"The Germans are surrendering the camp."

"Bullshit."

"They are. No fooling. When I went out there was a car out front painted white. Von Munsing and another German and two of our brass got in it and drove off to meet a column of our tanks just west of here. The Kommandant is going to surrender the camp. He's doing it right now."

There were a few seconds of silence before Tom finally whispered. "Well, could be."

Bob's voice sounded dubious. "A white car, you say?"

"Yeah. A Ford. Painted white all over."

"A Ford!"

A stage whisper came from somewhere up above. "Hey, you guys! Pipe down down there!"

Tom's whisper was soft and calm. "We'd better talk about it in the morning."

"But that's just it, Tom. By morning we'll be free!"

"I can wait till morning."

Bob grunted. "Me too."

Annoyed, Jim dropped his shoes to the floor, crawled into his blankets, and lay back wide-eyed, feeling his tooth throb and his heart beat. After a while he heard Tom's soft whisper.

"Good night, Jim."

"Good night, Tom." Suddenly Jim was smiling up into the darkness and feeling strangely warm. Surprisingly, he fell asleep that way.

Jim awakened slowly in the familiar mumble and bustle of the prison bay. He brought his arms from under the blankets and stretched thoroughly. Suddenly he sat up and looked about him between the hanging clothing and the towels. The bunks of Tom and Bob were empty. Beside him, on another lower bunk, Jack Noble was lacing up a shoe. "What's going on, Jack?"

"Nothing. Why?"

Jim slid his stockinged feet to the floor and stood up. Legs dangled from some of the upper bunks. Prisoners walked about munching Reichs bread or smoking. Jim looked at Burt Salem and Al Koczeck quietly buttoning up their greatcoats. He brushed past them out onto the main floor. Men milled about in confusion, grumbling, wisecracking, laughing, sour-faced, blank-faced. Everything was entirely normal. Frowning deeply, Jim walked back to his bunk and sat down, closing his eyes tightly.

"Appel!" someone down the bay shouted. "All out for appel! Everybody out!"

The floor rumbled as the prisoners headed for the exits. Jim felt a shoe nudge his calf. Bob stood beside Tom looking down at him. "You going to appel in your stocking feet?"

Jim reached down, pulled his shoes on and tied them. He looked at Bob and Tom as they walked toward their block's formation gathering in front of the Abort. "I don't get it."

Bob looked down at the ground. "Don't worry about it, Jim."

"But I just don't get it. I don't get it!"

Tom placed a hand on his shoulder. "Don't flap, Jim."

They followed Jim across to Major Smith, who was standing before the formation. "Pete, what happened last night? Didn't they go through with it?"

The major grinned through his beard. "Didn't who go through with what?"

"The goons. They were going to surrender the camp. I was there when they started out."

The smile faded from the major's face. "Now, wait a minute. Maybe I came in late. What are you talking about?"

Tom spoke flatly behind Jim. "We'd better fall in. Here come the goons now."

Major Smith nodded. "I'll see you after the count."

Jim stared at the Wehrmacht lieutenant and at the sergeant-major as they approached the formation. He had to hurry into place when the major issued the command.

"Blawck . . . tennnshun!"

Major Smith and the German officer exchanged salutes, and the Germans counted them off by fives.

"Block . . . at ease." The major motioned for Jim to come forward, turned his back on the formation, and spoke in a lowered voice. "Now what the hell were you saying, Jim?"

"I figured you would know about it. Real early this morning von Munsing and some of our brass left in a white car to negotiate a surrender with our people to the west of here. It should have been over by now. I saw them go myself."

The major nodded gravely. "Anybody else see them?"

"Well, Colonel Baker was there. And Colonel Akron. And a few of us who happened to be out just then."

The major nodded. "I'll have a talk with Red or the Old Man. In the meantime I wouldn't mention it any more if I were you." He nodded toward the Germans taking appel. "The goons are obviously still running things."

"But, Major, I saw them."

"Maybe something went wrong. You might have built up false hopes." He stared briefly at a distant goon box that was still manned by a machine gunner. Then he looked down at the ground and stirred the dirt with his toe. "Or somebody might think you've gone round the bend. You've been behind the wire a long time, you know. Why not just wait and see what happens?"

Jim turned and walked back to his place in the formation. Without looking at Bob or at Tom he lit up a cigarette and smoked it, glaring toward the distant goon box. When appel was dismissed, Tom broke the silence between them. "Come on, Jim. Let's take a circuit."

Still silent, Jim walked with them. Looking out beyond the tents that splattered the old parade ground behind the Abort, they could see the sentries strolling as usual along the outer fences. They crossed a line where a fence had been removed and walked between prison blocks occupied by RAF prisoners with their blue remnants of uniforms and blue laundry hanging from the lines. After more tents and milling men they came to the southeast corner of a large square field strangely free of tents or buildings. Its north boundary was the double barbed-wire fence and goon-box towers of the outer edge of the camp. To the west was another crowded compound. To the south as they walked with a ragged parade of morning strollers lay the first compound they had lived in after their delousing shower. Now its parade ground was cluttered with a jungle of makeshift shacks constructed by Balkan prisoners out of scrap lumber, cardboard, and gunnysack cloth.

Jim nodded to where several prisoners were talking through the fence with two tattered Balkan prisoners. "I wonder if they would know anything. All the time they've been in this place they ought to have a grapevine."

Bob sighed. "Aw, Christ, Jim. Drop it, will you?"

They rounded the bend and walked along the guarded north fence. Jim stared at the first sentry as they passed. He wore Wehrmacht green and his rifle was slung barrel down over one shoulder. They passed a goon box and looked up. The machine gunner was sitting relaxed on its railing. They passed on until they came abreast of another sentry standing outside the fences. Jim stopped and looked at him. He muttered out of the side of his mouth. "I'm going to talk to this goon." He waved and called out. "Wie geht's?"

The sentry looked surprised and smiled. "Gut, danke. Wie geht's Ihnen?"

"Gut, danke. Wo ist Ihre Heimat?"

The German's tanned face grinned wider. "Im Sudetenland."

"Und wann gehen Sie da?"

"Heute Nachmittag."

Jim looked at Tom and Bob and at several others who had paused in the circuit to listen. He looked back at the German. "Heute?"

"Ja, ja. Heute Nachmittag." The sentry spread his arms. "Heute ist der Krieg zu ende für uns alle."

Bob nudged Jim. "What's he saying?"

Jim spoke rapidly. "I asked him when he was going home. He said this afternoon. He said this afternoon the war is over for all of us."

The slit in Bob's teeth showed in a grin for the first time that morning. "He said that?"

Jim turned back to the German. He gestured at the forbidden zone between the perimeter path and the fence. "Können wir daran kommen?"

The German shrugged, still smiling. "Ja. Warum nicht? Kommen Sie doch." He unslung his rifle, and the prisoners cringed back a step. "Wir haben keine munition." He snapped the bolt back twice. There was no ejection.

Jim spoke excitedly to the faces around him. "He doesn't have any bullets in his gun. They're standing guard with empty guns!"

"What the hell!" somebody exclaimed. "They run out of ammunition?"

"No bullets!"

"Yeah. I'll bet."

Jim grinned first at Bob, then at Tom. "Come on." He led the way across the forbidden zone to the fence. He smiled back at the German. "Warum keine munition? Hat der Kommandant—er—ah . . ." He looked around at the others who had gathered up close to the fence. "Does anybody know how you say 'surrender' in German?"

"I schpeak zum English." The German chuckled.

"The hell you do. Well, what I want to know is, has your Kommandant surrendered the camp or not?"

"Ja, ja. Er hass all our bullets early ziss morgnink zu your colonel giffen. Zoon ve all now go home."

"What's he talking about?"

"What's he saying?"

Jim held up his hands. "Quiet, will you? Let me find out."

Tom nudged Jim. "Ask him why they're still standing guard."

"Yeah. If the camp is surrendered, why are all you guys out here standing guard?"

The German's tanned face frowned. "More z—z—slower, please."

"Why are you still on guard with empty guns?"

The sentry shrugged. "You haff hear of zer S.S., nicht?"

"Yeah, sure."

"Zer S.S. haff not zurrendered. Ve must play like ve are still in command or zer S.S. . . ." He drew a finger across his throat. "Verstehen Sie? Ve must make belief ve vill fight viss zem."

"All the Wehrmacht?"

"Ja. No one but zer S.S. vill truly fight now. Ve must make belief or zer S.S. . . ." Again he drew a finger across his throat.

"Youeee!"

"Man, oh, man!"

Excited prisoners broke away from the group and ran across the field toward the main part of camp. Others stayed, their thin faces split by glad smiles. Tom smiled. "Then it's all a fake. Just an act."

Bob was grinning. "It sure fooled me."

Jim pulled a pack of Old Gold cigarettes from his pocket and held them out through the rusty inner fence. The German reached them through the outer fence and was barely able to get them over the wire coiled in between. "Danke. Danke schön."

The German looked up at the goon box. "Ve must go in now. Zoon zey come. I must now go. Please to have meet you."

Jim called after the sentry. "Where you going?"

"Into der Lager. Soon zey come. Zie Amerikaner. Aufwiedersehen."

"So long, Fritz."

All along the fence the machine gunners were climbing down the ladders from the goon boxes. The strollers were walking north along the fence toward the front of the camp. Tom, Bob, and Jim turned and started walking light-footed across the field. Jim laughed, shook his head, and gritted his teeth with joy. "Well, it wasn't as quick as I thought, but it won't be long now."

Tom actually showed his teeth in a smile and patted Jim's shoulder. "You were right, Jim. You were right all the time."

Bob Montgomery sighed. "You know something? When I got up this morning and found everything just the same as it's always been I thought you had gone round the bend. I figured it had finally got you."

Jim kept on laughing softly. "I wasn't so sure myself. But what the hell? It's all over now but the shouting."

Tom ducked under a blanket hanging from a line between two of the British prison blocks and came up with the smile gone from his face. "It's all over but the shooting, you mean."

Jim stopped laughing. "What do you mean?"

"Don't forget the S.S. They're around here somewhere. If Hitler ordered us shot, the Wehrmacht may have ignored the order. But the S.S. won't have any qualms about that."

RAF prisoners were dashing about, shouting from block to block the news that the sentries had all left the fences and goon boxes.

Tom shrugged. "There's no use flapping about it, but it's there. If the guards had to put on a show for them, that means the S.S. are here and are going to put up a fight. Hell, they have to. Our people don't take S.S. prisoners any more. Not since the Malmédy massacre. So if they've got to die anyway, they may want to take someone along with them. It'd be awful easy for them to take some of us."

Bob sighed. "I haven't seen an S.S. around here."

Tom nodded and jumped over a crumbling slit trench. "Let's hope you don't."

Major Smith joined them as they walked along. "You were right, Jim. Von Munsing tried to surrender Moosburg to the Tenth Armored Division last night, but the American general he talked to refused to accept the surrender."

"Refused to accept it!"

"That's right. Von Munsing couldn't surrender for the S.S., so now there's going to be a fight. We got all the guards' bullets, though."

"Yeah, I know." Up beyond the end of the prison block men started cheering. "Now what's up?"

Bob, Burt, Noble, Koczeck, and Junior Jones stood in the group standing by the closed compound gate, staring westward. Tom tapped Koczeck's shoulder. "What's the flap about?"

Koczeck rubbed his hands together. "The goon flag just went down. Somebody ran down the Nazi flag at the main gate."

The pole standing beside the large sentry tower about an eighth of a mile down the main road pointed starkly up toward white sunlit clouds. Four immaculately uniformed Wehrmacht officers marched with flashing black boots up the road from that direction. Jim nodded toward them. "Here comes von Munsing and his staff all dressed up." The four officers wore iron crosses and silver decorations pinned to spotless green tunics. Instead of pistols they wore short swords in scabbards decorated with polished silver. "I guess they're going to hole up in here until it's over. We're the farthest compound back."

Tom watched the four Germans pass in through the compound gate and walk in dignified step into the compound. He looked again at the barren flagpole. "Do you reckon von Munsing struck the colors?"

Jim grinned. "What say we walk up that way and have a look?" He nodded toward the open compound gate. "I don't see anybody around to stop us."

Bob grunted. "I think we'd better stay where we are."

"What the hell difference does it make?"

Tom started for the gate through which a few Kriegies were already venturing. "O.K. Let's go, Jim."

Tom and Jim passed through the compound gate and started down the main road that stretched through the center of the jumble of barbed-wire fences and dirty gray buildings on either side. Jim shook his head as they walked. "I can't believe it. I can't believe it's true. This is a great day, Tom. A great day!"

Beyond the Vorlager gate and the outer gate the sloping-roofed Moosburg cheese factory nestled in sunshine against rolling green hills. Two airplanes suddenly popped up over the curve of the hills. Tom pointed. "Here they come. P-47's!" As he spoke the two Thunderbolts whistled and roared overhead, their silver white-starred wings rocking. Two more shot over as the first pair curved upward over the town, dipped their wings, and dove with chattering guns toward the ground. One explosion followed the other. "Dive bombing!" Explosions three and four shook the earth as the first two silver fighters in line-astern formation whined through perfect slow rolls directly over the prison camp. Men of many lands joined in a cheer as the P-47's darted off to disappear beyond the cheese factory and the hills.

"Wahoo!" Jim's teeth flashed as he bounced up and down. "How was that for a victory roll?"

Suddenly the cheering stopped. Near silence settled over the camp. Tom stared straight ahead at the main gate flagpole. A jet-black banner moved steadily up the pole and billowed out. On its silken bulge in the wind were jagged lightning streaks. Together they spelled S.S. Tom's face was taut, his lips thin. "Oh, God. They've taken over."

They moved forward slowly to join a group of silent prisoners of several nationalities standing at the locked gate leading to the Vorlager with its administration buildings and Wehrmacht barracks. All stared at the slowly flapping black flag. Beside Jim a ragged Pole crossed himself. Beyond the fence, among the buildings of the Vorlager, Germans wearing mottled brown and green coveralls, cloth caps or steel helmets, and carrying rifles and machine guns hurried about from one place to the other in seeming confusion. Jim spoke out of the side of his mouth. "Maybe we'd better get back to the other end of camp."

"Wait." Tom frowned in the direction of the fast-moving Germans. "Are they S.S.? I thought the S.S. wore black."

"Those are camouflage suits. Come on. I don't like it here."

Tom ignored the suggestion. "That guy with the Luger must be the top dog."

The German with the pistol wore a brown cloth-peaked cap instead of a helmet. He was shouting orders in unintelligible German. Machine guns were being set up facing a long low building similar to the prison blocks in the compounds. With shoulders swaying athletically the officer strode over to the door of the building and pounded on it with the butt of his Luger. He screamed something to whoever was inside. A voice inside answered something. The German officer stepped back beside one of the machine-gun crews. "Feuern!" he screamed. Instantly the machine guns went to work. Their chatter was like a million riveting hammers. Glass tinkled. Wood splintered. Chunks of gray stucco fell out of the sides of the building. Inside, men screamed. The door fell open on its hinges.

Two Wehrmacht guards stepped into its opening and fell back inside. Prisoners standing inside the Vorlager fence began to run. Jim and Tom ducked around the corner of a cookhouse building and stayed there pressed up against the wall. The shooting stopped. "What are they doing, for Christ's sake?" an American voice wanted to know.

"It's the guards," another frightened voice answered. There were three more quick machine-gun bursts. "The guards refused to fight. The S.S. is shooting 'em dead."

Jim turned his pale face to Tom's. "Let's get to hell out of here."

Tom nodded. "This way." At a nervous trot he led the way between the cookhouse and the delousing building. They slowed down as they walked along the rear of the camp hospital. Tom shook his head and panted. "My God! Why didn't they shoot back?"

Jim snorted between heaves of his scrawny chest. "No ammunition. They turned all their bullets over to us. Remember?"

The ground shook from nearby explosions. As they came out from behind the hospital they found the road crowded with prisoners standing and looking curiously up toward the Vorlager. Junior, his face red from running, darted up to Jim. He thrust three holstered pistols and a burp gun at Jim. "Here. Take these back to the block and hide them for me, will you?"

Jim stared down at the guns left in his arms. "Where did you get them?"

"Von Munsing's house. I liberated 'em." Junior's full lips quivered with excitement. "I got to go back and liberate some food. I'll bring you some."

"Food?"

"Yeah. Red Cross parcels. The Kommandant's basement is full of Red Cross parcels. He's been stealing them. Hide that artillery good, for Christ's sake! I'll see you later." Junior darted off again.

Tom gazed thoughtfully toward the black S.S. banner and the cheese factory and green hills beyond it. He had stopped panting. "We didn't have to flap. All the shooting has stopped. Look at those guys on the roof of the cheese factory."

On the sloping roof the tiny figures of riflemen lay on their stomachs pointed westward. Jim nodded. "There's going to be a fight, all right. Too bad the bastards didn't kill off more of each other. Imagine von Munsing with a basement full of our food!"

Tom tapped the burp gun in Jim's arms. "You'd better put this hardware away. You wouldn't want the S.S. to catch you with that."

Jim grinned as they headed back toward their compound. He felt the weight of the machine gun's clip. "This baby is loaded. The burp gun is, anyhow. Here. Take these rods." Tom took the pistols and Jim hefted the burp gun. "You know? This is the fastest-shooting light machine gun in the world. It can cut a man in half."

"Well, don't point it at anyone."

There was a powerful whine to the south as a P-47 dove on an unseen target in the village. The stubby fighter pulled out of the dive behind a red church steeple at the top of which flew a red, white, and black Nazi flag. "Give it to 'em!" someone in the crowd by the compound gate yelled. "Go get 'em!" Prisoners cheered and shouted at one another. Several sat on the sloping roofs of the prison blocks for a better view.

Al Koczeck was dancing a jig in the open gateway. "Hubba, hubba, hubba! Hubba, hubba, hubba!"

Major Smith grinned. "Where'd you get the arsenal?"

Jim grinned back. "These are Junior's. He got 'em from von Munsing's quarters. The house is full of swiped Red Cross parcels." Jim pushed on through the crowd and stopped. A few feet away, and approaching, was the German Kommandant followed in step by his three aides. They halted, staring tensely at the burp gun held pointed at them waist high. The Oberst looked up glaring hate from beneath the shiny black bill of his cap. Jim stared back without relaxing his tight grip on the gun. His lips curled slowly into a thin cold grin. The Oberst looked down into the barrel of the gun again. Jim sniffed, turned, and walked up the steps into the prison block. As he walked past the partition of the small infirmary, he glanced in through the doorway and noticed that it was empty except for Captain Daniels, who was setting rolls of white gauze on the table. Jim hurried on into the vacated prison bay and found his lower bunk in the maze of tiers. He felt beneath his tick, felt the hard bulk of his hidden manuscripts, and grunted. He started to stick the burp gun in with them, but whirled at the sound of footsteps. "Oh, it's you."

Tom smiled and tossed the three holstered pistols down onto the blankets. "Who else? Everybody else is out waiting for the main feature to start."

Jim shoved the three pistols in with the burp gun and the manuscript. "That ought to hold them for a while." He smoothed out the bunk and stood up. "Let's go. I don't want to miss a minute of this." He led the way out of the aisle and paused to look in again at the infirmary. "Come on out, Danny. You don't want to miss the show."

Danny smiled back over his shoulder. "I think my place is right here. There may be casualties. I hope not, but I wouldn't want to have to be searched for in an emergency."

Jim nodded, smiling, and went on out. The air was filled with roaring as more Thunderbolt fighters swept overhead. In the distance above the green hills beyond the cheese factory a high-wing monoplane drifted about like a kite in the sky. Tom pointed. "Look! A light plane. It's a Fairchild."

Nearby Bob's spaced teeth glistened in a grin. "Yeah. It's an artillery spotter."

The roofs of the prison blocks were covered with prisoners. Rifles began to go off, little popping noises in the distance. Men swarmed up the barbed-wire fences, using the cross strands for ladder rungs. The fast stutter of German machine guns joined the deep rapid chatter of the fifty-caliber guns of the fighters diving down on Moosburg. Men ran laughing from place to place along the fences, clambering up a few strands to look westward, then back to look southward at the diving planes. Burt Salem ran among the taller men like a rabbit, crying the same thing over and over again in a high emotional voice. "God damn! God damn! God damn!" Jack Noble jumped back and forth over a slit trench. Prisoners in the compounds lining the side of the road leading to the Vorlager shouted in foreign tongues.

"There they come! There they come!"

A great shout went up. Jim climbed up the fence, ripping his clothes on the barbs. The shouting grew louder and more sustained. Slowly, majestically, over the crest of the green slopes beyond the cheese factory, appeared first one crawling blue-gray tank, then another and another and another. Jim screamed with joy, his screams unheard in the screams of the others. On down the slope they crawled, firing their long guns as they came. There was an explosion, dirt and smoke flying just outside the front gate, then another which tossed dirt and rocks into the air beyond the outer fences. The third blast hit the outer gate and sent a crashing fountain of splintered posts and lashing barbed wire into the air. The screaming of the prisoners rose to a crescendo. And then the tanks rolled like great crawling insects down the green slopes, four abreast.

Pinnnngg! A bullet hit a pebble on the road among the prisoners standing before the compound gateway. Ping! Pinnnnnngunng! Two more bullets sent dirt flying and ricocheted on toward some prison blocks. A prisoner fell to the road and lay there, his legs thrashing.

"Hey! They're shooting at us!"

Prisoners leaped from the fences and dropped from the roofs. Some dove to the ground, others jumped into slit trenches, and many, like Jim, cowered down to watch the onward coming tanks. A pebble lifted from the ground at Jim's feet and went clattering into the end of the prison block. He looked in the opposite direction. "There he is!" He pointed toward the distant red steeple with its Nazi flag flying over Moosburg. "There's a sniper in that church steeple! He's firing into the camp!"

He and Bob scrambled to their feet and climbed up the fences again. The American tanks were still coming, their cannon barking sharply and jerking with recoil. Two more prisoners were hit, and lay squirming on the road. Noble clung to the top strand of the fence screaming: "Look up on the cheese factory! Look up on the cheese factory!"

Two of the tiny figures on the roof of the factory were crouched over a machine gun. It was pointed toward the prison camp. Jim took one short glance at the cheese factory roof. "The dirty bastards!" Then he continued to cheer the oncoming tanks with the other yelling prisoners. Bullets plunked among them, but they kept on cheering and laughing, watching the battle. A score of Balkan prisoners on the roof of one of their prison blocks scrambled onto its east slope to dodge a burst from the cheese factory. Jim looked at Tom clinging to the fence beside him and laughed hilariously. "You damned fool! Why don't you take cover?"

Tom laughed back. "Why don't you?"

A few places down the fence a Kriegie fell back into the arms of those behind him. He groaned and clutched at a bleeding thigh. Jim stopped laughing. "I think I'll go tell Danny there's some wounded out here." As he darted up the steps of the prison block there was a thud, and a chunk of plaster fell out of the wall by his head. He ducked going through the doorway. He turned into the doorway of the infirmary and called to Danny, who was sitting on one of its neatly made-up empty bunks. "Danny, there's quite a few guys wounded out there." Danny, white of face, was grasping his stomach. Jim stepped closer. "Danny." Danny rolled his eyes up. Jim bent over him. "What's the matter, Danny? What is it, boy?"

Danny let out a big breath and stammered, "I'm hit."

Jim fell to his knees and stared at Danny's clutching hands. "Where, Danny? Where? Not—not in the belly!"

Danny nodded. He pulled his hands away and began unbuttoning his shirt and pants. "It doesn't feel too bad."

"I'll get some help. I'll get a doctor."

"No. Wait." Jim stared in horror as Danny revealed a slightly bleeding hole in the clean white skin just above his navel. Danny probed into it with a thumb and forefinger as Jim got slowly to his feet. The probing red-stained fingers came away from the wound, and Danny grunted. "Here it is."

Jim stared at the flattened lead and copper pellet Danny held out in the palm of his hand. "Jesus! Jesus, you got it out?"

Danny nodded. "It came through that wall. Mostly spent, I guess. But it puts me out of action."

"You think it might be serious?"

"It could be. Depends on whether it went in far enough to puncture the peritoneum. Hand me one of those bandages, will you?"

As Jim handed over a bandage from the table, two men brought in the Kriegie who had been shot from the fence. One of them spoke up. "You were right, Danny. We got a customer." His eyes focused on the white patch Danny was taping to his belly. "Hey. You get shot, too?"

Danny nodded and motioned to a chair. "Put the man down. Is it a flesh wound? Get a compress on that leg." He lay back in the bunk. "I'm all washed up. I think I'd better not move until I can get to a hospital. You and the rest of the crew will have to take over."

Jim stood looking at the trail of blood leading from the doorway to the wounded man in the chair. "Anything I can do, Danny?"

Danny smiled, rolling the spent bullet around in his fingers. "No, thanks. The regular crew can handle it. Go on back out and watch the show."

Jim nodded solemnly. "You would get hurt on the last day. You take it easy, Danny."

Danny grinned up out of the bunk. "Sure. See you later."

One of the infirmary crew was tying a reddening compress to the thigh of the man in the chair. Jim motioned to the other one and stepped into the hall. His forehead furrowed as he faced the man. "You know anything about medicine?"

The man shrugged. "Only what I've picked up from Danny. Why?"

"What's the peritoneum?"

"The inner lining of the abdominal cavity. It covers the stomach and a lot of other organs."

"What happens if it gets punctured?"

"Peritonitis." The Kriegie looked back at the infirmary doorway. "Is Danny's peritoneum punctured?"

"Maybe. You'd better watch him."

The Kriegie shook his head. "That's all I can do. Watch him."

Two prisoners entered the block as Jim was leaving. One of them was holding his bleeding shoulder. The sound of thousands of men shouting hit Jim like a wall as he stepped into the open. Out by the main gate machine guns rattled and rifles popped. Jim scrambled up onto the fence between Tom and Koczeck. Tom turned his head and shouted to be heard. "You missed seeing those goons on the cheese factory get shot dead. One of 'em fell off. There's another one still up there where he got killed. Those S.S. really are fighting to the last dirty bastard!"

A tiny motionless brown form lay on the sloping roof. The Fairchild spotter plane was cruising back and forth about five hundred feet above the blasted gate. Jim ground his teeth together and breathed hard. In the compounds to the right of the road prisoners were standing on the roofs of the prison blocks. Suddenly on one of the blocks a great flag billowed, blue, white, and red forming an ecstatic cross in the wind. A solid roar of voices welled up from that direction. Koczeck almost fell from the fence. "That's Norway, isn't it?"

From another roof point along the road the red, white, and blue tricolor of France rolled downward. Prisoners lay flat on the roof nailing the top of the flag to the eaves. Jim looked back over his shoulder at the crowded roof of his block. "Where's ours? We ought to have one!"

On another roof a long stick went up and a Polish flag fluttered in the air to another mass roar of victory. The popping and rattling of guns beyond the blasted gateway began to let up. Another cry went up as a crowd of British prisoners passed a Union Jack up to the men on a rooftop. Noble called up from the ground. "Where's ours? Don't we have a flag?"

A Netherlands flag rolled down the front of another building, making six flags in all in a blaze of colors adorning the prison blocks along the right side of the doorway in contrast to the black and white grimness of the S.S. flag over the main gateway. Only an occasional pop came from that direction. Then it was drowned out by a deep mass yelling up by the gate. Burt looked back and forth along the fence. "See anything? What's going on up there?" Slowly the yelling grew louder and nearer. Slowly it swelled back toward them. Suddenly it hushed as the S.S. flag started to drop down the pole. Then the yelling exploded all over the man-packed camp. Burt threw back his head. "Ya-a-a-a-y-e-e-e-e!"

Koczeck jumped to the ground and kept on jumping up and down. "Hubba! Hubba! Hubba!"

Bob, Tom, and Noble clung to the fence screaming through wide-open mouths. Jim screamed from a taut throat through his clenched teeth.

Swiftly, surely, the stars and stripes of a great red, white, and blue American flag shot up the main gate flagpole and waved in the sun.

The shouting raised itself a pitch. Ears tingled with it. The camp blurred with it. It kept on, a mighty all-out scream of thousands of voices. Men hugged each other and cried. Some rolled in the dirt, still shouting, wrestling with one another. Men clapped their hands, beat each other on the back, threw their hats into the air, ripped shirts from one another's bodies and shouted with all the power in their lungs. Jim danced in a circle on the ground with Tom and Bob, their arms around one another. Suddenly he felt a sharp shooting pain that darted from his jaw to the top of his skull. He spat out the splinters of the rotten molar he had caved in. He and the others kept on screaming and dancing; and every time they looked up, there it was, red, white, and blue, strong in the breeze and the sunlight, flying above all. Jim stopped screaming and dancing and sobbed into his hands, tears running through his fingers. "Oh, thank you, God! Oh, God! God . . ."

Burt leaned close and shouted, "There's another one over there!" He pointed toward the village. Where the red Nazi flag had flown on the red steeple an American flag now fluttered. The shouting began to lessen. Men smiled at one another, red-eyed, with wet cheeks. The light observation plane was cruising back and forth directly overhead, and loud crashing shells were bursting in the air just above the treetops of the forest behind the camp. Burt surveyed the row of many-colored flags along the crowded prison road and sighed loudly. "It's just like a world's fair. Hey! Here comes a tank!"

Slowly down through the crowd on the road a big brown tank was coming. Two helmeted American soldiers kneeling on the sandbags that covered its hood reached down to shake the upstretched hands of the throng that crowded around it. Shouting and laughter carried over the distance. Tom tapped Jim on the shoulder. "Jim, get a load of the goons."

Jim turned to look. Stony-faced, stiffly, von Munsing and his three aides were marching toward the compound gate, hands on the hilts of their short swords. Jim laughed and started walking. "This I gotta see. Come on."

Prisoners jeered and followed the Germans down the road. "Hey, superman! For you the war is over!"

"Goon boys! Where you going with those cheese knives?"

"Hup. Hup. Hup. Hup."

Von Munsing stared straight ahead as he marched, the other three Wehrmacht officers following respectfully at his heels.

"Bread and water for you, horse face!"

"Naw. Let him eat spuds! With worms in them!"

"Hup. Hup. Hup. Hup."

They came up to the big tank, now covered, turret and all, with sitting, laughing, shouting Kriegies. Von Munsing halted, clicked his boot heels, and addressed one of the brown-faced GI's on the tank in crisp, precise English. "Where is your officer in command? I wish to present myself to your officer in command."

The American soldier's lip curled. He jerked a fist back toward the outer gate. "Out there, Kraut."

Jeering Kriegies opened a way to let the Germans through. Many in the crowd followed. Five American soldiers stood behind the tank. They wore helmets, field jackets, and olive-drab trousers tucked into well worn combat boots. They carried rifles and Tommy guns held loosely but ready. Their brown faces didn't smile and they looked large in their bulky jackets. Jim muttered out of the side of his mouth to Tom. "Look at those boys. Did you ever see Americans that looked like that?"

Tom looked back at them. "No. Those are the toughest-looking hombres I've ever seen. It gives you the creeps just to look at them."

"Yeah. I sure wouldn't want to fight them."

They moved with the crowd following the Germans through the gate into the Vorlager. Stretched out face up before the bullet-riddled guard barracks lay a long, regular row of German corpses. Two American soldiers carried out a limp body by its arms and legs and tossed it into place in the row. Jim looked away as they passed. It was the teeth in the open mouths and the eyes that bothered him.

Tom grunted. "Your friend from Sudetenland was there. Did you see him?"

"No."

There was shouting up ahead in the crowd at the shattered gate.

"He's all right!"

"He's O.K.!"

Surrounded by grinning Kriegies, Oberst von Munsing stepped up to two unsmiling American soldiers standing with slung rifles in the gateway and clicked his boot heels. "I wish to present myself to your general."

One of the soldiers answered. "Sure. Sure, Fritz. Wait your turn."

"He's the son of a bitch that ran this place!" somebody cried out.

Jim and Tom pressed into the mob to have a look beyond the fences. A small group of Wehrmacht and Luftwaffe soldiers grinned sheepishly, guarded by four mean-looking GI's with Tommy guns. A huge broad-shouldered sergeant was frisking another Luftwaffe soldier in the middle of the road. Jim put his mouth close to Tom's ear to be heard in the noisy press of men. "Jesus! I've never seen such tough-looking guys. We never had anything like that in North Africa."

The sergeant finished patting the German's legs and stood up. His voice boomed. "How 'bout dis one? Anyone been hurt by dis Kraut?"

The noise subsided for a few seconds and then someone shouted. "He's all right!"

"Yeah! He's O.K.!"

The sergeant gave the German a shove that sent him stumbling toward the guarded group. "Get over dere. Next!"

Von Munsing was pushed out onto the road and recovered his military stance with dignity. He clicked his heels and addressed the sergeant. The crowd became silent. "I wish to present myself to your general."

The sergeant's massive jaw hung open as he stared at the Oberst. He turned to the crowd against the fence. "Who is dis joker?"

Angry shouting broke out. "He's the Kommandant!"

"He's the commander of this camp!"

"He ran this place!"

The shouting subsided. The sergeant turned to the Oberst. "What's dis about a general?"

Von Munsing remained stiffly at attention. "Take me to a general or a colonel. I demand my right as an officer to surrender my sword to an officer of superior or equal rank."

"Gimme dat!" The sergeant reached down and jerked the scabbard, breaking the gold chains by which it had hung from the belt.

The German's face whitened. "I am your superior in rank. I insist that you take me to your colonel or general."

"Shaddup!" The master sergeant swung back his leg and planted a mighty kick into the Oberst's butt. "Here's a souvenir for one of you guys." The sword and scabbard came sailing over the fence. Hands clutched for it, but it landed right in Jim's unexpecting arms and he held it securely to his chest. The master sergeant faced the crowd. "What you want we should do with dis monkey?"

A terrible roar swept through the fence. "Kill the son of a bitch!"

"Cut his balls out!"

"Shoot the bastard!"

"Give it to him good!"

The master sergeant nodded grimly. With a rugged shove and another boot in the butt he sent the Oberst stumbling across the road. "Get over dere!" He motioned to two American guards. "Take dis rat up to da cage. And don't take no guff from him. No guff at all."

One of the guards brought his rifle stock with a thud into the Oberst's back. "Get goin', superman!" His voice roared as he brought the rifle stock around for another blow. "On the double!"

"Faster!" yelled the other guard, swinging a fist into the side of the Oberst's head.

The crowd roared through the fence. "Kill the bastard!"

"Let him have it!"

The Oberst staggered off down the road buffeted from side to side by the blows and kicks of the two guards. The cheering increased when he fell down only to be kicked to his feet again. As the three figures grew smaller, the one in the middle fell again and yet again. Finally they disappeared around a bend in the road, the German officer dragged along by his arms. The master sergeant's voice roared out. "Next!"

As one of the Wehrmacht majors was shoved out onto the road, Tom spoke sideways to Jim. "Let's get out of here and have a look at that sword."

They squeezed back out of the press of yelling prisoners. American soldiers were passing German corpses up into trucks in the Vorlager. Here and there groups of laughing Kriegies were gathered about GI's or jeeps. Jim slid the short sword from its scabbard as they walked. Its blade was of polished silver inlaid with gold. A German eagle perched on a swastika at its hilt. Jim passed the sword to Tom. "I was pretty lucky to catch it."

"Yeah. It's a nice souvenir." A group of Englishmen passed arm in arm wearing various types of German caps and helmets and singing an RAF song. "Better than hats."

Heavy artillery suddenly started firing with great crashing reports somewhere in the direction of the cheese factory. Shells swooshed overhead in the direction of the Isar River. Jim grinned. "The war ain't over yet."

Tom grinned back. "For us it is."

A German motorcycle carrying two laughing Aussies clattered in and out among the crowd milling on the camp road.

They waited while a brown field ambulance moved past with honking horn. Six laughing American prisoners hurried past carrying a white goat, dead, its throat dripping red, dangling from hoofs tied to a long pole. Jim called out. "Hey! Where'd you get that?"

One of the men held up a German pistol. "Liberated it!"

Jim laughed and waved back with the ex-Kommandant's sword. The great hunger within him came suddenly into his awareness like a blow to the stomach. They hadn't eaten that day. His mouth filled with moisture. "Come on. It's about time we saw about some chow."

"Yeah. If we're free now we ought to be able to get something to eat."

They hurried along through the gay throng on the flag-lined road. Above them signal corps men were attaching large white loudspeakers to the electric poles. Ahead, in the American compound, the tank was still buried under a blanket of grinning Kriegies. Another cluster of men was crowded about the rear of the ambulance. Jim pushed through to its open doors. "Hey, Danny! You leaving us?"

Danny sat with three other Kriegies on a bench inside the ambulance. Two men lay on stretchers on the floor. All wore some kind of bandage. Danny grinned back. "Yep. It's clean sheets in a hospital for me tonight, Jim."

"How you feeling?"

The ambulance's engine started up. "O.K., Jim. I don't think it's complicated. Just not taking any chances, that's all."

"Well, don't forget what I told you. If you ever have any trouble getting a practice set up you can take my appendix out any time. Even if I have to come to Spokane for it."

The ambulance started to move. The men inside waved back at the waving, shouting crowd.

"See you later, Mike!"

"Give my love to them nurses!"

The ambulance moved off through the gate and the sea of men on the road. A loudspeaker already set up on the poles boomed. "Testing. One, two, three, four. Testing."

A Kriegie called out from a group clustered around a nearby jeep. "Hey, Weis! Weis! Come here, will you?" Jim walked over with lifted eyebrows. The Kriegie who had called stood beside a tall broad-shouldered captain in combat uniform. "Koczeck is in your combine, isn't he, Weis?"

"Yeah. Sure."

"The captain here is looking for him. Think you can find him?"

Jim looked in surprise at the grim brown face of the captain. "Sure. I think so. You a friend of Al's?"

The captain nodded. "That's right. I hoped I could find him in here someplace."

"Well, we can find him."

Tom fell in on the other side of the captain. "Are you a friend from St. Paul?"

"Yeah. How is he?"

Tom shrugged. "He's O.K. Just like the rest of us."

The captain grunted. Jim spotted Bob standing before the prison block. "Bob, you seen Al Koczeck lately?"

Bob held a sandwich made of Spam and biscuits in one hand and a tin cup in the other. He swallowed before answering. "He's inside bashing some of the chow Junior liberated. You better go in and get yours."

As much of the public address system as was installed on the poles blared out: "Attention, all ramps! Attention, all ramps! Attention, all ramps!"

Jim stared upward, where a signal corpsman was still adjusting a cluster of speakers. "What in hell are ramps?"

The captain answered. "Recovered Allied military personnel. You're all ramps now."

The loudspeaker continued. "Attention, all ramps! This is your senior American officer, Colonel Good, speaking. This is a great day for all of us." A short cheer went up all over the camp. "We are no longer prisoners of war, but we are still in the army and under army law and discipline." The thousands who listened were silent. "This is still a combat zone and a war is being fought here. You all can hear our artillery trying to root out the S.S. fighting in the woods directly behind the camp." As he talked the guns barked every few seconds and shells whooshed through the air overhead. "You are all ordered to remain inside the camp until such time as we can be evacuated in an orderly fashion." A groan went up from the throngs. "That may take several days, as these advance forces are miles out in front of our main line of supply." A bigger groan went up. "These forces have been living off the land as they have advanced, and they are not equipped to feed us immediately." The crowd groaned again. "However, field bakeries have been set up and there will be an issue of GI white bread this afternoon." The crowd cheered lamely. "Now pay attention to this. No man. I repeat. No man, either enlisted man or officer, will be permitted to leave this camp unless authorized by me to do so. Any man caught outside this camp or caught leaving this camp will be placed at the bottom of the list of those who will leave the camp at the proper time in the proper fashion. Under no circumstances will any man take off across country to try to get back on his own. That's an order. Any man who attempts to take off across country will be court-martialed. That I promise you. That's all, gentlemen."

The throngs buzzed. Jim shrugged. "After two years, what's a few more days?"

Tom smiled slightly. "Anyhow, we get white bread."

The captain frowned. "Where's Al?"

Jim led the way up the steps. "Right in here. You must be a pretty close friend to look him up like this."

"He's married to my sister."

Jim stopped and stared at the captain. "The hell you say." A big smile brightened his face in the gloom of the prison bay as he watched the captain looking about distastefully at the blanket-draped maze of bunk tiers. "You wait right here. I'll get him for you."

Tom and Jim found the aisle of their tier and walked in. Noble, Burt, and Koczeck were seated on lower bunks gaily eating food from an open Red Cross parcel. Koczeck looked up and splattered crumbs from his full mouth. "Hubba, hubba. Sit down and help yourselves."

Jim grinned down and motioned with a thumb over his shoulder. "There's someone out here to see you, Al."

"Who?"

"Come and see."

Koczeck labored to his feet, taking a bite out of a jam-covered biscuit. Jim let him pass. Koczeck squinted through the gloom of the bay. He spat out what was in his mouth, dropped the biscuit, and lunged forward with a soft cry. "Ben!"

"Al, boy!" They hugged each other tightly, Koczeck's head pressed against the broad shoulder of the taller man. Tom and Jim stood back grinning. Burt and Noble stood looking on, wondering, in the aisle between the bunk tiers. The captain gently pushed Koczeck back at arm's length. "Let me see how you fared, Al."

They stood there looking at each other, both wet-eyed and warmly smiling, not knowing what to say. Finally Koczeck spoke in a stammering voice. "Wh-wh—How—How did you find me, Ben? Where did you come from?"

Ben grinned down at him and knuckled a tear from his cheek. "I knew where you were. You don't think Sis would let me come all the way across Germany without telling me where to find you, did you?"

"You—you've heard from her lately?"

The big man nodded. "Just the other day. I've got some new pictures of her. And the boy, too. Come on, Al. I've got a jeep, and my headquarters is just a few minutes from here." He looked around at the filthy bunks crowded into the dark bay. "Let's get out of here."

Koczeck looked about at his combine mates. He spoke in a voice light with delight. "Fellas, this is my brother-in-law, Ben Leslie. Ben, meet Jack Noble, Burt Salem, Tom Howard, and Jim Weis." While they were shaking hands Koczeck looked about. "I got another buddy, Bob Montgomery, around here somewhere."

Ben put an arm around Koczeck's shoulder. "Come on, Al. Let's take off for the rest of the day. I can fix you up with something better than these rags, give you a bath and something to eat and show you those pictures." He smiled around at the others. "You can bring something back for your friends tonight. You boys had any Four Roses lately?"

"Four Roses!"

"Not lately."

Koczeck frowned. "I don't know. We been ordered not to leave."

"To hell with orders. I can get you through the gate in my jeep. Come on."

Koczeck looked at Jim. Jim nodded, grinning. Koczeck started toward the door. "All right, Ben. Let's go."

The rest followed and stood in the doorway watching as Ben, with a big arm about Koczeck's shoulders, led him between clusters of ex-Kriegies, GI's and their vehicles to the jeep. Jim watched the jeep wend its way along the crowded road toward the front gate. His vision blurred so that he could not see. Tom turned to him with equally moist eyes. "Well, what are you crying about?"

Jim chuckled with a small catch in his throat. "You know, I think all the rest of my life it's going to be very easy for me to cry?" He wiped his eyes with the backs of his fists as Major Smith approached striding through the crowd with a frown on his black-bearded face. The major stopped before Jim.

"That was Al Koczeck who just left here in a jeep, wasn't it?"

Jim nodded just as the loudspeaker barked to life.

"Attention, all ramps!" The great blanketing chatter of thousands of men lifted. "Attention, all ramps! We have just received information from our own authorities that will interest you all. Oberst von Munsing has committed suicide! Von Munsing, the former Kommandant of this camp, took his own life a half-hour ago by swallowing poison. I repeat. Oberst von Munsing has committed suicide by taking what is believed to have been cyanide poison. That is all."

Here and there among the spread-out city of prison blocks and tents, cheers, yelps, and whoops shot into the air. Louder cheers arose from the foreign prison blocks as the news was translated to them. Major Smith's teeth flashed through his beard. "So the old stiffback could dish it out but he couldn't take it himself. Instead he had to take poison."

Jim looked thoughtfully at Tom. "I don't know . . ."

Tom nodded with a thin slanting smile on his face. "Maybe he did. And then again, maybe he didn't."

Major Smith's face grew serious again. "Now about Al Koczeck. Where did he go?"

Jim looked around at the others before answering. "That was his brother-in-law he was with. He knew Al was here, so he came in to look him up."

The major waited for more that didn't come. "Where did they go?"

Jim shrugged. "I dunno. Out to his brother-in-law's outfit for a visit, I guess. They got a lot of things to talk about."

"Without authorization?"

"What do you mean?"

"You know what I mean. No one is permitted to leave without authorization."

Burt butted in. "Aw, Major. This was a relative. It's the first one in his family Al has seen in over two years."

Major Smith ignored Burt and kept looking at Jim. "Well, it's too bad for Koczeck."

Above them the public address system began to play a swing phonograph record. Jim spoke softly. "Why, Major?"

"You heard the order. I hate to do it to an old Kriegie like Koczeck, but I'm the block commander. I've got to turn him in. His name will be dropped to the last of the list. It could mean an extra week here for him after the rest of the old Kriegies have been evacuated."

"But, Major, this guy is Al's wife's brother. Al is coming back tonight. You just didn't see it, that's all. Al went to see some pictures of his wife and a boy he's never even seen yet."

The major's jaw set firm. "What difference does that make? Hundreds of men saw him leave, not just me. And a lot of 'em know I saw him leave. I'm his commanding officer. You ought to know the spot I'm in, Jim. You're a good soldier."

"But Jesus, Major—"

"An order is an order. There are no exceptions to that. I have to put Koczeck at the bottom of the list. You ought to know that. You're a good soldier."

Jim stared back at the major's hard face before speaking. "Not that good a soldier." He looked away and walked past the block commander. He felt hollow and sick inside. His nerves twitched slightly. His eyes were blurred again. It was getting too easy to cry. He wiped them and with his right hand gripped a rusty strand of the compound's barbed-wire fence. He felt Burt standing beside him. The gay buzz of voices all around him was unreal. He gazed blankly at the Red Crosses painted on the sloping roofs of the camp hospital and at the drab gray roofs of the buildings beyond.

Burt spoke in a low angry voice. "I call it chicken shit. Just plain petty chicken shit."

Jim nodded and lifted his eyes to the red, white, and blue of the Stars and Stripes flying over the main entrance. He sighed. "You can't run an army without it." He felt a hand on his shoulder and heard Tom's calm voice.

"Come on, old man. Let's go in and eat some chow."

They turned and went into the block to bash some of the food liberated from the hoard in the late Kommandant's basement.

Outside the unshuttered windows, Stalag VIIA was ablaze from the floodlights mounted among the loudspeakers on the utility poles. Inside, the bay was a bedlam. A liberated German radio blared BBC music from a table set among a crowd of listeners in the middle of the floor. In one corner an accordion played, and jive rhythms of a jam session in the next block bounced in through the open windows. Everywhere men were eating. There were K-rations bummed from willing GI's, Red Cross food scrounged from the warehouses and the dead Kommandant's basement, white bread from army field kitchens, and fresh meat and eggs liberated from the German countryside by men who didn't take orders too seriously.

Koczeck, in new GI pants, field jacket, and combat boots, sat with the rest of his combine, three on each side of the aisle, facing each other atop two bunk tiers. He tilted a bottle of Four Roses back for a swallow and handed it across the aisle to Bob. "Have a slug."

Bob grinned, tongue against the slit in his teeth. "I never cared much for rye one way or the other, but it sure tastes good to me now."

Jack Noble looked up from a V-mail letter he was writing to his fiancée. "Maybe I ought to try it at that. Just to see why you like it so much."

Bob took a slug and handed it to Noble. Noble sniffed at the open neck. "It sure doesn't smell very good."

Koczeck leaned on one elbow. "I don't care if I do get left behind for a week. It was worth it to get rid of the bugs."

Beside him on the upper bunk Burt scratched an armpit. "You mean they ain't back on you yet?"

"Nope. I got the full treatment. First we went down by a little pond. I took off all my Kriegie clothes and threw them into the pond. Then we went back to this farmhouse and I got in a tub of hot water. I just lay there soaking and scrubbing for about an hour. I bet Ben brought more hot water at least five times. Then I dusted off all over with this DDT stuff and put on all new clothes. Haven't had a bug since."

"How come they haven't got back on you?"

"It's this new stuff; DDT they call it." He brought two small white cans from his field-jacket pocket. "It kills all bugs and they stay off you afterwards. It makes me immune."

"DDT you say? How about letting me try some of that?"

Koczeck handed a can to Burt, who began reading its label. Tom watched Noble still experimentally sniffing at the bottle. "Don't smell it, Noble. Drink it. Just throw it up and let it pour down your throat."

Noble looked at the bottle an instant longer, then tilted it up and let the liquid pour into his throat. He brought it down quickly, coughing, red in the face and gasping for breath. Tom reached over and took the bottle from a waving hand. Jim handed Noble a slice of cheese. "Here. Eat a bit of this for a chaser."

A passing ramp stood at the open end of the aisle. "Hey! Where did you guys get the whisky?"

Koczeck grinned down at him and rubbed his hands together. "You got to be in the rackets, son."

Burt began sprinkling DDT powder inside the open collar of his shirt. Tom passed the bottle over the busy man's lap to Koczeck, who passed it across to Jim. "You got missed that time. Have a slug."

"Thanks." Jim took a drink, feeling the burning liquor slide down his gullet, and followed it up with a mouthful of cheese. He passed the bottle back to Koczeck. "Your brother-in-law give you any new pictures of that bambino I sweated out with you?"

Koczeck grinned with delight and thrust the bottle between his knees. "Yeah. Yeah." He reached in an inside pocket of the new field jacket and brought out a small manila envelope. He pulled a photograph from it and handed it across the aisle. "That's him. Taken less than a month ago."

Bob and Noble leaned close on either side as Jim studied the portrait of a chubby-kneed little boy with dark curly hair and a big dimpled smile. Jim chuckled. "Wow! What a monster!"

Bob grinned across the aisle. "You sure you're the papa of that?"

Koczeck rubbed his paws together. "I'm his pop!"

Burt was sprinkling DDT into the open fly of his trousers. He stopped when the picture was passed to him. "Say, that's some pickaninny!" He passed the picture to Tom and resumed sprinkling his crotch.

Tom took a good look at the photograph and passed it back to Koczeck. "Nice-looking lad, Al. You're a lucky boy."

"Thanks." He took a drink, passed the bottle to Bob, and sat with a whimsical smile on his face, looking at the picture.

A BBC newscast was coming over the radio in the center of the bay. Ramps crowded around it cheering as each item of victory was announced. At the other end of the room the accordion was playing "On the Sunny Side of the Street." Burt buttoned up his fly and sat squirming. "Man oh, man! Are you sure this DDT stuff kills bugs? They're hopping all over me!"

Koczeck answered without looking up from the picture. "They're in their death throes. They'll be dead in a little while. You should have bathed first."

"I'd rather have live ones than dying ones, then."

Jack Noble picked up a thick slice of GI white bread. He reached his bare hand into a big can of apricot and pineapple jam and smeared the handful on the bread, licking his fingers afterward. Major Smith entered the aisle and reached up to lay a hand on Koczeck's knee.

"Al, I told you what your punishment was for breaking orders this afternoon." The major bit his lower lip beneath his black beard before he went on. "Well, I've come to tell you I've changed my mind. I can't do that to you. How about it, Al? Let's forget the whole thing. You leave when we do."

"Why, gee. Yes . . . well, gosh, thanks, Major."

"It's all forgotten, then." The major reached up for Koczeck's hand. "Shake on it, Al."

Koczeck shook hands eagerly. "Sure thing. Have a drink, Major?"

The major shook his head, grinning. "No thanks. See you men later." He turned and walked away.

Jim watched the major's back for a minute and then jumped down from the bunk and followed him. He pushed through the crowd and caught up with him just the other side of the loudly blaring radio. "Major!"

The major turned and faced him. Nearby, the accordion was playing softly. "Yes, Jim?"

"What made you change your mind?"

Major Smith looked down toward the floor. "I couldn't do it. Not the way it is now. How can I punish a good man who has been under me for two years when a dirty son of a bitch right up with me, higher even, does even worse and will probably get away with it? Maybe even get a medal for it."

"I don't get you."

"It's Condon. The dirty son of a bitch took off this afternoon."

"You mean to go to town or something?"

"No. I mean lock, stock, and barrel. Cross-country. He packed his stuff and left to hitch-hike to Paris. When he gets there he's going to tell them he escaped before we were liberated. How in hell can you run an army with pricks like that who get up as high as lieutenant colonel?" Major Smith looked down at the floor again. "Anyhow, after that I couldn't make myself punish Koczeck for taking an afternoon off to be with his wife's brother."

Jim nodded and began to grin. "So Condon did it." He began to laugh softly. "Condon. Thank God the bastard turned out to be good for something."

The major started to smile. "Yeah. I guess you're right. See you later, Jim."

As he started to go, Jim stopped him. "Major?"

"Yes?"

"I know one thing now."

"What's that?"

"This time things aren't going to get worse before they get better."

The major's teeth flashed. He waved and walked off through the crowded room. Jim turned and crowded his way back to his friends. Koczeck laughed down at him from his upper bunk and clapped cupped hands together. "Hubba, hubba, Jim. The major isn't so tough at that. He isn't so tough after all. Hubba, hubba, hubba."

Jim climbed back onto the upper-bunk level. "No." He grinned. "No. He really isn't at all." He took the bottle and looked out through the opened window at Kriegies wandering freely among the buildings of the floodlighted camp. He took a big hot swallow of the whisky and passed the bottle on. With the late camp Kommandant's sword blade he carved a slice from a brick of American cheese and popped it into his mouth for a chaser.

Glossary

Abort	A privy
Appel	Roll call
Bash	A mixture of various foodstuffs
Big X	The senior officer in charge of escape activity
Burp gun	Tommy gun
Canary	A radio
Fan	A propeller
Flap	Alarm, excitement
G	Constant of gravity
Gen	General information concerning operations
Gib. belly	Gibraltar belly, or diarrhea
Goon	A German
Goon box	A sentry tower
Hack	A synchronization of watches
I.F.F.	Identification Friend or Foe. A device used on aircraft to distinguish friend from foe
Kriegie	A prisoner of war
Little X	The second officer in charge of escape activity
Office	A plane's cabin or cockpit
Ops	Operations
Paddle foot	An infantryman
Penguin	A member of the ground staff, who, like penguins, do not fly
Poontang	Sexual intercourse
Pranger	A crowbar or any short steel or iron bar
Pukka gen	Reliable information
RT	Radio transmitter

Teat	The electric button which when pressed fires the guns
VHF	Very high frequency
Vic	V formation
Woof	To spoof, to joke
X Committee	Escape Committee

CPSIA information can be obtained at www.ICGtesting.com
Printed in the USA
BVOW05s2014070814

361874BV00001B/127/P